CITY OF MAGES

KIERSTEN MICHELE
A.J. CERNA

MAGIA BOOKS

SOMBRIA
Calao
Plaja
Llodora
Ruinedlands
Frutífere Plains
River Norte
Royo Desert
Pesca
River Muerto
Lejon
L'Lim
River Peste
Cielo
River Mied
Sémpere Sea
River Sur
Lake Mied
Attalea
Hurozon
River Arrib
Arbol
Endes Mountains

They had come before.

The mantra ran through her head, beating in her chest, along with her heart. They had come before and she was still here. Her mother had been alive then. She had been there to protect her and to hide her. Now she had no one—not here.

They had come before and they would come again. Over and over again until she was caught, or she fled.

This had become her life, and she wasn't ready for the consequences.

Chapter 1

Alara

Alara had never forgotten the smell of burning flesh. Smoky. Rich. Metallic. She felt it sear through her, filling her lungs, threatening to choke her as she watched the scene play out.

She had lit someone on fire—again.

This was how she would fail the Haven. Fail Emaru. Fail everyone.

Time seemed frozen in the moment her fire magia had reached out to spark the flames across Raquel's tunic. The other magite stared, wide-eyed in horror as her sleeve was eaten into ash. Senye Emaru stood behind Alara, a firm hand on her shoulder, squeezing her hard enough to bruise.

She could have turned on her teacher. Yelled that it was her fault for pushing her—threatening to fail her out of school. But the councilwoman wouldn't have even flinched under her verbal assault. She'd only give Alara the same look of icy disappointment she had given countless times before, whenever the girl had lost control of her magia.

So Alara did the one thing she trusted herself to do—she moved decisively forward, ripping off her thin leather vest and throwing it over Raquel's arm before she even had time to scream. The heat and light of her magia immediately went out, throwing their small group back into darkness.

The night stilled again as they stared wide-eyed at Alara. It wasn't the first time her magia had failed her or the group. But it was the first in a long time that she'd accidentally set fire to something while trying to use her mind-stalking ability. She knew what they were all thinking: even a seven-year-old would have had better control.

Raquel threw the singed vest at her feet. "Alara! What in El'dyo's name is the matter with—"

"We will talk about what just happened later," Emaru said, putting an end to Raquel's complaints, though Alara knew her guardian and teacher was less pleased with her. Her tone was biting—more biting than the chilled mountain air. "But for now, I believe we have company."

It didn't take Alara's mind-stalking abilities to know the enemy bruyas had spotted them and were headed straight toward their huddle. Their footsteps were soft but distinct in the silent night. The villagers of Hurazon had locked themselves away in their homes hours before, leaving Alara and the other magites guarding the perimeter in silence. It left the village eerie and quiet as they waited. Even the faint buzzing of insects was dampened by the thick air, soft and hushed.

The plan had been to sneak up on the bruyas and surprise them as they attempted to raid the outskirts of the village. There had been reports of bruya sightings in the area for the past few months, and Emaru had taken on the task as a final test for the magites nearing graduation. This task would show their skill with magia, both in protecting the village and capturing the rebels, and prove that they deserved to join the ranks of full-fledged mages.

"For El'dyo!" Emaru said as the shadows in the cloud forest before them shifted.

The others repeated her words, raising their own weapons and arms. Alara threw her vest back on and snatched her wooden staff from the ground. The heat of her magia pulsed in her chest as if still trying to reach out to the smoldering remains of Raquel's tunic. Their eyes met for only a second, and she saw a flash of fury. She would definitely hear about it later—she probably owed her a new tunic.

Alara was snapped from her thoughts as an arrow whistled by her head, thudding into a tree a few yards behind her. A moment later, the world exploded. Balls of flame met jets of water. Steam hissed and danced in the air as the two collided.

Beside Alara, Raquel took up her bow and shot arrows into the chaos, her hand moving gracefully as she used her wind magia to aim and turn the arrows in unnatural ways. A few hit their targets—wind-filled crystalized receptives exploding against skulls and wrists, unleashing concussive gusts of wind. Nothing deadly. The Haven didn't kill. Not even those who threatened their country.

Hearing the sounds of heavy footfalls behind her, Alara whipped around to see a dark-eyed bruya coming at her with a spear. She launched to the side and swung her staff to block the man's blow then swiped at his legs. Like Alara, he only wore thin armor over his chest. His legs were clothed, but unprotected.

She caught him off guard, and the bruya fell onto his back with a dull thump. But before she could celebrate, a blast of wind shot her off her feet and sent her skidding across the dirt.

By the time she stood back up, the bruya was running at her again, this time his spear forgotten on the ground and his arms raised up toward her. Another sharp gust of wind pelted her shoulder, and she stumbled back, hands searching in the dark for her staff. She knew a third strike was imminent. This would have been a good time to use her magia. Any other fire magite would be able to blind him, singe his hands, or block his strides with well-aimed shots of fire.

Instead, Alara braced her body for the third blast of air, letting it strike her just as she launched herself to the right. She flew back a few feet, hitting the ground with a bone-aching thud. Her jaw throbbed as she smiled. Her staff was now only a foot from her hand. His eyes widened as she threw herself at him, staff raised. She struck him across the knees and twisted to jam the butt of the staff into his gut. Even the leather armor he wore couldn't protect his diaphragm from the sharp hit. He fell forward with a wheeze.

"Cuffs!" Alara shouted, realizing the pair she had worn on her belt were no longer there. Had they fallen during the scuffle? Or when she was trying to save her classmate after her accidental murder attempt?

"I've got you." Mitteo came up behind her. She turned back to grab the cuffs just as his foot caught on a root, knocking him face first into the dirt a few feet away, the cuffs clattering to the ground. By the time she'd finally snatched them off the ground, the bruya she had downed was already gone. She bit her lip as Mitteo stumbled up, face muddy and red. The idea that this magite was going to be graduating from the Haven soon, while she was about to fail out sent a wave of unfettered anger through her. The boy was an earth magite and still tripped over every damn root.

She opened her mouth to berate him, but before she was able to get the words out, a wall of heat burned across her vision and fire veered sharply to the left, just missing her.

She didn't have to look to know that Emaru had saved her tail with a well-timed burst of air. The mage waved her hands calmly in front of her, the magia strain not even registering as she redirected the gust toward the bruyas, using their own powers against them. She gave a sharp flick, and a fire attack from a long-haired bruya ricocheted off an invisible wall, flying toward his own ally.

"Use your magia to corner them!" Her face was fierce, and even in the dark, Emaru's gray eyes seemed to glow.

Alara gripped her staff and looked back toward the fight. She raised her hand and took a deep breath. She could feel the heat of the torches in the village's main plaza, their flames leaning toward her. She reached back toward her own center, to the thread of magia that danced there. But as the wave of heat crawled up her chest, she let out a strangled cry and dropped her hand. The magia immediately dissipated and her body went cool.

"Try again," Emaru said.

"Right now? Don't you think—"

"Right now, Alara!"

She lifted her hand again, but couldn't bring herself to reach toward the flames. Dread curled in her stomach at the feel of her buzzing magia. She shook her head, her arm falling limp to her side.

"Useless child," Emaru said. "Go help Raquel, then!"

Alara tried not the feel the shame shuddering through her in cold waves as she sprinted to where the other girl fought. Raquel moved gracefully between firing arrows and sending bursts of wind at bruyas. As Alara watched her dodge the magia attacks, a small sense of hopelessness rang through her. The Haven's strategy would always baffle her.

The magites were fighting to capture. The bruyas were fighting to kill. They were ruthless in their use of magia. Anything to destroy the Council's rule. Personally, she didn't think the bruyas deserved saving, not that she'd ever let Emaru hear her voice such things.

One bruya broke off from the group and moved to flank Raquel.

Alara grabbed the bolas from her belt, relieved they hadn't fallen wherever her cuffs had. With a sharp twist of her wrist, she sent the bolas flying. The rope struck the bruya just below their knees, the stones wrapping around their legs, snapping tight. The figure went down hard.

Alara sprung forward, hoping to catch the bruya and knock them out. But before she could reach them, the bruya had gripped the rope around their ankles, disintegrating them into ash, then jumped to their feet.

She skidded to a stop. It was a younger boy, likely around her own age. His hair was long, falling into his face and partially covering his eyes that grew wide as she approached.

Alara moved into a fighting stance, ready to take him on. But rather than meet her head-on, the boy turned and bolted in the opposite direction. She watched as he melted into the forest.

He wasn't the only one. As it turned out, all the bruyas were retreating, tearing through the underbrush from where they'd come.

She took a deep breath and let the humid air fill her lungs, heavy and cool. Sweat dripped down between her shoulder blades under her tunic. The night was again hushed and quiet until the sounds of the forest came alive as the shadows stilled between the moss-draped trees.

The magites themselves were no worse for wear, still standing. Still breathing. Still living. They were scattered across the rocky clearing, the flames of Hurazon flickering just behind them.

They had survived the attack in one piece.

Alara's smile widened involuntarily, and she thrust her staff up in victory as she took in the tired faces around her. Her gaze found Senye Emaru's, and the look on her face sent her heart stuttering.

"Fool," Emaru said. Her voice was cold and pierced the air like a knife. "I should never have brought you along. You are clearly not ready."

CHAPTER 2

ALARA

The words were a slap to the face. Alara lowered her head, tears prickling the corner of her eyes. She could feel the gaze of the other magites on her, particularly Raquel, who was likely wearing her usual told-you-so smirk. Taking a deep breath and choking back the tears, she turned to Emaru with a determined look.

"We chased them away, didn't we?" she said. "We protected the villagers and their property."

"For today, maybe," Emaru said. "But the mission was to *capture* the bruyas, not scare them away. They could be back tomorrow or the next day. They may even move on to raid another village. You are thinking in the short-term, Alara. And that's not even mentioning your other failures tonight."

Alara bit back a response, her face heated. She had always felt the Haven put too much emphasis on students using their magia. She would have been better off tonight not using hers. There'd have been no chance of losing control. So long as the job got done, what did it matter?

But in this case, it didn't, and to Senye Emaru, it'd be yet another reason why Alara's abilities needed to be engaged and fully mastered. That very thought filled her with a sense of shame.

Emaru turned to the other magites. "This isn't over. If you can, get some food and rest. We'll meet at evening meal. Focus on what went wrong tonight and what we can do differently next time. Think back to our previous lessons."

"Yes, Senye Emaru," a few magites said, bowing their heads in acknowledgement before scattering. The eastern edge of the sky was starting to gray and Alara realized with a weary start that morning was already coming.

She turned to follow the group back toward the plaza, but Emaru placed her hand hard on Alara's shoulder. "No, not you."

She sighed, defeated. Avoidance wasn't going to be an option.

Raquel caught Alara's eye and gave her a small smile and wave as the others walked away, her lopsided tunic growing clearer in the slowly creeping dawn. Alara looked away, too tired and ashamed to even think about Raquel.

She already had to deal with whatever speech Senye Emaru had planned. For all she knew, this could very well mean the end of her career at the Haven.

Senye Emaru steered her toward a large tree stump on the edge of the woods. Alara collapsed, exhausted, as her teacher gently took her own seat. She didn't look up to meet her gaze and instead focused on the ground. She knew what she'd see if she looked up—Emaru's bright gray eyes shining with disappointment, the loose strands of her black and silver hair falling gracefully over her creased brow.

"I put my neck out for you to get you on this mission," Emaru said. "Jorye doesn't think you're ready. And Lena Cruz doesn't think you ever will be. But I thought maybe if I just challenged you more, pushed you a little harder, you'd finally prove them wrong." Her voice was soft, which made Alara's chest feel even tighter.

She wished Emaru would just yell at her.

"Alara, ever since I met you, I knew you were special. Do you know why?"

Her shoulders slumped as she answered. "Because I'm a mind-stalker."

"You're not just any mind-stalker. You're a powerful one—more powerful than me. And you know how big my ego is."

Alara had to give a weak smile back. Emaru had said it as a joke, but it was truer than even she realized.

"With your abilities, we could save so many more bruyas. We could bring them to El'dyo's path and allow them to use their magia for the good of all of Sombria. Your powers could do that. *You* could do that."

"Or," Alara said, doing her best to fight back the tone of defiance that came so naturally to her, "I can do all that *without* having to resort to my mind-stalking abilities. I'm better at fighting without my magia. You saw me! I can use a spear better than any other magite."

"You can't just punch your way through every problem."

"Hence the spear."

"I'm not joking, Alara." Emaru's voice somehow took on a more serious tone. "We wouldn't have had to fight so hard if you could have narrowed in on the bruyas and given us the ability to strategize. You *should* have been able to sense exactly where they were. You *should* have told us their numbers. And we *should* have saved some of them tonight."

Alara chewed the inside of her lip. She and Emaru had had this fight so many times she'd lost track. "You know I tried, don't you? I tried to use my mind-stalking, but it was just a mess of energy and people. When I pushed harder I... Raquel could have..."

She couldn't finish the sentence; acid burned bitter in her stomach.

"Stop lying to me and stop lying to yourself!" Emaru's voice was sharp. "What happened with Raquel was due to your own unwillingness to control your magia. Your fire magia shouldn't come out when using your mind-stalking abilities. You're better than that."

"Or maybe you just need to admit that your precious daughter just isn't cut out to be a mage!"

Emaru's eyes widened. It was as though Alara had plunged a knife straight into her chest. It had hurt her to say it, though perhaps there was more truth to it than even she wanted to admit.

"Where do you think that'll take you?" Emaru said, her voice low. "You want to be a member of the councilguard, yes?"

"I'm already a better fighter than many of them. Ardo doesn't have any magia, and *he's* a councilguard."

"Exactly. Ardo *doesn't* have any abilities. You do. The councilguard does not tolerate untrained mages in their ranks. The Council will not budge on this." Emaru gave a heavy sigh and stood up from the stump. "Today when the relief arrives, you're going to head back to the Haven. You're done with this mission."

"But—"

"No, Alara. Your chances are running low. If you don't open yourself up to your abilities, you will *never* be a mage. That means you will *never* join the School of Protectors, and you will *never* be a member of the councilguard." She turned and stalked away, not even giving Alara a chance to respond.

She was left slouched on the stump, her dark knotted curls falling across her face. She looked down at her hands, staring numbly at the mud caked in the lines of her palms. A few callouses beneath the mud were red, one even bloody, likely ripped open by her staff during the fight. She hadn't even felt the stinging until she saw the blood.

Bleary-eyed, she looked up past the tree line and noticed the stars had faded away. She could just make out pale pink in the eastern sky, coming over the rolling green mountains. When would the next round of guards come to relieve them? How much longer did she have until they took her home? While councilguards didn't interfere with these missions and tests, they were always around in case of an emergency, as backup to the in-training magites—something she feared she'd always be.

Exhausted, but too defeated to go back to the tents and risk running into Raquel, Alara wandered along the eastern edge of the town. Most of the trees had been cleared away from the main parts of Hurazon. The town was made up of multiple stone-lined ledges, the land flattened in layers for building. Even here, so close to the ocean, the land was sloping, rising quickly away from the River Sur that ran at the center of the valley. Trees loomed large on the outskirts of the town, some brushing up against houses as they grew. Ferns, bushes, and underbrush edged out from the woods and crowded the boundaries of the town. Dew was heavy on the leaves this morning and they sparkled in the wan light of dawn. It was the end of the wet season and everything glowed with green from the constant rain of the previous months.

Hurazon was one of the larger towns on the outskirts of Sombria. Given its position along the western coast, it served as one of several key ports. As large as it was, however, it was still dwarfed by Cielo, the sprawling city that wrapped around the mountain of the same name. And within the confines of the mountain itself was the Haven, where Alara had lived most of her life.

The mornings in Hurazon weren't exactly quiet; there were plenty of villagers milling about their homes to feed their alpacas, l'lamas, and guinea pigs. Others watered their crops or tended to their morning cook fires. Yet it was still unbelievably empty compared to the Haven and Cielo.

She almost found the relative silence calming, despite the anger still raging inside her from the conversation with Emaru. She replayed it in her head, coming up with new arguments to convince her she was wrong—that she would be a great council-guard with or without her powers.

She approached a small stone ledge bordering the south side of the village, a few yards from the churning waters of the river. It rushed with the recent rains, its banks already wide here as it headed toward the bay and the open sea

The stones that were placed tightly together to create the ledge were overgrown with moss, which added padding as she sat. She ignored the dew that soaked through her thin trousers, and looked out into the densely packed forest. Shivering slightly in the morning air, she realized she was still wearing her fighting gear and didn't have a scarf or poncho to shut out the cold. Goosebumps crawled up the length of her arms and sent a chill through her body with each passing breeze, though she was far too stubborn to head back into her tent after having just sat down.

She absently ran a finger along the ridges of scar tissue that lined her lower cheek and neck, running through her argument with Emaru repeatedly. She became emboldened with each pass she made of the conversation… until she inevitably made it back to the very end, where Emaru reminded her of the Haven's way.

That unless she became a mage, she could not become a councilguard.

She sighed, breathing out her last bit of defiance as her teacher's words sank in.

Her head sat heavy in her hands, her skin pale from lack of sleep. Closing her eyes, she played with the thread of magia that danced in her chest. It was warm and sent a wave of heat through her as she touched it, making her shudder. As it rose, a tingle materialized at the back of her mind, her mind-stalking abilities weaving with her fire magia. It was a barely-there sense of something—someone. Alara gave a heavy sigh. One mage was coming up behind her. *Emaru.*

Alara let out a bitter bark. "I'm opening myself up. I know you're there. Are you happy?"

She spun around with a scowl, weariness drowning out her tolerance for Emaru. But it wasn't Emaru who she made eye contact with when she turned. Instead, a dark-skinned girl who looked about her own age stood a few meters away, clasping a small bag. Her tan dress was embroidered simply with red and yellow yarn, marking her as a villager.

"You!" Alara jumped up, her own eyes going wide with shock. "You have magia!"

"W-what?" The girl's voice trembled, and she took a step back. Alara caught movement out of the corner of her eye, seeing Raquel turning the corner around a squat stone building. She was looking at both of them in shock, a bowl of quinoa in her hands. As the village girl turned to flee, Raquel didn't hesitate. The bowl fell to the ground, yellow grains of quinoa scattering in the dirt. In an instant, Raquel had pulled out her bow and shot a receptive-tipped arrow directly at the girl's head.

She let out a quick yelp as a blast of air exploded at the back of her skull, and she crumpled to the ground.

Chapter 3

Alara

"You didn't need to knock the poor girl out," Alara said.

Raquel and Emaru lifted the dazed girl into the cart that had just arrived from the Haven. She hadn't spoken and was holding a hand to her head where Raquel had hit her with the receptive-tipped arrow.

Raquel shrugged, looking back at Alara. "I thought she was a bruya."

Alara motioned toward the embroidered dress that the girl was still wearing. The fabric was rough, but clean and well fitting. The skirt hit the girl at the knee and flared out from her waist. Bruyas didn't wear any particular uniform, but the ones that Alara had seen were always disheveled and dirty, and they certainly did not wear brightly embroidered dresses.

"Does she seriously look like she's been living in hiding in the cloud forest to you?" Alara said, noticing the village girl's eyes flickering awake.

"She's so much older than magites normally are," Raquel

said, her voice lowering to a whisper. "Why hasn't she been found before in the testings?"

This last question was directed toward Emaru, who was climbing out of the cart. Her lips were pursed and eyes narrowed. She ignored the question and walked away to speak with a group of gathered villagers.

Raquel turned back to Alara, her brown eyes flashing. "You sure she has magia? You're not exactly flawless with your powers."

Alara couldn't quite argue that point. "Emaru tested her, too. She definitely has abilities."

She looked toward the wagon again. The girl was now hunched in the cart, eyes cast downward. Her dark, loosely curled hair stuck up a bit haphazardly, and there was a streak of mud on her chin. But she still managed to look defiant, a grim expression on her face. She was also tall, her shoulders broad with muscle. What kind of job did she do around the village?

"That's the father, I assume," Raquel said, moving her head toward the man Emaru was talking with.

Looking him over, she could see the resemblance. He had the same dark skin and hair, cropped close to his ears. While he was taller than even his daughter, his body was round and soft, making him look less formidable than her. Dull eyes hid beneath bushy eyebrows, his soft chin lined with a graying beard.

The man's brows furrowed in confusion, and he shook his head as Emaru spoke. Alara and Raquel occasionally looked back at the wagon where the girl sat stone silent. Finally, Alara saw the man give a curt nod before turning away, not even sparing a glance toward the wagon.

"I don't think he knew," Alara said.

"El'dyo," Raquel rolled her eyes. "Blameless villagers can be so stupid."

Emaru returned to the wagon and looked up at the girl, who still sat hunched and silent. "Quenti," she said softly.

The girl's—Quenti's—honey-colored eyes flashed, and she finally swiveled them sharply toward Emaru. They sparkled with something that Alara couldn't quite read.

"You have nothing to fear, child," Emaru said. "My name is Senye Linda Emaru, and I am in charge of the school at the Haven. I have spoken with your father, and he understands the situation. He's packing your things and then we will be on our way to your new home."

No response. Alara couldn't tell if this was a sign of defiance or confusion on the girl's part.

"I imagine this is all a bit of a shock for you, but we'll have plenty of time to talk on the journey." If the girl's silence and lack of decorum bothered her, she didn't show it. Emaru flashed an enormous smile. "This is the beginning of your new life!"

Quenti still didn't respond, but Alara thought she saw the spark of anger in her eyes as she turned away and let her hair fall in front of her face.

Alara must have fallen asleep at some point, because the sun was already high in the sky, the air thick with the afternoon heat, when she opened her eyes.

The cart bumped along the Via Sura, jostling her and Quenti, who sat silently in the back. Other than the two of them, along with the village girl's small canvas bag of belongings, the cart was empty, having dropped off its supplies at Hurazon with the replacement guards.

The path they were on wound its way along the river, in the valley between green mountains that sloped on either side of it.

This part of Sombria was known for its near constant mountains and hills. Each village or town on this side of Cielo was built along the narrow valleys that wove between the steeps slopes, the single road connecting them all to the Haven.

The recent rains had made the stone path slick, but the l'lamas were surefooted as they pulled them along. Emaru and the few councilguards returning to the Haven rode alongside the cart on the council-bred l'lamagas—which stood at least four hands taller than the ones pulling the cart and were significantly larger than any of the l'lamas ranchers raised in the outskirts of Sombria.

Alara looked over at Quenti, whose eyes stared straight ahead of her, focused on the l'lamas pattering in front of them. Alara leaned over, trying to catch the girl's eye. "So… that was your father back there?"

Quenti's eyes flickered to hers and then back to the l'lamas.

"Did he know you had magia?" She paused for a moment. "Did you know? How did you not get picked up in the annual testings? I've never heard of magia coming out so late."

Quenti sighed deeply, but remained silent.

"I don't even remember when my magia started," Alara said, leaning back against the cart's tailboard. "I guess I've always assumed I had it. What powers do you have?"

Nothing.

"I'm a fire mage and a mind-stalker—not very good on either account," Alara clarified.

She knew she was rambling, but the silence was making her uncomfortable, and she was still too tired to properly censor herself. But Quenti gave her nothing. After the initial recognition that told her the girl could hear her, she hadn't glanced at her once. She may as well have been speaking another language.

Giving a huff, Alara crossed her arms and looked away from

Quenti. *Fine.* She made eye contact with one of the council-guards riding along next to them and gave him a smile.

Ardo, one of Emaru's personal guards, pulled up alongside the cart where Alara sat.

"Good morning, sleepyhead." Ardo's smile was large and bright, and his pale gray eyes wrinkled at the corners.

"Haha."

"You missed all the excitement."

"I'm sure. What was it? A wild guinea pig crossing the trail? I haven't seen one of those in a whole day."

"You missed the pumisi attack earlier. It jumped in the cart and tried to eat you, mistaking you for a dead body. But don't worry, I fought it off single-handedly." His eyes flashed with amusement at this own joke. "You can thank me later."

"My hero…" Alara said dryly, but she smirked back at him. He was only a few years older than her, but that hadn't stopped the two of them from becoming fast friends. He also so happened to be one of the best physical fighters among the councilguard, despite being a blameless, and Alara couldn't help but admire him for that. In her never-ending desire to prove her worth to Senye Emaru, she had originally sought out the strongest oppo-nent she could find so she could take him down—proof of her superior ability without magia. While she never defeated Ardo in one-on-one combat, she had gained his respect, despite her low magite ranking.

"How's the new girl?" he asked, gesturing to Quenti, who was still ignoring them.

Alara shrugged. "I think she'll settle in over time. I can't imagine being picked up at this age—with a life already built somewhere else."

Ardo nodded solemnly. "It's hard to say goodbye to your home."

It took her a moment to remember that Ardo hadn't grown up in the Haven or even Cielo. She actually wasn't even sure where he was from. She opened her mouth to ask, but Emaru's voice cut her off.

"Ardo, can you scout ahead for a place to rest and water the l'lamas and l'lamagas? I think we're all starting to slow down a bit."

"Duty calls." Ardo gave Alara a quick wink before pushing his l'lamaga forward in a trot, away from the group.

Alara turned back to the village girl. "The roads seem bumpier than on the way here, huh? Although I guess you wouldn't know."

Quenti didn't bother to look her way, and Alara slumped back into the cart and closed her eyes.

By the time they made camp for the night, all she had gotten from the girl was a sideways glare. This was going to be a long trip. She would have much preferred to be riding on a l'lamaga alongside Ardo and the other councilguards, but there were no extra mounts that could carry her.

A long trip indeed.

A few mornings later, when they woke up at their camp, she could almost feel the rain coming. The air sat heavy with humidity and haze whiting out the treetops in the distance. Her hair curled stubbornly, and she had to pull it back a few times to keep it from sticking to her forehead.

At breakfast, Alara watched Quenti sit, still sullen and silent as the others ate and talked around her—a pattern that had developed over the past few days. After that first day, no one bothered trying to speak with her, and she seemed perfectly content with this.

Dark circles sat under Quenti's eyes. Alara had noticed them on the first morning, and they'd only been getting deeper as the journey continued. Multiple days in, and they were now dark purple bruises residing under bloodshot eyes.

Had the girl slept at all since they'd left Hurazon?

Leaning over to her, Alara shoved the warm tortilla in her hand under Quenti's nose. Her eyes met Alara's for a moment before she looked back down. Without speaking, she grabbed the warm snack and stuffed it down hungrily in three bites.

"Thanks." The single word was soft and quick, but Alara took it as a win.

They ate without speaking, but as Alara passed Quenti more tortillas, the silence seemed at least a little less oppressive.

"When did you get taken? To the Haven, that is."

Alara gave a small start at the sound of Quenti's voice. It was deep and a little hoarse, having gone unused for a few days now.

"Um…" Alara said, pondering the question. "I was four—I think."

After breakfast, they packed up again, and as Alara and Quenti jumped into the cart, Emaru climbed in behind them. Alara suppressed a giggle at the way Emaru sat stiff and awkward, her long legs folded under her not quite gracefully. A woman of her ranking was used to sitting in chairs or atop l'lamaga mounts, not on the floor with blameless or magite peasants.

"We should arrive at the Haven before mid-meal," Emaru said. "How's the ride been so far? It's quite a long trip from the outskirts."

Quenti shrugged and predictably didn't respond.

"Well, when we get to the Haven, I know you'll likely be

excited to settle in and rest, but I also want to prepare you for a few things and make sure you have a lay of the land." Emaru ignored Quenti's stubborn silence.

"We will be going through to the schools where the dorms are and where you'll be staying," Emaru said. "Everyone starts in the School of Researchers, but depending on where your talents, strengths, or passions lie, you can move to train at the other schools later. We'll have to figure out where to place you in terms of level—we rarely get magites your age coming through. I'm sorry to say you'll likely end up with the six- and seven-year-olds for now."

She paused and eyed Quenti. "I spoke with your father. He didn't know you had abilities."

Quenti shrugged.

"I'll admit he didn't seem to be the most attentive fellow," Emaru said, "but it did seem strange that he remembered no odd details. Usually, those with abilities at least exhibit telltale signs that their guardians pick up on. I've never seen a parent so blatantly oblivious to a child's magia before." Emaru let the unspoken implication linger in the air for several seconds.

Quenti paled slightly, but her expression didn't change, and she shrugged.

"Do you know what abilities you have?" Emaru asked.

Quenti's eyes narrowed, and Alara waited for Emaru to realize that she wasn't going to answer, but then Quenti surprised her. With a sharp wave of her hand, the haze in the surrounding air thickened until a small cloud formed, hovering just above them in the cart. Another wave of her hand and a light sprinkle of rain began. Alara gave a small gasp of surprise as the cool water hit her face.

But before she could really appreciate the rain, Emaru blew the cloud away with a wave of her hand. "Impressive."

Quenti shrugged. "I don't have much control. I'm sure others could do better."

Emaru smiled brightly. "Control we can teach."

Alara was about to ask if Quenti could make another rain cloud, but the unspoken request was made moot when a loud crack of thunder vibrated through the forest and the sky opened up with a roar. The councilguards let out a grumble and pulled the hoods of their ponchos up, but Alara let out a childish "whoop!" and turned her face up to the sky. The dried dirt that caked her skin from the last couple of days melted into mud and fell in rivulets from her skin.

She spent most of her days underground in the Haven, and it was a rare joy to enjoy the rain. Emaru gave her a wry look as she pulled her own hood over her head, but said nothing as Alara's brown hair plastered to her face.

Her clothes were heavy and soaked through by the time the rain stopped and the clouds dispersed. The forest also thinned around them, allowing more sunlight to filter in through the trees. Before long, they broke through the greenery and into open fields. The din of Cielo drifted across the fields, and Alara gazed upon the distant city as they approached.

They were joined on the road by other travelers. Some pulled carts with l'lamas and others trekked on foot, their sandals and boots slapping against the wet stone of the path. Out of the corner of her eye, Alara saw Quenti's eyes widen at the sight.

From afar, Cielo resembled an oddly colorful mountain, but as they approach, Alara could make out the terraces that wove around the city, covered in colorful stone buildings and bright wool tents. Speckles of movement could also be seen as the citizens of Cielo bustled around the narrow streets. Based on the din and commotion, it was a market day. She couldn't help but smile at the look in Quenti's eyes as they got closer—Cielo really was breathtaking.

"Beautiful, isn't it?"

"It's… big," Quenti said, her eyes not moving away from the landscaped mountain. Alara frowned slightly at the coldness in the other girl's voice, so mismatched with Alara's own joy at seeing home.

As they neared the city walls, their cart and convoy separated out from the crowd, onto a small path, and toward an enormous set of doors built into the stone walls, away from the open gate of Cielo. Two councilguards pushed the doors open, and Alara let out a small gasp as a wave of cool air hit her wet skin.

The cart made its way into a dark tunnel, which connected to the twisting underground tunnels of the Haven buried under Cielo. Alara let her eyes adjust to the dim lighting of the cavern and looked back at Quenti, whose awed expression had been wiped away. Her back was stiff and her face drawn as the cart came to a stop.

"Welcome to the Haven," Emaru said, her smile bright in the torchlight.

Chapter 4

QUENTI

The trip to Cielo gave Quenti too many hours to think. Each day that passed, her hope of escape drained from her. She knew that once they reached the teeming tunnels of the Haven, there was little hope of coming out. Her mother had told stories of the city beneath the mountain and the magia users that disappeared into its depths.

Terror gripped her throat and refused to let go, growing with each mile traveled. She had failed her mama. After all the times she had saved her, here she was heading directly to the center of their country, to the Council her mother had all but despised.

She spent each night huddled against the cold, away from the dying fire as her captors turned in. Plans of escape flooded her mind every evening. But it had been a hopeless thought. Each night, her eyes burning with exhaustion, she watched the guards pace their campsite, unerring as they took their shifts. Her weariness weighed on her body like a stone as she watched the guards standing dead still against a tree, eyes focused on her. By the fourth night, without her permission, her eyes closed and didn't open until the bustling of the camp woke her, the sky a pale mauve.

She knew she needed to sleep if she had any chance of escape. She tried sleeping in the day, to ignore the prattling of the idiot girl beside her and the banging of the wagon along the stone path. Sunlight filtered between the trees, sending a constantly dance of light and dark across her eyelids. It was impossible to relax, surrounded as she was.

By the time the cart had made its way into the shadow of Cielo, her entire body was heavy and sluggish. She hadn't even managed to find a moment to slip away when she was left to do her business. There was always a female councilguard casually leaning on a tree near enough to grab her if she ran.

Quenti looked up as the city rose above them, her eyes burning and body numb. The mountain loomed large—larger than any of the more shallow hills around. And rather than the rich green of the cloud forest, it sparkled with color in the late morning sun. The white walls of the city sparkled and a rainbow of rooftops stretched across the cascading levels of streets. At the top, a dome made entirely of crystal and stone overshadowed the entire city. She couldn't help the small gasp that fell from her lips at the sight.

But when the dense doors had shut behind them and the icy councilwoman—Emaru—had jumped down from her l'lamaga, Quenti's mind went into high alert. There was no time for exhaustion. She was in enemy territory now. She almost smiled at the irony of this thought—enemy territory—the capital city of her own country.

As Quenti followed her dull-witted companion—Alara—out of the cart, the councilwoman waved her hand toward them. A sharp breeze pelted the two of them, almost threatening to knock her backward. She seized up involuntarily, anticipating a follow-up attack until she noticed its purpose. The flurry of air was cold, but it dried the loose water on her skin and clothes quickly. Quenti felt her caution morph into annoyance. She could have driven the water away using her own abilities, thank you very much. In a mark of defiance, she did just that, pushing the remaining moisture off of her body and clothes, leaving it almost completely dry within seconds.

The councilwoman smiled, which was the exact opposite reaction Quenti had hoped for.

Damn.

Quenti knew it was petty, but behind enemy walls, every detail of her abilities could be used against her. She took a deep breath and smelled the musty scent of damp earth, nothing like the clear, crisp scent of her hometown.

She cast her eyes around the large cavern where their unloaded collection of carts and camping supplies sat. The coachmen ushered the l'lamas and l'lamagas off through a corridor to the right, which she assumed led to a stable of some sort.

The councilwoman guided them forward to where the cavern narrowed into another corridor. She stood straight as she walked —almost stiff—making her tall, thin frame oddly formidable. Her dark hair was streaked with gray and pulled back in a severe bun at the nape of her neck. Quenti winced as she stared at the woman's hairline, which was pulled taut, with the base of the hair bearing a red tint. This detail, of all things, made her realize how much she did not want to be on this woman's bad side. Anyone who could put up with that much self-inflicted pain likely warranted some form of fear.

Within the caverns of the mountain, the once-prevalent sound of the rain was nearly imperceptible. Though if she concentrated hard enough, she could just make out the sound of water moving within the recesses of the mountain. She placed a hand gently against the cool wall and closed her eyes. It was made of pressed soil, but it was firm beneath her palm.

When she opened her eyes, Alara was right in front of her. Of course.

"You know, it's not actually the sound of rain you're hearing." The dull-witted girl had an annoyingly proud tone in her voice.

Quenti's face reddened in irritation as she removed her hand from where it rested. "I don't care."

"It just seemed like—"

"I don't care." She turned her head and sped up, catching up with the councilwoman. As far as she was concerned, this long tunnel was nothing to admire, but just a means of her eventual escape. Her stomach growled and legs shook, as if reacting to the thought. She'd escape after she got some food and rest.

After turning left, the wide corridor narrowed into a hallway. The ceiling was likely at least four feet above Quenti's head, but with the walls closing in on them, it was hard to escape a feeling of claustrophobia.

Torches lined the hall, lit with what she assumed was mage fire, given the unnatural white smoke filtering up and into the small vents in the ceiling. She bit her lip to stop from gasping— she didn't want to get that stupid girl's attention again. Each torch had its own small crystal receptive embedded in the base. She had heard of crystals that could hold on to a mage's powers long after they had stopped casting them. A trader passing by Hurazon had once shown off a small pink quartz that he claimed was a receptive, though no one in the village believed him. The fact that he couldn't prove it was doubly suspicious.

Crystal receptives were considered incredibly rare—mined only from a few specific locations along the eastern border of Sombria—and their hefty price reflected this. The idea that so many were being used to simply light her way made her feel queasy. Of *course* the Haven would use this sought-after resource for such a mundane purpose. A quick glance at the others showed she was the only one sickened by this—though Alara's obliviousness wasn't surprising.

Several minutes passed, and the councilwoman led them down various junctions within the tunnels. Occasionally, they'd cross paths with another group going the opposite direction, but no pleasantries were exchanged.

Everyone's probably concentrating on how to get outta here. That had to be it. Quenti herself felt turned around; every hall and door they passed looked the same.

After another ten minutes, the walls parted suddenly, and the corridor widened as the sound of voices and rushing water broke over them. One turn later, they entered an enormous cavern—though, somehow, enormous failed to capture its immense size. She couldn't help the small gasp that escaped her lips, and she cringed at the smile that the other girl gave her. She wouldn't give Alara the satisfaction of a sideways glance. The cavern they stood in was so large that her entire village could fit inside. And it seemed, in fact, an entire village *had* been built inside.

Above them, the ceiling stretched so high that even the bright lights below couldn't illuminate it. Although they were certainly within the confines of a cavern, the expanse was such that it was almost like being outside again. Almost.

But the strange and unnatural reverberations within the walls gave it away. Things sounded different here, sharper, yet more garbled. She took in the scene in front of her, overwhelmed with colors, unable to focus on any specific part. A market was set up in the center of the cavern—one bigger than anything Quenti had ever seen. Hundreds of small tents and tables were scattered around as people streamed between them, chattering and laughing. The bright colors of potatoes, woven cloth, and spices blended together, as the smell of mint, aji, and roast fish sat thick in the air.

Quenti was drawn to the sound of a rushing stream and she saw a twisting canal that wrapped around the market and under a series of bridges. Some of the stalls were propped up tight against the river, and men in thin reed boats handed customers fresh fish from baskets hung along the edge of the canal walls.

Beside her, the young magite let out a breath, and she saw the soft smile of contentment ghosting her lips. The councilwoman, on the other hand, was unaffected. Quenti didn't know who she should be annoyed at more.

An icy hand pressed between Quenti's shoulder blades, pushing her toward a small bridge leading to the center of the cavern.

"Come on now." The councilwoman stepped ahead, her strides long and determined.

Quenti stumbled after the woman, trying to keep up as she did her best to make sense of the scents and sounds around her. One particularly strong whiff of roasted cuy caught her attention, and her stomach grumbled in interest. Meat was a rare delicacy in Hurazon, and the small animal even more so. She'd only had cuy once in her life, when her father had traded for it after a particularly large haul of fish. They had cooked it out on the fire pit in front of their house while her father had loudly commented on his own success in affording the meal.

"Nothing beats the smells of this market." Alara's voice pulled Quenti out of her thoughts and back into the moment.

There was no time to think about food or home. She needed to plan a way out. Her focus roamed from the stalls back toward the edge of the cavern as she counted the exits, determining which one led out to Cielo. But she thought again of the high wall that surrounded the entire city. It wouldn't be as easy as just walking out, though she tried not to let that thought suffocate her.

She followed the councilwoman as they turned down another unmarked hallway on the other side of the cavern.

"Is this how you trap all your captives here?" Quenti said. "Confuse 'em with a maze of tunnels. Are there any booby traps I should be worried about?"

"You'll learn the paths soon enough," Alara responded with an obnoxious smile. "We have maps in the student library that you're free to look at." She nudged Quenti gently, in what she probably meant as a friendly gesture. "And you're not a prisoner."

Quenti's lips pressed tight together in something between a grimace and a smile. "Right. So I can leave?"

Alara's face froze for a second, her wide doe eyes blinking. Quenti's lips stretched into a humorless smile. This girl was either brainwashed or a damn good actor.

Ahead of them, the councilwoman spoke without pausing her stride. "You are free to leave after all of this if you choose."

Quenti bit her tongue. *I'm sure it soothes their souls to pretend they don't kidnap children from their parents to raise as weapons for their government.*

"But first let us show you what we have to offer. Give us some time before you make up your mind about us. Your father will be waiting for you if you wish to return, I'm sure."

Quenti didn't respond to this. An image flashed in her mind of her father sitting by the hearth with a strong bottle of ferment in their empty house. She shook off the emotion that threatened to clog her throat and refocused on trying to memorize the endless twists and turns they were taking.

After what felt like hours, they came across a stone arch

carved into the tunnel. It wasn't so much a door as it was a threshold to another part of the Haven.

Alara whispered beside her, eyes focused brightly on the intricate carvings. "Welcome home."

This isn't my home.

Quenti turned to glare at Alara, but the other girl was already turning away, heading toward a new hallway that veered off to the right.

"Alara, where are you going?" the councilwoman asked.

"Eh?"

Quenti saw the brainwashed girl's body go rigid before turning back to them.

"I was going to go back to my room," she waved halfheartedly at the bag strapped to her side. "To unpack before my debrief?"

"I think your bag can wait. You're coming with us."

Quenti smirked as the blood drained from the other girl's face. At least she wasn't the only one unhappy right now.

"But my report…"

"Your report for the class that I run? Yes, I think we can figure that out later. We need to discuss some other things first, such as your future at the Haven. No, I haven't forgotten about that. And this may include Quenti here as well."

Quenti's eyes flickered back to the older woman at this, and she knew her own face had gone pale. *Include me how?*

"Include her how?"

"I'm rooming with Quenti?" Alara's voice was loud, and the councilwoman's eyes flashed in reproach.

It turned out that idiotic girl was going to be her prison guard.

"I don't have a second bed!" Alara said. The councilwoman's face was pinched with irritation—so she *does* show emotion—but she simply gave the girl a smooth smile.

"An easy fix, but I'm glad for your concern." She stepped closer to the girl, the threat clear, even to Quenti. "I've been soft with you over the years. Maybe all of this is my fault. You've fallen behind the other students, and it's only getting worse."

"My grades in classes are better than most!"

"In theory and basic fighting skills, maybe. But in the practical applications of magia you haven't passed a single mission exam. Which, if you want to be a councilguard, is where it counts."

Quenti felt she had become invisible, and she used the time to take in the councilwoman's office. The room was cluttered but not messy. Papers and books were neatly stacked and organized across the multiple tables and shelves that lined the walls. A map of Sombria spread across one desk, small carved figures scattered across the parchment in some formation that meant nothing to her.

"There are plenty of blameless who are successful councilguards. I don't need my magia to help the realm."

"I will not have this argument again, Alara," the councilwoman said as she pinched the bridge of her nose. Alone and safe within the confines of the office, she looked almost human as she gave a heavy sigh.

"I have my place here," Alara said.

"You spend most of your days with your blameless friends practicing spear fighting rather than your magia. It's time to stop playing councilguard and become a proper mage."

Alara's eyes widened, and Quenti shifted again, no longer

able to pretend she wasn't listening—not that she didn't enjoy listening to this incredibly personal family squabble.

"My apologies, Quenti," the councilwoman said. "As I was saying, you will room together. I feel you may balance each other out well. Alara could learn to loosen her control over her magia and you'll need to learn how to control yours. Anyhow, you will need to settle in to the Haven, and who better to help than one who's lived here since she was a child?"

Alara gave a small huff. "Can I go now?"

The councilwoman gave a quick nod. "I'll still expect your mission report in my office box by tomorrow."

"So, does this mean I'm not kicked out?" Alara responded, pale.

"Not yet."

CHAPTER 5

QUENTI

The idiot girl left Quenti alone in her—*their*—room shortly after she had thrown her bag down, not even bothering to change. Quenti had to bite her tongue to stop herself from commenting on the stench of l'lama on the other girl's clothes, but she doubted she smelled much better.

Once Alara was gone, Quenti found herself slumped on the other girl's bed, her mind racing and body tense with anxiety. She went over the conversations between the councilwoman and Alara again in her mind.

She may have a prison guard for a roommate, but it seemed her guard wasn't even that good at using her powers. No, it was more than that. This girl didn't even *like* to use her powers. A stupid girl, indeed. If the councilwoman—Senye Emaru, Quenti recalled her name—thought Alara was going to be able to keep Quenti under control, then she was just as foolish as Alara.

She fingered the gold cuff bracelet that rested on her wrist. Senye Emaru had genially locked the damn thing on her arm, as if she weren't aware she was effectively being cuffed by this woman.

"Don't worry," Senye Emaru had said. "All magites wear this at some point in their careers."

As soon as the metal had closed around Quenti's wrist, a pressure had settled in her gut.

Now, looking at the bracelet, it was unassuming and simple in design. It stretched about two finger lengths in width, with a small piece of quartz acting as a clasp where the ends met. There didn't appear to be any specific locking mechanism, and yet as she touched the metal, she couldn't find a way to open it back up. It held tight against her wrist, too tight to slip back over her hand.

Grimly, Quenti reached for her magia, her fears realized as she felt the weight pressing against her. She could still touch it, grasping it lightly and tugging at it in her mind, but it felt weakened and clunky as she manipulated it.

She waved her hand toward the small basin of water that sat in an alcove in the corner. The clear water rose up in small droplets and she spread them out through the air, covering the room in a mist. With a sharp jab that seemed to take more energy than it should have, the cloud swirled and condensed again into a small funnel of water, hovering and dancing through the air. She couldn't help the small bubble of relief that hummed through her as the water danced around the room. The bracelet seemed to dampen her strength, but she still had her powers.

In an ironic twist, even with her abilities dulled, she was, for the first time in her life, free to use them without fear. Back in Hurazon, she had always used them in secret, with one eye focused on her rear. At every turn, she had expected to be caught —by a peer, another villager, by—

She stopped herself there. Dwelling on the past wasn't going to get her out of here any faster, and neither was making pretty patterns with water.

She had just sent the water splashing back into the basin when there was a knock on the door. She immediately jumped up, back straight, like a child caught stealing sweets.

"Um… come in?" Quenti sneered slightly at the waver in her own voice.

The door swung open silently and Quenti saw a mage—no, a *magite*—a few feet back from the door, their arms completely full with some type of roll.

"I got a bed for you. Well… a mattress, anyhow," the young boy said, shrugging. "They said they would get a frame in here for you by tomorrow."

Quenti nodded and vaguely waved her arms to invite the boy in.

He took two steps into the room before spinning on his heels and looking around, an eyebrow raised.

Quenti scrunched her own face up as she took in what he was noticing. The entire floor of the room was littered with clothes, books, and literal weapons. A long spear was peeking out from under a rough woolen dress, the bronze tip blinking sharply in the torchlight of the room. She had been so caught up in her own head that she failed to notice the state of Alara's quarters.

"Where… do you want it?" the boy said, just as Quenti snapped.

"What the hell does she do in here?"

He let out a small snort of laughter.

"You're rooming with Alara, right?"

"Or a tornado. I forget."

"I don't think she's ever had a roommate before, and she's been here longer than anyone else I know."

"I got as much," Quenti said. She gave a small huff and

began shoving clothes and books aside in one of the corners with her feet, attempting to clear a spot large enough for a bed roll.

"My name's Ander."

"Quenti."

The young boy—Ander—was quiet for a few minutes as she cleared a space and motioned for him to put the roll down. Her eyes widened in surprise as he opened his arms and sent the roll into the corner with a gust of wind. It hit the wall with a small thud and landed slightly crooked.

"Impressive," she said. "Unnecessary, but impressive."

He blushed slightly at this. He looked to be about twelve or thirteen and he was wearing a pale yellow tunic over cream trousers.

"Sorry. I try and practice as much as I can."

"So you're a wind mage?"

"Magite." His eyes widened slightly. "I still have six years until my terminal exams."

Right. All that stupid nonsense. Quenti looked the boy up and down. She never understood how the Haven could take children at such a young age.

"How long have you been at the Haven?"

"I was sent here about four years ago," he said. "You should have seen me before. My parents didn't know what to do with me." He smiled fondly, lost in the thought.

Her chest tightened.

Brainwashed.

"I remember one morning when I got angry at my little sister and I accidentally sent her flying out the window. My mom didn't know whether to ground me or jump for joy. She sent for the Council the next morning to have me tested."

"Do you ever get to go home to visit your family?" she asked, voice warm and mind already calculating how much movement there was of magites in and out of the Haven.

"Once we start going on missions, we get to spend some time at home, but not until we get our powers under control. Without control, we're a danger to our families and villages."

Yup. Brainwashed.

Quenti's jaw clenched and she kept silent, knowing she'd probably say something she'd regret if she did open her mouth. Ander's lips tightened slightly, and she blinked, trying to wipe any telltale sign from her face. She'd usually speak her mind, but even if she didn't, her face usually spoke for her.

His shoulders suddenly shifted, and the tightness in his face melted away. "This is for you, too." He shrugged off the bag he was holding that she hadn't noticed until now. "It's your uniform."

She took the offered bag and looked inside at the contents. A dark blue tunic, pale trousers, and a long black woven piece of fabric.

"Blue for water. When we graduate, our *aguayo*," he motioned toward the black scarf, "is exchanged for the color of our powers. Mages wear the black tunics and the colored *aguayo*. You'll learn all about it in your basics class." Suddenly his face twisted in a look of bemusement. "At least all the littles learn it during their first classes."

She recognized what the issue was. "Ah. I imagine I am older than most… littles."

"I didn't mean—I'm sure—" he stuttered out.

Quenti laughed at the blush in his cheeks. "I just hope the desks aren't too small for me."

He smiled and relaxed once more. "I should go. Senye Cruz wanted to see me after I dropped these off. Oh! And she said that you're to meet at Senye Emaru's office tomorrow after first meal to get your schedule."

He practically ran out the door, leaving Quenti alone once again. She looked around the room, taking in the scattering of weapons, disappointed to see everything the girl owned seemed to be a club or larger. Nothing she could hide in her tunic—not that she was much good with any weapon. The only thing she had ever gotten good at in Hurazon was fishing and pissing off her father.

She went to shut the door Ander had left open and saw a man leaning against the wall in the hallway, reading a book. But the second her head peaked out, his shoulders tensed and his eyes scanned over her. She had a feeling there was going to be no wandering around the Haven by herself quite yet.

She gave him a cheeky wave, taking a small amount of satisfaction at the slight alarm on his face before closing the door to the room. She slumped on the newly placed mattress and tried to stop her mind from spiraling.

Hours later, Quenti was sitting on her mattress, eyelids heavy, body buzzing with anxiety, when Alara walked in. Alara's eyes narrowed slightly as she took in the corner Quenti had set up for herself, but didn't say anything as she marched in and dropped the shawl she was wearing onto the floor beside one of the spears.

"Do you usually store your weapons in the middle of your room?"

Alara crossed the chamber without speaking and picked up the two spears Quenti had seen earlier, as well as a set of bolas and a long wooden staff with a bronze star at the end. The girl may not have been good at using her powers, but she held her weapons with a confidence and ease that made Quenti not want to be on the other side of an attack. Alara set them against the shelves near her bed.

The room was silent and Quenti was still, watching her as she bundled up fresh clothes in her arms and marched back out of the room. Was she angry about having a roommate? She almost —*almost*—empathized with her. But then again, one of them was angry for being kidnapped from her home, the other because she had a new roommate.

She can deal.

Quenti let out a growl of frustration, her head landing heavy on the hardened wall behind her. The pain did nothing to ease her anger, but she took a few breaths and tried to get herself to just *think*. She didn't have many options right now in terms of avenues for information. Apart from Ander, and whatever the Haven might actually store in the library, it seemed Alara was her best bet.

The girl may have been terrible at using her abilities, but she'd lived in the Haven for practically her entire life. If there was a way out of this place, Alara would know.

The question was how to pull the information from her.

When Alara returned to the room, clothes fresh and wet hair plaited down her back, Quenti swallowed back a snarky comment and pasted on her best smile.

"I hope the corner I chose for my bed is okay?"

She froze and gave Quenti a slightly startled look. "Oh… I mean, yeah. It's fine." She smiled weakly. "Have you settled in well?"

"Yes, unpacking my single bag of clothing was exhausting, but I managed," Quenti said without thinking. Alara's smile faltered and Quenti gave a slightly over the top flinch, "Sorry, I'm just tired." *And kidnapped.*

Alara bit her lip. "It must be hard. I barely remember coming to the Haven, so it's not really something I ever had to worry about. You probably miss your dad."

Quenti ignored that last statement, schooling her face not to react. "You were that young when you came here, then?"

It seemed this was a topic that Alara didn't want to talk about either. She simply shrugged, busying herself putting away the clothes that littered the floor.

"Did you get your schedule from Emaru yet?" Alara asked, collapsing heavily onto her bed, the clothes now thrown into a large pile in the corner. Apparently, that was what she considered clean.

Quenti shook her head, "No, I think I'm going to be thrown in with the six-year-olds though."

"I guess that makes sense."

"I'm trying not to be too offended."

"You have to learn the basics," Alara said before pausing, "but then again, you seemed to know how to use your powers a bit already."

Quenti's heart rate spiked slightly, her face froze for a second. But no… Alara wasn't a mind-walker. She was a mind-*stalker*, and a poor one at that. Plus, even if another mage had tried to read her thoughts, Quenti would know; the touch of another mind had always been familiar to her, like the soft touch of a hand on her arm.

"So you're a fire mage?" Perhaps changing the subject was safer anyway, and she wanted to start to get to know her… captor.

"Um—yeah. Well, magite. As you heard, I haven't quite passed my tests yet."

"Well, you're clearly not stuck with the seven-year-olds, so you can't be that bad"

"That's not quite Linda's—Emaru's—perspective."

"She seems a bit like a stick in the mud," Quenti said, eyeing her reaction.

Alara's eyes widened and she let out a small snort. "El'dyo, never let her hear you say that or she'll send you flying."

Well that's one way out of here, Quenti thought grimly.

"All right. Show me."

"What?"

"Your magia," Quenti said. "Show me what you can do!" She sat up and leaned toward Alara, putting on her best curious face. Not that she had to fake it—she really wanted to see how bad Alara was with her magia.

"I'm starting to think an excited Quenti is a dangerous Quenti."

"Come on. Show me what you've got," Quenti challenged again.

"No, thank you."

Quenti jumped across the room and landed with a thud onto Alara's bed, "Come on! You've got to be better than me if I'm the one stuck with the babies."

"No. Really."

"Maybe the councilwoman's right. You won't ever be a councilguard with that attitude."

She had hit a nerve. Alara's dark eyes flared and her cheeks flushed. For a moment, Quenti almost thought she could feel the heat of Alara's powers like a mind-stalker.

"Fine," Alara snapped, locking eyes with her. The few torches that lined the room suddenly flared fully to life. Flames shot to the ceiling. Sparks crackled angrily as they jumped about.

And then the heat was gone, and Alara's eyes widened with alarm.

"The rug!"

Quenti turned to see that some sparks had landed on a rug centered in the room—a rug that had previously been hidden by piles of clothes. It was smoldering, fire eating away at the woven pattern.

"Well, put it out," Quenti said looking puzzled at Alara.

"I can't! I don't have water."

"With your powers, stupid!" Quenti was caught between annoyance and utter confusion.

"What!? I don't know how to do that."

"Seriously?"

Alara just gave her a helpless look.

Sol help us…

Quenti turned to the fire and felt the cool wave of her *magia* rising up from somewhere deep in her body. The water in the basin that she had been playing with earlier gracefully twirled into the air and landed onto the rug, steam and smoke hissing.

Quenti turned back to Alara grinning. "You are an absolutely amazing disaster."

And I won't even mention the fact that you could have used the basin yourself to put out the fire.

Alara flinched.

"Do you even realize how powerful you are?"

"You just called me a disaster."

"A powerful disaster, don't get me wrong. You barely even batted an eye and almost caught the entire room on fire."

"I'm confused if you think almost burning my room down is a good thing."

"If that's you when you're out of practice *and* with these stupid things on"—she shook her cuffed wrist in Alara's face—"I wouldn't want to be on your bad side when you learn to use your powers."

"Those are to help magites as they get used to their powers," Alara said, completely guileless.

"Ha. Help. Right. So do you all wear these until you become mages?"

"No, most take them off once they get far enough into their training to have some basic control."

"So you're still wearing yours because...?"

Alara ignored the question and laid back on her bed, eyes closed.

Quenti was still sitting on the edge of the bed as she examined the girl lying completely defenseless before her. Defenseless in more ways than one. This *magite* actually believed in everything the Haven stood for, and seemed to assume everyone else did too.

"So where can a girl get dinner around here?"

Alara didn't move from her position on the bed, but her stomach betrayed her with a loud rumble.

"There's a dining hall for the students."

"Anywhere we can go where I won't be stared at by a bunch of magites?"

"The market will likely still being going on in the central cavern. If you have a few bronze pieces, you can get some great fresh produce from the north region."

"Does it look like I have any money?" She hadn't meant it to come out peevish, but she knew her annoyance was evident.

Rolling off her bed with a groan, Alara slipped on her sandals. She didn't seem to notice or care about the bite in Quenti's voice. "You'll get your allowance soon enough. Come on. I'll buy tonight."

The market hadn't quieted down from that afternoon, and Quenti's eyes were wide as they wandered around the aisles, taking in the selection of food. The air was heavy with spices, roasting fish, and corn. In all her life, in all her trips to the markets near their town, she had never seen so much food. She counted nearly twenty varieties of potatoes at just one booth and saw another one piled high with enough dried meat to feed a family of seven over the entire dry season.

Before long, her arms were piled with fresh fruit, three types of roasted potatoes, and two ears of corn. They ate at the benches along the edge of the canal, and she was finally happy—at least happy that her stomach was full. The corn was smoky, salty, and sweet, and she felt an ease settle over her shoulders as she savored the final bites.

"So do you just spend all day'n night in this mountain?" she asked, swallowing her last bit of corn.

Alara shrugged, "You can wander out to Cielo on free days, but most the time magites just stay around here. The Haven is its own underground city."

"No wonder you are all so pale."

"Some of us, yes. It's usually how you can tell a blameless from a mage out of uniform."

Quenti shook her head. "Sol, how do you do it? I'd miss the sun—the forest—the animals."

She saw the small wince, and she wasn't sure it was from the curse or the sentiment. Her mom had raised her under the old religion, but she knew it was all but forbidden in Sombria to speak of Sol and the Many gods. If Alara caught the slip, she seemed willing to ignore it… for now.

"I can take you around to the back of Cielo the next day we have off. The city terraces don't wrap all the way around, and the cloud forest climbs right up the side of the mountain. It's only broken by the occasional window. It's quite peaceful."

A small spark of hope jolted through Quenti and she bit her lip to hide a smile.

Alara finished off her own roasted potatoes with a contented sigh. "We should probably head back. Curfew will be starting soon. Magites are expected to be back in the school an hour after sunset each night, though there is no curfew on being in our rooms."

Quenti got up without complaint, stuffing an extra granadiya in her pocket for a snack later.

Alara led them back through the tunnels toward the dorms and she found herself slowly falling behind her, shortening her steps and slowing her pace purposefully.

Despite the heaviness in her eyes, she wasn't ready to fall asleep just yet. She wanted to see more of the tunnels that twisted under the mountain. And this was likely the best opportunity she would have for a while. To her left was one that led to a set of narrow steps disappearing down, deeper into the mountain.

"Quenti!" Alara's voice was sharp behind her.

"Where does this go?" She was already partway down the tunnel.

"Not to our room!" Alara said, her voice growing clear as she followed Quenti with short, irritated steps.

"I want to see more of the Haven," Quenti said, mostly honestly.

"It's just about curfew."

"I thought you said there wasn't any curfew."

"There is for the Haven, just not our rooms," Alara huffed. "And you'll be starting class tomorrow. Don't you think you should rest?"

"Oh, please. I'll be dancing circles around those little children tomorrow, even with this stupid cuff." Quenti jangled her wrist above her head as she continued down the steps.

"We're going to get in trouble."

"Emaru said you needed to get a little out of control!"

"I don't think that is what she meant!"

"Yeah, but we can always play dumb." *Not that you'd have to do much playing on your part.* With that, Quenti quickened her pace, taking the steps in twos and smiling to herself as she heard Alara's footsteps behind her.

Chapter 6

Alara

Alara saw the dancing lights before she heard the soft din of raised voices. She had been following Quenti down the narrow hallways for a few minutes already and was getting anxious.

"Hey, we should head back now."

"What's down there?" Quenti eyed the dancing colors that glowed through an opening down the hall.

"Nothing special. And definitely nothing we should be messing with." She tried to grab Quenti's arm, pulling her back. But the girl was unperturbed by Alara's hand and kept walking forward, dragging Alara along after her. The commotion up ahead told her exactly where they were going.

"It could be dangerous!" Alara gasped out.

"How would you know unless we check it out?"

Before she could express her apprehension or argue again, Quenti bounded forward.

"Quenti, the dark marketplace is dangerous!"

"And it has a name!" Quenti said. "*Dark* marketplace? So

creative. And how would you even know about this *dark market-place*, Senye Goody-goody?"

"I've lived here long enough to hear things and…" Before she finished, they rounded the corner, and her voice died, along with the rest of her thoughts. "Oh."

The tunnel opened up into a long cavern.

Alara had indeed heard about the dark marketplace—Emaru had spent many an evening ranting about the continued struggle to shut it down and her own annoyance that the rest of the council was content to let it go on, albeit frowned upon. But she had never dared go looking for it and had never seen it in person.

It wasn't as large as the upper marketplace, but it sure was alive. The cavern brimmed with people, noises, and lights as magia shot through the air. The same torches that lined the halls across the entire Haven were lit and burning along the cavern, but the flames danced with color. Mage fire shot through the air and glowing globes of water sent a kaleidoscope of chroma shining across the ceiling.

Directly in front of them, a dancer moved, her hands flicking and waving in the air as a pink-and-green-tinted firestorm swirled around her. Alara watched with wide eyes as the mage twirled and jumped between the flames without hesitation. The onlookers cheered and threw bronze pieces into the nearby basket.

"Emaru is going to kill me."

"Does she stalk all the magites 'round here?" Quenti asked, looking at Alara sideways.

"What? No."

"Why you, then?"

"She doesn't…" Alara glanced at Quenti before looking away again, her eyes transfixed by the dancer whose head was thrown back and eyes closed as she continued to jump between the flames. "She's the one who found me… after my parents died. She took me in."

"Oh."

Silence fell between them for a brief moment.

"We really should get back!" Alara looked around them at the bustling crowd. What if someone she knew recognized her?

"Five more minutes, Mama. Please!" Quenti's eyes went wide and she arched her eyebrows at Alara.

"Seriously, no."

Quenti gave a toothy grin before jumping away. "Fine! But you'll have to catch me."

Alara grabbed at Quenti's tunic as she twisted away, but the thin wool slipped past her fingertips. Damn it. What was this girl, five?

Alara pushed through the crowd, swimming past a sea of elbows and shoulders that closed in tighter the farther she went. The cavern was long but narrow, and she kept her head down, trying not to make eye contact with anyone she passed. Not many knew her face, but she couldn't imagine what Emaru would do if she heard Alara had been spotted down here.

The Council knew the illegal trade existed here. Alara had in fact first heard about the dark marketplace directly from Emaru. Every once in a while, when it was worth the effort, the council-guards would be sent down to raid the place and arrest a few people. It never seemed worth their time to shut the entire enterprise down, but Emaru and the other councilors wanted to make sure the people didn't get too comfortable flaunting their magia. Looking around at the sparking lights and fire in the air as people laughed and chatted, she wasn't sure the strategy was working.

As she came to an opening in the crowd, she could just see Quenti's curls disappearing ahead of her into a large group. She tried to focus on Quenti up ahead, but the assorted booths drew her attention. Some tables held a large array of rare foods and others held colorful stones and gems. At one booth, she noted that distinct shine of receptives: quartz, pyrite, jasper, and chrysocolla. Some pieces were small, barely the size of a fingertip, and others were as large as Alara's palm. Considering how tightly the Council controlled any magia receptives, she was pretty sure they were illegal.

Alara was still staring at the booth of receptives when she ran into a warm body.

"Hey!" Alara said instinctively before realizing it was Quenti. "No more running off, okay? We have to get going before anyone sees us."

The other girl ignored her, her eyes focused on a booth next to the receptive stall. A tall dark-haired mage was performing a sort of puppet show, his hands waving smoothly to create intricate animals from water. They bounded around the small stage set in front of him, l'lamas dancing around as a puma tried to attack them, missing each time by a hair's length. Quenti's own eyes were wide and bright, and before Alara could register what she was doing, Quenti had given a sharp wave of her own hand, and a condor made of water droplets formed, circling the puma's head.

The performer looked up, his grin wide as he made eye contact with Quenti, whose own face flushed pink. Alara took her moment of distraction to grab her by the arm and pull them her away from the performance booth.

The crowds pressed against them as Alara tried to get her bearings in the dimly lit cavern. She had never seen such a mix of mages and blameless in a large crowd—the two groups usually kept their distance from each other. Centuries of division between those with magia and those without ended in a war that had almost destroyed the world and caused a rift that even the

Council couldn't quite heal, though it wasn't for the lack of trying. Many blameless still saw the mages for what they were—descendants of a people who had once incited what could only be called a mass attempted genocide. It was an event that mages, to this day, worked to make amends for.

To her surprise, Quenti was no longer trying to run away from her. Her roommate's mouth was in a wide grin and her eyes roamed around, sparkling in the torchlight.

Alara thought back to the almost perfectly-formed condor that Quenti had conjured. It wasn't a powerful display of magia, but it showed an amount of control and finesse that she had never mastered.

"Who taught you how to control your abilities?" Alara finally said.

Quenti looked at her and gave a small frown, but didn't answer.

Alara didn't press her, and instead tried to focus on getting back home. She'd given up trying to go against the flow of the crowd, and instead went with the current, hoping it would loop back to where they started. They passed into a separate room where the distinct sound of wood and bronze meeting echoed. As she strained to see over the heads of the onlookers, she and Quenti were pushed forward. They found themselves standing on the edge of an open circle of people, jeering and hollering at the two fighters in the center of the ring. The man threw his spear at the woman across from him just as a burst of air flew from his other hand. The woman jumped out of the way and turned, throwing a blast of water at him. It missed by a few inches, but she threw another shot that landed straight on.

Alara was mesmerized. She had never seen such a perfect union between physical-and magia-based combat. She knew some of the best councilguards could use these techniques together, but most relied on one form or the other in their fights.

"Mama taught me." Quenti's voice was in her ear, cutting through the noise of the crowd. "And Khuna."

Alara met her eyes with a questioning look.

"She was a girl… from the village next to mine."

"Is she in the Haven now? Maybe we can find her and—"

"No." Quenti's voice was sharp.

"But—" Alara tried to speak again, but the roar of the crowd around them drowned out her words, and she realized the fight had ended. The wind mage stood in the middle of the ring, his fists raised and a smirk playing on his lips.

"Who's next to challenge the Gran Diego!" An announcer stood on a platform behind the ring and called loudly over the crowd.

Quenti gave her a wide grin. "Do it!"

"What?" Alara backed up. Most people would be joking, but there was a terrifying spark in her companion's eye.

"Right here!" Quenti yelled this time, shoving Alara into the circle.

Alara stumbled forward, her hands raised. "No. She's joking."

"She thinks Diego here is a joke," Quenti said. "You hear that? Tell 'em what you told me: 'No better than a baby bruya,' right?"

The man on the platform grinned. "We have a challenge."

Before she could argue further, the announcer tossed a spear at her, which she caught in the air without thinking. There was a loud whistle and suddenly the air mage—Diego—came at her from across the ring. She spun to the side, gripping her spear in a defensive position. She readied for him to lunge again, but missed the wave of his hand. A blast of dirt and sand kicked up from the ground and hit her in the face just as he lunged at her. She blindly ducked out of the way again, but the butt of his spear caught her knee.

Above the roar of the crowd she heard Quenti yell, "Blast him!"

Alara twisted her spear around and threw out her hands, trying to call to the torches that hung around her, but the heat didn't come, and the mage was lunging again.

With a cry of anger, she twisted out of his way at the last moment, relishing the surprise in his eyes as his momentum threw him past her. She slammed the butt of her spear against his back, sending him sprawling on the ground.

Her eyes scanned the crowd for Quenti, a part of her wanting to show that she wasn't completely useless. But she couldn't see her in the crowd of people any longer. With a— probably showy—twirl of her spear she turned back to her opponent, readying for a follow-up attack. Before she could throw her spear, another wave of air hit her at the knees, and she fell forward, off-balance.

A flare of anger surged in her and the heat in her chest sparked. A burst of flames shot from the torches along the walls. Completely unaimed, the fire shot through the crowd, driving the onlookers to the ground, and hit near the feet of her opponent. While it didn't strike him, it distracted him enough that she could turn and take aim at his side with her spear.

"Stop!" a familiar voice rang out as her spear was jerked from her grasp.

A large hand rested on her shoulder, and her stomach dropped.

CHAPTER 7

ALARA

"Good evening, Alara."

"Hi, Adelmo," she said glumly.

His lips pulled down into a frown, creasing his wrinkled forehead, although his blue eyes still sparkled with a hint of humor. His silver beard was short and unkempt—as though he hadn't shaved since she had last seen him—making him look older and more tired. Next to him, upper arm gripped in his other large hand, stood Quenti.

"Now would one of you care to explain to me what Alara Ayar was doing down here at this time of night entering illegal skirmishes?"

"I… uh… we—" Alara stuttered, searching for an answer that made any sense at all and didn't land them in a load of trouble. She turned to Quenti for help, but she was looking around, apparently distracted.

Alara glared daggers at her. She regretted not leaving Quenti on her own when she ran off the first time. She could be safe and warm in bed, and most importantly, not in trouble right now.

Face red with shame, she met Adelmo's eyes. "We got lost?"

"You got… lost. Inside a fighting ring?"

She stared dumbly at him for a second, her mouth open slightly, as if she'd come up with a sudden genius retort. It didn't come, and she closed her mouth finally, silent. She shifted uncomfortably on the balls of her feet and looked away, no longer wanting to meet the intensity of his blue eyes.

"Well, this is awkward." Quenti finally piped up, laughter still dancing in her eyes. "Okay, this was sorta my fault. I tripped and hit her, pushing her into the ring. Next thing we know, they're throwin' a spear at her. I'm just so clumsy."

Adelmo looked Quenti up and down and then turned his gaze back on Alara, who was still trying to not make eye contact.

"Right," he said. "Very clumsy indeed. Well, we'd better get you cleaned up before you head back to the dorms, then. Otherwise, Senye Emaru may find out how clumsy you can be."

Alara looked down at her pants and tunic and saw them smeared with mud. Even her skin was covered in a thin layer of cream-colored dust, lightening her complexion in the dull light. Biting her lip, she lifted her hand to her hair and gave a groan at the tangle of dirt and brown waves her hair had become. It was going to take forever to get it clean again, and she had just bathed that afternoon.

"Come on." Adelmo was already a few steps ahead of her, his hand still leading Quenti along with him as he pushed through the oblivious crowd.

The onlookers' attention had been drawn away from them again to the ring, which now held two new competitors.

It took a few minutes of weaving between people, but they finally burst through on the other side of the crowd. Adelmo led them down a dark and thin tunnel to the side of the fighting chamber. It was empty and the sound of the dark marketplace and din of the audience faded with every turn they took.

Quenti's teeth shone bright in the dark, and Alara gave a huff of annoyance to see she was still smiling after all of this. Alara wasn't sure who she was angry at more: Quenti for leading her down there and pushing her into that ring, or herself for not having ditched the troublemaker when she had the chance. She was not looking forward to the disappointed looks from Adelmo over the next few weeks. He wasn't the type to tattle to Emaru about this little excursion, but she doubted he would let this go quickly.

As turned around as Alara had gotten in their time amid the dark marketplace, as soon as they ascended a set of stone steps, she knew exactly where they were. If she turned right they would find the healing quarter of the Haven and left would take them to the Council's quarter. But Adelmo continued leading them straight down a familiar path to her, the one out to Cielo.

As they passed through the stone arch marking the threshold into the outer city, Quenti threw her head back and took a deep breath, taking in the starry view. "El'dyo, I missed this."

Alara didn't respond, still fuming at the last hour's events. But even she had to appreciate the fresh night air that grazed her face. The moon had waned to almost nothing, and the streets were dark with shadows, the only light coming from a few lanterns and the stars that peppered the navy sky.

The roads were cobbled, winding, and thin. Having been built over hundreds of years, the city limits had slowly expanded as the power of the Council and the Haven grew, attracting more and more blameless. Three distinct walls surrounded much of Cielo. As the population grew, the old walls became defunct. Now, they were more symbolic, sepa-rating the terraces and neighborhoods, though the doorways always remained open, allowing citizens to filter through without trouble.

Where they were now was one of the oldest parts of the city though, where the original blameless had settled. Even still, the streets were barely wide enough for two carts to pass by each other. Against the building, small walkways raised up away from the streets, but these were only wide enough for one person to balance carefully. The three of them walked in the center of the empty street, the stones curving under Alara's thin-soled boots.

"Hey, Senye Strong Grip, where are we headed?" Quenti said, voice dry and unconcerned.

Ignoring her, Alara kept her face toward the sky, appreciating the breeze.

Adelmo didn't look back as he responded, "Home."

Quenti looked around the quiet, sleeping city, her eyes wandering slowly up the buildings, many two stories high in this district. "I thought all the Council's mages lived inside the Haven?"

Alara gave a short snicker before remembering she was still upset at Quenti. Adelmo, however, let out a large and gruff laugh, his face beamed, and he threw a wink at Alara before looking back at Quenti.

"I ain't no mage, kid."

Adelmo's home was a short walk from the Haven entrance, and they made the rest of the trip in silence. As they passed by the stables, Alara peeked in to see the l'lamas and l'lamagas sleeping in their stalls, ears twitching as they dreamed. As soon as they entered Adelmo's house, Alara made a beeline to the chest in the corner without so much as an order from the old man.

To her, his house was almost as much her home as the Haven itself was. In her years residing within the walls of Cielo, she hadn't made very many friends, but Adelmo had always been a sort of parental figure for her—much to the chagrin of Emaru, given Adelmo's blameless blood. Though, in spite of Emaru's protests, Alara had always found ways to sneak away from the Haven to spend her free afternoons with Adelmo in his stables, helping care for the Council l'lamagas. It was the one bit of defiance Alara allowed herself as a magite.

She opened the weathered wooden lid, snatched a well-worn tunic and pair of trousers from inside the chest, and retreated into the water closet to change. After putting on the clean outfit, she quietly went to work filling a bucket with water from the barrel outside.

Quenti sat on a stool near the door, looking dumbfounded at what she saw, and Alara couldn't help but take the slightest bit of satisfaction in her confusion. Adelmo ignored both and made tea next to the fire.

"Okay, so why do you have a change of clothes here?" Quenti finally asked, her voice laced with irritation.

Alara said nothing, though she could hear her just fine. After everything that girl put her through, Alara allowed herself this childish moment of superiority. Instead, she silently wrung out her tunic and pants, washing away the filth of the evening. She hung them out the window of the house before dumping the dirty water outside.

Adelmo handed Quenti a mug of coca tea. Upon receiving it, she absently tapped her fingers onto the leaves floating on top, soaking them in the steaming water.

Adelmo cleared his throat. "I might have taught Alara a thing or two about physical combat while Emaru wasn't looking. I'm sure she's figured it out by now," he shrugged, "but she hasn't told me to stop yet."

Quenti grinned at this, taking a sip of her tea. "How'd you learn to fight?"

Adelmo smiled and waved toward a small club that hung on the wall. It was marked with the Council's symbol: two rings linked together. "The same way all councilguards learn to fight."

Quenti's eyes went wide at this.

"Mind you," Adelmo said, "that was a long time ago, before time had its way with me, leaving me with sore knees and a bad back."

Alara watched from the corner of the room, her own tea clasped in her hands. The others sat close to the fire, despite the warm night, but she had positioned herself as far as she could from the crackling flames. She tried to not hear Raquel's smug voice in her head: *what use is a fire mage afraid of fire?*

The two were chatting amicably. She didn't like how relaxed Quenti looked. How was Alara the one anxious about getting in trouble when it was Quenti that got them into this mess?

To make matters worse, after the initial confusion, Quenti had taken to Adelmo's home like her own—which was actually very annoying. She continued to chat with him, asking him questions about the councilguard and the history of Cielo.

Alara's eyes grew heavy and she set down her mug, leaning back against the bale of hay in the corner. She vaguely wondered how long her magite clothes would take to dry before her eyes finally closed, the sound of Quenti and Adelmo's soft voices lulling her to sleep.

CHAPTER 8

ALARA

Alara woke with a start. The room was silent and cool, the fire having burned out in the hearth. With a panicked jolt, she jumped over to the window and threw back the wool curtain. The sky outside was gray with dawn light.

"Shit!" Alara cursed.

A grumble behind her made her head swivel, and she saw Quenti lying in a pile of blankets near the smoking fire. Adelmo lay on his cot across the room, snoring lightly.

"We are in so much trouble! Get up, quickly. We need to get back to the dorms before morning meal and classes."

She threw off her plain clothes fighting outfit and slipped back into her red tunic. It was still damp and had turned cold in the air overnight. She suppressed a shiver, ignoring the chill in her limbs.

Quenti still sat in her impromptu bed, legs stretched and hair disheveled. Alara's eyes blazed with fresh anger at Quenti's calm face.

"El'dyo, get up!" she hissed. "We're not supposed to be out in Cielo at this time of day."

Quenti gave a long sigh. "Okay, fine. Let's go."

Giving a small wave to the snoring form of Adelmo, Alara and Quenti ducked out from the house. The city was just starting to wake from its slumber. Some of the houses were smoking from the morning fires, and a few vendors wandered around, on their way to start the day.

She knew where they were going. She had been out to Adelmo's more times than she could count and could probably find her way back to her room blindfolded. But she wanted to be careful, knowing that even this early there was activity stirring in the Haven: cooks waking up to head to the kitchens, cleaning staff, and probably even a star magite or two trying to get a jump on their studies.

At one point, Alara heard a sound around the next corner, and she threw out an arm to stop Quenti. The other girl shot her an annoyed look, but stood quietly as they waited for the person to pass.

They were only a few passages away from their room when Alara heard the distinct sound of voices coming toward them. She looked around, but since the passage they were in was so long and thin, and there was nowhere to hide.

Councilwoman Lena Cruz and Mitteo—when had *he* gotten back from the mission?—rounded the corner speaking quietly to themselves. Mitteo noticed them first, his eyes widening in recognition. Senye Cruz followed his gaze and her eyes landed on Alara. Her face creased into a deep frown.

"Alara." She turned and looked Quenti up and down. "I assume you are Quenti, then. Neither of you ladies should be wandering about this time of morning." She exchanged a look with Mitteo, who only stood by silently. Then she gave a sharp jerk of her head. "Come."

There was no doubt she was talking to them. Alara ducked her head and followed, shooting an unacknowledged glare at Quenti. The other girl was finally looking a bit pale and anxious for the first time since arriving.

Alara's stomach dropped as they rounded a few more passages and came into Senye Cruz's office.

She motioned for Alara and Quenti to enter. "You wait here. I'll be right back."

She turned and left, Mitteo still trailing behind her. Alara rolled her eyes at this. He was always following after Senye Cruz like a trained puppy dog. She had to assume the only reason he hadn't failed out yet himself was the fact that he had one of the councilmembers in his pocket. Alara may not have known how to use her magia, but at least *she* was a competent fighter.

Alara sat tentatively in a chair by Senye Cruz's desk. Her back was rigid as she tried to come up with an excuse for why they had been out so early in the morning. Quenti, on the other hand, wandered around the room, her fingers tracing the books and papers haphazardly thrown about.

"Stop, snooping. You're going to get us in even more trouble."

Quenti rolled her eyes, "Calm down. I'm just looking." She ran her finger along a particularly large tome that was balanced on the edge of the large desk. "History of the Bruya Wars: An Analysis of Both Sides. Sounds *fascinating!*" she said, though her tone indicated it was anything but. She flipped through a few of the pages before slamming it closed again.

Alara watched with nervous eyes. The waiting game was already starting to wear on her. She was almost relieved when Senye Cruz's office door opened again. Quenti stood up straight and sidled over to the chair next to Alara as the councilwoman crossed the room silently. She took her seat across from the two magites and did not speak for several long seconds, eyes sharply moving between Quenti and Alara.

Quenti remained stiff, her own eyes focused on the woman across from her. And then, after a moment, Alara noticed Quenti's shoulders suddenly relax and her jaw tighten, as if she had seen something in Senye Cruz's black eyes and made a decision.

"So, ladies, would you like to explain where you were last night?"

Neither of them spoke. Alara's throat felt dry and her mind swirled with lame excuses.

"Alara," Quenti finally cut in, "was just giving me a tour of the Haven and Cielo in the evening. We got turned around, which was totally my fault, and ended up in Cielo after dark." Quenti's voice was calm and her face held no hint of a lie. "We ran into Adelmo and he offered to house us for the night rather than have us wandering around after curfew."

Senye Cruz's eyes flickered between the two of them. Alara felt the blood drain from her face, but she didn't flinch when Senye Cruz's eyes bore into hers.

"Hmm. I won't report you for punishment this time. But you should both know better than to be wandering around when you shouldn't be." Her eyes settled on Quenti again and her voice was sharp. "If we catch you out and about again after curfew, the punishment will be severe. We take these things seriously. Do not test our limits."

She paused for a long moment as Alara and Quenti's heads both nodded in agreement, her sharp brown eyes still focused on Quenti.

Without warning her face shifted and she smiled brightly.

"Well, off you both go. You don't want to be late to classes, and morning meal will be starting soon."

Alara practically jumped from her chair, rushing out the door before Senye Cruz could change her mind. Quenti followed at her heels. She was being uncharacteristically lenient, but Alara didn't care—Senye Cruz was strict, and the fact that they got off with just a slap on the wrist was something she didn't want to jeopardize.

If she kept her head down and made sure not to get in the way of any other councilmembers this week, maybe she could avoid getting kicked out of the Haven altogether.

"Who was that?" Quenti asked as they rounded the corner away from Cruz's office.

"That is Senye Cruz, another member on the Council."

"Like Emaru?"

"*Senye* Emaru," Alara corrected. "And yes. Only Senye Cruz is a councilmember that you do *not* want to get on the wrong side of."

Quenti didn't ask anything else as Alara practically stormed back through the tunnels to her—their—room. Quenti even managed to look a bit on edge—a change from the complete nonchalant attitude she had held since coming to the Haven. Perhaps she was finally starting to understand the gravity of their situation. This was a step in the right direction.

Maybe Alara could actually get some peace back.

CHAPTER 9

QUENTI

Quenti's heart beat a hard rhythm in her chest as she silently followed Alara back to their room. It was so loud, she was amazed the other girl couldn't hear the unsteady thumping. But then again, she seemed preoccupied herself. When they returned to the room, Alara didn't even look her way as she picked up a stack of books from the corner of the room, shoved them in a bag, and rushed out.

Quenti left the room a few minutes later, unsure of when first meal began or ended, and knowing she eventually needed to find Senye Emaru's office. She had a feeling this was one of those things that Alara was supposed to have helped her with. She rolled her eyes, alone with her annoyance. Perhaps she'd remember to make an extra biting comment or two the next time she saw the fledgling magite.

If there was a next time.

She let herself dwell only briefly on what she had learned. There was a way out. There were stories of magites and mages—or, *gasp*, bruyas—who had escaped the Haven without permission, never to be seen again. Of course, some of these stories had alternate, less happy endings to them.

Some believed those that betrayed the Haven were found and killed, while others talked of them joining the bruyas beyond the borders or crossing the sea to escape Sombria altogether. Happy or sad tales aside, the important fact was that escape was no longer impossible. Not everyone stayed trapped here.

Quenti shook herself from these thoughts. There would be time to think and plan later, but for now she had to act normal—or whatever passed for normal here.

It only took ten minutes to find Emaru's office. Or more accurately, it took ten minutes to run into a magite that was willing to walk her there. It was just down the hall from where they had just met Cruz, and she made note of this, already starting to build a map of the Haven in her mind. She needed to know these things if she was going to make use of her new information.

But she didn't have time to think about such things once Emaru swept her into the office and started talking.

The woman loved to talk.

There were going to be classes and extra lessons and tests to make sure Quenti was up to speed with her reading and writing skills—which she most definitely was not. She would be spending her mornings with the little ones and her afternoons in private lessons. And following the look she must have given Emaru when she mentioned writing, she was told her evenings would be spent practicing with a quill and parchment until she met some standard she was quite unsure of.

The Haven sent out ambassadors to the villages to teach reading and writing to the little ones, but the skill was unnecessary for most adults living on the coast and most just let the lessons of their youth drift away. Quenti could read better than most, her mother having been an avid reader of history who had passed down her passion to her daughter. However, writing was a skill she had had little use for.

Emaru did not seem to agree with this assessment.

As they exited her office, the councilwoman walked through the measures in place for keeping the students safe—guards and locked doors and curfews and regulations on powers. Quenti couldn't help but hear the threat in all of this.

Do not break the rules.

Do not step out of line.

Do not try and escape.

But the threats couldn't break the bubble of hope growing in Quenti's chest. There was a way out.

CHAPTER 10

ALARA

The rest of the day was a blur. Alara was still tired from the previous night's events and the spikes of anxiety she had been coping with since yesterday. It was amazing to her how exhausting it was just to be… nervous. And going over the events again and again in her mind didn't exactly calm her.

Thinking back to her fight with the wind mage in the dark marketplace, she couldn't believe she had let Quenti get her caught up in that situation. In the moment, it had seemed like the right thing to do, but Alara should have stopped the match herself—thrown down her spear or something. Instead, she fought, almost blasting her opponent and the onlookers with an uncontrolled burst of fire.

She let out a groan and slumped forward onto the surface of her desk.

"You feeling sick?" Mitteo asked softly next to her.

They were sitting near the back of the classroom with the professor droning on about the early history of Sombria and the continent of Inti. The ancient history class was supposed to help magites learn more about the early times before the Bruya Wars and how the premages lived.

It focused on the early sciences of magia and survival, which Alara usually loved learning about, but today she couldn't stay focused, and she kept drifting into her own mind.

"I'm fine," she said, giving Mitteo a weak smile before trying to focus back on the lecture. She must have been out of it for longer than she thought because a few minutes later they were being dismissed. The class was done, and she officially had three lines of notes to prove her attendance.

"So they haven't kicked you out."

Raquel. Ugh.

She let out an awkward laugh as she turned toward Raquel, who had walked up behind them as they were leaving the classroom.

"No, not yet."

"Emaru looked furious that night. I'd say I haven't seen her that angry before, but let's face it—it's like her go-to mood."

Alara's laugh was genuine this time. "So how did the mission end up after I left?"

Mitteo, Raquel, and the other magites had stayed an extra night to complete the mission.

Raquel gave a pout, but Mitteo was the one who answered. "Nothing. Didn't catch a single bruya after you left, but the raids have apparently stopped."

"For now," Raquel cut in sharply. "Seriously, Alara, when are you going to grow a backbone and start acting like a mage. Sombria could use someone with your fire strength—the Haven could."

Alara could have responded, but she was already sick of

having the same argument with Emaru. Instead she just gave an exhausted sigh.

"El'dyo, you are such a waste of talent." Raquel turned down the next hall, sending a biting smile back over her shoulder. "Oh, and Alara, you still owe me a new fighting tunic."

"She's right, you know," Mitteo said. "If you don't start controlling and strengthening your powers soon, getting kicked out is inevitable. Then where would you go?"

"I'll be fine," Alara said, ignoring the sinking feeling in her stomach. "Maybe you should practice some more, yourself. I'm not the only one who was a mess out there. Talk to Senye Cruz about controlling those stomping feet of yours. It's a wonder the bruyas weren't scared off for miles that night." She turned and marched down the hallway before Mitteo had a chance to argue with her. She knew it was a cruel thing to say, but she despised the look of pity that had been in his eyes.

She knew she should have headed down to the practice rooms to work on her fire skills—as she was scheduled to do—but instead, she found herself wandering toward Adelmo's home. She felt a nervous energy buzzing underneath her skin and needed to get out some aggression.

He wasn't home when she got there, but she let herself in, knowing he was probably with the livestock somewhere and wouldn't mind. She didn't even bother changing into her fighting outfit and just slipped out of her sandals. Propping up the straw dummy, Alara started sparring. Her hits were sharp and fast. She felt her anxiety melt away and all thoughts of the past and future fall silent. In that moment, all she could focus on was where the next blow would hit and where to place her feet to best keep her balance.

At some point she became aware that she was being watched. Aiming one last kick at the dummy, she spun, expecting to see

Adelmo. Instead, Ardo leaned in the doorway, a sideways smile playing across his tanned face.

"Shouldn't you be out training somewhere?" Alara asked, turning back to the dummy.

"I already make the other councilguards quake in fear of my talents. I have to give them a chance to catch up." Ardo stepped into the room, his eyes watching as she continued to move around the dummy, punches landing across the torso with soft thuds and sharp hisses of Alara's breath.

"With an ego like that," Alara said between punches, "you're just asking for El'dyo's ire."

"El'dyo and I have come to an understanding."

Alara rolled her eyes, but she was still smiling. "Don't let Wila hear you talking like that. She'll have you burned as a heretic."

"The old crone can try."

Alara ignored the comment, not altogether disagreeing with the sentiment. She didn't quite despise Wila the way she did Senye Cruz, but the stone-faced woman's constant quoting of scripture always set her on edge.

"Make yourself useful," Alara said.

Ardo understood immediately, grabbing two narrow clubs propped against the wall and tossing one to her. She caught it without question and lowered her stance, readying herself for the fight.

He made the first move, the wood sweeping low toward her knees. He moved fast, but she saw the shift of his legs before he swung the club, making the motion easy to block. She responded, swinging her own club toward his head. He blocked it, taking a step back as he did. They sparred in silence for a few minutes, and her arm started to ache.

"You're fighting high again," Ardo said blocking another swing at his face. Taking advantage of her open body, he sent a jab into her ribs with his free hand. "You're not playing to your strengths."

"What are my strengths?"

"You're small—people won't expect you to be able to beat them."

"I don't think that's a compliment," Alara said.

"You need to use your opponent's height and strength against them."

"Why do you assume they'll be taller and stronger than me?"

Ardo swiped her feet out from under her, leaning over her with a smile. "Everyone is taller than you. And you should always assume your enemy is stronger too, so you're never caught unaware."

Alara growled at this before swinging again as she jumped up.

As the two sparred, she felt her frustrations start to grow once again, along with a fire inside her chest—the same fire that had almost gotten her in trouble the night before. Rather than let it consume her again, she shoved it back down. Senye Emaru would've been disappointed, but this was a *physical* fight she was in, not some bruya brawl.

Ardo caught her swing again toward his face and hooked his leg behind her knee. She stumbled forward, angry at not seeing the move coming. Yet he always seemed to know what she was about to do. Perhaps she was becoming too predictable.

"How's the new girl?" Ardo asked, letting her regain her footing.

"I could not care less," she snapped.

He chuckled. "Always the friendly one."

"I'm friendly. She's just… impossible." Alara stopped fighting, her arms going wide with exasperation.

"I believe that is the exact term Senye Emaru uses for you." He moved over to Adelmo's table, wiping the sweat from his brow as he sat. She followed suit, recognizing that she and Ardo were more at home in Adelmo's house than anywhere in the Haven. A councilguard hanging around with a magite wasn't exactly outlawed, but it also wouldn't gain a resounding seal of approval—particularly from Emaru.

"Senye Emaru is also impossible," Alara said peevishly.

His laugh was warm and deep, and she ignored the feeling it sent through her chest.

"Should I bother asking if you're supposed to be in class right now?" A voice rang out from behind her.

Alara turned to the doorway as Adelmo slipped into the room, his own face slick with sweat, cheeks red from the sun.

"Alara?"

"Independent practice time," Alara said. She motioned briefly toward the fighting equipment, eyes wide with what she knew looked like fake innocence.

"And I'm sure this is exactly what you're supposed to be practicing right now."

Alara flashed him a large smile. "I'm awfully sure my schedule didn't specify."

He shook his head and gave her his patented *I'm disappointed in you, but am going to guilt you with my silence on the topic* look.

"Well, how's she doing then?" Adelmo asked Ardo as he lowered himself carefully into one of the chairs.

"She's still fighting too high. She's almost becoming predictable." He spoke to Adelmo, but his eyes focused on her. "I guess predictable is what happens when a soldier refuses to use half their tools."

Ardo's lips twitched as she opened her mouth to argue. He was expecting a fight. El'dyo, perhaps she *was* predictable. She quickly closed her mouth, grinding her teeth together in frustration.

Ardo stood, grinning wide, completely unaffected by her glare, much to her frustration. "I should go. No rest for the wicked." He nodded to them before he slipped out of the doorway and disappeared down the street.

"He's a nice young man, isn't he?" Adelmo said.

Alara shrugged, slightly perplexed by Adelmo's comment. She watched as his gaze shifted to the fighting equipment they had left lying on the ground. He was quiet—lost in thought.

She stood and began picking up the clubs, hanging them back on the wall where they belonged. She pushed the dummy back into the corner of the room before turning back to Adelmo. He was still silent, gaze following her movement, but mind elsewhere.

"Adelmo?"

His eyes sharpened back to focus, and he acknowledged her with a small humph.

"What were you doing in the dark marketplace last night?"

To her surprise, he chuckled softly at the sudden inquiry. He didn't look guilty. "Just because I can't fight anymore doesn't mean I don't enjoy watching a good spar. The fights in the dark marketplace are some of the best to watch. Unregulated, the fighters do a better job at blending their physical skills with their magia skills. And every once and awhile, you even get a blameless fighter in there, holding his own against a mage." He shrugged. "Even you almost held your own. Just imagine if you had full control."

Alara groaned, her forehead banging softly against the table as she slumped forward in her chair. "Not you too, Adelmo!"

"You were blessed with these gifts, but you keep insisting on fighting them."

"Blessed… right. And they call those without magia blameless for a reason."

CHAPTER 11

ALARA

Over the next few days, Alara did her best to avoid Quenti. She spent her free evenings wandering the Haven like she used to as a young girl or seeking out Ardo when he wasn't on duty. They spent one evening together sparring in an empty study room, trying their best to stay quiet as their spears cracked against each other.

Alara knew that Emaru wouldn't approve of her hobbies and found it infinitely ironic how such remnants of prejudice even remained in a councilwoman charged with keeping the peace in Sombria.

After they exhausted themselves, Alara enjoyed their whispered talks of fighting tactics and Ardo's hopes of becoming a captain of the councilguard. She could almost pretend that nothing had changed over the last week.

Despite living together in the same room, it ended up being easier than she expected to avoid Quenti. The new magite didn't seem inclined to spend extra time in the room either, and Alara only saw her occasionally in the early mornings as she was waking up. For her part, she was only too happy to get dressed and sneak out before her new roommate woke. She knew Emaru would probably be annoyed that she wasn't helping Quenti adjust to the Haven, but Alara needed her space to stay sane. At least for now.

When she woke up one morning, she started her usual routine of silently grabbing her clothes and boots and tiptoeing out. It took her until she was at the door to notice that Quenti's bed was empty and she was the only one in her room.

"Huh."

She must have gotten up early that morning and left already. Alara tried not to roll her eyes and she noted the time indicated on the wall. Curfew had just ended and she doubted Quenti had waited until then to leave the dorms. What other trouble had she gotten into without Alara? Part of her wanted to care, but after remembering that one frustrating night spent with her in Cielo, she just sighed.

And if Emaru asked about how Quenti was doing?

I don't know, I was too busy sleeping.

Shaking her head to clear her thoughts, Alara changed into her day outfit, slipped on her boots, and rushed out the door, not eager to accidentally run into Quenti.

They had the day off of classes, so she spent the morning curled up in a chair in the library with a hot cup of mint tea, reading. She probably should have been reading about the history of premages or the political dynamics of post-war Sombria, but she was enjoying the fictional account of a blameless soldier during the Bruya Wars who had to fight for her family's land. Her fellow magites called it cheesy, but the book was checked out more often than not from the library, so *someone* out there was enjoying it as much as she was.

When her stomach started to growl, she packed up her things and wandered over to the market. After grabbing a stuffed tortilla to-go, she headed to the stables. Adelmo was with the l'lamas, running his hands through their wool and cleaning off the large bits of embedded hay and twigs.

She finished her tortilla and then lent a hand to Adelmo, her own small fingers combing through the l'lamas wool quickly. It was coarser than an alpaca's wool, but she still enjoyed the feel of it. They worked in silence for an hour or so before both the l'lamas and l'lamagas were clean and content back in their stalls.

"You here to practice?" Adelmo asked as they sat down on the hay in the stables.

"I just needed to get out for a bit. Every time we go on mission, I get spoiled by being out in the sunlight. I love the Haven… but I miss the sun when I'm inside too long."

"You all end up so pale living your lives under the mountain," he said with a shake of his head.

Alara smiled and looked down at her own complexion. "Hey, I'm still darker than you most the time!"

In fact, after being on mission for over a week, she had actually darkened a bit more than usual. Although it was never stated, one of the markings that separate mages from bruyas was their skin tones. The bruyas, who lived their lives outside, were usually at least a few shades darker than the mages who spent much of their lives in the Haven, away from the sun. Alara sometimes pitied the mages who didn't pale for lack of sun and always held on to their darker complexions—she knew there was always a slight air of suspicion around them.

"Well," he said, "You might as well practice a bit. If your fight the other day is any indication, your combat skills are getting weaker. They're *supposed* to get stronger the more you practice."

"Ha! Yeah right." Alara said in fake offense. "I could still beat you, old man."

Adelmo laughed at this as he set up a dummy across the stable from Alara. "Let's start with the spear."

Alara and Adelmo lost track of time as they traded blows and took turns attacking the beaten and battered straw mannequin. It wasn't until the bells rang around Cielo that she realized it was early evening.

"I need to go!" She dropped her spear. After changing back into the dress she'd worn that morning, she combed her fingers through her hair, hoping to make herself presentable as she sprinted out of the stables and toward the Haven.

She knew he wouldn't follow—he worshiped El'dyo in his own way, but it definitely didn't involve sitting in the Haven worship hall for an hour.

Alara rushed through the empty tunnels, holding up the skirt of her dress as she ran, happy she had the foresight to throw it on that morning. It was as if she'd actually started to subconsciously account for her poor time management. Part of it was that it was one of the few dresses she actually enjoyed wearing, and it featured intricate and delicate embroidery around the collar, clearly done by mages. Her skirt reached just below the knees and was made up of white and red layers. She hoped the mud staining the hem and her boots from her sparring with Adelmo would go unnoticed by Emaru.

The worship hall sat in the center of the Haven, a level above the marketplace, and when Alara finally got to one of the stairwells that led up to the worship hall, she was happy to see she wasn't the only one.

Other stragglers headed toward the hall and she fell in step with them. Some wore the traditional scarves that marked them as mages, but plenty of blameless and magites were scattered in with them. The worship services served both the mages and the blameless of Cielo, though the two groups rarely sat together in the pews.

When she made it up the stairs, she squeezed between a few mages and darted over to Emaru and her usual seat. The councilwoman was already there and simply gave Alara a bland look as she slid into the open space next to her guardian with a sheepish smile.

At the same time, Wila walked to the front of the hall and began to sing.

Just in time.

The hall filled with the voices of the worshippers and Alara sang along, with little thought of the words she was saying. It was the same call to praise each Saturday evening, the words were automatic after spending a lifetime in the Haven.

"Welcome all under El'dyo's gaze." Wila's voice rang through the hall despite it almost sounding like a whisper. She was the only woman Alara had ever met that managed this balance.

"We gather this evening, as we do all evenings, to celebrate the light of El'dyo. He who defeated his own shadow to bring us to life. But today I want to remind us all that El'dyo's shadow is not the only darkness that we must face and overcome if we want to bathe in his light."

Alara found her mind drifting with the soothing tones of Wila's voice. Her eyes wandered around the worship hall, appreciating the beauty of the room. While the rest of the Haven was by no means ugly, it tended to be more utilitarian in its designs. The canals that ran along the tunnels and the lanterns and torches that glowed in the night had strict purposes, but the shaped bronze and endless gemstones that lined the ceiling between windows and threw light across the worship hall when the sun hit them just right were an unnecessary flourish.

Looking around the hall, she caught the eye of Ardo sitting a few rows back. He was off duty, his normal armor and black clothes replaced with a bright woven shirt, loosely fit. He was grinning at her openly and she smirked back, giving a small eye roll as he feigned sleeping.

Child, Alara mouthed the words, and Ardo grinned again, eyes wrinkling.

Alara felt a sharp jab of an elbow in her side. She caught Emaru's eye as she realized her head had been craned back, clearly not paying attention. She settled herself into her seat, eyes forward, sheepish at being caught.

"Through his story, we must remember we are all like Josye. None of us is immune to the power of greed and pride."

She remembered the story of Josye well. A follower of El'dyo his entire life until his child died, he had turned to his magia to punish those he blamed for her death. After each person he killed, his greed and anger only grew until he turned his blame on El'dyo himself and tried to strike him down. Josye died, consumed by his own magia, leaving behind his wife and other children to fend for themselves.

"All of us can fall for the pretty words El'dyo's shadows whisper in our ears if we turn from the light in a moment of weakness. But if we call to him in these times, instead of turning away, he can give us the strength to overcome our darkness, just as he did his own at the beginning of time."

As everyone around her started singing again, she let the lilting notes wash over her. Her thoughts drifted again, but she made sure to keep her eyes to the front of the room, aware of Emaru, stiff-backed, beside her.

When it was time to go, she and Emaru left together, heading toward the councilrooms rather than the dorms. It had been a weekly tradition for them to meet for Saturday supper after worship, and Alara was always excited to eat Emaru's cooking and avoid the magite cafeteria.

As Emaru stirred the bean stew that had been cooking over the fire all day, Alara sat down at the table, enjoying the smell of garlic and onion in the air. Her guardian wore the mage *aguayo* draped across her shoulder over a dark red dress. The scarf itself was a weave of yellow and pink shades, showing she was an air mage, with thin bands of white woven in to show her talent as a mind-stalker. And along the edge of the scarf she had a single bronze band that signified her rank on the Council. Mage councilmembers had a single band and blameless members had two. Alara wasn't wearing her *aguayo*, having left it in her room earlier that day, but it was a simple black weave and would be until she passed her exams and graduated to a mage. Someday she would have a bright red, orange, and white scarf of her own.

Assuming she *did* graduate.

Scooping up a serving for each of them, Emaru sat down at the table across from Alara. They ate silently for a while. Emaru wasn't the warmest person in the world, but Alara always liked her better when they were alone than when she was acting in her role as teacher or Council mage.

"So how have classes been this week?" Emaru finally broke the silence.

"Fine," Alara said, her mouth stuffed with a large helping of beans.

"Is Quenti adjusting well?"

Swallowing, the magite gave herself a moment. "Um—yeah. I guess."

"How's she settling in to the dorms?"

"Good." She paused, unsure what Emaru wanted and realizing she probably couldn't give it to her anyways. "Great. I think. How has your week been? I know Mitteo and Raquel said the raids stopped in Hurazon after we left."

If Emaru noticed the change of subject, she didn't comment on it. "Yes, although we got word of more raids up in Uodora."

"Really?" Alara was truly surprised at this news. "That's farther north than they normally travel."

"They seem to either be getting braver or this weather is driving them to desperation."

Alara shifted uncomfortably at this information. The bruyas were not to be taken lightly, but at least until now they had only bothered the southern outskirt cities more than anything. They never wandered far into the realm, and the Haven seemed safe within its center. But if the bruyas were even attacking villages in the north, maybe they weren't as safe as she had thought.

"The rains have also been causing some chaos on the terrace farms near Calao. We've sent a group of water and earth mages to help the farmers already there try and clean up the mess, but the crops may not be salvageable. Some of the lower terraces were completely flooded in the last rainstorm."

Emaru's eyebrows furrowed and she looked tired as she took another bite of her beans. For just an instant, Alara got a glimpse of how old Emaru likely was, even if she didn't always show it. Her hair was a mix of black and silver, and the fine lines that used to sprout from her eyes had turned longer and deeper over the past few years. The only thing that hadn't changed was the thin white scar that ran along her left cheek and into the hairline above her ear.

"The Haven can help to at least lessen the damage," Alara said. "The earth mages can always help plant new crops to grow this year."

Emaru seemed to shake out of her slump and smiled at her. "They'll figure something out. We haven't starved yet, through droughts and tornados. A little water isn't going to kill us. But it's good to hear you acknowledge how our powers can be used for good."

Alara rolled her eyes at this and prepared herself for the speech she had heard a million and one times from Emaru since she was little.

"When you were young and—"

"—you found me in the charred ruins of my family's house, you knew I'd be special." Alara finished with a smirk.

"I should have left you there." The words were cold, but Emaru followed them up with a smile. "I don't know who raised you to have such an attitude." She paused, then her face dropped back into a small frown. "But in all seriousness, you have more power than you can know. And yes—if left uncontrolled and wild it could be dangerous—but if you spent the same amount of energy trying to control and train your magia as you did learning to throw a spear…" Emaru gave a sigh. "Quenti is a bit—wild— but if you can teach her some restraint and she can teach you to control your magia, it'd do you both some good. You are going to be a powerful mage. Perhaps, you'll even have a place on the Council someday."

"I'd rather be captain of the councilguards!" Alara beamed as she said the same line she'd been firing back at Emaru for over a decade.

"And you think dancing around your own powers will help you get there? Francisco didn't become captain by pulling his punches and denying his strengths."

Alara's lip twitched.

Instead of firing back with her usual retort, she simply reached across the table a grabbed a warm tortilla from the pile.

She shoved the soft dough into her mouth, eyes focused on Emaru with just a hint of rebellion. The older woman grimaced as Alara tried to close her mouth, but she saw the spark of the laughter her guardian was trying to hide.

"The tortillas are delicious," she said, swallowing as best she could.

"El'dyo help me." Emaru rested her hand on her forehead. "I failed at raising you." She grabbed one of the tortillas, neatly rolling it before taking a much smaller bite.

They spent the rest of dinner with Alara carefully sidestepping conversations around Quenti or her powers. It was like the flowing movements of a fight as Alara diverted each question. She knew Emaru saw the steps but allowed her some respite.

When Alara finally returned to her room that night, she was tired and a dull ache throbbed behind her eyes. The room was dim and still empty. As she readied herself for bed, she tried to remember the last time she had seen Quenti. Had it been two days ago? Or maybe three? Whenever it was, it wasn't enough to keep her up for long, and she fell asleep the instant her head hit the pillow, enjoying the quiet of her empty room.

When Alara awoke at the start of the following week, she was still alone. By this time, a level of concern had started to creep in. Some of the other schools, like the School of Secrets and the School of Protectors had their own dorms, but if Quenti had been drafted into those, Emaru would have definitely told her over dinner. So, if she hadn't changed rooms, where in the world was she? The bed didn't even look slept in, and her roommate's magite clothes still littered the spot next to her bed.

As she wandered toward classes that morning, her mind cycled through all the things that could have happened to Quenti. She could have gone off exploring the Haven on her own and gotten lost in the hundreds of tunnels that wove through the mountain—some of which the Council didn't even know about. Or perhaps she had fallen into one of the canals. After all, the rains had left the waters deeper and the currents stronger. Of course, Quenti was likely good enough with her magia to not drown—she hoped.

Could water mages still drown?

When a class of young magites passed by her in the halls, Alara called out to one of them she vaguely recognized. "Hey... you..."

"Nico," the small boy said, his face pale and freckled in the torch light.

"Nico, have you seen Quenti today? The new magite that's about my age?"

He looked over his shoulder at his other classmates, who were moving away from him. When he turned back to Alara, he didn't quite meet her eye, but shook his head quickly. "I have to go."

She watched him practically run to catch up with his class, his brown curls bouncing. "Well, then."

She barely made it into her classroom before the chimes rang for the start of the school day. She quickly ducked into her chair near the back of the class and started pulling out her textbooks with grim determination to completely ignore the questions still racing in her head regarding Quenti. She needed to focus on her studies and not get kicked out of the Haven.

"Alara Ayar."

Her eyes snapped up to the front of the classroom. Her professor was standing next to a slightly younger-looking woman

—a blameless that Alara vaguely recognized from the councilrooms.

"Please go with Jimena here. The Council needs to speak with you."

ALARA

Alara was only vaguely aware of the stares and whispers that followed her out of the room as she trailed behind Jimena. The young woman didn't even look at her as she led her down the hall.

This is it. This is when I get kicked out. She thought she would have felt more misery at the prospect, but as she followed after the woman in front of her, she just felt tired.

The walk to the councilrooms felt longer than normal. When they finally arrived, Jimena only gave a short knock on the door before opening it and leading Alara in. Before she could say anything, Jimena had disappeared back out the door.

The room was a large circle, the walls lined with woven tapestries of bright reds, teals, and pinks. A small fire burned in a hearth set against the rounded wall, the smoke drifting up and into the walls of the Haven. The Council's circular table sat in the middle of the room, its surface a scattering of maps, books, and papers. Six chairs held the six councilmembers who were in the middle of a heated argument. A couple other seats sat a little away from the table and Alara wondered if she should sit. She wasn't quite sure how long her shaky legs would keep her standing at this point.

"This is unacceptable," one of the women at the table said, the wrinkles on her face deep with concern. Although they had never talked in person, Alara knew Senye Juanez was the oldest member of the Council in both age and tenure, and one of the three blameless that helped rule the realm.

"They are becoming a dangerous liability that needs to be stomped out if the Haven is to survive," one of the men said—another blameless. His green eyes stared daggers at Emaru, who sat still and silent across from him.

Alara knew the members on the Council didn't always fully agree with each other, but there was a tension in the room that she hadn't expected.

For centuries, the Council sat balanced with three mages and three blameless. As the original founders intended after the Bruya Wars. This forced them to compromise and find agreement among themselves, despite the bad blood that had once festered between those who held magia and those who didn't. But as Alara stared at the six councilmembers before her, it didn't feel like the bad blood resided only in the past.

She made eye contact with Jorye Molina, the third mage on the Council, who cleared his throat and gave a tight smile. "Our guest has arrived."

Five other pair of eyes swiveled toward her, and her heart lurched. A jumble of words and pleas formed in her head, a dozen arguments for why the Council should keep her on in the Haven.

"Alara," Senye Cruz spoke. Until now she had been silently watching the exchange between the others.

Before she could continue, however, Senye Juanez cut in

sharply, "Your roommate Quenti appears to have gone missing. What do you know about this?"

The taste of copper filled her mouth, and her face flushed. This was not what she had expected at all. Her eyes flickered to Emaru who looked her impassively. The other five sat in silence.

"I—" she stuttered. "I have no idea. I haven't seen her in a few days." Emaru's eyes were intense and dark; the three blameless scowled at her. Senye Cruz seemed to be wearing a smirk of satisfaction—she had probably predicted that Alara would screw this up. "I haven't been in the room a lot, and I just thought we kept missing each other. I didn't think—"

"You didn't think it was important to tell me that you hadn't seen her in a few days." It wasn't a question.

She felt sick.

"Clearly," Senye Cruz cut in, "the child should not have been entrusted with this task. The decision to give her supervision of a feral new magite was a mistake." This time the councilwoman's cold eyes were directed at Emaru, who didn't meet her gaze, but continued to glare at Alara.

"Did she run back home?" The other female blameless spoke this time—Senye Wila. Her eyes were bright and her voice smooth. "There is a precedent of new magites getting homesick."

"We have reason to believe she was lured out of the Haven by bruyas," Senye Manuel Mando, the third blameless, said.

"Bruyas…?" Alara tried to make sense of her thoughts. She couldn't imagine Quenti being stupid or naive enough to get involved with bruyas. Then again, maybe she'd been foolishly brave enough to think she could use them to get back home. "Seems… stupid, doesn't it? Even for her."

All six sets of eyes bore down on her.

"Sorry," Alara said, her voice weak and her face red with

anxiety. "I mean… Quenti seems a bit brash. But to run off with the bruyas? Maybe she *has* just gone home."

"We've sent messengers down to Hurazon to notify her father, but she hasn't been seen on the Via Sura nor was she seen leaving the Haven. It's doubtful she made this escape without some help —from bruyas or…" Senye Juanez let her words trail off.

Alara tried to keep her breath steady. The weight of their gaze was crushing.

"I don't know where she is," she said, probably more defensively than she intended. "She didn't say anything. I… there was a girl she talked about from the neighboring village. She seemed important to her, and she said she wasn't at the Haven."

Senye Molina pushed a map of the southern realm across the table at her, his eyes warm. Alara traced her finger along the Via Sura and found the marking for Hurazon. Just northeast of it was the village of Attalea. No other marked points on the map sat near the other town. She pressed a finger on the map at the scratched handwriting. "Attalea. It's probably this one. I mean, I assume."

No one said anything. Senye Molina looked at the map, his thick eyebrows furrowed.

"Perhaps we'll have to check there then," Emaru said, her eyes still focused on her as though she were trying to read her mind.

Alara had to reminder herself that the councilwoman wasn't a mind-walker, but she still felt a shiver down her spine.

"Can I go?" Alara's words were slow and soft, her eyes darting back toward the door. She just wanted to get away from the tension and have room to think about the fact that she had failed yet again—and at the simplest of tasks.

Emaru's voice was sharp. "You're going on the search."

"What? Why? I already told you what I know."

"Because you can use your mind-stalking skills to find Quenti again. Her mind is familiar to you, and she likely will trust you more than us—assuming she hasn't been brainwashed by the bruyas."

"She didn't trust me enough to tell me she was running away. I doubt she'll trust me now."

"Nonetheless, your mind-stalking skills are invaluable in this case. Even if the girl has just run off homesick, the road is dangerous alone. The sooner we find her, the better. For her own safety."

"But I'm..." She hesitated, but slumped her shoulders in resignation. "I'm not even good at using my magia." There was no point trying to pretend. If they didn't kick her out for losing track of Quenti, they weren't going to be forgiving about her magia any longer.

"You are walking a thin line at the Haven. This is a second chance to prove you can graduate and are eligible for the School of Protectors."

"I need more time to practice," Alara said. "I'm trying, I promise, but I just need more time. I'm not ready." Her eyes were pleading now, but the only amount of warmth was from Jorye, whose eyes were slightly creased in pity.

Senye Cruz spoke this time. "Perhaps she is right. She's uncontrolled, lacks precision in her magia skills, and likely will be of little use to any of us."

"Alara," Emaru said, her eyes focused on Senye Cruz, "can you please step out for a moment while we discuss some things."

She rushed out without a second glance and leaned against the cool wood of the door as she closed it behind her, head spinning.

It seemed like hours had passed, although more likely it was only a few minutes, before the door opened and Emaru stepped out into the hallway.

"We've discussed the situation," she said, "and I emphasized that obviously you have a choice in all of this. You do not need to come with us to search for Quenti."

Alara let out the breath she wasn't aware she had been holding and gave Emaru a look of pure relief.

"However…"

Shit.

"…before you go back to class, I want to show you something."

Emaru's face was soft, but Alara felt like she was about to step foot in a trap. Then again, there wasn't much of a choice with Emaru staring down at her with that familiar frown on her lips.

She finally nodded stiffly and let herself be led down the hallway. They wound though the Haven's tunnels, toward Cielo. When they finally stepped out of the Haven, it took a second for her eyes to adjust to the sudden bright light that streamed unfiltered from the cloudless sky. The temperature rose at least twenty degrees as they made their way outside. It wasn't even noon and the air was heavy with the heat of the day, evidence that the drying season was almost upon them.

As they stepped onto the street, she realized they were on the west side of Cielo on one of the lower terraces. The buildings here were old and squat. While many of the stone structures of Cielo were fitted together without mortar, carved perfectly for their purpose, the ones here were haphazardly balanced, mortar, moss, and mud slathered between the gaps. The streets of Cielo were almost always bustling at this time of day, yet here they were quiet. Only a few people wandered about or lurked in doorways, watching as they passed. The atmosphere had turned a bit fetid, the buildings pressing in on both sides. A single cart wouldn't have even fit along the street here.

"Do you know what happens to magites who do not succeed within the Haven?" Emaru's voice was soft.

She shook her head. In all the time she had worried about failing out of the school, she had never wondered about what would happen after. Perhaps a part of her just thought it would never actually happen. Maybe she just imagined she'd move back into Emaru's quarters and spend her days fighting with Adelmo in the stables, grooming the l'lamagas.

"They are outsiders. Neither mage nor blameless. Feared for their magia, lacking the control or strength to succeed as a part of the realm. Some try to return to their families and the villages they came from, but they are very rarely accepted back. Magia has proven itself dangerous and in turn, those who don't learn how to control it are as well. For some, the magia—uncontrolled and untrained—leads them to madness. Those who survive long enough, usually end up here. Not a part of the Haven, not quite a part of Cielo. They beg, they work the fields, or find other means of making a living."

She stopped in the shadow of the tallest building on the street. Alara stared at a woman who was leaning in the doorway. She wore the traditional mage tunic, but her legs were bare, the edge of the fabric hitting her well above the knees, a belt tightly fit around her waist. Its collar was cut low and her chest threatened to spill from it as she leaned over. The woman made eye contact with Alara and winked. Her face flushed and she quickly looked away.

"I know I've been soft at times with you," Emaru admitted. "I've indulged your passion for tactical fighting over building your magia, but you must understand that I do care about you." She put her hand on Alara's shoulder, her light gray eyes looking into her own with a pleading softness. "This is your last chance to prove to the Council that you belong here. I can't protect you anymore after this. If you truly want to become a councilguard, you need to prove to them that you can do this. After you've joined the ranks, you can swear off magia if you still want to."

Alara looked around again, avoiding the eyes of the woman still leaning in the doorway near them. Although she had always loved coming out to Cielo from the Haven and basking in the sunlight, she felt a dread settle in her gut standing on the streets. She wanted to help the realm. She wanted to fight for the realm. It's all she had ever wanted since the day her parents had died. And now, she was about to lose it because of her own fears and stubbornness. She squared her shoulders and met Emaru's eyes with a fierce look.

"I'll go. I'll use my powers. And I'll bring Quenti back."

Emaru gave her a large smile and briefly touched her cheek, just above her burn scars. "I knew you'd make the right choice."

They turned and Alara felt a wave of relief as they left the narrow streets of the slums, heading back toward the Haven. She had never felt so happy to feel the cool, wet air of the underground tunnels hit her face.

"Pack a few days' worth of clothes and your weapons in case we meet any bruyas. You can meet us at Sura Gate tomorrow at sunrise."

Alara stumbled a second, a jolt of panic surging through her body. She looked up at Emaru. "You're coming too?"

CHAPTER 13

ALARA

Just after sunrise, Alara found herself on a l'lamaga headed out through the south gate of the Haven, surrounded by a small band of councilguard soldiers. The morning air was still cool and crisp, but the cloudless sky foretold of the coming heat for the day.

Emaru led the group, her caramel l'lamaga at the front of the line as she directed them toward Via Sura. Alara was more than a little happy when she arrived at the gates that morning to see that Ardo's squad would be going with them as well. He now rode beside her, their l'lamagas a matching cream.

She was silent as they made their way south from Cielo and the Haven. Her nerves were on edge and her thoughts racing with all the things that could go wrong on the trip. She'd been on missions before, but now she wasn't a part of a magite team or class. This mission wasn't going to depend on group effort. The entire course of this trip—and Quenti's future—rested on Alara's powers to lead them in the right direction.

She looked around at the team that had been assembled to

bring Quenti back. The fact that Emaru and some of her personal guards were on the trip spoke to the importance of it. Whether this importance came out of care for Quenti's safety or ensuring Alara passed this test, she wasn't really sure.

After all, Quenti wasn't the first student to go missing. There was a tendency for young magites to try and run back home when they first arrived at the Haven—frightened and homesick for their families. Usually, they were caught long before they made it out of the shadow of Cielo, and the family would inevitably be called to visit and reassure their child. But Quenti was older and more trained with her magia. Too much for her own good, apparently, as she'd managed to escape Cielo.

Alara tried to think back to their interactions. She knew Quenti hadn't been in love with the Haven, but from what she could gather, it didn't seem like she missed Hurazon or her family. But then again, Quenti seemed the type to jump first and think later. She could imagine her sneaking out of the Haven and Cielo just to prove she could—only to get eaten by a wild puma. Alara shuddered to think of the dangers that lurked in the cloud forest for a lone traveler without much protection or supplies.

"Don't look so glum." Ardo's voice cut into her thoughts. "You'd think we were marching off to a funeral."

She looked up and saw his pale eyes creased with a smile. "We just might be," she said, giving him a weak smile in return.

"You know, I only met Quenti once or twice, but she seemed the type to put up a fight, even in the face of pumas, jaguars, and flash floods. She's just scrappy enough to get herself into trouble and then keep herself alive."

She let out a short laugh at this. "That sounds accurate. Of course, even if Quenti is off enjoying her adventure and staving off wild animals, there is still my magia issue. This is my last chance to prove I'm not a failure as a magite, remember?"

His smile faded away slowly, his thick eyebrows furrowing deeply. "I don't know much about magia, but I do know you, and I've never known you to let yourself fail."

She looked away quickly from the intensity of his eyes, annoyed at herself as she felt the blush creeping up her cheeks. She needn't have worried. When she looked back, his eyes were focused away from her and toward the right. She could only just make out the River Sura behind the thick foliage, but she could hear it without straining. The water was rushing, fast and loud. She could see the marshlands that stretched out from the river, proof of the rains that had been plaguing the realm for the past month.

It was a few hours before they came across the first settlement along the road. While north of Cielo was relatively well populated, villages in the southern lands tended to be few and far between because of the mountainous terrain. The road that meandered along the river was bordered on both sides by taller hills and thick cloud forests, not exactly the most ideal living conditions for most.

The settlement they came to was small—hardly even a village —with just a few sparse stone buildings set along the side of the road between them and the river. Alpacas grazed in the grass along the road. A few small children ran around barefoot on the stone streets, laughing among themselves. They slowed as Alara and her escorts passed, the heavy pattering of the l'lamagas' footsteps bringing out a few villagers from their houses.

Ardo and a few of the other soldiers jumped down from their mounts, opening up the satchels tied to their l'lamagas' backs. There were colorful potatoes and maize within the sacks along with some dried beans. The villagers took the food eagerly, smiling at the guards and placing balls of colorful wool into their hands in exchange. As the children stood nearby, now still and watching the exchange, Emaru waved her hand and sent a shower of dark orange flowers down from a tree overhead. The high-pitched squeal of children filled the air as they jumped and yelled, running through the rain of color.

Alara couldn't help but smile. This was a reminder of what she wanted to be a part of. The Haven and the Council did not just protect the realm, they brought hope and joy to the people that lived across the entirety of the lands. She wanted that, more than anything.

Ardo stood, surrounded by cheering children, as he twirled his spear in complicated patterns above his head, making them scream and laugh as the spear dipped and swept over their heads. His hands and fingers moved in a smooth movement without even a flicker of hesitation or uncertainty. Her stomach swooped with the movements, breath catching as he snatched the weapon from the air and brought it back to the ground.

They eventually left the village behind, Alara moving her l'lamaga alongside Ardo's. "The children love you."

He laughed and gave her a wink. "It's all for show. Being able to twirl my spear never helped me kill an attacker."

"It's more than just show and you know it. The way you move your spear…" Alara paused and tilted her head at him, "It's almost like magia."

"Ah. I am unfortunately not blessed with such gifts."

"No one is blessed with magia." Alara's voice was bitter.

"You are, whether or not you admit it. I wish I could do what the mages can do. Magia—it isn't just making flowers fly and children smile. The mages keep the people fed, keep the realm borders safe, and keep the sick from dying." He paused for a long moment and Alara thought he might be done talking, but finally he spoke again. His voice barely above a whisper. "You're a part of that. I envy you."

She didn't know how to respond. Was it possible to look at her magia as a gift instead of a curse? Perhaps she had when she had been younger—much younger—but she didn't remember and didn't think there was any going back at this point.

When they made camp for the night, Alara was sore and tired. The air was warm and thick with humidity, and the steady pace of the l'lamagas made her drowsy. She spread her *aguayo* out on the ground as a blanket and laid back in the shade of a tree. The river was farther from the trail here and she could just barely hear the steady rush, but it couldn't have been too far, as scouts came back soon enough with filled canteens.

A hand reached out to her, offering her one and she looked up to see Emaru sitting beside her.

"The sun is going down," Emaru said, "so hopefully we'll get some respite from this heat soon."

"It's times like this I miss the cold tunnels of the Haven," Alara said, taking a swig of the clean, cold water—filtered by the water mage in the group. At least the river was still icy cold.

"Close your eyes."

Alara squinted at Emaru questioningly, but she simply repeated herself.

"Close your eyes."

She did so, her other senses coming into focus more as she did.

"Now, tell me, where are the mage guards right now?"

Alara suppressed a sigh of frustration. *And so start the tests.*

She could feel the warm breeze that pushed through the trees from her left and the dapple of sunlight that broke through the shade of branches above her. She could hear movement to her left as a few councilguard soldiers gathered wood for a fire.

"There are some to the left, in the clearing."

Emaru clicked her tongue. "A blind blameless could tell me that with the racket they're making."

"Son of a bruya," Alara cursed under her breath.

"Language, Alara."

She suppressed a groan.

"Now, how many are there?"

Alara closed her eyes and focused again. This time she called on the heat in her chest, doing her best to ignore the anxiety that came with it. She plucked at the flaming threads that sat at her core and pulled them, connecting them with the magia that circled her mind. She tried to control her pulse as it jumped and skittered with every wave of heat that passed through her body. Her awareness pushed forward. She could feel the hint of magia cores to her left. "Two mages helping with the fire and supper."

"Good. Now what about the patrolling guards?"

Breathing heavily, she focused back on the threads of heat and tried to push her mind out farther away from the clearing. As she did so, her body temperature spiked again and all awareness of the clearing or the present were swept from her mind. There was only heat and flames and screams. So many familiar screams. Calling out for her. As if she could save them. As if she wasn't the reason they were all dead.

She let out a gasp, pulling herself back into her body and the present. Her eyes flew open, the blood rushing from her face.

Emaru didn't look angry, but there was a hardness to her eyes that made her heart skip another beat. She was going to ruin her last chance and she was not ready for the disappointment that would cloud Emaru's face when she did. But her stomach was churning with acid and grief and memories she didn't want to think about.

They sat like that, Emaru being more patient with her than she expected. Alara was running her hand back and forth across the fabric of her pants, feeling the weave there and focusing on her own body. Finally her stomach settled. She was able to hear the wind in the trees and the quiet rustling of camp being set up and dinner being cooked.

Alara closed her eyes again and grabbed onto the threads, yanking at her powers and feeling a trickle of sweat bead down her back as the heat rose in her, and she stretched her mind out, looking for the guards. "There is one mage southeast and another west of us and…" A wave of heat hit her and she let out another deep gasp. When she opened her eyes, Emaru was looking at her with a small smile. She looked almost satisfied for once, and Alara felt another wave—this time, one of joy.

Her guardian's smile disappeared and she gave Alara a curt nod. "We'll practice again tomorrow."

As she walked away, a branch snapped behind her and she turned to see Ardo. He sat down on the ground beside her with a lopsided grin and her stomach fluttered.

"Shouldn't you be working or something?" she asked him as he stretched out on the grass beside her.

"I'm not on watch until later and no one wants me anywhere near supper. I can ruin a plain potato."

Alara laughed and laid down next to him, looking up at the clouds that were slowly moving across the sky. The sun must have hit the horizon somewhere behind the tree line because the blue of afternoon had started to fade into a purple and pink along the western sky. She smelled roasted meat and figured the food would be ready soon. But the rumbling that came from her stomach told her the meal couldn't come soon enough; she hadn't eaten anything since their brief stop in the first village. As she moved her arms to prop up her head, her hand brushed against Ardo's side and she felt her face grow warm.

It was starting to get annoying at how aware she was of his

presence lately. She had known him for years now, but over the past few months, something had shifted, and that shift had stupidly made her more conscious—how he moved, how he smelled, and where his hair fell in his eyes. With that shift also came a constant worry of how she looked and smelled and how her hair stuck out in random directions.

"You have to appreciate what magia is able to do for us. It can be really beautiful," Ardo said softly, his gaze directed to the cookfire and the guards moving around it. She looked over and saw Emaru using the air to throw a wool blanket over a low branch. The colored cloth whipped in the wind, rippling as though it were alive as it flew over the branch and drifted back down, forming a small tent. Near the fire, another mage filtered their water and let it float above the fire in large orbs. As it began to boil in the air, she dropped them into individual mugs, coca leaves already ready to brew.

"Maybe water and air magia can be useful," Alara said, "but fire is a different story."

"What about cooking dinner?"

"It's not like that can't be done *without* magia," Alara smirked. "And all I've ever managed is to burn guinea pig to a crisp."

He shook his head. "How have you managed to get this far in your studies?"

She was surprised at the sharpness in his voice. His eyebrows were knit and he looked at the mages as he spoke.

"You can control fire—stop fire. You can stop a village from being burned down by a random lightning strike. You could truly fight fire with fire if you ever ran into a bruya and become the best soldier the councilguard has known."

"I don't think I could ever take the title from you." She smiled and laughed, but Ardo didn't.

"You could."

He placed a warm hand on her arm before getting up and walking over to the others. She ignored the warmth that seemed to linger from his touch. With a deep breath she looked toward the others. Based on the smells in the air and the commotion, supper was ready.

She followed Ardo, her stomach rumbling deeply. She moved to sit next to him, but caught Emaru's eye. She looked at Alara with a raised brow and nodded toward the empty spot next to her. Alara's eyes flashed to Ardo as she moved to the other side of the fire with her guardian.

They ate in silence, Alara taking an extra potato when she saw that the others had gotten their share of food. The heat of the campfire was warm against her skin, even as it began to die.

Emaru finally spoke as the guards started moving around the camp to clean up supper and prepare for their watch shifts. "What were you and Ardo talking about earlier?"

Alara realized she was following Ardo around the camp with her eyes and looked down quickly. "He was just preaching about how I should appreciate my magia. You would've been proud."

"And did you listen to him better than you listen to me?"

"I wouldn't dream of it."

Emaru's lip twitched. Whether in humor or annoyance, she was unsure.

"Close your eyes."

Alara's shoulders slumped slightly, but she didn't argue. She was too tired and sore to bother with that fight. As she closed them, she could still see the red of the flames dancing across her eyelids, contrasting with the now-darkened forest.

"Concentrate on the threads of energy within yourself."

She was well practiced in this part of the dance. She could feel the threads of heat within her own chest, swirling just beneath the surface. The threads from the fire reached out softly from where it burned in front of her. And she danced around the edges of the threads, not quite touching them, but knowing they were there.

"Do you have them?"

Alara frowned and took a soft hold on the threads within herself, the barest touch sending warmth through her. She gave a stiff nod.

"Now open your eyes and connect your threads to the fire. Bend them to your will and make the flames dance."

She weakly pulled at the threads of energy from her chest and felt them connect to those the dying fire was sending off, crackling before her. Without much conviction, she sent a flame leaping from the logs. It was small, only a foot or so tall, but it sent a sharp wave of heat at her. She flinched and shook her head. "My flame is pathetic."

"Strategy and focus can make up for weakness." Emaru flicked her hand toward the fire, and Alara's weak flame jumped up with a gust of wind, rising out of the logs with a roar of heat.

Alara immediately let go of her magia and the fire fell away, leaving a small flame licking at the logs.

"I don't know how I raised such a coward." The words were sharp and they felt like a slap across Alara's face. She didn't argue them though. She wasn't quite sure if she could. Perhaps that's all Alara was—a coward.

The next few days passed much the same as the first. Any time they reached a settlement or farm, Emaru or the others would dole out some food and perform a few simple spells to make the children clap. Between these visits, Emaru would occasionally ride up beside Alara and test her again.

"How many mages are behind us?"

"How many in front of us?"

"Where is our scout?"

Alara tried to focus and usually was able to get a few of the questions right before she felt the searing in her chest, pulled her magia back, and slumped against her l'lamaga. Emaru never seemed particularly disappointed, but she also never seemed quite satisfied, either. But by the third day, Alara truly did feel like she was able to stretch her mind farther than before. She still had no idea how she was going to find Quenti though. She could have gone in a million different directions, and if she was out of range of Alara's abilities, she could be passing by them without anyone noticing. The whole endeavor felt hopeless.

It was late morning of the fifth day and Emaru was drilling Alara again, her l'lamaga padding directly behind. Alara had her eyes closed, feeling the movement of the mount, slow and smooth beneath her.

"How many behind us?"

The answer came quickly. "Three."

"Ahead?"

"One."

There was silence. Alara didn't turn around, but stretched out her mind behind her, searching for where Emaru would be. There was nothing. She stretched farther and with a jolt, realized when she brushed across another core—one she recognized instantly as Emaru's.

Recognizing magia was nothing new to Alara, but being able to recognize a specific person—that sent her whipping around, a smile wide on her face as she immediately made eye contact with her guardian, who had drifted off to the left and behind Alara, among the other guards.

Emaru must have recognize the look of excitement on Alara's face because she smiled brightly and gave her a soft nod.

The joy in Alara's gut faded quickly though, as they came across a farm and a couple of houses that marked the edge of a village. They had reached the outskirts of Attalea.

It was time for Alara to start using her magia for real.

And she did *not* feel ready.

CHAPTER 14

ALARA

Just as in the smaller villages they had passed on the way to Attalea, the locals exited their homes as Alara and her caravan rolled in to the center of the main plaza. The town was by far the biggest they had passed, with numerous houses and farms scattered around the small shops that stood at its heart. Many of the stone buildings were less worn here, the cracks between stones still clean and free of moss. There was a small fountain in the middle of the square that looked much older than any of the other buildings, the central feature long since broken away, with water bubbling from the cracked stone pedestal in the middle.

Children laughed as they jumped around the legs of the l'lamagas, both shocked and ecstatic at the size of them. But the adults in the village looked more worn and tired than Alara had seen before. Had they been dealing with recent raids from the bruyas?

The councilguard soldiers dismounted and started handing

out the last of the food they had taken with them to donate. The few mages sent out swirls of water dancing through the air around the children, who whooped and chased after the orbs and ribbons. Alara watched appreciatively, and a part of her ached to use her magia in such a way to make the children smile so genuinely.

As Alara watched, she caught the eye of an older man who was standing on the edge of the group. His face was worn and creased deeply with wrinkles, skin a dark brown from the sun and hair a pale white. He looked at her with sharp dark eyes—the irises almost black. She shifted on her l'lamaga and tried to look away from him, but something in his gaze made her pause. He stepped forward and for a second, she wondered if he would come speak with her, but by then, Emaru was already off her mount and had stepped between them, whispering in his ear. The two of them walked off away from the crowd of people that watched the mages perform.

Briefly forgotten, Alara dismounted and wandered into the shade of the tallest building in the square. It was a small worship hall set along the northern edge and one of the few buildings in a sad state, with moss growing where the edges of large stones met. She pulled back the wool blanket that covered the door and glanced into the small room. The benches were set up to hold likely no more than forty people and were slanted toward an altar that stood at the front. It smelled of damp soil and stone inside, and the floors were muddy and worn. It was nothing like the worship hall in the Haven with its crystal and bronze decorations and perfectly swept floors. It looked more like an abandoned building than a center for worship, and she had to wonder what El'dyo would think of it.

She heard Emaru call her name and quickly stepped back

into the square, temporarily blinded by the bright sun upon exiting the dark building.

"There is no Khuna here." Emaru's voice was sharp with frustration. "And they haven't heard anything from a Quenti or seen a girl wandering around alone."

All eyes fell on Alara now and she felt the blood drain from her face, leaving her mind blank and buzzing. "I…"

"It looks like we're going to have to do this the hard way," Emaru said, her lips somehow pursed in disappointment as she spoke. "We'll just have to sweep the forest, with the assumption she'll have followed the road or the river. If she was even headed this direction. Alara?"

Her heart beat in chest and the heat in the air pressed down on her, making her lightheaded.

"I… I need some space." She took a deep breath and looked back at Emaru whose face was still pinched in frustration. "If I separate myself from everyone, perhaps I can concentrate better."

Emaru seemed satisfied. With a few sharp directions to the councilguards, they mounted their l'lamagas and rode back toward the northeast end of the village, where they had entered from. As Ardo hopped on his own mount, he turned briefly and gave Alara a tight smile before following the rest of the guards.

Magite and guardian were left alone. The villagers had dispersed again, the children bored of the visitors now that the magia had stopped, and the parents had returned to their work for the day.

She realized that Emaru was waiting on her for the first move, so she finally took a tentative step toward the southern end of the square. The buildings seemed to drop off in that direction and she wanted some space to think away from the town.

They found a small clearing not too far off, and Alara sat, her scarf folded beneath her. Emaru took her own place, sitting cross-legged in front of her.

"Close your eyes and breathe."

Alara followed the directions, her heart already starting to race. This was it, her last chance to prove she could make it at the Haven—and she had no idea if she could do it.

"Focus on finding your magia. Feel where it sits and take hold of it. It's okay to fear the magia, to recognize the power and dangers. To understand the curse El'dyo settled his followers with. But you must use your fear to control your curse. Bend the magia to your will and don't let it overpower you. Fight it for control."

Her mind flashed back to her early lessons when she had first arrived at the Haven, Emaru's voice softly walking her through these exercises. Each time, she'd follow the directions, try to fight the magia, and every time the magia won. The heat would overpower her, burning her from the inside out, and she'd end up locking it back away, feeling hopeless.

She tried to push these thoughts from her mind and grabbed at the threads of energy swirling hot in her chest. Emaru's own core oscillated beside her. She stretched her mind out around her, searching for the familiar prickle. For just a brief moment, she thought she felt something. A small thread of magia—too small to be the mages in their group.

Alara tried to focus her mind on the spot, pushing all her awareness toward it. Though just as her mind started to settle, a wave of sharp heat hit her, and her concentration faltered. She gasped out loud, but tried to keep a tight rein on her magia, feeling the sweat trickle down her forehead.

But no matter how much she tugged at it, the heat kept rising in her body. The flames licked at her skin—flames she knew only existed in her mind—but she flinched away all the same. Her heartbeat was hard and fast in her chest and the blood rushed through her ears, blocking out the sound of Emaru's voice trying to soothe and direct her. She heard a woman's scream sharp in her ear and then the cries of a dozen more—men, women, children. She was no longer in the clearing, but surrounded by bright red searing heat.

Suddenly, a heavy hand fell on her shoulder and her eyes opened wildly. She whipped around, trying to understand where the screaming was coming from. But it dissipated in an instant and the clearing was silent, save for her own breathing and Emaru's soft voice.

"Alara, you're letting your magia control you instead of the other way around. You are its master."

Her hand released Alara's shoulder, but she could still feel the heat where it had sat.

"Try again."

"Can I take a break?" Alara jumped up from the ground before Emaru could argue.

"Of course. Why don't we take a walk."

"No," her voice was sharp, sharper than it had ever been with Emaru. "I mean I need a break… from you."

She tried to ignore the look of shock and hurt that flashed over Emaru's face. Still, the councilwoman nodded and Alara quickly left the clearing, taking long strides to dodge the thick layer of trees. She tried to focus on the coolness of the shade on her skin as she lost herself in the forest. She knew generally that she was headed away from the town, but wasn't paying close attention. She'd find her way back eventually; she just needed to get away from everyone.

Her quick strides finally slowed down as her heartbeat returned to normal. The humidity in the air stuck to her skin and dripped down her face, but she relished in how cool it made the breeze feel. Looking around, the forest started to thin and she kept moving forward.

As she broke out of the woods, she slumped onto the ground in the shade of a particularly large tree. She ran a hand through her knotted hair, pulling it away from her sweaty skin. She knew she was going to have to go back to Emaru eventually. She was going to have to either find Quenti or admit defeat. But what did that even mean? A life lived in the slums on the outskirts of the Haven? What other choice did she have?

You could run, a voice whispered inside her mind.

She shook her head, pushing the thought away before it had time to form. There was no one for her to run to. At least living as an outcast in the Haven, she'd still have family, friends, and familiarity. So long as those people were willing to associate with a failed magite.

"El'dyo, give me strength." Alara whispered. She didn't often talk directly to El'dyo, having never been particularly pious, but it felt as good a time as any. The breeze hit her damp skin again, and a cold wave of resolve hit her. She pulled herself up from the ground and brushed the loose mud from her skirts.

Taking a deep breath through clenched teeth, she closed her eyes and sent out her awareness. Her heartbeat quickened in her chest, but she ignored the steady rhythm and focused instead outside of her body. The plan was to reach out to Emaru. Just far enough to show she could do it. But before she even made it out of the clearing, something else tugged at Alara's awareness. Her focus faltered for a second and she felt her core flare with a desire to reach out.

She stumbled forward, shuddering at the feel of her magia. Even as she let go of her hold, she could feel the heat of something in the back of her mind. It wasn't a human—it wasn't big enough. But it was a spark of magia. Alara took a deep breath, emptying her mind and letting her core cool. She looked around the clearing. It wasn't large, just a small break in the forest centered around an outcrop of rocks. She looked up at the tower of stone that hovered a few yards away and a small shiver crept up her spine. Something about the place felt familiar. It was like a strange sense of déjà vu or foreboding.

Walking forward, she touched one of the larger stones that sat at the base of the rock tower; it felt rough and cold under her hand. Without quite knowing why, she knew where to look. She found herself crouching along the stones, examining the base where the rocks met the wet soil underneath. There was a small gap between two of the larger stones, forming a small cave the size of a guinea pig. As a cloud passed across the sun, the light in the clearing flicked off and on again, and she saw a glint in the small hole.

Alara's eyebrows furrowed deeply as she reached in and grasped the white handle of a dagger. Her skin scraped across the stone as she pulled it out, drawing a small bead of blood along her knuckle. A few pieces of rotted wool were stuck to the blade's handle and she saw more remnants of the cloth in the small crevice of stone. She turned the dagger over in her hand, careful not to touch the sharp blade. The sun glinted off of the bronze blade as she turned it. It was cleaner than she expected, given that she had just pulled it from the mud and she ran a finger across the handle, noticing some carvings in the alabaster.

A sharp snapping of a branch caught her attention and her head shot up, the blade now raised in front of her. She let out a small gasping giggle as movement caught her eye and a large monkey swept across the canopy above her. She slipped the blade under her belt and moved back toward where she had come from. The sense of familiarity still pressed in on her and she caught the faint whiff of smoke. Was there someone living out here?

She moved forward, veering slightly to the right of where she had left Emaru, noticing with a smirk that she was now following behind the brown monkey that swung above her. Perhaps he knew where they were going.

Before long, she found herself in another clearing. This one much bigger than the last, and she could almost see the edge of the village from here. The remains of some house sat in the center of the clearing, moss and trees weaving through the scattered stones. These weren't fresh ruins and yet she felt like she could still smell the acidic sharp scent of burned wood and something else—sickeningly savory. Burned flesh.

Alara stumbled away, running as best as she could through the thick trees and undergrowth, tripping over the roots and ignoring the sting of branches whipping at her face. She didn't pay attention to where she was headed. She just had to get away from that smell. It was too much; it was wrong. She ran until the smell finally disappeared from the air, and she felt like she could breathe again. Looking around, she realized she should have made it back to the village by now… if she had been headed in the right direction. But she had clearly turned around at some point. The forest was thick here and the sun was blocked out by the dancing canopy high above her. Even the monkey had swung off somewhere and left her alone. She was lost.

She turned to her left and walked a few yards, thinking the clearing had to be this way somewhere. Then she stopped and wondered if it was better to head back the way she had come and try again. But she didn't want to stumble back into the second clearing, the memory of the fleshy scent still fresh in her mind.

She closed her eyes and took a few deep breaths. Damn Emaru for always being right. She gritted her teeth and reached for the threads of her magia, grasping them lightly and sending them spreading out around her, searching for Emaru. It took almost a minute, but she finally felt the familiar tingle at the back of her mind. She had met someone's energy. But it wasn't Emaru… After another second she realized who it was.

Her eyes flew open and she looked sharply to her right.

Quenti.

CHAPTER 15

ALARA

Without thinking, Alara immediately bolted in the direction of Quenti's energy. Had she actually found her? As she rushed through the trees, all she could picture was Emaru's proud face and Ardo's wide smile as she came back with that troublesome magite.

She kept the threads of her magia softly held at the back of her mind, letting them direct her where to go as she dodged around trees through the thickening forest. The rush of the nearby river gurgled just out of sight as she broke through the trees into a wide clearing.

And out in the open stood her target—the person who would bring her back into good graces of the Haven.

Quenti whipped around as Alara emerged from the trees. Her face went white at the same time as a wide smile stretched across Alara's face.

"You're here!" Their voices rang out in unison.

Quenti took a step back, her eyes darting around. "Who are you with?" she asked sharply.

"We came to find you!" Alara said, ignoring Quenti's question. "El'dyo, I was worried you had gotten yourself kidnapped by bruyas."

Without warning, Quenti launched a jet of water toward her and ducked into the forest on the other side of the clearing. Alara dodged the haphazard attack and bolted after her, automatically sending out the threads of magia to track her.

"Quenti, stop!" Alara tripped over the roots of a tree and felt a sharp throb in her knee, but jumped up and kept running. A minute later, she broke out of the forest, Quenti standing frozen ahead of her.

Here the river rushed loudly, drowning out the sounds of the forest behind them. Alara stepped toward her and noticed she was standing on the edge of a cliff, the river rushing a few dozen feet down below.

"Go away." Quenti's voice was cold.

"Quenti, we came to help you." Alara's knee was throbbing from her fall and she was losing patience with Quenti's foolishness. The girl was clearly trying to get kidnapped or eaten.

Quenti let out a bitter laugh. "Help me?" In one smooth motion, Quenti pulled an arrow from the quiver across her back and nocked it into a bow, aiming it directly at Alara's chest.

Alara hadn't even noticed she'd *had* a bow and quiver on her until that moment. She took an instinctive step back. Did she even know how to use a bow? Though, with them only being a couple of yards apart, she didn't have to.

"We're not here to hurt you," Alara said, donning her best diplomatic tone. "Emaru's back at the village; we can help with whatever trouble you've gotten yourself into."

"Emaru's here?" Quenti's face somehow lost even more color.

"Of course. I told you. We were all worried."

Quenti looked like an animal caught in a trap. Her breath was quick and her eyes wide. Alara feared that she would accidentally let the arrow loose at any moment. But, against her own survival instincts, she took a step forward.

"Quenti, we need you to come back." Another step. Another. She reached out and gently nudged the nocked arrow aside.

To her great relief, Quenti slowly let the arrow loose and dropped the bow to the ground.

"Good. Now let's go."

"You really shouldn't be here," Quenti said, her voice soft as she glanced over her own shoulder at the rushing water below. "I don't want to have to hurt you. Just let me go."

Alara sighed deeply, both in exhaustion and as a way to delay having to respond. She had no idea what was going through Quenti's head, so no way of knowing how to calm her, and she wasn't exactly trained in the art of diplomacy.

Just as Alara opened her mouth to speak—though she still had no idea what she was about to say—the snapping of twigs sent both their heads spinning toward the tree line.

Ardo stepped out first, his face red with the exertion of running. Two more councilguards followed, spears lifted and poised to strike.

Alara immediately felt a wave of relief and she let her lips form into a smile. She met Ardo's eyes and saw the ease she was feeling reflected in his own gray irises. He stepped forward and Alara immediately felt Quenti's arm wrap around her waist. She felt a tug at her belt and the cold metal of the dagger she had found earlier pressed against her throat.

"Don't come any closer!" Quenti's voice was strong, but Alara could feel her hand trembling.

Alara's stomach dropped and she froze.

Ardo in a blur drew his bow and nocked an arrow. The look of calm in his eyes replaced with fear and desperation.

"Let her go. Now!"

"Put your bow down and I'll let her go."

Alara could see his arrow lower an inch, but the other two guards didn't move, their spears still pulled back in the ready position.

"You will let the girl go." One of the other councilguards barked.

Alara's heart slammed in her chest and she could feel her pulse beating hard against the edge of the knife. In the deep recesses of her awareness, she felt the heat of magia building within her. A soft voice whispered inside of her to release the energy and strike out at Quenti, who still held the dagger close against her neck. But Alara looked between the two councilguards who had their spears leveled at Quenti, and she could see the hate in their eyes. To them, Quenti was likely nothing more than a common bruya at this point. She wasn't sure they had gotten the memo from Emaru that the girl needed to come in alive and well. Given the situation, releasing her wild magia wouldn't help anything. She and Quenti might both end up with spears in their chests.

"Can we all calm down?" Alara choked out.

"You have three seconds to drop your weapons!" Quenti yelled, ignoring Alara completely. "One—two—"

No one moved, although Ardo's eyebrows were drawn tight together.

"Three." Quenti stepped back, pulling Alara with her.

The councilguard on the left growled. "Ardo, shoot. Now!"

Alara's eyes went wide as Ardo drew and took aim, but she saw the hesitation flicker across his face as he held the bowstring taut. But Quenti had taken another step backward.

The world fell away.

One moment, Alara could feel the grass against her sandaled feet, and the next there was nothing. The air rushed past her ears and she wasn't sure if she saw or imagined Ardo dropping his bow and running toward her as the cliff rose up in front of them.

She let out an involuntary gasp and waited for the impact, her eyes closed tight. But there was nothing. The world had stopped spinning, even as the air continued to rush around her. She opened her eyes to find the river still a few feet below, Quenti still gripping her tightly—although the blade was now gone from her throat.

Looking up, she could see the edge of the cliff where they had just been, now a dozen or so yards above them. She could just make out Emaru's pale face, with her hand thrown out over the edge. She was using her magia to keep them from falling any farther. A wave of relief hit Alara until she saw the strained look on Emaru's face. She didn't have the energy to pull them both back up.

"Quenti, let Alara go. Please."

Silence. What was Quenti thinking? Was she going to let them both fall? The grip on her arm loosened—but Quenti's arm around her waist tightened painfully. Alara had just enough time to see her arm stretched out toward the river before the icy wall of water hit them, propelling them forward.

The grip of Emaru's magia slipped from them, and she yelled out, but it was quickly drowned by the rushing onslaught of water. The water knocked the air out of her lungs. Her eyes stung. Her skin numbed. She had to get away from Quenti and this hellish water. She gasped and struggled, flailing wildly and jamming her elbow behind her. She heard a gargled gasp, and the grip on her waist loosened.

In triumph, she pulled away, thrashing and kicking her legs.

Until, for the second time, the world dropped out from under her. She felt Quenti's hand clasp onto her wrist just as they hit the bottom of a waterfall with a crack.

CHAPTER 16

QUENTI

Quenti wasn't thinking.

She had acted on pure instinct when she had jumped, pulling Alara with her, whose mere presence had jeopardized her freedom. She just had to get away from them. If only it had been that easy.

As the current tugged against her skirts, she felt the added weight of Alara, who now clung to her wrist, a sign that she recognized her current position. Like it or not, she was the only thing keeping Alara from drowning in the rapids. Though, even with her abilities, wading through a fast-moving river wasn't the easiest thing to do, and the weight of an entire extra person made the task doubly taxing.

No one would blame her if she just let this foolish magite go, right? No. She didn't deserve that. She tightened her grip on Alara's wrist. She may not be able to kill the girl in good conscience, but she could at least keep her from finding her way back home. After all, the sooner Alara returned to the councilwoman and the others, the sooner they'd all chase her down again.

She propelled them through the river; there wasn't time to think things through—with each passing minute, the fatigue set in more and more. She could feel herself slowing down already. Her body grew heavy, her powers draining as she fought against the water. It now pushed against them as she slowly lost control of the current. She had guided them into another river a few miles back, and between the exhaustion and newfound resistance, she couldn't keep this up for much longer.

Using the last of her strength, she brought them to the shore, pulling Alara up against the rocks before dragging herself out of the water with a shudder. Her magia, which was usually an explosion of power within her was now just a dull pulse in her core. It wasn't until she was lying on her back, staring up at the steep hillsides on either side of the river that she realized how tired she was. Her whole body trembled, and her fingers burned with a numbing cold.

Beside her, Alara sat up with a start, shoulders heaving.

"You—you could have killed me!" she gasped out, eyes wild and hair plastered to her face.

Quenti waved her hand weakly, trying to push her out of the way so she could sit up. "Please," Quenti said between breaths. "I'm a water mage. I had it handled."

"You're not a *mage*."

"Fine. *Magite. Bruya.* Whatever you want to call me."

"You think you have a right to the word magite after you tried to slit my throat?"

"Bruya it is, then!" Quenti said, already getting fed up with the direction of the conversation. "And please, I couldn't slit your throat if I tried. Have you looked at this stupid thing of yours?"

She pulled out the dagger and slashed at her own arm. It didn't leave so much as a scratch on her skin. "It's dull as a spoon. Hardly even worth being called a dagger."

Alara's eyebrows furrowed, studying the blade in Quenti's hand. She tried to reach for it, but Quenti quickly slipped it back into her belt without comment. She didn't trust Alara, even with even a dull weapon.

Alara didn't protest, but an annoyed look crossed her face. "Why did you run?"

"Why do you think?" Quenti pushed her hair back from her face, the feeling slowly coming back to her fingers.

"We were trying to save you." Alara attempted to stand. Whether from the sodden clothes or her own shaky exhaustion, she stumbled a few times before she could get her feet under her.

Her teeth clenched at Alara's words. "Save me?" She was standing now, any weakness having been burned from her body by anger. "I was trying to save myself from *you*."

"Save yourself how?"

She sighed. What had she been expecting from this? "You really are a sweet, brainwashed child, aren't you? Ever stopped to think about what the Council has to gain by keeping all magia users under their thumb?"

"You mean apart from a half a millennium of peace and prosperity?" Alara said. "Need I remind you that—"

"—that mages were the instigators in the great war, blah-blah-blah. Yeah, I know." As much as she wished no ill will on Alara, she was starting to regret saving her. "Go on, then. I'm not holding you against your will. You're free to go back, I guess."

Alara narrowed her eyes and looked back toward the way they came. "How far did we go?"

Quenti had already done the calculations in her head. "A

couple dozen or so miles—two waterfalls. You should be able to make it back to them in a couple of days or less if you walk through the night."

"A dozen—how…?" Alara's eyes were wide.

"A *couple* dozen. And did you already forget that I'm a water mage?"

"*Bruya.*"

"Whatever."

"*Fine,*" Alara said, crossing her arms and throwing herself onto the ground. "They'll come looking for me if I just stay here."

Quenti laughed. Just how stupid was this girl? "You'll be eaten by a wild puma long before they find you. And you'd at least need to get to the split we took, since they won't know which way we went. That'll be like…five or so miles. It's even downhill. Completely doable, especially with your powers to protect you. You might even make it down before nightfall."

She could see Alara's eyes tracking the river back toward the horizon, making her own calculations. At this point, Quenti wasn't quite sure what the best move was. Even if Alara did make it down to the split and the councilguards found her—it would give Quenti hours of a head start to make it into the cloud forest and disappear. But then again, Alara *was* a mind-stalker, and though she wasn't exactly in tune with her abilities, she had found Quenti twice already.

On the other hand, if she brought Alara with her, she'd only slow her down. Of that she was sure. But at least that way Alara wouldn't be able to tell the councilguards which way she had gone.

"You could come with me," Quenti's voice shook Alara from her contemplation.

The magite's head whipped around, her eyes narrowed. If she was trying to intimidate Quenti, it likely would have only worked if they were both ten years younger. In spite of any combat skills, her short stature didn't exactly inspire fear and intimidation. "Or… you could wait here as the sun begins to set and pray to El'dyo you don't get eaten. The two of us can brave the wilderness much better together than apart."

Quenti started to walk away from the river. "Either way, I'm going to go find a place to make camp. You're welcome to join me if you aren't too annoying."

"Why can't we make camp here?" Alara said waving her arms around the flat open ground they were on.

"Oh yes, let's just stay here next to the lovely water source saying, 'come get me, predators, *please.*'" Quenti continued to walk away, eyes now trained on the incline ahead of her and the deepening shadows as the sun fell behind the western side of the mountains.

She could almost hear the thoughts whirring through Alara's mind before the sound of stumbling footsteps followed behind her.

They walked less than a quarter of a mile uphill and through the dense forest before Quenti found a spot she was content with. The undergrowth was sparse here and the land relatively flat.

She could just hear the river in the distance if she strained her ears. It mixed in with the sounds of the forest, birds calling back and forth in the high trees, and a small group of monkeys chattering together just outside the clearing.

Alara crumpled on the ground, dropping her head into her

hands. She thinks she's tired? She wasn't the one who tamed miles of river to escape a kidnapping councilwomen.

After taking a labored breath, Quenti took stock of her sodden pack of supplies. The quinoa she had left was beyond saving, but the jerky could be dried by the fire. She grabbed some branches scattered about the clearing and made a small pile away from the trees.

Her legs folded beneath her as she collapsed to the ground next to the pile. She took some deep breaths, staring at the damp wood, trying to reach for the cool core of her magia. It was weak and hard to grasp, but after a few minutes, she managed enough to suck the water from the branches, sending the droplets to a small cup she had pulled out of the pack.

A few feet away, Alara was still sitting, head in the hands, breathing heavily. Quenti could practically taste the panic and fear in the air. What a disaster.

"Can you at least make yourself useful and start a fire?" she said, throwing Alara a small flint and metal ring. She nodded to the branches she had collected as Alara gave her a blank stare. "I've dried them off, so they should light easily."

"Right. I…"

"Look, if you want to sit around and wait to be rescued, you can go back to the river and waste time there."

"No," Alara said, her face flushed. "It's just… I don't know how to start a fire."

"You're a fire mage." She couldn't believe her ears. A fire mage that couldn't start a fire. That girl really *was* a disaster.

"Wrong. I'm a *magite*."

"You and your names!"

"And a bad one at that," Alara said, ignoring the barb. "Have you forgotten already? Besides, do you know how to swim just because you're a water bruya?"

"Yes." Quenti looked over at her with a mixture of pity and disgust. "It was like the first thing I learned."

"Well, I've never much liked fire. So it never was at the top of my priorities."

"Sol help me. What do they even teach you people at the Haven?" Quenti dragged herself up and grabbed the flint back from Alara. She pulled the branches together into a small pyramid, before striking the flint a few times. Her frustration over the past few weeks seemed to build in her chest as she tried to get the sparks to light over and over again.

"Do *you* know how to start a fire?"

"Of course I do!" Quenti snapped. Though she had always struggled to start fires, no matter how many times she had been taught as a child. Her mother had always said it was because it went against her nature—not that she would have said that in front of Quenti's father.

"Let me see it," Alara said, interrupting her thoughts before they could spiral any deeper.

She stepped back, letting her take the flint and ring from her.

"Can you just… back up a bit more. Just in case?"

Quenti rolled her eyes, and while she didn't say anything as she stepped back, she did reach into her core and grab onto a thread of her magia, lightly, readying herself if she needed to throw any water at the problem—or her face.

Alara was silent and still as she kneeled in front of the wood. Quenti couldn't see her hands, but she heard the sharp sound of flint hitting metal.

Even with her abilities, it took a few minutes, and Quenti was about to snatch the flint back from her when a spark suddenly flared to life. The wood in front of Alara caught, flames roaring almost instantaneously, blackening the wood.

Her eyes went wide in amazement. So she was able to do it, after all.

Alara froze, a look of terror locked onto her face. She fell back from the fire, her powers flickering out as the inferno settled into a small fire. But the blackened wood was proof of what had just happened.

"I did it." Alara's voice was loud and strong despite her ashen face.

Quenti rolled her eyes and pushed her aside, taking over tending the fire back into something more substantial. She almost felt sorry her as Alara quickly retreated to the edge of the clearing.

"You're not going to stay warm from over there."

"I'm fine here," Alara said.

All the same, Quenti grabbed her sodden cloak from her bag, waved her hand over it to wring out the water and then threw it at Alara.

"You seem to have a plan," Alara said, eyeing the rest of the supplies Quenti had laid out beside her pack. She seemed particularly interested in the small array of weapons Quenti had packed—a bow, a quiver of arrows, a small club, and a set of bolas. It wasn't her fault the councilguards were careless with their supplies.

"Yep. Although, you following after me was not a part of it."

"Well, gee," Alara said, her voice coated in irony. "I am so sorry about that. I just really wanted to join in on the fun."

Quenti quickly lost the momentary pity she felt for her. "I needed to get out of there. I didn't ask you to find me."

"Save you."

"Recapture me."

Alara's eyes dropped and she actually looked unsure of herself.

"So where are you going?" Alara finally asked, still not making eye contact.

"*We*, now… We're going to meet Khuna."

"The girl that taught you magia? The villager?"

It was her turn to avoid eye contact now. "Yeah. Her."

"What is she even doing out here? Is there a village this way?"

"Yes." She was stabbing at the fire now. A part of her knew she was probably more likely to ruin the fire at this point, but it was an excuse to not look at Alara.

"You must have been close with her to run away like this." Alara's voice was questioning.

"We were—are." Quenti stood up and brushed the loose dirt from her cream skirt. "I need to catch us some fish for dinner. The quinoa is useless, but maybe you can go find us some fruit or nuts. You know how to not poison us, right?"

"I'm not an idiot."

"Aren't you, though?"

Alara's eyes narrowed.

"Okay, forgive me if I assume someone who grew up with a market the size of the Haven's never had to scavenge for food!"

"I want to be a member of the councilguard—it's useful training."

"So you want to be a councilguard but are *still* too afraid to use your gifts?"

"Gifts? We call them curses at the Haven. At least until they're mastered. And what's it to you? You have a problem with that?"

Quenti looked her over. Alara was fit but still on the small side—a few good inches shorter than her, not that she was particularly tall. Alara seemed to be able to read her thoughts, as the look in her eyes practically dared her to argue.

"Right, then you will understand why I'm taking these with me," Quenti said as she grabbed the small store of weapons and walked out of the clearing without a glance back.

What was she supposed to do with this girl? She couldn't very well just *leave* her out in the middle of nowhere... Could she? But what would happen to them when she showed up in Arbol with a councilguard-in-training?

Chapter 17

Quenti

Quenti sat carefully on the edge of the water and stared into the murky depths. Their trip up the river had brought them a bit into the mountains and deep into the cloud forest, but they were still too low for the water to be clean and clear. It wasn't quite the muddy mess of the river near her childhood home, Hurazon, but it still took squinting to see the fish rippling beneath the surface.

She closed her eyes and plucked at her magia, letting the coolness run through her. She opened her eyes and gently reached out, touching the river with her magia, letting it settle momentarily. She waited patiently, the magia threads held gently. Her father always told her she was too impatient, but then again he had never seen this side of her. This side of her could sit on the edge of the water perfectly still, so long as her abilities were engaged. She was just too impatient to wait for stupid fishing nets to work.

It took a couple minutes for the timing to line up, but she abruptly snatched the water toward her, a wriggling fish caught in the bubble. With a small prayer to Sol, she let the fish fall onto the earth beside her and sucked away the last of its water with only the smallest bit of guilt as its movements slowed. It was definitely more humane than letting it suffer. She did this a few more times until she had a small pile beside her, and exhaustion pulled deep in her core again.

She had used her magia more over the last few days than she had in all the years she had grown up—at least before she met Khuna.

The thought of her brought another wave of emotions over her. Emotions she was too tired to fight off. She was excited to see her again. Anxious about what she had been thinking these past weeks when she hadn't shown up as planned. Worried of what her people's reaction would be when she showed up with Alara in tow. None of this had been a part of the plan.

But she remembered Khuna talking about mind-walkers who lived in her village, walkers strong enough to erase a memory or even rewrite someone's mind. Strong enough, she hoped, to send Alara back on her way, none the wiser as to where she had gone. Or maybe the mind-walker was strong enough to erase the brainwashing Alara had gone through at the Haven.

Quenti snorted at this as she finally rose, collecting her catches from the ground. Nobody was strong enough for *that*.

"What happens if I go with you… to wherever you're headed?"

Alara had been staring at the fire when Quenti returned. The shadows of dusk had completely enveloped the clearing and Alara's fear of the dark had apparently outweighed her discomfort with fire.

"I can't exactly stay forever," Alara noted.

"You might find you like it above ground," Quenti said with a smirk.

Alara didn't seem amused by the comment.

"Look, once we get there, I'm sure you can get some supplies and head back then. You'll be better prepared to return to the Haven if you have more than some clothes and a dull dagger. And maybe they can even spare an escort to help." Her eyes didn't meet Alara's, and she knew the other girl had noticed.

"Right... an escort..." Alara said, her sentence drifting off, laced in doubt.

Quenti ignored the uncertain tone and turned her concentration back to cooking the fish she had laid out on a stone nestled in the hot coals of the fire.

The fish was buttery on her tongue. Not only that, but it was divine to just get something warm inside of her after all the river riding and hiking.

They sat in silence, Alara across the fire from her, with only the crackling of burning wood and the soft hum of wildlife to keep them company. The sky had darkened and with it the shadows in the forest had turned black and deep. The air was still moist and held some of the warmth from the day and the fire radiated dry and heavy heat. She felt her body relax for the first time in weeks as warmth and comfort spread over her. She had spent the past countless nights huddled against the shadows, too afraid to light a fire while still in the borders of Sombria, where —even now—she was being hunted.

"So, how did you get so good at using your magia?" Alara asked, staring into the fire.

Quenti flinched, just a bit, in surprise at the broken silence. "I already told you." And a magite of the Haven probably knew more than she should already.

Alara paused, seemingly mulling over her non-answer. "I mean, why didn't you ever get picked up in the testings?"

Quenti didn't speak immediately, her mind racing with images of all the testings that she had indeed participated in. She chewed on the piece of fish in her mouth until it melted into nothing, and her throat was left empty and dry.

"Mama didn't trust the Haven. She didn't trust the Council," she said finally.

Alara didn't interrupt the long pause that followed, her eyes still focused on the fire.

"So when I was young, she taught me not to use my magia around others. And if someone did see me use it, she would make them forget."

Alara's mouth hung open. "Your mother's a mind-walker?"

"Was." She gave a sad smile, trying to push back the ache in her chest. "She died a few months back. Pneumonia. The way it happened was so… ordinary. Way too ordinary for someone like her."

"I'm sorry," Alara said, her voice softer than she had ever heard. "You know, mind-walkers are incredibly rare!"

"They are. Which is why the Council seemed so interested in me. Once your not-mother-guardian figured out Mama was likely a mind-walker, they thought I might be one too," Quenti said.

"Are you?"

Quenti shook her head. "If I was, do you really think I would have needed to kidnap you and jump off a cliff to escape the councilguards?"

"So you admit it was kidnapping," Alara said with a lopsided smile.

Quenti blanched. Even if made in jest, she felt the sharp bite of shame and swirl of anxiety at what would happen when they got to Khuna's village.

"That was your father back in Hurazon?" Alara broke the silence again, apparently aware of the sudden thoughts spinning through her head.

"Yeah." Quenti didn't elaborate. She didn't like talking about Papa.

"He didn't know about your magia." It was a statement, not a question.

"No. He and Mama didn't always agree on things, particularly when it came to the Council."

"So you don't want to go home?"

Quenti let out a cold laugh and waved her hand. "No. That jerk'd just send me right back to the Haven."

The sleeve of her tunic rode up and Alara's eyes widened as she glanced at her bare wrist.

"Your bracelet's gone."

She pulled down the arm of her tunic, covering her skin again and gave her best nonchalant shrug.

"How did you get it off? They're impossible to remove!"

"I found a key. It wasn't hidden or anything. Stupid on their part, really."

But not as stupid as she had been for letting Alara see her bare wrist to begin with. The last thing she needed was for Alara to go back to the Haven, asking questions about whether someone had helped her remove her bracelet.

But before they had a chance to do their dance of pursuit and avoidance, a branch snapped in the forest just behind Alara.

They both fell silent, her ears straining to hear. Another branch snapped, and the bushes rustled a few yards into the shadowed forest.

There was someone or some*thing* nearby.

Chapter 18

Quenti

Quenti tried to signal to Alara, but she was turned, eyes fixated on the darkness.

"Emaru?" Alara whispered.

Quenti's eyebrows furrowed. Emaru and her soldiers should be at least a day's walk from them still… unless they went all-in on using an aguen's water abilities to follow them. She crouched and reached into her bag for the stolen handful of arrows without taking her eyes off the shadows. There was another rustle of leaves.

She worried Alara might call out again, but instead, she stood up and took a step back. She looked at Quenti, eyes wide, apparently recognizing the situation for what it was. Her eyes darted around their camp, no doubt looking for the weapon she no longer had. Quenti groaned to herself. Now would be a good time for Alara to have her trusty spear.

Her hands shook as she tried to notch an arrow. She wasn't a good shot. A fisher and trapper, yes, but no archer. She only hoped she was decent enough to spook whatever was lurking out there.

"Get behind the fire," she ordered.

Alara listened without hesitation. "What do you think it is?" she said, her voice hoarse and quiet.

"Nothing good."

A second later, an enormous cat the size of a l'lama stepped out from the shadows and into the circle of light their fire gave off. Its fur, a deep rich green, shimmering in the firelight, and the ground beneath its paws undulated in its wake.

Quenti felt her stomach drop. She had never seen a pumisi before, but her mother had told her stories as a child, the kind of stories that kept children from running too deep into the forest alone.

"Shoo! Go away!" Quenti shouted instinctively. Was she actually telling a near-legendary beast to shoo? "Go! Get out of here!"

"By all means, say please while you're at it."

Quenti didn't reply, but gave her an annoyed look. "Leave us alone." Her voice was firm and loud, but her entire body trembled as the giant cat took another step. The ground shuddered, and a log fell over in the fire, emitting a wave of sparks.

"I don't think it's listening to you," Alara said.

Quenti didn't look over, but raised her bow and pointed it at the wide body of the feline.

"Do you know what you're doing with that thing?"

"Enough."

"Perfect, we're betting our lives on 'enough.'"

"No, I'm telling you to shut up."

She let an arrow fly. It flew fast and true—straight over the pumisi's head.

"For the love of… give me your bow," Alara said, reaching out for it.

Quenti ignored her, letting another arrow fly. This one struck the beast but glanced off its thick hide. Intelligent feline eyes flickered to her, looking more annoyed than anything. Then they rested on the fish roasting in the fire.

"Give. Me. The bow!" Alara said. "Give me anything."

Quenti clenched her teeth. "I've got this." *And I don't trust you with a weapon.* She notched another arrow, aiming for the pumisi's head. This time, the arrow grazed its ear before sailing wildly into the night.

"No you don't, and I don't feel like dying," Alara's voice was loud, any pretense of keeping quiet gone.

The pumisi shook the ground as it moved again. Yellow eyes turned again to them. The dirt around its paws swirled and rose into the air, caught up in the animal's natural magia. Mouth open, long fangs sparkling in the firelight, it let out a silent roar, and the entire forest seemed to creak, the ground around them jerking and shuddering. She fell backward, bow falling at her side. Alara rode out the quake, knees bent and fists clenched.

She looked back just in time to see the pumisi crouch, its tail writhing. She reached out for the dropped bow. Too late. The cat leaped. Before her fingers could even brush the wood, a burst of heat threw her back. The world shimmered in white and red.

A sharp cry filled the air, and she saw the beast land in a heap on the ground, fur singed black. The inferno collapsed back in on itself, fading back into their simple campfire.

It let out a soft yowl before pulling itself up and bounding into the woods beyond.

Quenti looked up at Alara, who stood beside her, arms raised, her skin radiant with heat and light. And as Alara glanced down at her, the glow dimmed then snuffed out altogether.

"Thanks," she choked out. Her throat was hot and dry. She looked down at the bow, useless beside her, and tried to ignore the swell of shame bubbling up. "You were… good."

"Are you okay?" Alara said, her eyes darting around frantically. Quenti followed her gazed, seeing her sleeve singed, but nothing else was hurt or out of place.

"Yes. Fine."

She was suddenly aware of how cold it was. The fire was only smoldering embers now, the fish had burned down to nothing.

"I killed the fish."

Quenti let out an involuntary laugh, though she still had the metallic taste of fear on her tongue as she pulled herself up from the ground.

Alara stared glumly at the charred remains of dinner.

"I can catch more tomorrow," Quenti said. "I have some jerky if you're still hungry." She motioned toward her bag.

Alara shook her head, turning away from her and making a bed of leaves farther from the fire than was probably necessary. Quenti shook her own head at Alara's slumped shoulders. She had just scared off a pumisi, but instead she looked like she'd just murdered someone. She should be proud—ecstatic.

Quenti cleaned up the remnants of the fish, tossing them as far into the trees as she could without stepping out from the waning light of the embers. She was being overly cautious considering there was no meat left, just ash. After drying out a few more pieces of wood, she tossed them onto the fire, stoking it until they lit.

When she finished, she gathered her *aguayo* over her shoulders, picked the small club from her bag and sat down on the edge of the woods closest to the firelight.

"We should keep watch tonight. I can take the first shift," Quenti said, looking where Alara lay. But she wasn't listening. For a moment, Quenti remembered the glow of Alara's skin after she had used her abilities. Now her eyes were dark and somber, skin back to its normal pale brown.

"The Haven really did get inside your head."

Alara's eyes refocused and looked over to where Quenti was sitting. "I don't know what you're talking about."

"I can read your face like a book," she said, smirking.

Alara didn't reply, rolling over to look at the sky.

"You know you were glowing after the pumisi attacked. Literally glowing. I've never seen anything like that before. I've never even seen a fire mage at work before, in all honesty."

Alara gave a small *hmph* of acknowledgment.

"But now you look—ashamed."

"I should have been able to control my magia better."

"Better? You lit the entire clearing on fire and all I had to show for it was a singed cuff."

Alara was silent in response.

"Is this what the Haven teaches? How to fear your magia?"

"I don't fear it."

"That's a load of l'lama shit."

Alara rolled over on her makeshift bed, looking at her incidental captor for the first time since the conversation began.

"El'dyo gave magia to teach control and discipline," Alara said after a moment of silence. "So we could prove ourselves faithful. But I just don't understand why I need to use my magia to show discipline. Isn't it better to prove that I don't need it at all?"

"So El'dyo gave us magia… so we wouldn't use our magia? You seriously believe that."

"It's not about believing. It's in the teachings. We know it to be true."

Quenti groaned. "Our magia wasn't given to us by anyone. It wasn't something to be given. It's just us. It's life."

"That's blasphemy."

"That's just what they say of anything that clashes with the Council's rules." It was her turn to look away in frustration now, her eyes focusing on the stars bright above her.

She sat for a moment, remembering the stories her mother used to tell her about Sol. Just another secret kept from her father—the old religion long ago banned by the Council. But Quenti always loved the stories. It was a faith filled with hope and balance and life, not fear and power.

By the time she looked back across the clearing, Alara was already asleep.

"Guess I'll take first watch then."

Sometime later, after Quenti added wood to the fire for the third time that night, she nudged Alara awake with her club, and she woke quickly, but silently. Wordlessly, she nodded and stood up to move toward the fire.

Before she had gotten two steps, Quenti stopped her with a small grunt. Saying nothing, she handed her the club and lay down on the bed Alara had made, turning away and closing her eyes.

CHAPTER 19

ALARA

Alara found a comfortable-looking spot among the roots of a large tree and sat down, her back against the smooth bark. The soil between the roots was cool beneath her, and she felt the dampness seeping through her skirts. Normally, she would have worried about getting her clothes so dirty. Emaru had often yelled at her when she came back to their dorms with grass and mud stains all over her clothes. She had learned to keep herself clean as she ran around and trained with Adelmo—mostly to avoid Emaru's sharp looks. Though she probably wouldn't yell at her in this case.

She leaned her head against the tree trunk and looked up through the canopy of leaves above her. She could just make out a small piece of the inky black sky above their clearing, where the stars shone brightly.

She tapped at the club in her hands as she tried to stay awake. She could just run now that she had a weapon. Find the river and make her way to Attalea. A voice in her head urged her to do just that. Leave this crazy girl and get back to Emaru—and

Ardo. She looked into the dark underbrush surrounding them and thought about the pumisi's yellow eyes again. She had saved them once, but there was no guarantee she could do it again. And directions had never been her strong suit. Where was the river? Down the hill, surely, but the fact she didn't know instinctively irked her.

She let out a soft groan and closed her eyes tightly. Perhaps Emaru was right—after all of her training and learning how to fight without her magia, she was still completely useless at saving even herself. With a quiet huff, she shook herself from her thoughts and focused her eyes on the shadows across the clearing. Like she had many times before in her councilguard training, she let her mind go blank and her body go still.

"Why didn't you wake me?" Quenti said, brushing her eyes awake.

"I wanted to keep watch." Alara's response was soft and curt. Amid everything happening around her, the responsibility of keeping her fellow magites safe was warm and familiar, even if her "fellow magite" in this case was technically her captor.

She stood, brushing off the dirt and leaves that had stuck to her in the night then wound her *aguayo* around her shoulders. She looked back at Quenti expectantly. "Are we ready to go, then?"

Quenti gave an almost growl as she slung her bag over her shoulder and marched past Alara. "You better keep up with me. Don't think you can use lack of sleep as an excuse."

Alara followed in silence.

They walked like this for hours. She could hear the constant gurgling of the river somewhere off to their right, so she knew they were following it. Following it away from the Haven. Away from home. She watched her feet carefully as they hiked along, stepping over twisted roots and around muddy puddles collecting among the underbrush. She was happy for the soft leather sandals she wore, but even then, her feet already began to ache by midday. Her legs were sore, and she noticed an annoyingly subtle incline of the ground as they trudged on, though she refused to voice her complaints. When she slipped on a root hidden beneath caked mud, she simply bit her lip as pain shot up her ankle.

It was past midday when Quenti finally broke the silence.

"Come out with it."

"What?" She didn't look up, still concentrating on where her feet were stepping, and her ankle still smarting from her slip earlier.

"I get you're mad at me, but I'm gonna go crazy if we spend the next few days in silence. So, get it out—yell at me and tell me all the reasons I'm awful."

"I think you kidnapping me pretty much covers it," she said, still not looking up.

Quenti didn't respond, and the silence fell heavy between them again, Alara's gaze still fully focused on the ground in front of her. Step. Look. Step. Look.

"I'm not brainwashed by the Council, you know?" Her voice was quiet, but it echoed in the silent forest.

"You could have fooled me."

"It's complicated."

Quenti stopped and leaned against a tree, looking at her with bright eyes.

Alara stopped a few steps ahead of her and gazed back at sharply.

Quenti sighed. "Look. All I know is last night after the pumisi attacked—after you used your magia to save us—you were excited. There was a spark in your eye, the same one I saw when you were fighting in the dark marketplace thing. You looked… alive. You wanted to do more. To practice more. And then it all shut down. You probably heard the voice of that woman guilting you for enjoying your powers and reminding you you're supposed to hate them. The spark went out, and you returned to"—Quenti waved a hand haphazardly at her—"*this*."

"How…?" She bit her lip and tried not to let Quenti see the tremors in her hands.

"It was the same feeling that I used to get when I was around my papa." Quenti's voice softened a bit. It was perhaps the first time she had seen any emotion other than anger or mischief from Quenti. "When I was younger, before I gained control, I would slip sometimes and use magia in front of him. Mama would always come sweeping into the room to erase his memory and give me another speech about keeping my secret. It was confusing trying to make sense of the excitement I felt when I used my powers and the terror in Mama's face every time I did." The next sentence was almost a whisper. "Khuna was the first person who wasn't afraid."

"Emaru isn't afraid."

"Oh?"

"No, her and the others… they try to get me to open up."

"But they teach you to fear your abilities first."

"To fear them so we can control them," Alara said. "It isn't just about Emaru or me or you," Alara said. "It's the bigger picture. The Haven is protecting us and the rest of the world from devolving back to where we were during the Bruya Wars. Without control, magia just led to escalating war and death."

"So every time you need to light a campfire, that's what's stopping you? Some old propaganda about the Wars from five hundred years ago?"

Alara was silent at this.

"I thought so."

She broke eye contact with Quenti and leaned heavily against the tree behind her. The bark was smooth and cool where her arms brushed it. "Like I said before. It's complicated."

Quenti just raised an eyebrow, but said nothing, clearly waiting for Alara.

"If I tell you, will you shut up?"

The air was cool, but the sun was warm—Alara would always remember how the weather felt on the day that forever changed her life.

A trickle of sweat slipped down her back, tickling against her skin. She concentrated hard on the frog statue in front of her. The frog was made of cool gray stone and a small stream of water shot from the palm of its foot, which was raised up in front of it like a human hand. It sat on a pedestal in the middle of the village square, its mouth thrown back and open wide.

This is where Alara's eyes focused. She clenched her small fist around the copper coin in her hand.

"Come on, Lara. Just do it already!" The loud shrill voice behind her was disembodied—a blur of brown hair and dark skin. The face had long since faded into lost memories.

Alara placed the coin on her thumb and flicked it, sending it spinning through the air. And with a small plunk, it hit the lip of the frog and veered off, falling into the base of the fountain.

She felt the weight of disappointment hit and heard the snicker behind her. "I knew you couldn't do it. My turn!"

She smirked and jutted her foot out. The boy behind her

tumbled onto the ground, and she jumped, grabbing at the coin in his hand, tripping as she did.

The stone of the village street cut into her knee, but she ignored the sting as she stood back up, triumphantly holding his copper coin in her hand.

She turned back to the statue as the boy tried to recover from his fall, scrambling up from the street and reaching for her, just as she flicked the second coin.

"Ha!" She elbowed the boy and pointed to where the coin had landed in the frog's mouth. "That's a point for me!"

"That was my coin! My point!"

"Oh, please. It doesn't work that way."

Another voice piped up from behind, this time higher and softer. "Lara won fair and square, Ro. Don't blame her because you're a loser." Alara didn't turn to see her—she didn't know her face, but she knew she knew her. Her name...

Then she was laughing. The faceless boy was laughing, and she felt herself grinning.

And then there was the whizz of an arrow, and the boy's features came into sharp focus. His brown eyes wide, tanned pink lips parted, freckled cheeks flushed with laughter, and his white tunic stained with red blood where the arrow protruded from his chest, just right of his sternum.

He fell and the world erupted in chaos. The ground spun under her, and she realized she was running. The other girl's hand was clenched in her own and she heard the shocked sobs coming from one of them—or both of them.

She had known this day might come. Her parents had trained her, and the village had had safety drills. Run. Hide. Stay silent. The bruyas would kill on sight.

When she reached her house, Mama was standing in the doorway, face pale and eyes wild. "Faster, Alara!"

Inside the small stone house with its wicker roof, a group of others stood, still and pale. Mama opened the trapdoor in the wood-planked floor, and the small group of children descended the stairs, followed by a few women and men—her parents among them. Their faces were faded, but she could still make out Mama's sharp black eyes. She could feel her calloused hands running against her hair, holding her against her warm body.

The sounds outside were muffled, but she could still hear the screams, the sharp splintering of wood, and the heavy footfalls of running.

Under the wood planks of the floor, they remained quiet and still. She could make out the heavy breathing of a few children and the soft rocking as the adults tried to soothe them. Her own breath slowed, almost calming. Her mind was clear as she waited.

Wood splintered above them as the front door of the house blew inward. Between the wooden planks above her, she could see them. The black boots of men. Dirt fell silently between the planks and into her face, brushing against her skin. Beams of light crossed the underground space as the sunlight made its way through the shattered doorway. The men threw around furniture, upturned tables and rugs, and pulled apart packed chests.

What are they looking for?

Another sound from just outside drew their attention.

They were going to leave.

She made eye contact with Papa from across the space. His brow furrowed in concentration. She recognized his eyes as the same rich brown as her own just as a spear came through the floorboards.

Everything around her was a blur, except for her papa's body as it crumpled to the ground. Screams erupted, and the floorboards splintered as hands pulled them away.

"Get out! All of you!"

A large hand came down on her neck and lifted her off the ground. The man holding her yelled, spit flying from his mouth as he did. Without warning, he slammed her hard against the stone walls of the house. She could hear him yelling but couldn't understand him. His eyes focused on the others, still looking up from their useless hiding place. Mama stepped forward, and something stronger than fear shot through Alara.

She could feel the warmth of the fire like a tingle against her skin, but it didn't burn her. The man holding her let go with a howl as the flames crawled up his arm and enveloped his body. The smoke was thick and black, and it stung her throat. Her vision blurred with smoke and heat. The air was hotter and thicker than it should've been. At that moment, she heard other screams joining the guards. Flames danced across the wood floors, eating up rugs and blankets—and Mama. She could only just make out Mama's face between the white flames, and she scrambled toward her, ignoring the searing pain consuming her.

She knew it was hopeless the second she clasped Mama's hand in her own and saw the blisters—red, angry, and charred. So sharply in focus that she would never forget. And the look in Mama's eyes as she finally collapsed against the ground, her breath stuttering for the last time, a look of pain and hate painted across her face.

CHAPTER 20

ALARA

Alara unconsciously ran a hand along her scarred face, waiting for Quenti to say something. The silence between them stretched on as she felt the hard bark of the tree digging into her back. She was no longer looking at Quenti, unsure of what she'd see, dreading the looks of pity or fear this story would bring with it.

Then again, she wasn't sure how one responded to the *I killed Mama and a bunch of children with my magia* story.

"No snide remarks?" Alara said.

"Is that what you expect from me?" Quenti's voice was soft.

She winced—there was the pity.

"The Haven isn't some evil entity trying to suppress me. They've protected me, helped me gain control and learn not to hurt myself or others. The magia we all wield is wonderful, but it also has the capacity to hurt and kill." She took a deep breath, her heart beating wildly. "I don't know how many people I killed that day. But I can't lose control again."

Quenti was silent for a moment. "There's a fine line between controlling your magia and suppressing it."

Alara pushed herself off of the tree she had been leaning against and shook her head. "Maybe, but I'd rather suppress my magia than lose control again."

Quenti didn't respond. They resumed their slow trudge through the forest in silence. Her heart still pounding, she felt a tinge of regret for having told Quenti her secret. That's what it had become—her dirty secret. She had learned when she was much younger not to discuss her past. Adelmo and Emaru were the only ones close to her that knew her story.

"You know it wasn't your fault, right?" Quenti's voice startled her, and it took her a moment to register the words. "When I discovered my magia, I screwed up plenty. I almost got Mama and me caught even after I gained more control. I hate to agree with Emaru, but if you practiced and trained, you could be amazing."

"Or terrible."

To her surprise, Quenti nodded at this. "Couldn't anyone, though, powers or not?"

She chewed on her lip. That was the closest to an apology she'd get from Quenti.

They trudged on, neither looking at each other nor speaking, the sun inching across the sky and sending light dancing through the trees. But the silence was somehow lighter than it had been before. For a few moments, she even appreciated the whistle of the warm breeze and rustling of wildlife in the branches above them. She rarely had the chance to appreciate the sounds of nature in the forest. More often than not, she was hunting bruyas, sparring, or trying to control her magia.

The anxiety that she hadn't even realized was there unfurled itself in her gut as they walked, and she allowed herself to be lulled by the forest ambience. The air felt thinner today, and the shade seemed a few degrees cooler as she passed between pockets of sunshine. Yet, her feet still ached with each step, taking her farther and farther from home. She thought of Adelmo and his stable full of l'lamagas and imagined herself slumped in the saddle of one, breathing in the musty scent of animal. She was so lost in her own thoughts that she hadn't registered the lengthening shadows until Quenti stopped them in another small clearing.

Alara foraged through the forest nearby to feel useful while Quenti marched down to the river to fish. She found a few lucumas hanging low on a nearby tree. The fruit's flesh was a verdant green, and they were large and heavy in her hands.

Dinner was subdued, their conversation quiet and stilted, neither speaking about Alara's history that she had revealed.

In fact, the next few days passed much the same, in almost companionable silence. Occasionally, one or the other would make a mundane comment about the surroundings—"Look, there's a condor up there" or "That tree trunk is huge"—but never anything important or meaningful. As if neither wanted to open the door for argument.

She was over sharing feelings—it was exhausting.

It was only on the third morning that she questioned what the hell they were doing. The land had continued to slope up as they followed the river deeper into the mountains, and her feet had gone numb from their days of walking. Her stomach ached almost continually, hungry for more than just fish and berries. The meager food supplies Quenti had stolen from the Haven had run out two days ago, and this was by far the longest Alara had gone without washing or changing clothes. So bad was it that she was getting a headache from the foul stench that emanated from her whenever she moved.

"Can we stop?" she finally asked, leaning against a nearby tree. Its trunk was five times her size, stretching wide and twisting up into branches.

Quenti turned with a startled look.

"I need a break. And not just to sit. I need to do something about my clothes."

Quenti looked around as if to ask permission. From whom, Alara was unsure. "I guess that would be fine. My clothes could use a rinse, too."

She grinned, almost giddy as they turned to walk down toward the sound of the gurgling river.

When they got there, the sun had reached its zenith, the ground radiating heat. She sighed as she slipped out of her shoes and curled her toes in the warm soil. She had rinsed off at night a few times during their trip, but it had always been rushed and chilly in the setting sun. Now the air felt warm as she slipped her scarf, pants, and tunic off and jumped into the river.

The water was clear and shallow near the banks, although she could see it deepen toward the middle of the river. While not warm, it wasn't as icy as she had expected, having absorbed the heat from the sun over the course of the morning.

Still on the banks, Quenti stripped out of her pants and tunic before throwing off her undershirt and slipping into the water, almost naked.

The two of them dunked their clothes in the running water and laid them out on the shore in a sunny spot to dry. Neither of them moved to leave the river, though.

Alara stood in the water as it rushed around her thighs, savoring the combination of the warm sun and refreshing river.

Quenti went out farther than she had dared and dunked her head, hair plastering to her face when she resurfaced. Though, in stark contrast to most of the trek, her grin was wide.

She was about to ask why when a jet of water hit her in the face. She stumbled into the shallows of the bank and slipped on a rock, falling with a clumsy splash.

"Stop being a wimp and get out here."

She bit her lip, preparing for the backlash. "I can't swim."

Quenti just shook her head. "Did you forget how much I already helped you when we jumped into the river?"

"Jumped? You pulled me in."

"I promise I won't let you drown."

Taking a deep breath, Alara stepped out farther into the river, feeling the bank dropping steeply away until she was standing on her toes, the water rushing by her face. Her heart leaped hard into her throat and she retreated. But before she could stumble back, the water around her legs stopped moving against her, circling in a light current. Her toes slowly lifted off the ground. She yelped, but her body only bobbed in the river, even as the water at the surface rushed by.

"Tada." Quenti stretched out on her back, floating gently in stark contrast to the rushing river around her.

She tried to smile, but she couldn't shake the unsettling sensation that came with drifting at odds with the choppy surface of the water.

"Why do people do this?"

"Swim?" Quenti said with a laugh.

"This is not fun."

"Not how you're doing it. Kick your legs a bit—no, no— gently."

She jerked in the water as she tried to kick her legs against the press of the current. Water churned around her and she gasped as an icy cold wave cascaded into her mouth.

"Calm down! You're not gonna drown. Stop trying to fight the water."

She shot a glare in Quenti's direction before screwing her eyes shut. "I'm good to just float here."

There was a splash nearby and Quenti emerged next to her, her legs kicking back and forth. "Come on, like me."

Pursing her lips, she copied Quenti's motions, arms waving at her side like paddles. Before long, she felt her body moving in the water.

"El'dyo, I'm swimming!" A massive grin split Alara's face.

Quenti laughed, her own grin stretched wide. "Masterfully." She flung herself back again, her body lifting to float along the surface of the river.

She smiled and tried to let herself relax, feeling the sun warm her face. She experimented with kicking her feet a bit again, letting herself drift. After a few minutes, she lay back and closed her eyes against the sun.

She lost track of time as the two of them bobbed in the river. The water was icy against her skin, but the sun was bright and warm. The pain and exhaustion from the last few days seeped from her body.

Quenti pushed them back to the bank of the river, reluctantly, as the afternoon lengthened the shadows of the trees. Alara let out a small sigh of happiness when she found her clothes dry, warm, and mostly clean.

She and Quenti both laid back against the ground, letting the afternoon sun dry their skin. After days of walking, the muscles in her body were finally relaxing. But as she closed her eyes and her thoughts drifted, the calm of the day drained from her. The worries that had been tumbling through her mind during their trek rushed back.

Where were they going? How would she find her way back after all this? How long until she saw her own bed again?

"When are we going to get there?"

"It shouldn't be much longer," Quenti said.

Alara cracked an eye and saw her looking up at the sky, avoiding her gaze. "You said that two days ago. What exactly is 'not much longer' in your mind?"

Quenti shrugged before sitting up to slip her undershirt and tunic over her head. "We should get going unless we want to make camp here tonight."

Her eyes narrowed as Quenti finished dressing and collecting her things. She didn't move from her spot by the river. "No. You need to tell me where in El'dyo's name we are going."

"Oh, watch your mouth, humble Haven servant!" Quenti held her hand up to her mouth in mock surprise.

"I'm not joking. How many more days of 'not much longer' do we have?"

Quenti lowered her hand and looked back at her, not quite meeting her eye.

The realization hit her like a stone in her gut and she scrambled to slip her tunic overhead as she leaped up and stormed toward Quenti.

"You don't know?" Her voice was shrill and loud, but she was too angry to care. "You said you dragged me out here because it was safer, and you don't even know where we're going?"

"I know where—I mean, I know we need to go south until we hit an outcropping of rocks. I just… don't know how far." Quenti had the decency to blush as she stumbled over her words.

"That's all you know? An outcropping of rocks? Please tell

me you're joking." Quenti paled as she jabbed a finger into her captor's sternum. "Where are we going?"

"I told you. We're meeting Khuna."

Her eyes bored into Quenti's, and she saw the slight tremble in her lip.

"Who in El'dyo's name is Khuna, really, and how does she know we're out here?"

"They sent a message to her. When I was in the Haven. We just need to—"

"Who is she?" She was shouting now, her entire body buzzing with anger. The normal din of bird calls and monkeys moving through the trees disappeared, and even the buzz of insects hushed.

"Don't move." The voice coming from the edge of the woods was cold and hard.

She swiveled, her hand reaching for a nonexistent spear on her back.

There were ten bruyas, women and men, spread in a crescent around them, cornering them against the riverbanks. They wore green and brown clothing and had mud painted along their faces, their muscular arms gleaming in the afternoon sun, spears, clubs, and bows raised in an obvious threat. She realized with a shudder that these weren't just random bruyas—they were battle-ready soldiers.

After everything she had survived, was this is how things were going to end? At the point of a bruya's spear—without even a weapon in hand to defend herself?

Quenti was still pale beside her.

Alara's hands shook as she raised them in surrender. "Please, we're just—"

"I said, don't move." The female bruya that spoke spit the

words out in disgust. She stepped forward, spear still leveled at the two of them. "You move, I strike."

Alara's eyes flashed over to Quenti, who looked just as frightened. Her honey-brown eyes darted around the clearing and the bruyas that surrounded them. Was she calculating their odds of survival or looking for a way to escape?

But in an instant, Quenti dropped her hands and flung herself toward one of the female bruyas to their right, ignoring the sharp glint of metal pointed at her chest.

"Khuna!"

CHAPTER 21

QUENTI

The second her eyes had locked on Khuna's, all logic flew away. She was no longer aware of the sharpened spears that followed her every move as she leaped forward. It had been months since Khuna had last snuck into Hurazon to meet her, and seeing her suddenly lifted a weight off her chest.

Khuna smelled of rain and wood smoke. Quenti breathed her in as she felt arms wrap around her waist and the touch of rough, chapped lips against her own. They stood like that for a moment, neither moving. It was Khuna that broke the kiss and eased her away.

"You're late." Khuna cupped her face and looked at her questioningly.

"I know."

"Also, you're not where you were supposed to be. Our spies told us you were in the Haven. Did your father…" Khuna didn't need to finish the question.

She shook her head. "It's complicated."

"Clearly." Khuna's voice turned icy and Quenti followed her gaze to Alara, still standing in shock by the river. Khuna looked back at her, brows creased and eyes sharp.

"It's a long story, but she's with me. *Not like that.*" Quenti amended when Khuna's eyes narrowed.

"Alara meet Khuna. Khuna, Alara."

Alara's mouth set in a grim line. In an instant, any questions Alara had regarding Khuna were likely answered. Quenti grimaced. This was not what she had wanted.

"Khuna." A young male bruya stood, bow taut a few feet from them. "Would you care to explain why there are two of them? No one mentioned a *second* magite." His dark eyes didn't leave Alara as he spoke.

"I might have accidentally kidnapped her," Quenti said, directing her words to Khuna, whose brown eyes widened. "I got caught by the councilguards on my way out of Sombria, and she helped me escape. Once she was with me, I couldn't just leave her in the middle of the forest."

"Khuna, your girl is stupid," the male bruya said.

"Runeo," Khuna warned.

"Look." Alara stepped forward. The weapon-wielding bruyas shifted, and she stopped. "I don't want to be here. You don't want me here. I just need some supplies and I'll be on my way."

"The spy wants to leave so she can bring back her council-guard friends." The female bruya who had originally yelled moved forward, spear pointed at Alara's throat, now only half a foot away.

Alara was looking scared, and Quenti felt the guilt heavy in her gut. This wasn't how she planned it, but a part of her always knew this would happen. She just hadn't cared—or she had cared more about seeing Khuna again.

Quenti turned back to Khuna, placing a hand on her arm.

"Please, this is all my fault, not hers. She didn't want to come. There has to be something—"

Runeo—the male bruya with the dark eyes and thick brows— overheard her words and let out a soft growl. "Enough of this. Zinita is right. If we let her go, her friends will be here within a week." The grip on his bow tightened, sending a wave of nausea through her.

Khuna stepped forward, nudging Quenti to the side. She laid a gentle hand on Runeo's arm, though the look she gave him was anything but. "You're right. We will bring her to the elders to decide what the next steps are."

His dark eyes narrowed at Khuna's words, but he lowered his bow. "Agreed. Micos, tie her up."

He directed the words at a younger male bruya around Quenti's age, if not younger, standing in the back of the pack, staff in hand. He didn't move.

"Micos. Now," Runeo said.

The boy blinked, as though registering for the first time that everyone was looking at him. He jumped forward, hands shaking as he unwound a length of rope at his waist.

Alara clenched her teeth and let out a small growl as the boy bound her wrists. For her part, she didn't struggle, which Quenti was glad for. Her stomach was already twisted with anxiety enough as it was.

For a moment, she let herself appreciate the fact that she'd found them. Her new people. She leaned into Khuna and felt the other girl's warmth seeping through her skin. As Alara was marched past her, spear tip dug into her back, she heard the sneer whispered only for her ears.

"Bruya lover."

Quenti wasn't sure Khuna had heard. But it didn't feel like it mattered when Khuna wrapped around her in a short but reassuring embrace. "Come, the walk home is long."

Quenti felt a pang at the words.

Home.

Even with the warning from Khuna, Quenti was surprised to find them still walking hours later. They followed the river for another thirty minutes before reaching the rocky outcrop Quenti had been looking for this entire time. It had unfolded from the thick forest, gray stone set against blue sky. When they reached its base, they turned and followed a new path, uphill and away from the water.

Occasionally, she could see a faint trail—what they must have been following—but other times it seemed as if they were fighting their way through the low branches of the cloud forest with no direction.

Her breath came in quick gasps she tried to stifle. Her feet ached in the thin magite boots she was wearing, but she bit back any complaints. The bruyas seemed at ease as they moved through the trees, their sandaled feet gracefully balancing on slick roots, skipping over the same muddy puddles she stepped in every time without fail.

And then they broke from the forest, the trees ending without ceremony. Before them and below lay a verdant valley, hidden on either side by tree-covered peaks. Everything was green and still save for a condor that circled above, likely stalking some soon-to-be-dead prey farther down the hill. Quenti hadn't realized that she had stopped to stare until she felt Khuna nudge her to the left.

"Come on, it's still a bit longer. If you like this view, just wait 'til you see Arbol."

She nodded and followed as they paved their way along the steep hillside, higher still into the mountains.

When they had hiked higher than she felt was possible, they hit the peak and the path veered downward. Somehow, her feet hurt worse as they wound their way down and back into the forest.

She studied the others around her to distract her mind. Runeo, bushy eyebrows still furrowed in what Quenti had decided was anger, led the march. Micos and Alara walked a few feet behind. She wasn't sure if she felt glad or guilty to see Alara breathing just as raggedly as her. There were a few other bruyas who walked with eyes focused on Runeo, as though they feared losing step with him. At the back of the group walked Zinita, the female bruya who had first threatened them. She was nearly as tall as Runeo, and her eyes were dark and narrowed as she walked. Quenti shuddered at the unbridled hatred she saw there.

Without thinking, she reached for Khuna's hand, seeking reassurance. *Home.* That was Khuna had called it. What Khuna had promised months ago now while she and Quenti had laid intertwined in the woods near Hurazon. At first it had seemed just empty promises whispered into her ear like a folk song— meant to bring joy without truth. But then Khuna had repeated it in a mantra, no longer whispers, but desperate pleas.

"Come *home.*"

Khuna's hand was warm and dry against her own sweaty palm, but it didn't stop the twist of anxiety that still threatened to spill from her throat in a strangled cry.

Khuna wanted her there. She just wasn't sure anyone else did.

When they stopped, she looked around expectantly. What she saw did nothing to quell the anxiety.

There was nothing—or nothing new.

They were encircled by thick trunks of trees, wide enough to fit houses, but not hiding any she could see. She studied their surroundings, but still couldn't see anything beyond trunks and roots and shrubs. She caught Khuna's eye and saw a familiar, knowing grin.

"What—"

Runeo's high-pitched whistle cut her off. The group fell silent and still again. She swallowed down the nausea that rose in her throat. She tried to hide the fear in her eyes and waited patiently with the rest. Based on the reassuring tightening of Khuna's hand, she wasn't sure she was succeeding.

A couple of minutes later, a wooden platform more than a dozen feet wide and long emerged from the thick branches above them. She let out a small gasp as the lift landed with a soft thud in front of them, and Khuna led her onto the planks. About half of the group followed, including Runeo and Micos with Alara. With another whistle from Runeo, the surrounding ropes pulled taut, and the lift ascended. Quenti cursed as she glanced at the disappearing ground beneath them. She gripped Khuna's arm tight. As she made eye contact with Runeo, she couldn't help but catch the small glint of laughter in his eyes at her paling face.

She closed her eyes and leaned into Khuna. It felt like they had been ascending forever when she heard Alara's small gasp a foot away. Her eyes opened, almost reluctantly, but then went wide.

They had passed a thick layer of tree branches, and the ground was no longer visible below them. But just above was an entire village laid out between the trunks and branches of the colossal mahoganies. Rope and plank bridges stretched between massive platforms, buildings wrapped around trunks, and stairs spiraling above and below. The sunlight broke through the upper branches, still many yards above them, and in the dappled light, Quenti saw the hundreds of bruyas milling about the treetop village.

This was Arbol. This was home.

CHAPTER 22

ALARA

It took a few seconds for Alara to realize the lift had stopped. Her knuckles gripped white against the railing and her arms ached with tension. She could see amusement playing on Micos's face as he gently guided her off the lift. The young bruya gave her a smile. It seemed genuine, but it made her chest tighten.

"You get used to it," he said. "The first time I took it down as a bruyita, I almost peed myself."

She didn't know what to say—or if she even wanted to respond. Before she could decide, Runeo was next to them, roughly grabbing her arm.

"Hurry up, *mage*."

The tone should have annoyed her, but she was too captivated by the surrounding sights to notice. They made their way through the treetops, walking along wood planks tightly pieced together and somehow balanced on the tree branches. Under normal circumstances, she would have been terrified, but given how tightly the planks were packed together, it offered no opportunity to see the dizzying fall below. Besides that, there was plenty to see above the planks to keep her eyes occupied.

The city was a maze of bridges and stairways, stretching as far as she could see. While it made for quite a sight, she hadn't the faintest idea how the bruyas didn't get lost. Each tree looked the same, but everyone around her seemed to know where they were going. She wondered if this was how Quenti had felt when she was first brought into the Haven.

Hundreds of bruyas milled about the city, some walking fast with a purpose and others taking their time, chatting in groups. Laughter rang out across the treetops. Two young children darting between legs and across a rope bridge caught her attention, seemingly unaware of the fall that awaited them if they stepped the wrong way or lost their balance.

The bruyas gave her group a wide berth as they passed, but a few more curious souls followed behind their train, necks craning to see where she was headed, her arms still restrained. She lifted her chin and kept her gaze fixed above their heads. Her stomach roiled with an emotion somewhere between hate and fear as she tried not to make eye contact with anyone in the village.

They walked, weaving their way from platform to platform, crossing the village—or perhaps Runeo had only taken them in a few circles. She truly couldn't tell. But they finally made it to the front of a large wooden hut. It was larger than any of the other buildings she had seen. Balanced between five separate trees, the round structure sat along a large platform stretched between the trunks. Smoke ribboned from its top, where the thatched ceiling gaped at the center. Intricately woven curtains hung in the doorway and a small boy leaned against the frame, looking bored. Until he saw them.

"Runeo!" The boy straightened immediately. "I'll let them know you're here."

Runeo simply nodded as the kid darted into the building. Less than a minute later the curtains parted, and she was ushered into the room, Runeo's grip still tight on her arm.

Inside, the air was hot and thick. A fire crackled in the center of the room, though the light was dim, with only a few slivers of sunlight stretching across the floor, the torches and fire at the center fighting against the inherent darkness. It took just a few seconds for her to realize just how much fire was contained within the wooden—purely wooden—building. Her heart lurched, and she stumbled a bit before catching herself. Runeo had let go of her arm and pushed her forward. She took a few steps, edging away from the minor inferno that crackled in the center.

When she looked up, she saw three pairs of eyes trained on her. One of them—an older man with nearly white hair and a deeply creased face—moved his hand to rest on the hilt of the dagger that was tucked in his belt.

"Runeo, what is in the world is going on?" The woman's voice was warm and her eyes wide and dark. She sat beside the older man, holding an air of power about her. She was obviously older than herself, but her skin was still smooth. How much older could she really be? The woman's hair was dark black and tightly coiled, falling in thick spirals around her face. Beside her, on her left, was a third man, likely closer to Emaru's age, based on the graying of his hair and the soft lines of his face.

"Why is Quenti tied up?" the woman asked.

Runeo gave a small bow of his head and acknowledged her. "Quil'la." He then jerked his head toward Quenti. "That's Quenti. This one is a magite from the Haven who tagged along with her."

Quil'la stood up and Alara felt her body go rigid, bracing for a blow or a fight. But the woman's eyes slipped away from her without a second glance. She walked past Runeo and Alara before stopping in front of Quenti. Gently, the woman took the girl's face in her hands, the copper rings along her fingers glinting in the firelight.

"Of course, it's you." She gazed into Quenti's eyes, smiling. A thin finger swiped gently across the girl's face, brushing back a loose strand of hair. "You look just like your mama, don't you?"

Quil'la turned back to face Alara, and she was once again aware of how many eyes watched her.

Quil'la stepped toward her, head tilted and eyes narrow. It was almost as if she was trying to place her—as if she might recognize her—and her heart jumped at the thought of what it would mean if a bruya did, in fact, recognize her. But the woman only gave her a level look.

"You are?"

"Alara." Her voice almost cracked, and she felt her cheeks redden. Clearing her throat, she tilted her chin up and repeated her name again, clearer.

"Alara… Do you have a family name?"

"Leon," she finally said, giving Adelmo's family name. She was certain they couldn't tie her back to the Council with his name.

Quil'la didn't respond for a moment, her black eyes studying Alara's face. But finally she nodded. "And how did you end up here with Quenti, Alara Leon?"

"I—" She shot a look at Quenti. The anger that had finally started to thaw was returning. What right did any of them have to be angry? She didn't exactly come here willingly.

Quenti cut in, perhaps seeing the thoughts racing across her face. "I sort of—I mean, I accidentally…" Quenti paused again, as all eyes in the room swiveled on her. "The councilguards were threatening me and I didn't really think, and I grabbed her. And well, once we were out in the wilderness, I couldn't very well leave her alone. She's kind of useless by herself."

She opened her mouth to protest this last comment, but one of the older men that had been sitting beside Quil'la stood up sharply. He was taller than Quil'la by almost a foot and towered over the others.

"And how had those councilguards found you in the first place?" he said.

Quenti glanced at Alara. "I don't know how they found me."

Alara started at this, realizing that Quenti most definitely knew how the councilguards had found her. She was protecting her, even to her own detriment. If she didn't know how they had found her, then who's to say they couldn't have followed her again?

The bruyas spoke all at once, a ripple of anxiety permeating the room. Alara felt like she could sink into the background, forgotten. She stepped back, and then a hand fell on her shoulder. It wasn't rough, but she bristled all the same. Where in El'dyo's name did they think would she go all tied up like this?

"Look," Alara cut in. Her voice was sharp and more confident than she felt. "I just want to get back to the Haven. I don't care that Quenti escap—left the Haven. And I'm glad she's safe. If I can just get some supplies and a point in the right direction, I'll be on my way."

The room fell silent and she was once again the center of attention. Quil'la's eyes were almost sad as they turned to her, but she could feel the anger and hate thrumming in the surrounding air from the others in the room.

"We've kept our city safe for a good many decades by keeping our secrets hidden."

"I promise, I won't say anything. I don't even know where we are or how to find you again. I just want to go home." She winced internally at the desperation that was clear in her voice. Emaru would have shamed her for groveling to these bruyas.

The eldest man, who had been sitting beside Quil'la, his hand still resting on his blade, stood up. His face creased with a sneer, his hand tightening on the hilt of his blade as he stepped toward Alara.

"We can't trust this magite. There is nothing to stop her from coming back here in a month's time with a legion of councilguards."

Alara tried not to show the fear in her face as the venom in his voice cut into her. Her heart beat firm and fast in her chest, and she could taste the copper of fear on her tongue, but she kept her face level and sent a silent prayer to El'dyo.

"I swear, I just want to get home. I promise I won't tell the Council anything…" her voice faded by the end of the sentence. She knew the words were a lie as they left her lips—everyone in the room knew it too, and she saw her chance of making it out of this alive fading with her words.

"Can we cleanse her memories?" The voice was soft and she turned to see Khuna standing next to a pale Quenti, a gentle hand on her arm. "Send her home… *without* being able to find us again." She lowered her voice. "If we keep her here against her will or kill her, we're no better than them."

The room exploded once again, everyone talking all at once.

She was looking at Quil'la, who she suspected was the leader of these bruyas. The woman looked tired at Khuna's proposition. After a few minutes, she raised her hand silently and the chorus of voices dropped away.

"Mena is the only one with abilities strong enough for a cleanse like that, and she's at least a month away from returning from her mission. We'd have to send out word to the other outcrops to see if anyone has a mind-walker to spare. But that will likely take just as long as waiting for her and Beno to return.

"That being said, it is the most ideal solution to our problem." Quil'la turned to her, looking at her with those intense black eyes. "So long as this Alara Leon stays here with us until such a time that the twins return. And if you are here with us, I suppose it wouldn't hurt to make you comfortable." Without breaking eye contact with her, the older woman motioned to the young, lanky guard still standing behind Alara. "Micos, can you go tell Lili she's going to have two new guests? And Runeo, will you be so kind as to check for any weapons before untying our guest?"

His jaw tightened, and he gave a grunt as he moved toward Alara. "Yes, Senye."

She tried not to show her relief as the rope around her wrists loosened and fell away while Runeo haphazardly searched her bag before handing it back to her. She stroked her fingers across the raw skin of her wrists and forced herself to stand up straighter as Quil'la's gaze fell back to her.

"To be clear," Quil'la said, "you may not be a prisoner, but you're not a free guest either. Do not try our patience and we will get along just fine. When our mind-walker returns, you will be on your way, and we can all go back to our *separate* lives."

She felt like she was in a daze as the bruyas moved around her. She could make out parts of the conversation Quil'la was having with Runeo and Khuna, their eyes darting back to her every few words.

Then Quenti was there beside her, a soft, warm hand on her shoulder. "I'm sorry. I didn't want to cause so much trouble."

She wanted to be angry, wanted to brush Quenti's hand off of her and scream at her for dragging her into this. But she was tired, and Quenti was the only familiar face in the sea of dark-eyed bruyas. So she only nodded and let Quenti's hand continue to rest on her shoulder.

A few moments later, Quil'la was standing in front of them both again. "Khuna will escort you to Lili's house, where you'll be staying. She can help settle you in, and Khuna will be around tomorrow to give you a tour of the city. Go rest—you've both had a long few days."

She let herself be steered toward the door, Quenti following behind Khuna. As they exited, the wool curtain pulled back by an outside guard, Alara heard her name behind her and saw Quil'la still standing in the center of the room, staring at them as they left.

"Alara Leon, if Quenti vouches for you, then I will trust that. But know that my trust is quite fragile."

The curtain dropped, and the black-eyed woman disappeared behind it, her face grim.

CHAPTER 23

ALARA

lara was baffled to realize it was night when they left the hut. The city was now lit by torches lining the walkways, the moon still frail and dark above them in the sky. Despite the darkness, there seemed to be even more people wandering around, though the children now padded along behind their parents, instead of bounding around unsupervised.

Most of the bruyas headed in the same direction, toward a bright glow between the trunks.

"It's the communal supper," Khuna said, answering her unasked question. "Lili can cook some food back at the house, so you don't have to worry about going there tonight."

She nodded, still unable to form words, and turned back to follow behind Khuna, whose fingers intertwined with Quenti's.

Alara lost count of the bridges and stairs and turns as they trekked through the trees, but after several long minutes, they finally arrived at their destination. Lili's house wrapped around the trunk of a particularly wide and flat tree, a bridge leading across to a small porch and bright yellow curtain covering the open doorway. The windows glowed from inside, and before they even crossed the bridge, a young woman darted out the door.

"Hello! Hi! Come in!" Her voice was clear and smooth and her eyes bright. They weren't quite brown—almost a mossy green—and her face was sprinkled with freckles, her skin still tanned beneath them. Perhaps the most noteworthy part of her appearance were the thick green vines that twisted around her arm, up her neck, and into her hairline. As they walked into the brightly lit house, Alara saw the vines were made of dark ink drawn directly onto the woman's skin. *A tattoo.* Something she had heard of, but never seen. They were considered taboo under Council rule.

"Sol, you both look exhausted. Come sit and get some food in you!" Alara let herself be led to a table against the wall and fell into the wooden chair pulled out for her. A steaming mug of coca tea was set in front of her, along with a plate of potatoes, corn, and some unknown meat. Lili continued to fuss around them and Khuna stood awkwardly by the doorway, watching them.

Alara ate instinctively without tasting the food, looking around as she did. The quaint home was split into a few rooms, with half of the circular building being taken up by the space they sat in. A tree trunk acted as one wall, its bark painted with vines and flowers.

Despite its small size, the room somehow wasn't cluttered with furniture. There was the table Quenti and Alara sat at. Nearby was a small cooking area set up, along with a small hearth, where a fire danced merrily under a pot of water. Across the room was a rug and a scattering of cushions, and beside that, a mess of small bowls and brushes she realized were painting supplies.

In the other chair, Quenti let out a sigh of contentment. "This is delicious. Thank you!"

"It's my pleasure! I actually love cooking, but don't often have anyone to cook for. It's a pleasant change of pace."

"You can always cook for me, Lili," Khuna said, smirking.

Lili only rolled her eyes at this. "Hold your hands out."

It took a beat for Alara to realize Lili was looking at her as she spoke. Her heart skipped a beat, and she wondered if they planned to tie her up again. But as she laid her hands on the table, Lili gently placed a warm, wet leaf on both of Alara's red and raw wrists.

Her skin gave a twinge, but as Lili laid her hands over the leaves, the burning sensation disappeared.

"You're an earth mage—bruya…"

"Hmm, we're called *tierren* here." Lili placed two fingers on Alara's temple and in an instant, the deep ache in her bones seemed to drain away.

"Oh." her eyes went wide at this. That was not normal for an earth mage.

Lili laughed and gave her a wink. "Handy, huh? I have just enough mind-walking ability to do that. Always helps with healing."

Lili took the leaves off her wrists and went back to making tea.

She marveled at her now unmarked wrists.

The room was warm and smelled of wood. Everything felt completely unfamiliar to her, and her thoughts were clouded with exhaustion and a steady fear of the unknown. She didn't know where she was. She didn't know what was going to happen tomorrow. She didn't know much of anything.

Yet something else beyond fear pulled at her. After so many days in the forest, she wanted to give in and sink into the comfort of being warm and dry. But as Lili chattered away, smiling and plying Quenti with more food, Alara had to reminder herself that Lili was just another bruya among the thousands that she was now surrounded by. The enemy.

"Khuna, go on with you. You can come back tomorrow morning to see Quenti, but both of these ladies need to get some sleep," Lili said, gently directing Khuna out the door.

For her part, Quenti slumped in her chair, eyelids drooping. Alara doubted she looked much better, her stomach full for the first time in days.

A few minutes later, Lili shuffled the pair into the other room. Alara let herself be wrapped in a blanket and led to a mat on the floor. The last thought she had was how strange it felt, sleeping on something soft again.

That night, she dreamed of her mother and father and their screams as they died. And in her dream, she saw Runeo standing over their bodies, spear at his side. She then felt the spear in her own hand, its tip bloody.

She woke sweating in the dark. Dawn hadn't come yet, and the room was black and warm, but she couldn't fall back asleep. She stared at the dark ceiling and wondered how far down the ground was and if a single person could operate the lift.

The next morning, Lili had made breakfast—a collection of fruits and bread that made her stomach growl and mouth water. A small sigh of contentment broke between her lips as she swallowed a piece of the freshly baked loaf. She again had to remind herself where she was. Good food and soft bed aside, these people were still not friends, and she wasn't safe.

Quenti sat across from her, and Lili leaned against the wall with a mug of dark cafi in her hands. The pungent smell of the bitter drink drifted through the room.

"You both look like starved animals still."

Quenti smiled at Lili's comment. "You can only survive so long on fish and berries." She then grimaced. "I can't even think about fish anymore."

As the two of them continued to chat, Alara sat silently, mind elsewhere. She thought about Emaru and Ardo, wondering if they were looking for her. Where were they searching? They could be below them now and never even know it. She didn't quite expect the tightness in her throat that came with the very notion.

"I'm sorry, Alara." Quenti's voice invaded her thoughts. "This isn't what I wanted when you ran into me. I told you to leave me alone."

Alara tightened her lips into a thin grimace. "I thought you were in danger."

Perhaps I still do.

"You are both quite safe here," Lili said, responding to Alara's unspoken comment. Her voice held a warmth that made Alara almost want to believe her.

"I'm a prisoner. Let's call it how it is."

"We don't want this any more than you do," a voice broke in from the doorway. Everyone turned to see Khuna leaning against the frame. "This is the only way to keep our people safe. Safe from the prying eyes of the Council."

"What are you afraid of?" Alara said, biting back a bitter laugh. "If you stopped raiding the villages and came to the Haven, all of this would stop. The Council just wants to keep the peace. They want everyone to know how to control their abilities."

"Control that will be used for the Council's gain." Khuna shook her head. "We are perfectly content without their interference." She walked over to where they sat and picked a piece of red fruit off of Quenti's plate. "And control doesn't have to mean fear." She waved her hands and a small gray cloud swirled and formed in the air, letting off a sprinkle of rain that danced before falling to the ground.

"Can you not get it wet in here, please?" Lili said, smacking Khuna's shoulder.

Alara stood up now, facing Khuna straight on. "Control doesn't mean fear. Control means people not using their magia to gain power. The last time there was none, the bruyas waged war against the blameless and nearly eradicated them."

"So you're really one of them," Khuna said, with a hint of disappointment. "Come on Quenti, let me show you around."

Quenti gave them a small wave before she and Khuna went through the curtained doorway. Alara slumped back into her chair.

Lili sat where Quenti had just been and patted Alara's hand where it lay on the table. "You'll have to excuse us. We're all a little serious up here. Generations ago—before we moved into the trees—we used to be more trusting, more open to runaways and outcasts. We would take in anyone needing a place, including magites who failed out of the Haven or mages that got sick of the Council." Lili paused, staring into the dredges of her empty mug, her lips pressed into a thin frown. "Then someone betrayed our people. We don't even know who it was, but the councilguards found and surrounded us in the night. It was a slaughter."

With a thud, Lili placed her mug back onto the table and stood up, shaking the sadness from her shoulders like a coat. "Anyway, pretty much everyone has a great-grandparent or great-relative who died in the massacre, so it's not something anyone forgets. That was when we built this place."

She was cleaning away breakfast now, her smile wide and bright again. "My grandmother actually helped build some of the expanded parts of the city. She was a tierren, too. Much more powerful than I am, mind you."

"Is that what the tattoos signify? Being a tierren?"

Lili paused from her cleaning and leaned against the small counter. She looked down at her arm with the green ink that crawled up it. "In part, yes."

"Do all tierren in Arbol have them?"

Lili laughed this time. "Oh, Sol, no. My grandmother wasn't happy about it."

Alara was silent as she waited for Lili to continue.

"I got the tattoos after my mother passed," Lili said, turning back to clean the counter. "Each leaf represents a year she was with me. I wanted something to remember her by."

As Lili spoke, Alara's hand grazed the burned skin of her cheek without thinking. Lili had turned to face her, eyes bright as she watched the movement.

"We don't always get to choose our scars. I at least wanted to choose this one," Lili said with a soft smile. "And I'm a bit of an artist, so I might as well use my skin as a canvas."

Before she could stop herself, Alara's lips parted into a smile as her eyes flicked back to the mural, which swirled with bright colors. It answered her question as to who had painted the wall.

Suddenly, Lili's bright hazel eyes were wide in front of her face. "You look positively pale. I know you've had a long journey, but maybe we should go for a walk. I can show you around a little. Give you the tour."

"I—I don't know if I'm allowed outside."

"Oh, Sol. Runeo and those other grumps will get over it. Come on! You can borrow some clothes and a pair of sandals. Those won't be warm enough up here anyway," she said, motioning at Alara's tunic and pants.

Before she could answer, Lili swept her into the back room and starting pulling out skirts.

An hour later, Alara and Lili were making their way through Arbol. It had taken some convincing on Lili's part to leave the guard behind that had been stationed at her door. It's not like she had any way of running. What was it they thought she was going to do? She couldn't even see the ground beneath them, and she most definitely couldn't fly.

Her palms sweat as she tried not to lose her balance on the thin bridge that stretched between two platforms. The soft leather sandals she had borrowed from Lili were a bit too big, but the soles were flexible, making it easy to grip the flooring with her toes. She wore a skirt and tunic of Lili's as well, the former of which was a frenzy of colors—yellows, pinks, teals, and purples —woven into flowers and intricate designs. The tunic was a simple green, but the collar was embroidered with a delicate pattern that matched the lower half of the ensemble. Alara was a little baffled at the skirt, but Lili showed her how to wrap it so the slit sat in the front. The materials were thicker than what she was used to, but they were soft and easy to move in.

As she followed Lili around town, she was glad for the thickness of the wool. An icy breeze occasionally broke through the branches and danced across the exposed skin of her neck, sending shivers up her back. She felt less exposed now as she walked with Lili, her own outfit blending in with the rest of the villagers. Bruyas wandered back and forth, their brightly woven fabrics dancing among the green and brown background of the forest. The men's outfits looked much the same as the women's, save for the wide cut pants they wore under their tunics, instead of the skirts. She quickly realized the subdued green and brown outfits the bruya guards had been wearing yesterday were not their usual garb.

As they walked, they pressed through throngs of people. She was amazed how many were living in Arbol—and this wasn't even their only city. It sent a spike of fear through her, wondering just how many others there were hiding in the outlands. She had always imagined that small, fragmented groups scattered around Sombria were all that remained, but Arbol alone made it clear that thriving civilizations could go unnoticed within their borders. What would happen if they grew sick of their small raids and rebellions and attacked the Haven in force?

She tried to focus, counting bruyas as they walked, hoping she could return to Emaru with something that could help the Council. But it all felt pointless. Unless she escaped, there would be no way for her to return with any memories. Once the mind-walker did her work, all this would be a distant flicker in the back of her head.

As she snapped back to reality, she realized they were walking through what had to be a marketplace. A wide platform of branches and wood stretched out between the large trees, and small tables and stands were set up along the edges of the walk-ways. Some stands had piles of colorful woven clothes stacked around them and others roasted sweet-smelling meats. Her stomach growled despite the breakfast she had eaten earlier, and she turned to ask Lili if they could stop for some meat.

With a small lurch, she realized Lili was no longer beside her. She stopped in the flow of the crowd and turned, trying to look over the sea of heads. Even here, her stature seemed shorter than most, and she struggled to see more than shoulders and dark hair around her.

"Lili!" she called out, still struggling to stand still as the crowd pressed in around her. She could feel the buzz of magia in the back of her brain as bruyas circled around her, their presence assaulting her awareness. She saw their eyes narrowing as they passed by her, face pale and eyes wide. One bruya shoved their elbow hard into her side as they passed by her.

Frustrated, she felt a wave of heat rising in her, and her magia reached for Lili without conscious control. Her awareness spread and hit the wall of bruyas that circled her. She desperately tried to take a deep breath, but her chest was tight, heat building from within. She was panicking. The realization only sent another wave of hot fear through her.

Without thinking, she pushed her way through the horde of bruyas, no longer looking where she was going, but simply trying to get *out*. And then there was a hand on her shoulder, and a wave of relief. *Lili.*

But when she whipped around, eyes wild, it was Runeo whose large hand was pressing down on her shoulder. His eyes narrowed—dark—as he sneered down at her. "Where do you think you're going, *magite*? Why are you out here alone?" He practically growled at her, his hand pressing ever harder on her shoulder.

"I…" She tried to answer, but the heat of her magia was still building and she could feel sweat beading on her forehead, her skin damp and hot. She tried to step away, eyes still flickering around for an exit.

"Don't you dare." Runeo saw she was about to dart and grabbed her arm. He had to feel the heat rising beneath her skin. His eyes went wide, and he looked down at where his hand touched her skin. "You going to burn me, then?"

"I don't want to. Just let me go." She grit her teeth, desperately grasping for control.

"So you can run back to the Council? I don't think so."

"I'm not going to run." She spoke the words, though they rang false in her head. She knew she couldn't promise that.

"Trust me. I'm going to make sure you don't go anywhere." His voice was low, and for just an instant, she wanted to loose the spark of fire flickering under her skin. Perhaps it would serve him right. Her mind buzzed with static, the anger taking over, and she found herself reaching toward her center, to the flame that was dancing there.

"Alara, thank Sol!" Lili's voice broke through the buzzing in her head, and she looked to see Lili pushing through the crowds. "Let off, Runeo. She's with me."

He dropped her arms, and a wave of cool pressed through her.

"Come on, we should get back." Lili looked between the two of them, clearly understanding something had happened.

As they turned to go, Runeo grabbed at her, once again, fingers hard on her wrist. "Quil'la may not see you as a prisoner, but know that we're watching you. I won't let the likes of you hurt us again."

She tried to lift her chin, meeting his eyes. "I don't plan on hurting anyone, I can promise you that. Now let me go."

Her heart thumped hard in her chest as he loosened his grip. She scurried back over to Lili, feeling like a lost child scrambling for her mother. As she made her way over to the bruya, her body cooled, and she shivered at the loss of heat.

Had she just made a promise she couldn't keep?

Chapter 24

Quenti

"You should get some fresh air."

Quenti stood in the doorway of Lili's bedroom as Alara lay sprawled out on her bedroll, staring at the ceiling.

"There's plenty of fresh air in here," Alara said, not making eye contact with her.

She chewed on the inside of her cheek. Alara hadn't left Lili's house for days since the marketplace "incident." Lili didn't really know what had happened between Runeo and Alara—neither one of them was open to discussing it—but it had been clear the magite hadn't taken it well.

"Well, let me know if you change your mind. Khuna and I are going to the market and then to her house."

Alara didn't respond or even acknowledge the comment, but after letting out one last sigh, Quenti backed out of the room. A part of her was angry at Alara. Angry that she was making her feel responsible for her own misery. Then again, the other part of her rationalized, she technically *was* the reason Alara was here. She almost couldn't blame her for being upset.

But she shook off this thought quickly. Kidnapping Alara was never her intention. She had just wanted to leave the Haven. It had been *Alara's* choice to follow when she had stumbled upon her.

Khuna was standing in the front entryway when Quenti withdrew from Alara's room. Her eyes were questioning, and Quenti shook her head. "Not today."

Khuna shrugged, apparently unperturbed by Alara's choices. Perhaps she was just happy to have time alone with Quenti—a feeling she could empathize with.

"Where's Lili?" Quenti asked, looking around the small room, as if Lili was hiding under a cushion.

"Gone to visit her grandmother. Apparently she has not told her yet that she has two magites staying over."

"One magite," Quenti rebutted. She would not be lumped in with anyone from the Haven.

Khuna ignored her. "I tried to get us invited. I would have loved to see Wela Runtu's face during that conversation."

"Do people here really see me as a magite?" Quenti asked, her eyes finding Khuna's.

"It won't last forever," she said, squeezing Quenti's hands between her own. "We're all refugees in the end, or descendants of them."

She nodded, but Khuna's words did little to untwist the knot in her gut. Sparks of anxiety still crept up her spine and jumbled her thoughts. It had been nearly a week, and she still felt like an outsider walking through the trees.

It'll take an adjustment, she reminded herself each night, though that didn't stop the anxiety from flooding her entire body.

They meandered over to the sprawling market, enjoying a

few moments of quiet together. Neither of them talked at first, their hands intertwined, shoulders bumping as they walked. The air was cool, but the sun breaking through the trees was hot on Quenti's skin.

The market bustled with activity. Quenti couldn't keep the grin from her face as they wound through the crowds, stopping at every stall that caught her eye. So many of them were draped in beautifully woven fabrics, the colors of which she had only ever seen in nature. The work was leagues better than anything she could have gotten in Hurazon—or even what little she saw in the Haven. Other tables displayed intricate wooden statues that, upon closer inspection, Quenti realized were grown into the shapes, rather than carved.

One booth in particular that caught Quenti's eye sparkled with gold and silver pendants. A golden sun necklace stood out among the rest.

Wordlessly, Khuna plucked the pendant from the table, exchanged some copper with the store owner, and hooked the heavy chain around Quenti's neck with a wide smile.

"I've been wanting to buy my girlfriend jewelry for a ridiculously long time."

Quenti ran her fingers along the shining metal, for some reason, fighting a smile that tugged at her lips. This would normally be the point where she'd make some snide remark. But, for now, all she could do was hang on to this feeling. This… contentment.

"Where to next?" Khuna said, shaking Quenti from her daze.

"I am famished," she said, eyes still not leaving the pendant.

"My parents promised us tea, but we can head over there early. Papa'd be more than happy to make us something."

"I don't want to impose," she said, hesitant.

A warm finger lifted her chin and she met Khuna's eyes

staring up at her, their height difference more apparent at such a close distance. "My parents loved you before they met you. You would never be an imposition."

Something heavy and tight burned in Quenti's chest, and she leaned down to plant a quick kiss of Khuna's lips. As she turned to move away, Khuna grabbed the pendant around her neck and pulled her down once more, deepening the kiss in a way that made her blush at the public display.

After a minute, Quenti brought her hand to Khuna's chest and gently pushed her back. "I love you, but I am not getting any less hungry."

Her girlfriend's eyes darkened, sweeping across her body. "Is that an offer?" she said huskily.

"Not like that!"

Khuna only grinned before taking Quenti's hand a leading her out of the market.

"The farms are a few miles from here," Khuna said, waving an ear of seasoned corn around. "Far enough away that if anyone ever managed to stumble on them, it would still take time to find us."

"And who picks the farmers?" she asked as she grabbed a handful of assorted roasted nuts, which were unglamorously shoved into her tunic pockets. The two had been talking nonstop since leaving Khuna's parents behind. They'd eaten approximately five people's worth of food while there, and Khuna's father was only too happy to shove more food in their hands as they left.

They now explored Arbol, with Quenti trying to get a full grasp of how the tree-dwelling civilization remained a secret.

Khuna shrugged. "I mean… no one picks them. Why did your father end up as a fisherman?"

Quenti bit her lip. It had been a good while since she'd even thought of her father. Their relationship wasn't a memory she was eager to revisit any time soon.

"Khuna!" A voice came out of nowhere, shaking her free from her thoughts.

A little boy no older than five leaped into Khuna's arms. "Urco stole my ball and told me I wasn't allowed to play it anymore."

"Well, that just won't do, now will it?" Khuna said, hitching the small boy onto her hip.

The boy's eyes were a bright green, and they swiveled suddenly to meet Quenti's before going wide.

"Capac, meet Quenti. Quenti, this is Capac, my monkey of a cousin."

Capac said nothing, eyes still fixed on her. She tried to give him a smile, but it only made him squirm.

"Put me down! We need to go attack Urco," the boy said matter-of-factly.

"I left my spear at home, but let's see what we can do," Khuna said, obliging to put Capac down. "Lead the way."

Capac solemnly led them to a larger platform a few bridges away. It was empty except for four children no older than Capac. Between them floated a ball of stretched leather.

She could only assume Urco was the long-haired boy who was grinning with a joyful maliciousness that only young children can muster. His hand was outstretched as he used his air abilities to raise the ball just out of reach of the other three children.

Khuna stopped on the edge of the platform, frowning.

"Give me my ball back or Khuna will defeat you," Capac proclaimed.

Urco glanced up briefly, seeing Khuna and Quenti on the edge of the platform. "You've brought the mage spy! Traitor!"

Capac paled slightly, looking back at Quenti in suspicion again.

Khuna leaned down and whispered something in the boy's ear, and then motioned for her to come closer. She stepped forward, joining the impromptu huddle.

"Can you distract Urco with some clouds?" Khuna asked Quenti with a conspiratorial smile.

"I..." She looked at Khuna quizzically. Khuna shook her head sadly and waved her hand, pulling together a small drop of water from the air.

"Alas, I am too tired to fight. Save us, Quenti, our only hope."

Quenti smirked devilishly. "I think I can come up with something."

Khuna looked back at Capac. "You know what to do?"

The boy nodded.

"Then on my signal."

Khuna stood back up. "Urco, you have challenged our loyalties. Do you retract it?"

The small boy only stuck out his tongue and made the ball float higher.

"So be it," Khuna said.

With a look from Khuna, Quenti snapped her fingers and sent the water around them rushing into a cloud above Urco's head. She waved her fingers slightly, tempted to let it rain on the young boy, but she simply let it swirl around him.

The little boy let out a squeal of irritation and the ball flew higher still. Quenti had to laugh a little at the uncoordinated movement. It was clear he was trying to blow the cloud away while keeping the ball in the air, but he was too young and unpracticed. The ball wavered but didn't fall.

Before she could comment on the plan not working, she saw Capac moving his fingers. She looked up at the ball and saw with a sudden huff of surprise that vines were growing down from a branch above the platform. In a blur, they had wrapped around the ball and were moving down toward Capac's outstretched hand.

"Kid's got talent," she said. Capac's face brightened at the compliment before he dashed back to his friends, ball in hand.

"Lili's definitely had a hand in some of his skills," Khuna replied.

She watched the kids as they tossed the ball back and forth. Urco, to her surprise, had joined the group and was tossing the ball around as if the last few minutes hadn't just happened.

Ugh. Kids.

"Do they all have powers?"

Khuna's eyes were focused on the children as well. Her voice came out softly. "All but Pala, the shorter girl. She still has time, but…"

Her voice faded, the strand of thought lost.

Quenti tilted her head, looking at Khuna's profile. "But?"

Khuna turned suddenly, smile bright. "But I'm sure she'll find her magia soon. For some, it just takes a bit of time."

"Some children in Sombria don't find their powers until they are ten or eleven," Quenti offered.

Khuna wrinkled her nose. "Quil'la has a theory that the delay is born out of the oppression of magia. Most children here find their magical core by age three or four."

She looked back at the group playing, magia occasionally

sprouting between them as they manipulated the ball. "Your nurseries must be chaos."

"There is fun in chaos," a voice said behind them.

She turned to see Runeo striding up behind them, his hair loose around his broad shoulders.

"Be careful Alara doesn't hear you say that." Quenti smirked.

Runeo's eyes darkened, and she regretted the comment immediately. Khuna seemed to feel the shift as well and threw an arm around Runeo's shoulders.

She couldn't help but laugh. Khuna didn't even come up to his shoulders, after all.

"Come. I was in the middle of giving Quenti a tour of Arbol before Capac interrupted."

"I'm amazed she's still awake." Runeo turned to Quenti, his face serious. "Are you okay? Blink twice if you need help."

"Hey, all her talk about agriculture at this elevation was... enthralling."

Runeo gave a dramatic sigh and shook his head. "Oh Sol, she's perfect for you, isn't she?"

The mood was light as they walked through Arbol, with Runeo and Khuna bantering back and forth. Quenti watched them with only the slightest tinge of envy at their ease in each other's company. She had only ever had that kind of ease with Khuna, but even this felt different. They had the intimacy of people that had known each other from before they could walk.

It was the same ease she had seen between many of the Arborelis as they wandered around. There was a calm here that she had never seen, even in the villages. In Hurazon, there was always a slight tension in the air of waiting for something to go wrong. Or maybe it was just her.

"It's peaceful here." She was startled to see them looking at her and realized she had spoken out loud.

"Sometimes," Khuna said, her words careful.

"Everywhere has its conflicts." Runeo's voice was low and his jaw tight. "Not everyone has agreed with the elders' rules in how they handle the conflicts with the Council."

"Runeo had a friend—" Khuna started, but Runeo shook his head and stopped her.

"What happens to those who disagree?" she asked.

Khuna and Runeo shared a look that she couldn't quite read.

"They leave," Khuna said.

"Usually," Runeo added.

"The troublemakers leave, then," Khuna said, a tone of finality in her voice.

Quenti knew the conversation was done, despite the questions that were still spinning in her mind. The tension in the air made her skin crawl as they walked, and she tried to think of what to say to change the subject. Anything to bring back the ease that had come before—even if she hadn't been a part of it.

But before she could think of something clever or light to say, she recognized where they were. "Oh, Sol! We're back at Lili's. This place is a maze."

Khuna opened her mouth to respond, but Runeo cut her off. "Where the hell is Micos?"

Quenti looked at the empty doorway and shrugged, "Probably inside with Alara."

Runeo let out a curse under his breath as he stalked across the small bridge and into the house. "Micos!"

Khuna and Quenti followed silently.

"Micos! Sol damn him," Runeo spat. "When I find him."

"I'm sure they're fine," Khuna said plaintively.

Runeo ignored her and stormed out of the house, shouting Micos's name as he went.

"Do you think we should go after him?" she asked.

"I think we should go find Alara before he does," Khuna said.

Shame ached in her chest as she looked around the empty house. The voice whispered in her mind again, *this is your fault.* Everything that happened to Alara and everything Alara did was because of the decision she had made for her. Maybe the voice was right.

"He wouldn't hurt her, right?" She bit her lip.

"I don't know. When it comes to mages—I don't know."

CHAPTER 25

ALARA

Alara lay on the ground for another hour, eyes tracing the vines that wove to create the ceiling of Lili's home. The pattern was anything but natural, and she knew that Lili had to have used her magia to help the vines along. They twisted together across the ceiling, green leaves fluttering in the breeze that came through the window.

The architecture of Lili's home was beautiful. Beyond the mural in the living room, Lili had also used magia to tailor the branches of the tree her house was perched in. One of the walls of her bedroom was made from these branches, formed into an intricate design that depicted a forest and a river. It was the type of magia that the Council would consider a waste of time and energy. The mages would occasionally do small tricks to impress the villagers or the blameless, but it was all for show. Magia was for survival. But she felt a tingle of warmth at the beauty of Lili's skills and wondered what else these abilities could create.

Alara stood up, muscles stiff from her time pouting, and she gave herself a small shake. She was spending too much time thinking. Not good. A small flicker of heat snapped in her chest. It was Runeo's fault she was locked in this house. She had let his threats get to her and now she was slowly going crazy locked up here.

No, it wasn't his fault. It was hers for letting him get to her.

With a determined huff, she slipped on the sandals that Lili had given her. She glanced at her magite clothes for a moment before slipping into the Arboreli outfit she had borrowed from Lili. The soft wool pants and tunic felt light against her skin and she wrapped her embroidered skirt around her waist, the slit still giving room for plenty of motion. She grabbed a bright red shawl and wrapped it around her shoulders before leaving the room.

As she stepped outside, she was unsurprised to see the younger bruya who had tied her up originally leaning against the outer wall, eyes half closed.

"Good morning," she said casually as she brushed by him.

"Wait." He jumped to attention and hurried after her, the rope bridge that connected Lili's home to the rest of Arbol swinging gently. "You're not supposed to wander around alone."

She looked back at him with her best smile. "I'm not alone. Micos, right?"

He nodded without speaking, and she continued across the bridge. She felt him hesitate behind her, but she knew he didn't have an argument for her. After a moment, she felt the bridge move again as he followed after her.

She took deep breaths in the cool air, trying not to get overwhelmed by the rush of bruyas and colors that seemed to surround her like waves. It was amazing how the caves and tunnels of the Haven could somehow feel less oppressive to her than the wide open platforms of Arbol. At one point she had to pause, leaning against the cool trunk of a tree as she closed her eyes and breathed.

"So, are we going anywhere in particular?"

She cracked an eye open and looked over to where Micos stood. He looked around uncomfortably.

He's afraid to be seen with me.

She was sure that the entire city had heard about the Haven captive hiding away in Lili's house. Of course he didn't want to be seen with her.

"Anywhere but the market," she finally said.

"Well, you're definitely going the wrong way then."

She sat up and looked around, frustrated with herself. Nothing looked familiar from her trip out with Lili, and she had been sure she was taking another way.

"Which way, then?"

Micos took a small rope bridge to his right.

Now it was her turn to follow as he made his way from platform to platform. Some of the bridges they were crossing were actually made from branches of trees, woven together to form arches. It was clear they had some powerful… tierren, as they called them in the village. She wondered if Lili or her grandmother had been responsible for any of these intricate formations.

At one point, Micos even took her up a twisted staircase that wound around the trunk of a tree, leading them into a new layer of the village above where they had been. It was difficult to tell just how large Arbol was, with its twisting platforms and layers.

The Council hadn't fathomed just how big the bruya threat was.

"Where are we going?" she asked. The crowds had noticeably thinned since she'd first stepped outside, and now there was only the occasional passerby weaving among the trees.

Micos grinned. "My favorite spot in Arbol. And the best place for peace and quiet."

With that, he ducked *into* a nearby tree. As she stepped closer, she saw a small gap had formed in the wood, just wide enough for a small person. She followed him through the trunk, not wanting to get left behind and lost. Stepping forward, she was surprised when she realized the opening hadn't taken them into the tree, but rather through it and out to the other side.

Ahead of her, he took another staircase up, this one even more narrow than the one before. As they twisted their way around the trunk, the staircase seemed to wind into the upper branches and disappear. She resisted the urge to look down, but still felt a sickening lurch in her stomach as she followed after him. He had disappeared in the branches above her. The surrounding branches were thick enough now that she couldn't see below her, even if she had wanted to. There was some small relief in that—some.

Then the branches fell away around her and she gasped as the expanse of forest stretched before her in every direction. It was beautiful, like nothing she had ever seen. She saw Micos a few feet away, legs dangling off the small platform that balanced on a series of small branches. It was barely big enough for four people standing and perched on what seemed to be the tallest tree in the forest. The trees below them swayed with the wind, creating an illusion of a green sea rippling around them. In the distance, she could see the white peaks of the Ende Mountains, hazy but jagged on the horizon.

"El'dyo," Alara breathed out, gripping the trunk next to herself with white knuckles.

"This is the only place in Arbol you can see the whole sky. The world seems so big from up here." He smiled, looking out at the expanse. "You can step away from the trunk. There is a barrier of wind magia that will keep you from falling."

She loosened her grip on the trunk and stepped forward, still keeping a few inches from the edge. She took a moment to relish the sharp breeze and the wide sky above them. It was a relief to be out of the trees, away from the press of loose magia that permeated the air.

"What's this place for?"

Micos grinned. "Honestly? I'm not sure. From what I heard, it was built when we first moved into the trees. Perhaps as a lookout or as an escape. Not everyone here even knows it even exists."

Alara sat, legs crossed, knees just reaching the edge of the platform.

"We found it when we were just kids, my brother and I. We used to sneak up here when our parents were looking for us to make us do one chore or another. Runeo set up the air magia receptive down there to keep us from falling. Well, to keep *me* from falling."

She blanched at the name.

He looked at her with a small apologetic smile, running a hand along the back of his neck. "Yeah, he's my brother."

"Oh." She didn't know what else to say.

"He's not always such an ass. He's just… protective."

She bit back a bitter response, her cheeks flushing red with the unspoken anger. *Protective* was an interesting way of putting it.

They sat in silence for a while, Alara watching the sea of trees dancing in the wind below them. Micos was right. It was quiet here, and she felt a small amount of peace and calm settling into her chest, even as the voice in her head told her she couldn't trust it. Branches in the distance bent under the weight of a pack of monkeys, and she wondered what it would be like to swing off into the trees, not looking back at Arbol or the Haven. But then she saw Emaru's face in her mind and the ache in her chest of homesickness burned through her thoughts.

Micos stretched and stood up. "Come on. We should go."

He brushed by her as he made his way down the staircase and back into the cover of the trees. They walked in silence, but she noticed that even as they made their way back down to the main level, he wasn't taking her back to Lili's as she had expected.

It had only been a few minutes before the silence of the trees was broken by the high-pitched screams of children. She gave a start before hearing the laughter mixed into the cacophony of voices. She and Micos came around a large trunk and she saw a winding platform laid out in front of them, swarming with small children. The air buzzed with magia and she felt the sharp awareness in her mind before pushing it away.

Most of the children on the platform barely looked seven, yet they threw around magia as if it were nothing. Alara unconsciously took a step back as a particularly zealous child clapped his hands, causing a large fireball to fly into the air above them. Nearby, another group of children were running in and out of a small rain cloud that swirled gray in the air.

What in El'dyo's name was happening? There were only a few adults scattered around the edges of the platform, talking amongst themselves. Yet no one seemed to even notice the rush of magia darting through the air, including the flames shooting across the largely *wooden* area.

"Should someone be telling them to be more careful?" she finally managed, eyes wide as another ball of flame seared by one of the children, grazing their brightly woven tunic.

Micos shrugged. "How else are they supposed to learn how to use their skills?"

"But what if they hurt someone? Or catch the trees on fire?"

"There's always someone around if something goes wrong. I accidentally burned Runeo plenty of times when we were growing up before I learned better control. Now I only burn him when he deserves it." He shrugged again at her alarmed face. "Okay, that part was a joke. But even if it wasn't, there's was always someone around to help heal us, anyway."

"So you're a fire mage? Bruya… fire bruya?"

He made a face. "*Fuegen*, but yeah." He tilted his face at her. "You?"

She reddened a bit, unsure of why she was afraid to admit that she was the same. "So, is this how they train?"

"Train for what?"

"For fighting."

"We don't train to fight," Micos said. "Not most of us anyway."

"Alara!" Quenti's voice broke through the din of children's screams and laughter. Micos and Alara both turned to see Quenti and Khuna making their way toward them across a nearby bridge.

"You finally made it out."

Khuna's eyes were warm as she looked at Alara. "Micos, Runeo is looking for you." Khuna smirked. "He didn't seem too happy."

Micos grimaced and hurried away, giving them a small wave.

Quenti smiled at her. "Come with us. We're going to supper."

She hesitated, unsure if she was ready to face the crowds like she had seen back in the marketplace. But a small voice in her head urged her to gather more information, to discover how many bruyas were in Arbol, anything that could be useful in the future. She was no use to the Council—or anyone else—locked away in Lili's house.

A small shiver of guilt raced up her spine as she thought about speaking to the Council, her eyes still focused on the children racing around in front of them. Would they be taken by the Council—like Quenti?

Of course, if the mind-walker returned and cleansed her mind, none of this would matter. She tried to imagine what it would be to simply not remember the last few days, weeks, or even months. Would it really be that bad? Would she even notice?

"Listen," Quenti said, pulling Alara from her thoughts. "You've been at Lili's for almost a full week. Someone finally got you outside. You're not going back yet. Got it?"

Alara smiled in spite of herself. "Okay, I'll go," she finally said.

CHAPTER 26

ALARA

Alara's head was pounding by the time dinner had finished. It was bad enough being overwhelmed by the sheer number of bruyas who surrounded her, but she had also spent most of her time trying to block her awareness of every magia user in the dining area. She'd only been around this much magia in the Haven, and she now appreciated the thick walls of the tunnels that kept her mind-stalking skills dampened and safe from the crowds of mages and magites. There had also been little free-running magia outside of the practice rooms. She had never realized just how much sharper her sense was for active magia and wondered if Emaru knew she could differentiate.

"So you're a fuegen, right?" Alara gave a small start, realizing Khuna was now walking alongside her, her pale brown eyes focused on her face. "Quenti told me," she answered the unasked question.

Alara shrugged. "Yeah."

"I was always envious of the fuegen. It always seemed like a more useful gift than making rain clouds and fishing."

"I mean, it's useful if you want to hurt people, sure." Her voice was sharp and perhaps more bitter than she had meant it.

Quenti's shoulders stiffened. She was walking just ahead of them, but it was clear she was paying attention to their conversation.

"Perhaps," Khuna finally consented. "But we grew up learning the life-bringing aspect of fire, as well. Without fire, forests like these wouldn't exist. It cooks our food and keeps us warm."

"Burns down villages."

"And water can flood them," Khuna said softly.

Alara gritted her teeth. "That's different. A water mage can't accidentally flood a village, just like a wind mage can't accidentally blow down a tree. A fire mage, on the other hand…"

"Is that why they make you wear that bracelet?"

Khuna looked at her wrist, where the gold cuff hung. She instinctively pulled her shawl down to cover it.

"I choose to wear it," she said. "It keeps my abilities under control."

"Are you aware that those are the same cuffs they use on captive bruyas?"

Alara stopped in her tracks, her cheeks flushing red. Torches lined the walkway, lighting the path and making the shadows of the trees swayed in the wind. She turned to a nearby torch and raised her hand, pulling the fire from the wood. The flame danced unaided in the air for several seconds before jumping back to the torch.

"I can use my magia just fine when I choose to," she snapped. Before Quenti or Khuna could argue, she walked away. She could see Lili's bridge in the distance and knew they were almost—

She stopped herself before she thought *home*.

The next couple of weeks did little to calm her conflicted mind. In fact, she had almost settled into a peaceful routine in Arbol. In the mornings, she and Lili would cobble together a breakfast of quinoa and fruits. After which, Lili would sit cross-legged in the living room, adding to her mural and chatting about the best ways to make the different colors she used. Through this, Alara actually learned more about the local vegetation, particularly what was edible, poisonous, or what would stain your hands the longest.

Most afternoons, she would sneak away to the platform that Micos had shown her, forcing either him or Khuna to follow her whenever they were stationed outside Lili's home. The one exception was when Runeo was on duty, whose seething anger seemingly knew no bounds.

"What do you want, magite?" he had sneered the first time she had stepped outside. After that, he took to glaring at her until she ducked back inside, her face flushed red.

Those were the afternoons that she had spent cross-legged in Lili's room plotting how to escape, examining the branches that stretched out from Lili's bedroom window.

She noticed by the end of the week that Runeo's shifts were getting fewer and farther between, leaving her more free to explore Arbol with the others. Was this Khuna's and Micos' doing? Despite her unfriendly demeanor, the duo almost seemed to enjoy her company. Micos noted at one point that seeing Alara exploring Arbol wide-eyed was like seeing it for the first time.

Though she wouldn't admit it to anyone but herself, she did feel a unique sense of freedom among the trees in Arbol. So carefree was everyone with their abilities, it was almost contagious. It certainly helped that whenever humanly possible, Micos would poke jabs at her inability to use her fire magia.

"Not wanting to use magia and not being able to are completely different issues!" she assured him. The ability to manipulate flames was never the problem. It was the ability to effectively control them without hurting anyone that kept her up at night.

Micos had only shrugged at this, but the look on his face made her scowl.

She had proceeded to grab the flame he was playing with and almost burn herself in the process. Not her finest argument.

He offered a few tips and tricks to holding a flame without letting it get out of control. She had even managed to do so. Once.

"Don't treat it like a puma getting ready to attack you, but rather a l'lama you're convincing to carry your bag," he had said, juggling a series of fireballs between his palms.

She had only rolled her eyes at the remark and his unnecessary show of magia.

For Quenti's part, she was settling in well—a far cry better than she had in the Haven. While Alara floated between Lili, Micos, and Khuna, Quenti spent every waking moment with Khuna. Some days, seeing the couple intertwined on the cushions in Lili's front room made her heart ache with a loneliness that she hadn't been aware existed. Occasionally her mind would flash to Ardo's gray eyes or his laugh—a habit she refused to examine closer.

But seeing them together made her realize just how hollow Quenti had been during her short time in the Haven. Alara never saw her eyes light up as they did when she was with the bruya. A part of her wondered if Quenti would even spend the night at Lili's if it wasn't for her.

One evening after dinner, while she, Lili, and Quenti were drinking tea next to the fire, Alara made that comment to Quenti and watched the deep crimson blush rise up her cheeks and into her hairline. She didn't say anything, but she didn't have to. She responded by letting her curls cover her face while Alara and Lili laughed.

That night, for the first time in weeks, Alara didn't fall asleep thinking about the Haven.

The next morning she woke up alone in the house. She could tell by the warmth in the air that it was later than normal. The birds just outside the window sang a different tune from their standard early morning warble.

She slowly rose from her mat, brushing her tangled hair from her face and picking apart the knots that had formed in the night. Eventually, she gave up and tied her hair at the nape of her neck. She splashed some water on her face from the basin that stood beside the window. In the Haven, a physical system of small tunnels channeled water from rain and snowmelt into a central basin that distributed water to the various rooms. But in Arbol, water mages—aguen, she was told—collected rain and each morning's dew to distribute into the buildings through the help of wind funnels created by *airen*.

When she left the room, she saw the house was empty. A plate of cut fruit was left out on the counter, along with a mug of leaves for boiled water. She smiled at Lili's thoughtfulness before filling the kettle. Noticing the fire had burned out, she set to relighting it.

"What're you doing?" a voice in the doorway called out, causing Alara to drop the flint she was holding.

She turned around, startled to see Khuna's silhouette in the doorway. Alara's shoulders relaxed as she saw the smile stretched across the bruya's face.

"If you're here, then where is Quenti?" Alara said, tilting her head at the empty space behind her. "Aren't you two attached at the hip?"

Khuna grinned wider. "After ten years of sneaking around, it's just nice being in the same place." She went over to Alara's plate of fruit and stole a slice of lucuma. "But alas, Quenti's volunteered to help restore an older bridge. I decided I'd rather take guard duty than braid rope." She smirked. "I volunteered Micos to help her."

"Volunteered Micos?" She raised an eyebrow.

"I may have bribed him with some cuy meat from a recent hunt." She stole another piece of fruit off Alara's plate with a wink.

"I'm flattered you wanted to guard me so much. Should Quenti be worried?"

"I really hate rope weaving. And Pacha will be there. That woman's mission in life is to drive me crazy." Khuna slumped down in one of Lili's small cushions. She was wearing pants instead of a skirt, which was lucky given how she sprawled.

"Pacha?" Alara asked.

"One of the tierren in charge of construction. Lili doesn't much like her either, so it's not just me."

Alara gave a small nod and returned to the dying fire. She picked up the flint that had fallen to the ground and started working to relight it.

"You are a strange one, aren't you?"

Alara turned back to her and groaned, her eyebrows knit. Khuna was grinning—of course.

"What's that supposed to mean?"

Khuna nodded at the red embers in the hearth. "You could light the fire with your magia, immediately."

Alara frowned. "It's not that easy."

It was Khuna's turn to frown. "I've seen kids do it." She looked Alara over, as if trying to understand a strange new species of animal. "Is it the cuff?"

She covered her wrist defensively. "I told you, the cuff doesn't stop me from using my powers. I've even practiced my magia with Micos!"

"Then relight the fire," Khuna said, crossing her arms.

Alara turned back to the embers with a small huff. "Fine."

For a second, nothing happened. She closed her eyes and concentrated on feeling the small tendril of heat that always danced hidden inside of her. She opened her eyes and reached out her awareness to the heat that still emanated from the burned out fire. The ghost of the fire's presence still lingered, a shadow of the heat that had consumed it only an hour ago. Biting her lip, she willed her abilities to spark the fire, the thread of her magia not quite reaching the embers. A part of her knew she was still holding back, still afraid. A sharp breeze of warm air brushed past her face.

The hearth exploded with heat and light. Large flames jumped to encase the embers. Alara fell back, the blood draining from her face as the heat seared her cheeks.

She whipped around to see Runeo standing in the doorway, hand still outstretched, as he let out a not-too-friendly laugh. His face was clean-shaven today, revealing the sharp angle of his jaw.

"Why'd you do that?" Alara said, her heart pounding.

"Yeah, Runeo," Khuna agreed. "What in Sol's name was that about?"

He shrugged, his lips dancing in a smirk. "What? I was helping."

"I didn't need *your* help," She turned back to the kettle, trying to hide her shaking hands. "You could have caught Lili's house on fire—or even me!"

"So, the fire magite's afraid of a little fire."

"Afraid of burning down someone's house, yes," Alara said, the lump in her throat growing.

"You have that little control that you'd burn down a house without stopping it?"

"Yes! That's exactly what I've been trying to tell everyone!" Alara felt the heat in her chest rising.

"Sol," Runeo said, "the Haven's really in your head, isn't it? They lock you up in that little mountain and warp your minds until you hate yourselves and everyone else like you."

"I don't hate myself." Tears of frustration built behind her eyes.

"You hate your abilities. Is that all the Council knows how to teach?"

She stepped up to him, her face red and eyes flashing. "Don't you dare talk about the Haven or what they teach."

Runeo let out a bitter laugh. "They force you to fear your abilities and then teach you to hate those of us who don't!" He loomed over her, shoulders rigid, and his face a mask of brutal anger.

"Okay, Runeo," Khuna cut in. "I think you've said enough."

"We don't hate you because of your abilities, we hate you because you're murderers!" Alara said, ignoring Khuna. Her body burned with anger, and her chest tightened.

"Oh, so you think we're the murderers?" Runeo said. "Your people kill or enslave anyone who doesn't follow their teachings."

"And your people murdered my entire family!" Heat flared behind her. Her magia must have found the flames of the stove and filled them with rolling waves of fire.

The room went silent, and she saw the mix of emotions and thoughts flickering across the bruyas' faces.

"I…" She started and stopped again. She looked back at the stove. Charring had painted the stove and kettle black. Lili was going to be so disappointed in her…

Before either of them could say anything, she pushed past them, her eyes stinging with tears she didn't want them seeing.

CHAPTER 27

ALARA

A few hours later, Quenti found Alara, face puffy but dry-eyed, at the platform in the highest tree. Her body was curled in on itself, her back pressed against the tree and her legs tight against her chest.

"Hey." Quenti's head peeped around the corner of the tree.

"Hey." Alara's eyes remained focused on the green hills in the distance—north—toward home.

"Khuna told me what happened. Micos thought you might be up here."

Alara stayed silent, her mood too dour to react.

"I yelled at Runeo for you. Just a bit." She paused. "You can yell at him some more if you want. Or set him on fire… but only if you're ready."

She smiled for the first time in hours. "Thanks."

Quenti climbed the rest of the way up and sat next to her on the platform, then crossed her legs and brushed her shoulder against her.

"I'm sorry I brought you into all of this," she said. "I know it's not much of a consolation, but I never meant for all this to become so… messy. All I wanted was to be with Khuna. It was selfish of me."

The anger she had latched on to for the past few weeks abated… though just the slightest bit. Enough for her to respond with a very un-Alara-like civility.

"I know," Alara said. "I just want to go home."

They sat silently, watching as the sun reached its zenith and began its slow descent toward the horizon. She had always felt so self-conscious in crowds, but this was different.

"I might actually miss this place," she said, barely above a whisper. "I mean this platform, specifically. This view."

Quenti laughed and looked out over the sea of treetops. "I don't blame you. The tunnels are nice and all, but *Sol*, you can see the world from up here!"

Her smile fell. "Have you ever had your mind cleansed?"

Quenti didn't reply immediately, her eyes focused on a distant point on the horizon. "I don't know. I mean, I guess I wouldn't know?"

"What do you think it's like?"

"Maybe it's like sleeping? Like you close your eyes one minute, then open them, and it's another time. Or maybe—maybe you don't even notice." Quenti nudged Alara's shoulder. "Hey, maybe you've had your mind cleansed already?"

Alara shuddered at the thought. "I don't like the idea of someone messing with my head."

"At least you won't, you know, remember?"

"I suppose I won't miss this view then, huh?" Alara said, biting her lip. She wasn't even sure how to explain the lump sitting in her throat.

"You don't have to leave."

"You know I do. I can't imagine never seeing the Haven again—never seeing Emaru. She's the closest I have to a mother." For an instant, the image of Ardo flashed in her mind and she felt another longing pang.

"You ready to head back?"

No. A voice whispered in her mind as Quenti stood, turning toward the staircase. *Oh, right. Back to Lili's.*

Before Alara could answer, her stomach did so for her. The growl echoed in the air, and Quenti let out a laugh.

"Runeo left on a hunt earlier, if that helps? Khuna says he wouldn't be back for a few days."

"In that case, I would love some food."

A fire crackled in the hearth as Lili, Quenti, Khuna, and Alara talked, the air smelling of smoke and bark. Despite the pangs of longing that plagued her, she felt something like contentment sitting with her friends, high above the ground.

She swallowed. Is that what they were to her? These... enemies. Friends? They'd cost her so much. Could she really be one step away from becoming one of them?

She tossed and turned that night, long after the others had passed out.

And then there were the screams.

She wasn't even sure if she'd slept when the commotion erupted outside, causing Lili to stir. Alara sat up, her heart thundering from the distant screams echoing through the trees. And they were growing closer.

Lili jumped up at the same time as Alara, wrapping her blanket around her shoulders.

"What's…?" Alara started.

"I have no idea. Not good."

They rushed into the front room, surprising the bleary-eyed Quenti and Khuna. Lili reached the front door first, pulling back the wool curtain with a sharp tug, giving face to the chaotic bellows.

Copper tang filled the air, and then the panicked, dark faces of the bruyas surged past them. Micos entered behind Runeo, reaching a trembling hand toward Lili's hearth, re-starting the fire that had burned low in the night. The embers leaped to life, whipping vicious shadows across the walls.

As the fire settled and the darkness shrank back, she gaped at the scene before her. A male bruya with dark skin and cropped hair lay on the ground. His face shone with sweat, a red stain spreading along his side and stomach. Beside him stood a female bruya—one she recognized from the day she was captured. Blood dripped down her arm, a long deep gash along her shoulder still weeping. Everyone seemed frozen in some macabre tableau.

"Alara, boil water!" Lili shouted, a rare assertive side showing itself. "Quenti, go retrieve the white leaves from my healer bag and bring them to me."

Everyone moved all at once. Alara put a pot on the fire, carefully using her magia to strengthen the flames in hopes it would boil faster. She grinned, just for a moment, at her success.

After what felt like an eternity, the pot of water began to boil, and she snatched it from the stove, setting it next to Lili, who quickly dumped in the large white leaves as Quenti twisted her fingers over the mixture, causing the water to froth and churn.

Lili's hands glowed as they flew over the prone body of the bruya, who had finally stopped groaning. She hoped that he had just passed out from the pain, then grimaced as Lili scooped the soggy leaves from the pot of water and laid them across his open stomach. He hissed—so he definitely wasn't dead, yet!—and she laid her hands over the leaves, magia rolling off her in waves.

"Micos, can you cauterize Zinita's arm?" she asked without taking her eyes from her task.

He moved over to the female bruya—Zinita—who was shaking her head, eyes focused solely on the downed bruya. But he ignored her protests and set his hand along the bloody gash.

The heat of the fire behind Alara reached out to meet him as his hands glowed red. She couldn't help but gag at the smell of burning flesh, and a sharp groan rose from Zinita's throat as the cut sealed. Still, she didn't take her eyes off the man lying beneath Lili's moving hands. Alara was staring at the blackened wound. It was ugly, but it had stopped bleeding.

Because of fire.

Lili let out a sound somewhere between a sigh and a whimper. Sweat beaded on her forehead, dripping down her cheeks. After a few more seconds, she slumped back, shaking her head.

The air in the room shifted. Zinita let out a wail and sank to her knees. No one spoke, the only sounds came from the mourning woman. Runeo placed a hand on her shoulder and pulled her back from the body. She slumped against him, arms wrapping around him, weeping.

Lili leaned over the body and placed a gentle hand on his forehead. She whispered a small prayer that Alara didn't recognize and directed Micos and the others to take him out. "Contact the solkeeper to prepare him for burial."

She turned to Runeo. "What happened?"

"Zinita?" Runeo said, and she stepped forward, a streak of blood smeared across her face where she had wiped her hand by accident. It shone, wet against her dark, tear-stained skin.

"We were hunting near the border," she said. Lili grunted in disapproval as Zinita continued her story. "Yesterday evening, a group of councilguards stumbled onto our camp and before we knew it"—she took a deep breath—"two died immediately. We hoped if we got here fast enough though, we'd be able to save him."

Zinita's eyes flashed bright and focused on Alara, and she stepped back instinctively. "The councilguards have been scouring the borderlands looking for bruyas. An Alara Ayar has gone missing with another magite, kidnapped by bruyas. It seems this girl is important to the Haven. Councilwoman Emaru is looking for her personally."

"Quenti?" Khuna turned to Quenti with a look of confusion and concern.

"I…" Quenti's face was pale, and her eyes as the room shifted its attention to her.

"Let me explain," Alara said, her voice shaking. She stepped defensively in front Quenti. It was her lie, Quenti shouldn't be the one to pay for it.

"How about we stop listening to your lies," Zinita said with a sneer. "If it were up to me, we would have started interrogating you the moment you walked in."

Runeo stepped forward and towered over her. "We should arrest her immediately." There was a murmur of agreement from the other bruyas.

"Step away from Alara, Runeo." The entire room froze at the soft voice of authority. The bruyas parted, and Quil'la stepped into the overcrowded room, Micos following behind. "Now, would someone explain what is happening?"

"She lied about her name, probably to hide her connection to the Council," Runeo said. "She's a spy!"

Quil'la's face remained calm throughout his heated accusations, her eyes remaining focused on Alara's paling face. She gave a slight nod when the young man finished, but didn't break her gaze. "So far, she's done nothing to harm us. She hasn't tried to run away."

"She can't be allowed to just wander free. If she lied about her name, what else has she lied about?"

Quil'la held up a hand and shot him a sharp look. He immediately fell silent. "What would you have us do, Runeo? Kill her? We'd only incur the wrath of the Council. If anything, this proves how wise we were to think before acting. We can't have the entire Council breathing down our necks. When Mena returns, she'll make sure this girl can no longer be a threat to us. Then we can return Alara to her home and this can all be settled."

The room burst in murmured disagreement, but no one dared step forward to argue.

"Yes, Senye," Runeo finally said, stiffly nodding his head before storming out of the house.

Quil'la turned to look at Alara again. "Do not prove me wrong." The words were soft, but she could hear the unspoken threat. With that, Quil'la left, and the other bruyas followed her out, but not before Zinita stepped up to her, face twisted with pain and malice.

"Watch your back, *magite*," she hissed into Alara's ear. The woman shoved her shoulder sharply before turning and following Quil'la out the door. Alara was left gaping at the blood staining the wood floors.

While the Arborelis had followed orders, few clearly agreed with Quil'la's decision. How much power did she actually have over her people? And what would happen if they ignored her?

No one wanted her here, either. She couldn't blame them. She wouldn't want herself around either.

She clenched her fists and looked out the window at the gray moonlight seeping into the room. For the first time since she'd arrived in Arbol, she was resolute.

She could no longer wait around for this Mena to show up. It was time to leave.

CHAPTER 28

ALARA

lara sat on one of Lili's cushion chairs, a mug of strong, dark cafi clenched in her hands. The bitter drink almost broke through the fog of her mind. The house was silent and still, not even a breeze interrupting the mournful reverie. Lili had already left to care for the lesser wounded from the ambush, and Khuna and Quenti whispered softly to each other, too quiet to tell about what. Micos sat next to Alara, his eyes distant and face wan, a now-cold mug of cafi in his hands.

Though the bruyas had helped clean the mess in Lili's home, a dark stain still marred the wood planks.

He was just another bruya. Just another bruya. Though no matter how much she tried to remind herself that, she couldn't wipe his soft features from her memory. His eyes had been a soft gray, his nose wide and flat, and his lips a pale pink. She shivered and took another sip of the lukewarm cafi.

"He died because of me, didn't he?" she asked.

"No." Micos's focused on her. "He died because of the councilguards."

"But they were looking for me. That's the only reason they were out here." She stared into the dregs of her mug, refusing to look into his pitying face.

His eyebrows were deeply furrowed and his golden eyes shone softly in the fire light. "So, who are you really?"

Her shoulders tensed. "I'm not a spy."

"I have no doubts about that." Micos's lips twitched into a small smile.

"Your brother doesn't agree."

"Runeo can be an idiot. If you were a spy, you'd be a lot more..."

"Competent?" She raised her eyebrow.

"You said it, not me."

She sipped again and shuddered at the bitter taste lingering on her tongue.

His eyes softened as he waited patiently for her to explain. She wasn't going to get out of this. With a sigh, she explained.

"Linda Emaru—one of the councilwomen—raised me. She's practically my mother. We don't share the same name, but I didn't know if they would connect me to her. I was afraid of what might happen if Quil'la knew that I had direct ties to the Haven's Council."

He was silent for a while before he spoke again, his voice hoarse and barely above a whisper. "My parents died when I was a bruyita. I don't really remember them anymore, just the stories Runeo tells me about them. We were raised by Wela, our dad's mother."

"What happened to them?"

"My father got lost during a hunting expedition in the mountains—my mother went after him, and she never returned."

"I'm sorry."

"I sometimes wonder if it will stop hurting. How can I miss

someone that I can't even picture? But sometimes when I think of them…"

"I don't think it ever stops hurting."

"I suppose not." It was Micos's turn to sip from his mug.

"Who was he?" Alara asked, her tone uncertain. "The bruya who died." Her eyes locked onto the dark stain on the floor.

"Puka—he was an airen and a hunter. He always claimed that he killed a puma with his bare hands. I never did believe that."

"Was he Zinita's partner?"

Micos let out a subdued laugh, startling her. "Oh, Sol no, just friends. They were practically siblings. Runeo and them were born under the same moon. Always together as kids."

"I am sorry."

Micos only nodded at this before setting a warm hand over her own. She felt something loosen in her chest at the touch. The room lapsed into silence, and she let her thoughts drift, her gaze settling on a sleeping Quenti, whose head lay on Khuna's lap.

With a despondent sigh, she leaned back against the wall and closed her eyes.

Khuna, Quenti, and Micos left in the late morning. There was to be a ceremony prior to the fallen bruya—Puka's—burial. They had invited her, but she knew it was only out of politeness. No one really wanted her there.

As they left, she saw two unknown guards outside the door. Their faces were set in a cold look of determination, though she didn't even acknowledge them as she closed the wool curtain and retreated into the bedroom. The air was finally warming up for the day, and filtered sunlight began stretching across the wood plank floor. She looked around, summoning what sense of conviction she could, though the exhaustion from the night before muddled her thoughts.

She went over to the windows and peered down at the branches that stretched out below. How high up were they? She cursed herself for closing her eyes on the ride up all those weeks ago.

Taking in the room around her, she noted the scattering of sheets and blankets, the skeins of wool and clothes. Even if she tied everything together and pretended it would hold her, there wouldn't be enough material to get her down to the ground. Were there branches all the way down? Could she simply climb? She tried to imagine doing so in the dark of night and shuddered.

Maybe she was overreacting. If she just stayed in Lili's home, silent and unassuming, Mena would be back soon. Alara could have her memory erased and be on her way home, never even knowing the difference.

Deep down, she knew that was wishful thinking. The air had changed within Arbol, and no matter what Quil'la had said, she had definitely overstayed her welcome. The only question now was *how* she would leave.

She lost track of how much time she spent staring out the window, scheming her way out of this impossible problem. So consumed was she by her thoughts, she almost missed the flame that danced in the air between her palms.

Startled, she waved her hands, and the flame disappeared with a small puff of white smoke. She looked around. When had she created it? How? The only fire here was all the way in the kitchen. She shuddered at the thought. This place was driving her crazy, and now she was picking up flames without realizing it. She could have caught something on fire or burned herself.

Unconsciously, she ran a hand along the ridged skin of her cheek where her scar still stood out.

A bang in the other room made her jump, and she turned just in time to see Quenti and Lili burst through the door.

"What…" She fell silent when she saw Lili shaking her head. They whispered to one another for a moment and Lili ducked back out.

"You need to leave." Quenti's face was stone.

Alara's stomach lurched at the sudden declaration. "Leave as in…?"

"Leave as in leave, stupid. You need to get out of Arbol. Today."

"But… is Mena back?" Was she serious? She couldn't be serious.

"You can't wait for her. The bruyas are talking. Zinita and others…" Quenti paused and gave an apologetic look. "They're making plans to kill you. With or without Quil'la's blessing."

She stumbled back a few steps, her legs weak as the blood rushed from her extremities. The copper taste of fear bit at her tongue, and she dropped down onto the sleeping pad. "Oh."

Lili burst back into the room, carrying a large bundle and handed it to Quenti. She made a face and wrapped Alara up in a tight, one-armed hug. "Bye," she whispered under her breath before letting go and hurrying from the house.

"What's going on?" Everything was happening all at once; it was too much.

"I told you," Lili said. "You're leaving." With a grunt, she pulled out a long rope from the bag and dropped it onto the floor with a heavy thud. "I might have stolen this from that bridge I was working on earlier. With all the chaos from the attack, I figure they won't miss it. At least not right away."

Her eyes went wide, realizing the implication of what Quenti was saying. "El'dyo, you're not saying I have to climb down."

"You leave at dusk," Quenti said, her typical dry tone absent. "When the community dinner starts, there won't be many bruyas around. Lili's house is near the edge of the city, anyway, and no one will see you climbing."

"Climbing," she repeated, eyes focused on the window.

"With help," Quenti said, waving a hand at the rope that laid coiled in front of her.

"And if that's not long enough to reach the ground?"

"What kind of attitude is that?" Quenti said with a grin—a grin that fell away seconds later. "Okay, I honestly don't know if it is," she admitted. They both sat in silence, staring at the rope.

Quenti finally looked up, a spark in her eye. "If I stay up here, I can untie it when you reach the end. You can then retie it and climb the rest of the way down. Hopefully, it's at least long enough for that."

Alara gave a slow nod, the million ways this could go wrong swirling in her head. "Won't you get in trouble?" she asked.

"Lili and Khuna are going to provide me with an alibi. I'll be at dinner." She winked. "You didn't know you had friends in the enemy's camp, did you?"

Alara knew it was a joke, but a warmth she hadn't felt in a very long time spread throughout her chest, calming the whirlwind inside of her—slightly.

"Okay," she said. "Let's do this."

CHAPTER 29

ALARA

A few hours later, Alara precariously straddled the large branch that stretched under Lili's bedroom window. The forest was darkening, the weak light of dusk no longer breaking through the thick tree cover, leaving the woods in deep shadows, resembling what she could imagine as some form of hell.

She shivered and reached to tighten the poncho around her shoulders. She wore her bruya outfit, the thick material warmer and less likely to tear in the climb. Her magite clothes were tucked into the small bag that clung to her back, along with a few loaves of bread and some nuts Lili had snuck them earlier. With some reluctance, she had also tucked a small flint into the sleeve of her tunic, easily accessible in an emergency.

In the window, Quenti fussed with the heavy rope, quietly tying it to the thick branch.

Alara looked down as the heavy rope fell through the branches with a soft rustle.

"I'm afraid of heights," she said to herself. "I'm definitely afraid of heights."

"That's what you get for growing up underground." Quenti smirked. "Just don't look down."

"Right. Don't look the way I'm climbing. Sounds great. Thanks for that." She took a deep breath, trying to stop the revolution of butterflies inside of her. Against Quenti's advice, she spared another glance into the dark abyss below.

Yeah, she was going to die.

At least she wouldn't give Zinita or Runeo the satisfaction of doing it themselves.

"When you reach the end of the rope," Quenti said, "give it three quick tugs and two slow ones. I'll untie it and drop it down so you can reuse it the rest of the way."

"And assume there's actually enough rope to reach the bottom the second time."

"That's the spirit," Quenti said, oblivious to Alara's sarcasm. "When you get to the ground, remember to move away from the village and then go left until you hit the valley."

"Move away and go left? What sort of instructions are those?"

"I'm not a cartographer, Alara!"

"Which way is left?"

Quenti stood up straight, awkwardly pivoting back and forth as she got her bearings. "It's north. Away is north. That should get you back to the river. Probably."

"I love the confidence."

"Oh! I almost forgot." She dipped away from the window. When she returned, she had the familiar bronze dagger grasped in her hands. "For you. Think of it as a good luck charm."

"Great. I'll think of it as you returning something that belongs to me, anyway." Alara forced a smile and Quenti smirked in response. She took the dagger and tucked it into her belt alongside another—actually sharp—blade, a gift from Lili.

Quenti leaned awkwardly out the window and gave her a hug. "Don't let anyone see you. And don't fall."

"Your advice is priceless," she said with as much sarcasm as her shaking voice could muster before she started the descent.

She wrapped her hand tight around the rope, using her feet to find footholds in the branches, though they were few and far between. She had barely made it a few yards before her hands began to burn. At this rate, she wasn't going to have any skin left when she reached the ground. Not for the first time, she wished she had a more useful power, like healing.

Whenever she found a thick branch, she loosened her grip on the rope, letting her weight rest on it as she caught her breath. Each time, she avoided looking down or thinking about how much farther she had—or about how one mistake could send her hurtling hundreds of feet through the darkness onto the dirt below.

Time slowed to a crawl, her hands growing more fatigued with each breath. By the time she reached the end of the rope, the pain was all she could think of. She chanced a look down and cursed under her breath. She still couldn't see the ground between the thick branches beneath her. The palms of her hands were sweating, and she hoped to El'dyo that the rope would reach the bottom this time around. If it didn't, it's not as though she'd be able to climb back up either. The bruyas would eventually find her stuck and helpless in this tree. Either that or she'd fall and put an end to their concerns herself.

Several shallow breaths escaped her lips as she pushed the dark thoughts away and tugged on the rope, signaling to Quenti. There wasn't a choice. She just had to do it. She pressed up against the trunk of the tree and braced herself, holding onto her end of the rope. A minute later, she heard the snapping of branches above. The rope twisted and fell past her, hitting the branches below.

A second later, the heavy rope snapped in her hand and wrenched her sideways. She scrambled, trying to catch herself, fighting between grabbing onto a branch and keeping a hold on the rope. Just as her leg slipped, her other foot found the firm hold of another branch, and she stopped her precarious slide into thin air.

She pulled herself back onto the branch, using every ounce of strength she had, finally regaining her balance. It took all of a minute, but she was left panting and sore as she slumped onto the cool wood, the rope still clenched tightly in her other hand. After catching her breath and tying the rope, she slipped off the branch and continued her descent.

The next leg of the climb went faster, and before she realized it, she had reached the end of the rope. To her dismay, when she looked down, all she saw were the black shadows of the forest. No ground in sight. To make matters worse, it looked like the branches were thinning out, turning the final part of the descent into a big question mark. She squinted into the night, willing herself to see the ground. It took a minute for her to realize she was fingering the flint that sat along her wrist.

She smirked and whispered to herself. "Come on, Alara. You're a magite, aren't you?"

With a deep breath, she closed her eyes and stretched her awareness out, looking for nearby bruyas. Just as she grasped her powers, she noticed the warm glow of magia strapped to her belt. Her fingers brushed against the dull bronze dagger, mind suddenly spinning with questions.

"Get it together. Not the time," Alara said, taking shallow breaths. She reached out again, ignoring the nearby spark. She could feel bruyas a few hundred yards away through the trees—likely lookouts—and a sharp tinge of fear ran through her. Her eyes darted around her, taking in the thick branches of the cloud forest that wrapped around where she was hidden.

With a flick of the flint, she sent a small ball of flame gently floating down, lighting the branches below her. A few seconds later, she gasped in relief. The forest floor was only about forty feet below. Though relief was quickly quashed by anxiety as she remembered she was fresh out of rope and had no promise of branches the rest of the way down.

She released her powers quickly, letting the flame dissipate into nothing.

It worked. A shaky sigh escaped her lips as her eyes focused back on the rope that hung overhead, marking her escape and implicating Quenti and the others. She couldn't let that happen. She squared her shoulders and sent the small flame to the base of the rope.

"L'lama, l'lama," she muttered, recalling Micos's advice.

The rope flared to life and burned. It wasn't difficult to get something dry and flammable to ignite, but she used all her focus to stop it from burning out of control. The wetness of the canopy helped her keep the fire in check. By the time she felt the fire flicker out with the last of the rope, she was gasping for air. Keeping her abilities in check certainly took its toll. She needed to practice more.

After taking in several deep breaths and nursing her scratched and shaking limbs, she started the final leg of her climb. She kept a small ball of flame nearby to light her search for branches in the darkness, more confident in her abilities than ever before. Every few minutes, she sent out her awareness, taking care that none of the bruya lookouts had been alerted to the small light dancing in the forest.

It was a great short-term plan, but it inevitably took its toll with every branch. As she split her awareness between the floating flame and the bruya nearest her, her sandal slipped on the damp, smooth wood. Before she could catch herself, her grip slipped, and she was sent free falling.

She landed with a thud, instinctively rolling onto the soft forest floor. She had fallen around fifteen feet, and while the impact had done a number on her shins, she was no worse for wear, save for every muscle in her body aching, alongside her hands and her feet—everything really. The flame she had been holding onto had disappeared as she hit the ground.

She relit it—or at least she tried.

Tssk! Tssk! The flint at her wrists sparked and sputtered.

Come on, you son of a bruya. Light!

It was no use. For whatever reason, her magia wasn't cooperating. Perhaps her descent from the tree had scared it right out of her. Keeping her breath light, she waited for her eyes to adjust. When they finally did, she shuddered as she realized just how close she had come to hitting a large and twisted root.

At least luck was on her side.

She stood up, brushing the twigs and dirt from her. She rearranged her poncho and ran a hand through her tangled hair, brushing it out of her face. She wished she had saved a bit of the rope to hold back her hair. Instead, she dug through her pack and ripped off a piece of the sleeve from her magite robes, using that to tie it up. She almost laughed at how thin the material was. The past few weeks had gotten her used to the thick wool of bruya clothing.

She looked up into the shadows above her and sent up a silent thank you to Quenti and Lili before taking a deep breath, trying to reason out which way was north.

She steadied herself against a trunk and closed her eyes,

pushing away the exhaustion from the past twenty-four hours. That had been the most she'd ever used her magia, and the effort had stretched her thin. But she needed one more push. Hopefully her mind-stalking skills weren't spent too.

She reached at the small heat in her chest and picked at the thread, pushing her awareness out and letting it spread slowly around her. She touched the minds of a few nearby bruyas and turned in the opposite direction.

She moved slowly in the dark. With each step, she swept her foot in front of her, avoiding the large tree roots that scattered around the forest floor. She only slipped a few times as she walked. After an hour of achingly slow progress, she sent out her awareness one more time, feeling a wave of relief at the absence of anyone nearby.

She turned left—hoping Quenti's advice was accurate.

When she broke through the trees and saw the dark valley shadowed below her, her knees gave out. But she didn't have time. She took a few deep, gasping breaths and pushed herself up. She followed along the valley, finding the path she remembered from their first trip into Arbol. When the path veered and disappeared back into the forest, she followed. Even in the thick wool pants and poncho, her body felt cold and numb. Her feet ached, and she was tripping more and more now. But she kept walking. Straight down the mountain until she hit the river.

Hours must have passed, because she could hear babbling of the river. She jolted at the sound, losing her footing and stumbling over a root hidden in a small flowering bush. She looked around, realizing she could make out the shapes of the surrounding forest. Morning had come, and she had only just gotten to the river. With a bone weary sigh, Alara tried to push herself up from the ground, but for the literal life of her, she couldn't quite pull together the energy.

Without another thought, she dragged herself to a low-lying pine and ducked under the boughs of the tree. Leaning against the trunk, she let herself breathe, body relaxing for just a moment. Closing her eyes, she reached toward her core, fumbling in her attempts. It took a minute to even get a grasp on her magia. It was weak, but she held it firm with determination and sent out her awareness.

One more time, and then rest.

There were no bruyas that she could sense and she sagged in relief, only that strange dagger. Her magia flickered out like a dying ember, and she let the coldness of the night seep into her body. But she wasn't ready for sleep just yet.

She had felt the spark of life again. Fingers numb with cold and exhaustion, she pulled out the bronze dagger tucked at her side, squinting at it in the dark. It didn't look special. It didn't glow in the darkness, and it felt cold beneath her fingers, as any dagger would. She wanted to shake it or send her magia running through it, but didn't have the energy. Clenching her jaw in frustration, she tucked it back into her belt. Tomorrow. It was tomorrow Alara's problem.

A branched snapped, sending Alara's heart up into her throat. A horrid ache permeated her entire body. She squinted into the bright light filtering in through the leaves above.

And then another branch snapped, and this time it was followed by the rustling of leaves and the sound of voices.

CHAPTER 30

QUENTI

Quenti stared out of the window in the living area, feeling as though she were on vigil. She sighed at the black night that stared back at her. Lili and Khuna had fallen asleep a few hours before, with Lili taking up space on a pad in the middle of the room. Khuna had tucked herself beside Quenti, her head resting on her partner's leg as she let out a soft snore.

Quenti still had a mug of cold cafi gripped in her hands. Her fingers were stiff as she set the mug down beside her and leaned back into the cushions. Despite the exhaustion of the last day, the coil of fear twisting in her stomach overpowered any weariness she should have been feeling.

Had Alara made it? If not, how long until word reaches them? If she did make it, how long would it be until the rest of Arbol discovered their missing prisoner? More importantly, what would happen if they found out she, Lili, and Khuna had been the ones to assist the "dangerous magite?"

Just after dinner, Khuna had locked Lili's bedroom door and

maneuvered out the window and back into the living space. Lili and Quenti had taken the time to loudly yell about Alara locking them out of the room for the guard's benefit. So, they were safe for now. But how long would that last?

She ran a hand through Khuna's hair and closed her eyes, hoping for sleep to take her.

She didn't know how long she had dropped off for, but when she awoke, the night outside the window hadn't changed, and the hearth still flickered with life.

"Quil'la's command…"

"She said… morning… can't leave."

"We… question… just following…"

As she blinked the sleep from her eyes, she could just make out the snippets of a hushed conversation outside the doorway. She sat up, jostling Khuna, who groaned and looked around in confusion.

"What time is it?" Khuna asked sullenly.

"Night still," she said in a hushed tone. "I heard something outside."

Khuna's eyes sharpened. She stood up without hesitation and pattered to the doorway. She eyed the club that leaned against the threshold near her right hand before pulling the door open.

"Everything okay out here?" she said, voice bathed in a phony exhaustion.

Khuna was pushed aside as three shadows filled the room.

The dim light from the fire lit up a snarl on Zinita's face, while Runeo and another bruya she barely recognized pushed in behind her.

Lili was awake now. Her eyes narrowed, but she gave the three guests a tight smile. "I know I cook an excellent breakfast, but—"

"Where's the spy?" Zinita asked.

"Spy? I don't believe we know any spies," Khuna said, still leaning near the doorway. Quenti could see the club behind her partner, her hand inches from the handle as she spoke.

"Where's Alara?" Runeo said, threateningly.

"It's the middle of the Sol-forsaken night," Lili said, "so my guess is she's sleeping." Though her words were innocent enough, Lili had a fire in her eyes that Quenti had not seen before. She looked at Runeo as she spoke, and surprisingly enough, he had the decency to look ashamed.

Zinita, on the other hand, exhibited no shame as she pushed past Lili and Quenti, gripping the handle of the door to the bedroom, trying to shove it open.

"Why is it locked?" she growled.

"She was afraid of being kidnapped in the middle of the night," Lili said. "Apparently for good reason."

Zinita growled and jammed her shoulder against the wooden door. It creaked against her weight, but didn't budge. Quenti held her breath as Zinita took a step back before slamming the door again. It responded with a crack. Two more hits and the door splintered along the edge and swung open.

She and the other bruya both rushed into the room as Runeo stood back, apparently just watching the scene play out with the rest of them.

"She isn't here," Zinita said. Her eyes were wild, face flushed with anger. "The room's empty."

"There are some freshly snapped branches just outside the window," the other bruya said.

Runeo's eyebrow shot up. "She climbed down to the ground?" There was a hint of amusement in his voice. "Maybe she's braver than I thought."

"This one probably helped the bitch escape," Zinita sneered and stepped toward her.

"Quenti"—Lili calmly stepped between the two—"has been with Khuna and me all evening, so I'm not sure what you're implying."

The angry bruya glared at Lili, eyes narrow and unblinking, but she didn't move toward Quenti again.

"It doesn't matter," Zinita finally said. "We'll track her either way."

Runeo shoved Khuna against the wall and Quenti stepped forward without thinking, eyes automatically scanning the room for some sort of weapon. Lili stopped her with a gentle tug on the arm.

"Hear this," Runeo said, his voice rough and low. "If we find her, we will make sure she pays for Puka's life with her own. Don't think she won't." He snarled something else under his breath before shoving her away. Khuna hit the wall behind her with a thud.

"Come on," he continued. "She'll have landed somewhere under the house. We'll start there. If we're lucky, she's already a stain of blood on the forest floor." With that, Runeo stormed out, leaving Zinita and the other bruya to follow.

"That Sol-forsaken piece of…" Lili started.

Quenti winced at the stream of colorful expletives that flew from Lili's mouth. Her heart beat hard and fast in her chest and as she caught her breath. It took her a moment to realize what Khuna was doing.

She had slipped into her trousers and tunic and was buckling her sandals. Her club sat strapped to her waist, and she set about grabbing a set of bolas from the wall. "I'm borrowing these, Lili."

"You're…" Lili started in confusion.

"I have to find Micos. Runeo wants us to follow them. I don't think he trusts Zinita's judgement at this point either."

"He—when—" Quenti stuttered. "Is he a mind-talker, because none of what I just saw indicated any of that."

Khuna gave a half smile. "No need to be a mind-talker when you can just whisper. He said as much when he had me shoved against the wall." Khuna looked around the room and down at her belt. Apparently satisfied, she turned to leave. Quenti felt a small jolt of panic. Should she follow? This was her fault, in the end.

"I'm coming too," she said.

"Like Sol you are," Khuna said without hesitation.

"This is my fault. You shouldn't go alone."

Khuna moved back to her, resting a hand on her waist. "I love you. You are amazing. But you're *not* a fighter. We need to move quickly out there."

"And, what, I'll slow you down?"

"I didn't say that."

Quenti's jaw clenched. Now wasn't the time to be offended. Khuna meant well, but could be overly blunt. "I should still—"

"Please," Khuna's voice was pleading down. "Stay here and stay safe. Tell Quil'la what's happened at sunrise. That's how you can help. Either Alara will have had enough of a head start to get away, or—well, it's best Quil'la knows what's happening."

Quenti and Lili both nodded silently and watched Khuna slip from the house. Quenti's chest ached. She'd never felt more useless in her life.

"I think it's time for more cafi," Lili said. Her voice was tight, and she gave Quenti a smile that felt more like a grimace.

"How did I let this happen?" Quenti said. She hadn't moved. She was afraid her legs wouldn't hold her if she tried. "This is all my fault, isn't it?"

"Maybe it started that way, but you're not alone in this one anymore," Lili said softly. "Now sit and share some cafi and guilt with me."

CHAPTER 31

ALARA

Alara pressed herself against the trunk of the tree, wondering if its boughs were hiding her completely. She placed a hand on the actually sharp dagger at her waist and peered out between the branches. The light of the sun, fully risen, blinded her for a second before she could make out what she was seeing. A small group of councilguards trudged through the forest a few yards away.

Alara's heart leaped, and she was on her feet, the aches and the exhaustion forgotten. It had been a while since anything had gone right.

"Thank El'dyo!" she called out, scrambling from her hiding spot. Before she could say anything else, a set of spears was pointed at her heart, a look of contempt passing across the eyes of the lead guard.

Alara stepped back instinctively and put her hands up in front of her. "Sorry to surprise you. I was just excited to see councilguards out here. I'm Alara Ayar."

The spears didn't twitch and their sneers didn't falter.

"What the hell are you playing at, you dirty bruya?"

Alara's eyes went wide for a second. "I…" She looked down at the dirty tunic and shawl she was wearing and realized the mistake. "Right, my clothes. I stole them. I'm the magite who went missing. Alara Ayar." She looked around at the unfamiliar faces that had moved to surround her. These were likely scouts that guarded the borderlands—no one she would have grown up around. "Alara Ayar. Senye Linda Emaru would be looking for me."

One councilguard stepped forward, his sneer twisting in amusement. "You don't look like a magite to me."

"I just escaped from a bruya camp."

"And you think we'll believe you just escaped the bruyas without a scratch on you?"

"Sounds like a spy," one man said.

"Or a trap," another suggested, eyes narrowed, surveying the surrounding woods.

"Well, what are you then, girl? A spy or a trap?" The sneering man stepped forward, and it took all of her strength and stubbornness to stand her ground. He was close enough she could see a thin silver scar that crossed his forehead and into his left eyebrow, splitting it in two.

Alara squared her shoulders. "Neither. I told you, I am the missing magite, Alara Ayar, and I demand you take me back to the Haven."

"She demands," one of the men jeered behind her.

The man leaned closer to her and brushed a strand of hair from her face, his breath bitter and warm. "No one's going to buy that excuse about stealing bruya clothes. Perhaps if we removed them, we'd have a more objective… look."

She paled and stepped back, stomach twisting. There was a

smattering of laughter around her, and she felt dread crawling up her spine. This was not what she had expected.

Suddenly, she remembered the gold cuff that circled her wrist. She moved to pull back her sleeve, but the fast movement caused the surrounding guards to step forward, their spears almost touching her now.

She raised her hands again. "Hey, morons! I'm just trying to show you—"

Before she could finish, the guard behind her grabbed her arms. The one in front of her moved closer, pressing against her. Without a second thought, she brought her knee up, hitting him between his legs. He gave a groan and folded over. The man holding her arms jerked slightly in surprise, but his grip didn't loosen.

"I told you—" Before she could finish her statement, a whistle broke through the woods and an arrow grazed the side of her face, painting her cheek with the blood of the councilguard who had been holding her. She turned to see the rest of the arrow sprouting from his shoulder as he yelled out in pain, his hands finally loosening around her wrists. She twisted, a little off balance, and saw bruyas darting out of the woods behind them, more arrows flying.

"It's a trap!" cried one councilguard.

Without thinking, she dropped to the ground and rolled to the right, dodging feet as the guards focused their attention on the new arrivals. The small clearing broke into chaos as bruyas reached guards. The sound of spears meeting clubs and flesh rang in the trees.

Alara grabbed the blade from her waist and scrambled to her feet, trying to get her bearings as to what was happening. It took her only a few seconds to recognize Zinita and Runeo among the bruyas.

Her stomach dropped, and she readied her blade to attack. Who did she fight? Perhaps if she killed a bruya, it would prove whose side she was on.

Without another thought, she lunged toward Zinita, and another flash of color and movement caught her eye. Khuna and Micos were running out of the woods now, hands raised to attack the guards. She hesitated and stumbled back, her dagger clutched in her hand as the two groups clashed in front of her.

The decision was made for her as a snarling councilguard rushed forward, spear thrust out in front of him. She side-stepped his attack as he lumbered past her, too big to be agile. With a spin, she jabbed the blade into his side, just below the leather armor he wore. Seemingly unperturbed by the wound, he twisted around, holding out his hand as if readying a magia attack. Alara held up her own hands in anticipation when a spray of blood splattered across her face, an arrow jutting out of the soldier's throat.

Alara looked up, making eye contact with Runeo before he engaged with another nearby guard.

She grabbed the fallen enemy's spear, stumbling away from the center of the conflict. She felt right at home almost instantly, the familiar material smooth in her hands. It was the first time she'd felt empowered in what felt like years. Had it only been weeks?

She spun around, ready to join the fray, though unsure how she'd feel contributing to either side. Regardless, a cursory glance at the battlefield was all she needed to realize the bruyas were winning, likely because the councilguards had underestimated their threat. It was the type of mindset that Senye Emaru would not have allowed, and one that would be their deaths.

She shuddered. This wasn't what she wanted. A bruya side-stepped a guard before thrusting his dagger in the man's neck, twisting it as the councilguard fell. Soon, only one soldier remained, fighting in desperation as the bruyas circled in on him.

Her stomach knotted. As much as she hated it, this was her chance to leave. She turned and darted away, making it only a few hundred yards before she heard the snapping of branches behind her. She spun around, stolen spear thrust in front of her, eyes dark.

In front of her, Runeo stood, arrow raised and bowstring taut. "Drop your spear."

"So you can kill me easier?" Alara said. "I think not."

"I could kill you either way."

"Please, I just want to go home," Alara said, the desperation and exhaustion leaking into her voice.

"The councilguards didn't look agreeable to that."

"It was these stupid clothes. I shouldn't have been wearing them."

"Did you plan on approaching them naked?"

Alara's face flushed. "No! I… you know what I mean!"

"I should have let them kill you," Runeo said, though Alara thought she detected a hint of sarcasm.

"Why did you save me?"

"Maybe I just wanted the satisfaction of killing you myself."

Alara tightened her grip on her spear. "Don't think I'm going to make it easy."

Runeo smiled at this, and she felt an unexpected rush of anger. He may have been joking, but she hated anyone who gave her that patronizing look.

"I'd love to see you try," Runeo said. "What was it that Quenti called you? A bruyita?"

"It doesn't mean I don't know how to use a spear," she practically snarled.

His eyes narrowed, and his muscles pulled tight, the

bowstring steady as his aim settled on her. She took a slow, deep breath, her fingers running along the wood grain of her spear. The familiar calm of battle washed through her.

A sharp cry broke the silence, and they both froze, their eyes swiveling back toward the clearing where they had left the others.

A thunderous din of fighting rose in the air, louder this time. Runeo turned, running toward the sound, and after a moment's hesitation, she followed.

As they neared, the cries of councilguards grew louder. She reached Runeo, who had paused some yards from the scene, hidden behind a tree. The small clearing was now teeming with over two dozen councilguards. Her hand flew to her mouth as she saw the crumpled body of one bruya on the ground. She grabbed Runeo roughly by the shoulder as he tried to step forward. It was suicide to go out there, now.

They scuffled for a second as he tried to push past her, but then a voice stopped them both cold.

"Why don't you just kill us?" Micos's voice was loud, and she found him. He leaned against a large tree, his face red with anger. A trickle of blood ran down the side of his face and his arms stretched tight behind his back, presumably with ropes. Another bruya slumped next to him, her chest moving in and out slightly. She let out a sigh of relief to see Khuna's wild hair, but her smile turned into a frown when she recognized Zinita as the third bruya bound on the ground, eyes seething with hatred.

"Shut up, filthy bruya." One of the councilguard's boots made contact with Micos's side, and she flinched. Beside her, Runeo's body went rigid.

"We should head back," one guard said.

"What are we going to do with that one?" A female guard motioned at Khuna, who was still slumped over. Alara saw with alarm that there was blood matting her hair on one side.

"If she can't walk, kill her."

Micos leaned over Khuna and spoke in her ear. She cracked one eye open, wincing at the light, but nodded. Micos stood awkwardly and helped her stand. She swayed momentarily before gaining her balance.

Alara's stomach twisted. A small voice in her head told her to step forward. These councilguards were likely returning to the Haven. Returning home. Even if they didn't believe her until she got back, Emaru would clear things up. But she couldn't seem to get her body to move. The feeling of the other councilguard's fingers on her face was seared into her mind. But this was her chance to reclaim her life. To return *home*.

Before she could get her legs to function, the guards were leaving, their new captives stumbling after them. As they departed, a flash of gold caught the sunlight. Cuffs were wrapped around their wrists beneath their restraints. She traced along her own cuff as her stomach tightened.

When they were gone, Runeo turned on her, his eyes wild and teeth bared. She stepped back under his glare, but his hands gripped her shoulders, fingers hard as they dug into her skin.

"You," he said. "This is your fault, you Sol-forsaken, stupid—"

Alara lunged her head forward despite herself. Runeo's head snapped back as her forehead crushed his nose. His fingers on her shoulders loosened, though she regretted the instinctive move almost as quickly.

"You were hurting me," Alara said as Runeo recoiled back, hand on his head, though he did not try to grab her again.

"I'm hurting you?" he said through gritted teeth. "If my brother dies because of you, I'll show you what pain is."

Her heart skittered, not at the threat, but at the thought of Micos dying because of her. Tears welled in his eyes, and she thought back to the look of anger and terror on Micos's face as they dragged him away, a lump of guilt settling in her stomach.

"I'm sorry," she said, bringing her hand to her own head. With her adrenaline waning, the pain of her assault on his face was settling in.

He snarled and marched over to the clearing. Alara followed, seeing him kneel over the fallen bruya and draw a small sun on his forehead, using blood from the wound before closing his eyes. She stood by as he whispered something beneath his breath. A prayer, she assumed.

"We're going back to Arbol." His voice was cold and distant.

She bit her lip and looked in the direction where the council-guards had gone and then back at Runeo, where he knelt beside the body of another bruya she only vaguely recognized. None of this was happening the way she had wanted.

She still had a chance. She could take out Runeo and run back. Run home. Instead, she found herself nodding. "Okay."

CHAPTER 32

ALARA

Much to Alara's annoyance, Runeo insisted on tying her up before they set off.

"Believe it or not, I don't trust you."

"I'm not going to run," she snapped as he jerked her shoulders again, tying the knot tighter.

"And the last time you said that, a bruya got killed and three more got captured." His voice cracked. "Three who very well may be dead soon."

"We don't kill bruyas."

"Tell that to Cava," he said, motioning to the dead bruya.

And then it hit again. The guilt. She said nothing as he pushed her forward, rope tied off. She could only watch him as he kneeled down again, gently lifting Cava's body from the ground.

They walked in silence for over an hour. Her shoulders ached, but she didn't complain as Runeo trudged behind her at a steady gait, holding Cava aloft.

After what felt like an eternity, she broke the silence, her voice barely above a whisper. "I've never seen the councilguards act like that."

"I've never seen them act any different."

"The councilguards are supposed to protect… us…" She cleared her throat. "To protect the people of Sombria."

"To protect them from who? The big bad bruyas?" Runeo's voice was icy. "All we want is to be left alone. To be free from the Council's rule. Everything we do is for self-preservation. And yet, *your* people keep hunting us."

She shook her head again, trying to clear the fog of confusion from her brain. "Not hunting. Saving. We're trained not to kill. I've been on several missions, and that's the one thing that's drilled into us from day one."

"You said you're a magite, right?" Runeo said. "That makes you a mage-in-training, right? How many of those missions were supervised?"

Alara said nothing.

"You really are a sheltered flower."

"If the Council knew how those councilguards had been acting, they would have been demoted immediately," Alara said, the image of Emaru's steeled expression in her mind. "In fact, when I get home, I'll make sure of that."

Runeo scoffed. "Well, this is the reality that we live in out here. Welcome to the real world, magite."

Only he could make that last word sound like an insult.

Hours later, they made it back to Arbol. Runeo's face had lost some color by the time they made it to the lift, and as he handed Cava's body to another bruya, she noticed a growing stain of blood that marred his stomach. He shook her off when she tried to note it, pulling away from her touch. When the lift reached the top of the canopy, he stepped forward, grabbing her by the shoulder and dragging her through the city at a quick pace. As they crossed bridges, making their way toward the main chamber, she felt a strange sense of déjà vu.

This time, she recognized the young boy who sat outside the main hall ducking inside without a word upon seeing them approach. She felt a twinge of dread when they entered, seeing Quil'la and the two older male bruyas waiting in the chamber. A handful of others sat scattered around the room on small cushions.

She stood in silence, head down, as Runeo explained what had happened. Partway through the debrief, Quenti and Lili rushed in, a small group of bruyas in tow. In the back, Khuna's parents pushed through the small crowd and stood next to Quenti. The look in their eyes made her stomach twist and throat burn. Clearly, news of what had happened was already spreading. Alara watched Quenti in the corner, fighting the urge to plant her gaze to the ground. The girl's face was gray as Runeo described Khuna's capture, her shoulders shaking with every word. Beside her, Khuna's parents held tightly to each other.

"Who helped you escape?" A silence followed, and Alara realized Quil'la was looking at her, lips tight.

She hesitated, resisting the urge to look over at Quenti and Lili. "No one."

Quil'la's lip twitched at this answer, but she didn't argue. "And why did you run?"

She raised her chin, meeting her eye. "There were rumors of a plan to kill me. I feared for my safety."

Quil'la's eyes narrowed. "And I should believe this why?"

"I—"

"It's true," Runeo said beside her. "Zinita spoke of killing her in retaliation for Puka's death."

"Why did no one tell me?"

It was Runeo's turn to look uncomfortable. "I was hoping to convince her otherwise before anything happened. I didn't want… I didn't want another Utu."

Quil'la's face softened at his words, though Alara didn't follow.

"I'm sorry both of you had so little faith in my ability to rule." She paused. "Perhaps your actions were justified, but now I must explain to my people why their sons and daughters are dead or missing."

Alara's eyes burned, but she kept her chin high. "I am deeply sorry for Cava's death." Someone behind her let out a soft sob and her eyes darted down as she tried to push back her own tears. "But they will absorb the captured bruyas into the school. They won't kill them."

"Few bruyas that go into the Haven make it out. And none come out the same." Quil'la's voice was matter-of-fact.

Another sharp sob. Khuna's mother folded into her husband's chest, her shoulder shaking.

Despite her own trembling, Quenti reached out and placed a comforting hand on her back. The display of overt affection made Alara swallow thickly.

"Quenti and I made it out," she said.

"Sure, Quenti made it out," Quil'la said. "Quenti, who was a new and trusted magite. Who they shepherded into the school after discovering her abilities. It is the so-called 'savage bruyas' the Council fears."

"Then they'll need a little help." Her voice was growing in confidence and she squared her shoulders, the rope around her wrists pulling tight. "What about the underground network?"

Alara said, remembering an earlier exchange between Khuna and Quenti. "The one you worked with to help smuggle Quenti out."

"We don't risk the lives of many to save the lives of a few. Smuggling one person out is a far cry from the infiltration you speak of."

"We need to try," she insisted.

"Out of the question. We survive because we play it safe. Going into the Haven is a suicide mission, and not just for those involved, but for everyone here," Quil'la said with finality.

"It'd be suicide if you didn't have us," Quenti said. Alara's attention snapped to her. Her eyes were red rimmed and puffy, but her face was set in grim determination. "Alara and I both know the tunnels. Okay, well, Alara does. I know them a bit. Sort of. But she knows them better than some Councilmembers, I'd say. And I know the tunnel out."

"You would get caught."

Alara bit her lip and took a deep breath. "I'd be able to warn of any nearby mages."

Quil'la's eyes darted back to Alara and her eyebrows arched. "You're a mind-stalker. A strong one."

It was a statement and not a question, but Alara nodded anyway. She felt Runeo stiffen beside her.

"And do you and Quenti plan to storm the Haven alone?"

She didn't know what to say to this. The idea sounded ridiculous, despite how confident she had been just a moment before.

"Well, we—"

"Will have help." Lili's voice was firm as she stepped forward.

"Quil'la, you can't be considering this," Runeo said. "I will not place Micos's life in the hands of this fuegen who refuses to light a fire."

"Are you volunteering?" Quil'la raised an eyebrow at Runeo, and his face reddened. "You are considering it."

"For the sake of those lost, yes."

He looked between Alara and Quil'la, debating with himself. Alara glimpsed pain in his eyes, the same pain as when he watched get Micos dragged away.

Finally, he spoke. "Fine."

Quil'la's lips twitched in surprise, almost imperceptibly.

"Well then," Quil'la said with a nod, "Untie your new partner."

Runeo scowled, but he tugged at the ropes around her wrists and they dropped away.

She gave a small shudder as she rubbed her shoulders, trying to bring feeling back to her numb limbs. She glanced up at Runeo, but he was scowling, taking care to not make eye contact.

The chamber erupted in conversation, and she even noticed the other elders whispering in Quil'la's ear with what she was sure wasn't praise.

Quil'la held up her hand, and to her surprise, silence followed.

"The four of you have my permission to retrieve those lost, but know that this is not an official mission. Arbol will *not* interfere if anything happens. We will not jeopardize the safety of our people. You do this on your own volition."

"Then why let them go to begin with?" the older man next to Quil'la said, though she silenced him with a swift glare.

Quil'la turned back to the small group that had gathered at the center of the chamber. "Do you accept these terms? Should you return with the Council nipping at your heels, we will not welcome you into the city. Is that understood?"

Alara bit her lip, but nodded. Runeo gave a stiff nod, and Lili and Quenti's heads bobbed in unison.

Quil'la gave a small sigh. "So be it. Good luck, and Sol keep you."

CHAPTER 33

ALARA

That same evening, they camped along the river, some miles north of where the councilguards had fought the bruyas. They passed by the familiar clearing, the smell of blood heavy and metallic in the air. The group walked in silence, skimming the outside of the clearing and averting their eyes.

Some wild animals had already claimed the councilguards as a meal. Alara's stomach twisted, and a wave of nausea crashed over her. Then she remembered the one councilguard's cruel face and felt a small pang of satisfaction. She hadn't seen him die after he had been shot, but she was sure that he laid among the dead.

Quenti walked beside her and Alara felt her stumble as they passed the clearing. Her thoughts were undoubtedly on Khuna. She swallowed a click in her throat and reached for Quenti's hand, giving it a tight squeeze.

They had left only a few hours after their meeting with

Quil'la. Plans still half-formed, they had packed food and weapons, and Lili and Runeo said their goodbyes. Alara had looked up at Arbol as they descended on the lift and wondered if this would be the last time she saw it, something that wasn't relief twisted in her gut. Far from the feeling she'd expected. But she still longed for home, though the warmth that the Haven represented in her mind had gone cold.

"What's Lili doing?" Quenti asked Runeo, setting down the fish she caught for supper.

Runeo glanced over at Lili, who sat cross-legged at the edge of camp, face toward the sky.

"Saying a prayer for the dead. Councilguard or no, she wants their spirits to make it to the Dead Plains."

Quenti nodded at this, but Alara just gave a silent shudder. How would the councilguards feel about being sent to somewhere as ominous sounding and blasphemous as the Dead Plains?

"Have some tea." Quenti took a mug from Runeo and shoved it into Alara's hands. "It'll warm you up."

"I'm not cold," Alara said.

"I meant metaphorically. You look pale."

She didn't argue. "Did you know councilguards acted like that?"

Quenti gave a small shrug. "I always heard the rumors. Mama taught me to be very careful if I ever wandered outside the village. They don't act like that within the borders usually, but there are always a few exceptions." Quenti's eyebrows raised at what must have been her pinched face. "There are good councilguards, I'm sure. Your friend back at the Haven seemed nice."

Beside them, Runeo grunted but didn't shift his attention from the fish he was cooking.

She took some comfort in Quenti's words and pictured Ardo's

face in her mind, his smile crooked and bright. There were good people in the councilguards. No matter how hard the Council tried, there would always be bad apples. But still… to see it in practice…

If anything, she could report back to Emaru about what she saw. Clearly, the councilguards on the borderlands needed to be reprimanded and retrained. Perhaps a different approach could assuage some of the violence between the mages and bruyas.

"There were just so many pointless deaths." Alara's hand had unconsciously wrapped around the cuff on her wrist.

Quenti bit her lip, looking at the cuff. "It was terrible what happened to your family," she said. "But I don't know why you let it rule your life."

Alara's face reddened, and Runeo stiffened at Quenti's words. "It's not that simple."

"I dunno what happened, but it seems to me like you're still punishing yourself for something a child did in a moment of fear." Quenti's words were soft, her eyes warm.

"It's not about punishing myself. It's about protecting others."

"By wearing a cuff that keeps your magia bound and gagged?"

"I wear it because I can't control my magia without them. Because I don't know if I trust myself to learn without hurting others again."

"But imagine," Lili said, walking up to the fire, her hazel eyes almost glowing in the orange light, "what you could have done to protect yourself without all the bloodshed had you allowed yourself to use your powers freely."

"It's easy for you to say. You're a healer, a tierren. Your powers are literally about giving life." As she finished, she thought back to that moment she saw Micos using his abilities to heal Zinita's wound. He was so methodical and precise with his magia. Alara was many things, but methodical or precise weren't words anyone would ever use to describe her.

"I spent most of my childhood wishing I had something closer to what you have," Lili said, picking at one of the fish on the fire before Runeo slapped her hand away. "Sometimes we don't get what we want."

"Hands off," Runeo snapped.

Lili rolled her eyes and sat back on her heels. "Anyway, your powers can bring more than just destruction. If you learned control, you could stop fire from spreading, douse it even."

"It's not that easy," Alara said.

Runeo picked up the fish from the fire and distributed them to the others. He practically dropped the last fish in her lap. "Nothing in life is easy. But you can't expect to get anywhere hiding from your problems."

"That's ironic, coming from an Arboreli. All your people do is hide."

"Which is it, then?" Runeo said. "Do we hide all the time, or do we murder villagers on a whim?"

Alara glared at him through the flames that stood between them. They reacted to her anger, a wisp inching toward him before snapping back to the embers.

"We don't murder for fun, you know. We do what we need to survive and protect our own. We fight when we need to and hide when we can."

The flames danced sharply again as she opened her mouth to respond, but Lili laid a soft hand on hers.

"I think perhaps we should rest for the night," Lili said, softly

Runeo grunted, shoving another bite of fish in his mouth, but didn't protest. Alara closed her own mouth and took a calming breath, trying to disconnect herself from the fire. It took a few seconds to untwine the threads of magia that had knotted into the flames.

The next morning she awoke to the faint gray light of dawn filtering through the trees. The forest was thinner here near the river, and the sky was visible between the branches. The second thing she noticed was Runeo's grim face looking down at her from above, eyes sharp and lips thin. The third was the spear pointed at her head.

Alara's eyes flew wide open, and she jerked.

"Don't move," he bit out. The spear came soaring down, catching the dirt just behind her left ear.

She turned slowly and jumped back at the sight of the large snake skewered on his weapon, inches from where her head had just been.

"Breakfast?" he said, grinning at the green tinge of her face as the snake convulsed.

"No thank you," she said. She tilted her head and looked at him, eyebrows furrowed. "You keep saving me."

He said nothing, instead lopping off the head of the dead snake with his dagger.

"Does this mean you no longer want me dead?"

"I haven't quite decided."

The corner of her mouth twitched slightly up. *Was that a joke?*

"Thank you," he said, not looking at her, but examining the snake with some care, "for volunteering to help Micos."

All humor dropped from her expression. "It's my fault he got captured. He didn't deserve that."

"You could have left with the councilguards," Runeo said,

finally looking at her. His dark eyes seemed to bore into her soul, and she looked away quickly.

"I just…" She stopped. She wasn't completely sure herself why she hadn't stepped out that morning and turned herself over. "I'm still planning on going back. Once we get Micos and Khuna, I'll help you all escape. I still end up back home, which is all I've ever wanted. But Micos and Khuna getting caught was my fault."

Runeo nodded and turned.

"Had you been the one kidnapped," Alara said. "I might have just walked away."

Runeo's lips thinned to a flat line on his face. Was that a smile? Or an almost-smile?

"I think we all would have." Lili was beside her, Quenti some steps behind, holding, to Alara's great disappointment, *more fish*.

"Breakfast?" Quenti said grinning.

Runeo and Alara both groaned, and Lili let out a sharp laugh. "My feelings exactly."

They made it to the edge of Sombria two days later, climbing to the top of the cliff Alara and Quenti had jumped off of what seemed like a century ago. Two short days it took them to make it here, which really drove home just how slow and meandering their pace had been on the way to Arbol.

Now they walked fast and long, taking advantage of every moment of daylight. Alara only complained in her head about the aches in her feet, but she knew from the look of cold determination that stayed on Runeo's face that she shouldn't vocalize it.

"If we take the roads, we'll get there at least two days sooner." Runeo argued with a frustrated Lili.

"If we get caught on the roads—which we most definitely will—we'll never get there at all," Lili said. "Or we'll get there in shackles."

The group had stalled their progress in order to indulge in this debate, which had been going on for over ten minutes now, and neither side appeared ready to budge. Alara knew Lili was speaking logically. They had been lucky to not run into any councilguards so far on the trip, in part thanks to her own abilities. But even her mind-stalking magia wouldn't save them from the mass of folks who would likely be on the main roads, blameless and mage alike. Plus, as she had learned in her brief encounter with the councilguards, their clothing wasn't something the average soldier would overlook.

"Catch," Quenti said, tossing her a flurry of brown cloth.

It smacked her in the face before she could even move. "What?" It was a simple brown tunic and black skirt. Village clothes. "Where did you get these?"

Lili and Runeo had stopped fighting and had turned their attention to Quenti.

"We're near Attalea. I may have snuck into a yard and helped relieve a family of some clothes."

"Relieved them when?" Runeo said, eyes wide.

"Just now," Quenti said, a lopsided smirk on her face. "Thanks for keeping yourselves busy while I was gone, by the way."

Runeo glared at her.

"I wasn't seen," Quenti said, answering the unasked question. "There was a house on the edge of town and things are quiet. They were hanging in the yard. This solves the problem of sneaking up the road, doesn't it? It's what you wanted." She handed a black dress to Lili, who frowned at the dour material.

"One problem," Quenti continued. "I couldn't find pants for you."

Runeo's eyes darkened slightly and his lip twitched. "So this solves nothing. What, we steal *more* clothes, then?"

"We'll have to wait until nightfall, if we don't want to be seen," Quenti said. "All the other houses are farther in. I didn't see any easy clothesline targets."

Runeo shook his head. "I'm not waiting. We need to keep going now."

"Well, we can't very well just wander into the town midday and kindly ask for a pair of trousers, can we?" Quenti snapped.

"Why not?" Alara said, her smile wide.

Quenti and Runeo stopped arguing and looked at Alara like she had gone crazy. Which, she realized, she might just have.

"I mean, Runeo can't wander into town, but we could," Alara said, motioning to Lili and Quenti, and the clothes in their hands. "You said it seemed empty. What are the chances it's a market day? Otherwise, at this time of day, there would have been people working in their yards."

"You want us to walk into the market and steal pants?" Lili said, feet shifting uncomfortably.

Alara didn't speak for a moment, searching her bag before letting the tension from her shoulders drop. She pulled out the small leather pouch. "Not steal, buy." Carefully, she opened it and let the bronze coins fall into her other hand.

No one spoke. Finally, Runeo stepped forward, eyes studying the coins with trepidation. "It seems risky revealing ourselves, even in disguise."

"No more risky than trying to steal clothes in daylight or wandering down the road in bruya clothes," she replied.

"She has a point," Lili said, looking between them.

"I'd be recognized in Attalea," Quenti said. "And I don't

know what the villagers have been told about me. I couldn't do it. And they'd recognize you for sure, Alara."

"I shouldn't go alone," Lili whispered.

Alara shook her head. "I've only passed through the village a handful of times and never even interacted with anyone. Lili and I can go. We can meet you both back here."

"I don't like this," Runeo said.

"I don't think we have a choice," Quenti noted. "Unless you want to waste another half-hour arguing."

Chapter 34

Alara

It had been many years since Alara had dressed in plain village clothes, but it only took her a few seconds to loathe the impractical fashion. The skirt was long, having no slits to allow for movement in combat. It was wide, but fell to her ankles, making her feel as though she would trip at any moment.

Lili, on the other hand, wore a dress that fell to her knees, flaring with the heavy material beneath the top skirt. It fit her well, but the black wool fabric of the dress looked stark on her compared to her usually bright clothing choices. She wore a shawl to cover the tattoo on her arm and had brushed her hair to fall across the side of her face. Much to Alara's surprise, Lili looked like a presentable village woman. Her straight, bright hair somehow looked perfectly serviceable after days hiking through the woods.

She ran a hand through her own tangled hair, trying to make it lie flat. When that didn't work, she let Lili twist it into a plait that hid the dirt and knots they couldn't get out.

They stuffed their old clothes into sacks and handed them to Runeo and Quenti.

"So, if anyone asks where you're from?" Quenti quizzed Alara for a third time.

"Hurazon. We're Elena Ortiz's daughter, Tera…"

"…and cousin, Isabela." Lili finished.

"Good. Those two are so antisocial. I doubt anyone in Hurazon has even seen them."

"We'll meet back here with the clothes and head out," Alara said. "We'll need to skirt the village in case someone recognizes Quenti, but then we'll be on the road and in the clear by evening."

Rather than hit the village straight on, Lili and Alara headed toward the western path, planning to enter as travelers from Hurazon would. It wasn't uncommon for people to visit different villages to look for bargains or different materials, and she just hoped that no one would question their knowledge of Hurazon.

She felt Lili's energy shift as they entered. The dirt path turned to stone, and they passed the first few houses that sat on the outskirts. Alara remembered the town square from her trip here with Emaru and the councilguards months ago.

The road wound past a few more houses before it opened wider and into the central plaza. She barely recognized it from when she had been here last. It teemed with people, and stands lined the road, circling the fountain at the center.

Lili tensed as they set foot in the square, bumping by a few villagers as they walked. A small group of children ran by screaming, chasing after a small l'lama that seemed to have escaped from its family. It had a small pack on its back that was slipping off as it bounced along the cobblestones of the square.

Alara turned to find Lili no longer beside her, but instead chasing down the loose livestock. She caught the harness around its neck and laid a calming hand across its head. The animal danced impatiently on its padded feet before calming down. The children stopped their chase and looked up at Lili with awed expressions.

"Thank you, Senye!" The oldest boy, no more than six years old, said with a small bow. He took the harness from Lili's hands, eyes cast downward in respectful reverence.

She gave a nervous smile, patting the l'lama on the head one more time before backing away from the children and making her way back to Alara. She was silent, but her shoulders seemed a little less stiff as they continued on their way.

"Let's find a clothes vendor," Alara said, and Lili nodded.

It didn't take long to find a stall that fit their needs. A pile of cloth sat on the table, tipping precariously, with many pieces embroidered with bright yarn. Of course, there was nothing as gorgeous or intricate as the Arborelis' bright designs, but it was still impressive. The duo ignored the beautiful pieces and picked out a plain pair of black trousers and a tan tunic with a simple black embroidery along the neckline and hem. They only cost three bronze pieces, a bargain compared to what they'd run in Cielo. As she paid the woman, her eyes caught on a set of hooded ponchos, woven from undyed alpaca wool.

"How much for those?" Alara asked.

The woman looked at ponchos. "Four bronze pieces each."

Alara bit her lip. "I'll pay twelve pieces for four of them."

The woman frowned and shook her head. "Too little. Fifteen pieces."

Alara shrugged and backed away, waiting for an extra beat as she turned.

"Okay, okay!" the stall woman conceded. "Thirteen pieces."

She let herself smile before turning back. She counted out the bronze pieces, noting how few she had left after the exchange.

Lili balanced the new clothes in her arms, thanking the woman with an enormous smile.

Before they left the square, Alara bought some roasted corn wrapped in cloth with another bronze piece, unable to resist the smell as they walked by. Having lived off of fish for the past few days, she knew Quenti and Runeo would appreciate the change.

As pleasant as the side quest had been, she felt a weight lift as the sounds of the market faded behind them. She gave Lili a tight smile, relieved that the plan had worked.

"Lara?" a gruff voice called from behind them. It wasn't one Alara recognized, but against her better common sense, she turned at the sound of the nickname. No one had called that her since she was a child.

An older man stood a few paces behind her, his eyes widening. Alara squinted at the vague familiarity of the man. Had she met this man the last time she passed through with Emaru?

She took a step back, blood rushing from her face. "Who are you looking for?"

"Lara. It's Yaime—I'll admit I've aged since we last saw each other." He shook his head and stepped toward her, a hand outstretched. She stopped herself from backing away as he placed a rough palm on her cheek. "Sol, I thought you were dead. Killed in the raid."

"I... don't know you," Alara said. She had gone rigid on contact. "I think you have the wrong girl."

The man's face somehow sagged even lower as he stepped back. "It's been a long time, but I thought you would remember. I helped raise you, child. Taught you how to climb trees"—he looked over at Lili with an air of suspicion—"and I taught you and your mother *other* things."

Alara frowned at the secret she didn't quite understand. She racked her mind trying to remember the man's face, but her memories from before the Haven were smeared and blurry.

"If you were in my village, how did you survive the raid?" Alara asked, eyebrows furrowed.

He shook his head, eyes sad again. "I had left town to visit my nieces in L'lim. I didn't return here until weeks after. The village was in ruins and…" His voice choked off.

"Here?" Alara said, her pulse quickening.

It was his turn to look confused now. "Yes, I returned from my visit."

"I'm from Attalea?"

"It wasn't Attalea at the time."

She felt a warm hand on her arm and faced Lili. What was Lili seeing on her face? Her mind raced back to her studies in the Haven. Attalea was a fairly new town. But could she really…?

"Where did you end up? How did you survive?" The man was moving toward her again, hands reaching out as if to grab on to her.

She stumbled back. "We need to go."

"But—" The man stopped short, his hands grabbing the air in front of him.

"I'm sorry. I don't remember you. I need to go."

With that, she whipped around and started back down the path out of town. She was running, stumbling blindly over the cobblestones, slowing only when the path turned to dirt. She veered off the road and into the trees, slumping onto the root of a tree and letting her head fall against the mossy trunk.

She sat like that for a few minutes, her eyes closed. Her thoughts raced, settling on nothing in particular. Nothing useful anyhow. She said nothing when she felt Lili's presence beside her, the root bending under the weight of the other woman.

Lili placed a finger on her wrist and heartbeat slowed as the adrenaline drained away. She only opened her eyes when she was sure the tears had cleared.

"Are you okay?" Lili's voice was soft.

She nodded, taking a deep breath. "I'm sorry. I don't know why I… reacted so much."

"Thinking about the past can be hard. Confronting things we don't want to remember, even harder."

"I don't know why I don't remember him. I can't even remember what town I was from. How stupid can I be?"

Lili patted Alara's hand. "The trauma of death can warp what we choose to remember. You lost your parents in a violent way. That can take a toll on any child's memory."

She looked at Lili with sharp eyes. "It was bruyas who did it, you know." She had always suspected on some level that her captors had been responsible, though she had never verbalized it. "Are the Arborelis the only bruyas in this region?

"Are you asking what I think you're asking?"

Her lips tightened, but she remained resolute. "Yes."

Lili's face paled at the accusation, but she held Alara's gaze. "I don't know. I don't remember any raids destroying a village in the past decade, but tensions have always been high between our people and yours. And there are always rogue groups—even among us—who choose violence over peace." She broke eye contact and looked out into the woods. "I wish I could promise you it wasn't us, but…"

Alara felt the sharp sting in her eyes again and stood up abruptly. She gave a nod. "No matter. We have a job to do."

Lili smiled weakly, not quite reaching her eyes, but she too nodded and rose, picking up the clothes draped along the root.

"Let's get back to Quenti and Runeo. I'm looking forward to the corn. I can still smell it."

Alara nodded and followed Lili as they walked deeper into the woods, keeping to the wildlife trail they had taken originally.

Quenti and Runeo were waiting, pale-faced and nervous. When they came to the small clearing, he jumped up, eyes darting between them.

"What in Sol's name happened? You both were gone too long!"

"We weren't that long." Lili threw the clothes at him. "Just change and stop whining. We can head out now."

"Are you okay?" Quenti asked her.

"Everything's fine," Lili answered before she could even register the question. "And she was kind enough to buy us ponchos. And corn!"

That last line helped snap her out of her trance, reminding her of the mission at hand. "They have hoods. The ponchos, not the corn. They'll help to hide our faces if we pass by any people that may recognize us." It was cool enough in the mornings and at night that no one would find the hoods suspicious.

Runeo didn't bother to duck behind a tree while he changed, only turning himself away from the others. She averted her eyes, but noted the matching smirks on Quenti and Lili's faces as they watched.

"Ready," he said, turning around.

She absently ran a hand along the ridges of her scar. "We look good, I think. Properly boring. Once we get on the main road, it's only a few days' trek."

He was walking before anyone could respond to her. No one moved to follow him and he made it a few yards away before he whipped around. "What are you waiting for?" he snapped.

She gave him a bright smile before turning the opposite direction. She looked back over her shoulder as she walked. "It's this way."

CHAPTER 35

QUENTI

"We have a problem." Runeo jumped from the tree, landing on the soft earth without so much as a sound. "The area just south of here is swarming with councilguards."

"What, were they guarding the entrance?" Quenti let out an exasperated sigh. Their detour into Attalea had gone well, so it only made sense they'd hit another obstacle this close to their destination.

"I don't think so," he said as he walked past her. "The way they're spread out, it looks like they're just guarding the entire perimeter."

The group had arrived at the outskirts of Cielo the night before. Rather than go with Quenti's instinct of heading directly toward the city, they had circled north of the mountain and camped a few miles from where she guessed the entrance was.

Despite having recently escaped the Haven, she hadn't paid attention to the landscape under the cover of darkness. The most she could give them was a vague approximation—a fact that had left her stomach twisted with guilt for the past two days.

"Which means they might not even know the tunnel is nearby," Quenti said with a small amount of hope.

"Doesn't help us if we can't get past them."

She only gave a grim nod as she followed Runeo back through the thick trees.

They were still walking in sullen silence when they reached the clearing.

Lili and Alara had their supplies laid out on the ground in front of them, Alara counting weapons and Lili repacking the bags.

"Two bows, thirteen bronze-tipped arrows, seven wood arrows, four daggers, and two bolas," Alara said, eyes focused on the ground and still unaware that the others had returned.

"Don't forget the dull letter opener," Quenti chimed in.

Alara looked up at the sound of her voice. "I'll have you know, that dull letter opener has actually done well for me."

Quenti tilted her head at this revelation. The dagger looked incapable of opening a letter, let alone stabbing anyone. "How?"

"It's…biding its time."

"What's the situation?" Lili said, ignoring their side conversation.

"Multiple patrol groups circling just south of us," Runeo answered, attempting to snatch a small piece of dried meat at the top of one of their packs. She smacked his hand without looking up from her task.

"They're guarding the tunnel entrance?" Alara asked.

"I don't think so. They look more like they are just guarding the general area. Looks like they're expecting us."

Quenti swallowed. They had made it this far, but now, Khuna seemed more distant than ever. "There is no reason they would know we're coming," she said. "Who would have told them?"

"No one," Alara said. "This is how they do things. There are many secret entrances into the Haven. By design, no one person knows all of them, but they still need to protect and track everyone who comes in."

"But wait," Quenti said. "When I escaped, I didn't run into anyone on my way out. Was I just lucky?"

"It's possible," Alara said, "there's an uptick in perimeter guards in the days following bruya captures, for fear of retaliation or infiltration."

"For good reason, I guess," Lili said.

"Well, it's a good thing we have you around to enlighten us, magite," Runeo said dryly.

Alara smirked.

"We can take them," Lili said, her eyes sharper than Quenti had ever seen.

Runeo let out a gruff laugh and shook his head. "There are too many to fight. At least with the weapons we have right now."

To that, Lili did not argue. The four of them stared down at the small stash of weapons. Again, her stomach twisted. They had no plan beyond "get in and get out." Maybe Quil'la had been right to doubt them. This was a hopeless mission, borne from the desperation of love. Were the others thinking the same thing? When would they realize this and decide to walk away?

"Lili, do you think you could forage for food around here?" Runeo asked, looking around the clearing. Quenti smiled at that. She had no idea what he was thinking, but it was clear she wasn't the only one surviving on desperate hope.

"I'm a healer, Runeo, not a hunter," Lili said. "You know more about foraging than I do."

He glanced around, looking lost. He spotted a small growth of mushrooms along the trunk of a nearby tree and grabbed a few.

"Are we going to bribe them with mushrooms, or are you hoping they're poisonous?" Alara said.

"We can say we are traders if we're spotted."

Alara looked at him, her eyebrows raised. "That's not going to work. Not even a bit. Traders don't take the back routes and they don't carry one small bag of mushrooms. Or a slew of weapons."

Quenti frowned. "She has a point."

"You think?" Alara said.

"Well, does anyone have a better plan? I don't do stealth."

"We know," they all said in unison.

Alara's eyes lit up. "We still have our magite uniforms."

Quenti frowned. "But we only have two."

"That's all we will need."

Twenty minutes later, Alara and Quenti were standing in their uniforms. The material was wrinkled, and the cuff of Alara's sleeve was torn, but she rolled them up, hiding the hem and showing off her gold cuff.

As smart as this plan was, Quenti didn't like wearing the clothes again, even temporarily.

"Do you think this will actually work?" Runeo scrunched his face.

"I don't know," Alara said. "It's rare to have older recruits, let alone runaway bruyas, but I know it's happened before."

"How many of the councilguards know your face and know you've been missing?"

"Everyone likely knows I'm missing, but few would recognize me by my face alone. Only Emaru's closest guards ever interacted with me. Same with Quenti."

His eyes darkened at Emaru's name, but he said nothing. The topic of Alara's relationship with the Council hadn't been broached since Zinita's revelation, and she didn't think this was the time to debate it further.

"How far are we from the entrance?" Lili asked.

"It's hard to tell," Quenti said with a sigh. "I remember what it looks like, but I wasn't mapping it out as I was running." Twisting guilt. Shame. Hopelessness. Why was she even there if she couldn't help?

No. Stop thinking.

"We just need to walk carefully," Alara said. "I'll try to help us dodge as many of the councilguards as I can. Usually, squads come with at least one mage, so I should be able to track them. But if we run into trouble, remember: no visible weapons. And let me do the talking."

They made their way slowly, Alara rigid in concentration as she used her mind-stalking abilities to track nearby councilguards as they moved through the trees.

Somehow, amid the anxious stew brewing in her gut, Quenti managed to squeeze in a small bit of pride for her friend's growing abilities.

It took a while, but Alara steered them around two small scouting groups. All the while, Quenti scanned the surrounding area dutifully, in hopes of—

"Shh!" Quenti said, bringing the group to a stop. "To the left. I hear water! I think the waterfall I escaped through is this way."

They turned left, Quenti feeling a little lighter. After a few minutes, the roaring of water grew louder and clearer and the trees thinned.

"Hey, you."

Quenti's stomach dropped. The voice was imperious. She saw a small group of councilguards break through the trees some yards away, wearing black tunics and leather armor, spears casually draped over shoulders. They didn't seem to see them as a threat—yet.

Alara squared her shoulders and Quenti ran through their story again in her head.

This plan was going to work. It had to.

"Alara!" the voice from within the group of councilguards was warm and familiar.

"Oh, no," Quenti said under her breath.

This plan was not going to work.

She looked at Alara and read the mix of emotions in the brightness of her eyes and the tightness in her jaw.

Frustration. Mixed in with joy and something more.

"Ardo!"

CHAPTER 36

ALARA

Alara froze, trying to process this new development.

Ardo's tunic under his leather vest was green like the main councilguards—not the black it had been last time she had seen him. He had been demoted. Her heart gave a sharp thump as she recalled the look on his face moments before Quenti pulled her over the cliff.

"How…? When…?" Ardo stumbled over his words, looking back at Alara expectantly.

"I…" Alara's gazed flickered between the young council-guard and the bruyas beside her. Quenti's eyes were wary.

She couldn't forget the reason why they were here. It was bigger than whatever she and Ardo were. Without another thought, she jumped into his arms. She closed her eyes for a stolen second and breathed him in. "It's good to see you! I've missed you so much."

She heard her companions shifting uneasily behind her and continued quickly.

"I missed everyone. It just took so long for us all to escape."

She pushed back from a shocked Ardo, stealing a look over her shoulder at Quenti, whose shoulders relaxed.

"Escape?" he asked, gaze finally finding Quenti, eyes widening with recognition.

"The bruya encampment," Alara said. "It was terrible. Quenti was brainwashed, and they convinced her to run away. But when we got there…" She flung herself into Ardo's arms again.

"They lied to me," Quenti said, the slightly overdramatic quiver in her voice making Alara cringe. "They were savages. They just wanted me to help'em raid the villages because I knew the area."

Out of the corner of her eye, Alara could see the muscles in Runeo's face twitch as he clenched his jaw.

Come on. Keep it together, Runeo.

"We found these two," Alara continued. "They were kidnapped from the outskirt villages years ago and wanted to leave. Just like us. So we made a plan, waited, and escaped." Alara paused for dramatic effect. "I'm so happy to be home."

The last line wasn't a lie, but the words still felt clunky and awkward.

Ardo's eyes were still darting between the four of them, but they settled on Alara.

"I'm… I'm glad you're home, too." He rested a hand on her arm.

She finally felt her body relax. She hadn't realized she had been clenching her jaw just as tightly as Runeo.

One councilguard behind Ardo stepped forward, his brow furrowed in suspicion. "Then tell us why you're coming from the wrong direction. You disappeared in the south."

Quenti smacked Alara on the shoulder with too much enthusiasm. "I told you we went the wrong way back there!" She turned toward the suspicious councilguard. "She insisted she knew better than me."

"Why don't we escort you down to the entrance, so you don't get turned around again?" Ardo said, looking between them warily, battling between his instinct to believe Alara and the seed of suspicion already planted. "Senye Emaru's going to be so happy. She's been going crazy searching for you."

"We just need…" Alara started, unsure of where she was going. "Because… well…" She bit her tongue before the next words slipped from her lips. *We had planned to take the secret passage. The secret passage that no one knows about. Especially you.*

Everyone was focused on her and all she could do was stare at the ground. Even Alara would have admitted this wasn't her greatest moment.

"All right, then," Runeo said, his tone exhausted. With a swipe of his hand, the two unnamed councilguards were blown over and Ardo's spear flew from his hands.

His eyes widened in surprise and his gaze fell on Alara, a flicker of betrayal painted on his face, and she froze. Runeo tossed Quenti the spear as he pulled out his bow. She caught it and twisted its point toward Ardo, his Adam's apple bobbing next to the point.

"Don't hurt him," Alara said, eyes wild.

"I know that, stupid," Quenti said. "But we can't just leave him."

Runeo grumbled, frustration mounting. Before either Quenti or Alara had time to react, he had pushed between them and swung a clenched fist at the councilguard's face.

Blood spurted from Ardo's nose as he stumbled back. Runeo sent another punch into his gut and the guard crumpled. Alara let out a small gasp, one that mixed relief with anxiety.

Runeo then turned his attention to the other two guards, who scrambled to their feet, grabbing for their fallen weapons.

He sent a wave of air whirling toward them. The leaves on the forest floor swirled in a miniature cyclone, but the leftmost guard dodged the attack as the other swung his hand, shooting a blast of air back at Runeo.

It hit him on the chest, hard, and he flew back. The other guard snapped his wrists together, sending a ring of fire from the flint housed under his sleeves. A flaming wall shot up behind them, preventing their escape.

"Now would be a great time to be a fuegen," Runeo said to Alara.

Alara nodded and shut her eyes, grasping for her magia. She managed to snag a thread, but her mind was racing and the power slipped like sand through her fingers. As she tried again, the frantic buzz of anxiety only worsened and she struggled to even feel her magia. Frustration mounted in her. She knew she needed to use her magia, but looking at the uniformed council-guards she had grown up with, she also knew she didn't want to hurt anyone. Could she even control her magia if she *did* bring it out?

"Hey, magite," Quenti said, tossing a spear to her. "Catch."

Alara snatched the weapon out of midair without missing a beat, the faintest of smiles escaping her lips. "Non-lethal," she said. "Got it?"

Quenti frowned despite giving her a nod of affirmation. But Alara still thought she heard the girl mutter something under her breath about a *liability*.

Alara didn't have time to question her. She charged, swinging the butt of the spear toward the fire mage's gut. He dodged her obvious move, and she grinned, spinning around him and stabbing the spear into his right palm. For a moment, her love of battle made her forget who she was fighting against. He let out a cry, pulling his injured hand to his chest.

"I think we're bound to attract a little attention," Lili said, her voice anxious.

"I think we already have," Quenti said, standing on the edge of the clearing, away from the fight. Her dagger was out, but she was holding it wrong.

"Quenti," Alara said, swinging her spear at another guard, "You're going to accidently stab yourself with that!"

Quenti's cheeks pinked slightly and she looked down at the blade in her hand, as if it was to blame. She tucked it back into her belt, and Alara felt the water in the air around her condensing. It formed itself into a small bubble and Quenti threw it in the face of one of the guards. He staggered back, allowing Alara to strike him hard in the side with the butt of her spear, sending him sprawling onto the ground.

He was wheezing heavily, but didn't move to get up immediately. She stepped forward, unsure of her next move. A force hit her from behind. She tumbled to the ground and rolled over to see Ardo holding her down. His nose was dripping blood and his eyes were angry. She noted the stubble on his chin and the lines that seemed new—worn into his forehead as he looked down at her.

Ardo twisted Alara's wrists in his hand and pressed a small dagger against the soft skin of her throat. They froze, the sound of fighting only a muffled presence in the back of her awareness.

"Why…?" His voice was rough, but soft.

"It's not what it looks like," Alara gasped out as his hands clenched hard against her wrists. "You have to understand."

He shook his head. "I can't. Explain it to me."

"She's just trying to help me," Quenti said. "I threatened her if she didn't."

Ardo didn't even look at her as he replied. "Not you. Alara. Explain it to me."

"The councilguards," she said, voice strained. "They captured innocent bruyas. It was my fault."

Ardo's eyebrows furrowed. "You're trying to *save* bruyas? That's our job. You *know* that."

"It's more complicated than that. Please, just let us pass." Alara's hand curled under Ardo's grip. "Please."

The dagger against her throat sagged, and she felt his body shift.

But before he fully committed, Lili came up from behind him and placed a hand on his head. Ardo's body went limp, and he fell sideways.

Alara jumped up, feeling for his pulse. "What did you just do?"

Lili's eyes were wide. "I put him to sleep. I've done it when healing people before—when their pain is too great." She looked down at Ardo, pale. "Though I honestly didn't know if it would work."

Despite the momentary confusion, a look of determination returned to her face, and she turned to the mage that was still struggling to breathe on the ground. She lunged at him, grabbing his injured hand with a look of guilt. As the man cried out, she placed a finger on his temple and let him slip onto the soft dirt, unconscious.

She turned to where Runeo fought, grabbing the bola hanging from her belt, though she didn't throw them immediately. Runeo and the wind mage were moving too fast for her to get a clear shot.

"Quenti, distraction," Lili said.

She nodded, eyes glued to the fight. She closed her eyes and fog thickened around the face of the wind mage. He stumbled at the loss of his sight, but kept his footing. Lili used the moment's distraction to throw her weapon. It hit the wind mage's spear and jarred it out of his hands. In the second it took him to turn, Lili had already stepped behind him and placed her hand on his head.

His eyes went wide for an instant before he fell hard to the ground.

"How long will they be out?" Runeo said, his breath heavy.

"Long enough," Lili said. "I hope."

"We can tie them up and try to hide them, but someone's bound to find them, eventually." Quenti held a rope she had pulled from her bag.

Runeo took it and went to work. He tied the wind mage's hands, and Alara pushed him out of the way to tie Ardo's wrists herself, though Runeo made no secret about making sure the job she did was sufficient. She bit her lip when she finished and touched his cheek, holding it there for a moment. He was breathing slowly and Alara sent out a silent prayer that he somehow wouldn't remember the last ten minutes when he woke up. Her stomach clenched as she stepped back. How was she going to explain this all when she met with Emaru?

Runeo worked quickly, dragging the two guards' bodies over to a tree with low branches. Quenti and Alara dragged the unconscious fire mage to an area of high underbrush and tried their best to hide him among the leaves. Alara positioned the man with care, ripping a piece of her tunic to bind his still bleeding hand.

"Why didn't you just betray us?" Quenti said. "You were home."

"What?" Alara responded. "You thought I would do that?"

She shrugged. "I betrayed you for Khuna."

"That's not the same. I promised to get Khuna and Micos back safely. I won't go back on that."

Runeo walked over and they both fell silent. He saw Alara bent over the man and sneered. "Another friend of yours?"

"No. Just another human," she said, pulling the flint cuff and ring from the incapacitated fire mage's wrists. "Thank you for holding back, by the way." Her tone was oddly sincere. "I saw you had openings where you could have gone for a kill, but didn't."

"I'm no monster," Runeo said with a sneer as he walked away.

She looked to Quenti and they shared a smile. She let the relief of no lives being lost on either side settle into her chest.

"Where to now?" Lili asked.

Quenti took a moment to take a deep breath before she oriented herself. "Toward the river."

Alara led the group, letting her powers guide them as best she could. Her nerves were frayed and her magia kept slipping from her control, but the mind-stalking was easy enough to push through. The sound of the river grew louder and louder until it drowned out the breeze coursing through the forest trees. They broke through the trees and saw the small waterfall crashing down from a ridge along the back of the mountain Cielo was housed within. The waterfall was only a few yards high, but the pool was deep and the current fast as it flowed into the river they stood alongside.

Quenti motioned for them to follow as she edged the river. She didn't look back as she pressed against the damp stone and ducked behind the curtain of water.

On the other side of the falls, the light was diffuse and blue, shadow and light dancing as one against the gray stone wall. The shelf Quenti stood on was a few yards wide, giving plenty of room for the four of them to stand. But the ceiling was low, and Runeo stooped under the sloping stone above them.

He scowled as he scrutinized the glistening stone of the cliff and grimaced. "A wall? Awesome plan, Quenti. We'll really surprise them this way."

Quenti rolled her eyes at him. "The entrance isn't up here." She turned back toward the waterfall and jabbed a finger toward the dark waters below the rock shelf. Three pairs of eyes swiveled.

"It's down there."

CHAPTER 37

ALARA

Alara's eyes focused to where Quenti was pointing, and she shuddered. While the water closest to the rock shelf was calm, it was inky black, giving no indication of what lay hidden beneath its surface.

"I'm sorry, but what?" Alara said.

"Happy you learned how to swim?" Quenti said with a small grin.

"No. I'm really not."

Lili and Runeo looked no happier than Alara about the news.

"Look," Quenti said. "It ain't that far of a swim. Once you go under, the entrance is only a few feet down and the actual tunnel only took about ten seconds to swim through. When you surface, you're basically in the passage to the Haven."

Alara looked down at the pool of water. "So we swim through and climb out the other side." It wasn't a question. Just her repeating the mission aloud, hoping it would make it just the slightest bit less terrifying. It didn't work.

"That doesn't seem horrible," Lili said, though her confidence seemed to reflect Alara's own.

"And in case this wasn't obvious," Quenti continued, "it'll be pitch black once you go under. So you'll want to pay attention and keep your hands in front of you as you go."

Alara gave a small shudder. "Awesome, swimming underground in the pitch black. Got it."

"Alara, you should go first," Runeo said.

"What, why?" Alara's eyes widened and her face snapped to the his, though he looked back at her without malice.

"You'll be able to light the cave on the other side once you're through."

"He has a point," Quenti said. "You can help guide the way for the rest of us once you're there."

Alara looked between their three faces. She had no argument, but she wished she did. Why couldn't there be another fire user among the four of them? One that loved to swim and wasn't afraid of dying in a tunnel—in the dark.

Finally, she nodded, removing the flint cuff and ring that she had stolen from the fire mage. She had hoped she wouldn't have to use it so soon. Carefully, she wrapped them in her bruya clothes and tucked these in her pack, making sure it was as sealed as possible.

Runeo handed her a small rope to tie around her waist.

"Tug it twice when you get to the other side and we'll follow."

Alara didn't answer, but felt the daggers on her waist, making sure they were secure before looking back into the dark waters. She felt like she had just volunteered to jump off the edge of a cliff first.

"You ready?" Quenti said, placing a hand on her shoulders.

No.

"Two feet down, around ten seconds in the tunnel, and then

up on the other side. Remember, kick your legs, paddle your hands, and stay smooth."

"Here goes nothing." Alara gave a jerky nod before slipping into the water, acting before her common sense could catch up with her actions.

She was happy for the lightweight fabric of the magite attire as her trousers tangled around her legs. Her knuckles grasped the edge of the pool as her feet waded beneath her. She pushed off, testing her legs and arms as she went, trying to remember the feeling of swimming from weeks before. It seemed like another lifetime when she and Quenti had been lying in the river, basking in the sun. If only there'd been more time to practice.

She gave one last look before nodding and ducking her head under.

Once inside the blackness, her eyes became useless. She could tilt her head up and see the vague light of day above her, along with the shifting faces of Lili, Runeo, and Quenti as they leaned over the pool. But toward her mission, there was only darkness.

She propelled forward, legs kicking and arms paddling awkwardly as she tried to feel along the rocky edge, looking for an opening. She felt a cool wave of relief as her hands slipped into an opening in the stone. She pulled herself down deeper, happy to feel the tunnel was at least a few feet wide on all sides. Large enough to slip through.

She pulled herself through, trying not to bump against the jagged stone above her, but it was difficult to steer in the inky blackness of the water. It took only a few seconds for her to lose her sense of direction. She was moving slowly—slower than Quenti likely accounted for—but where was the end of the tunnel? Her lungs burned and her chest was tight with fear. After another second, she realized that despite kicking and paddling, she was no longer moving through the water.

Alara jerked, fingers searching desperately in the darkness for where her pack had gotten snagged. She struggled to unhook the material with numb fingers, but the wool was stiff and she couldn't see where it had caught.

The burning in her lungs only increased and she felt the panic setting in. She whipped around in the water, unsure of what direction she should to go. Blackness now stretched in every direction, unending shadow. The muffled sounds of water churning reached her and she turned to the left, blindly. Then there were fingers alongside hers, unhooking her pack from the rock and pushing her forward.

She paddled ahead, her chest aching for air. The surrounding water swirled, and she was being pushed through the tunnel. Several seconds later, her head was above water and musty cave air filled her lungs.

She coughed as she dragged herself onto the floor, happy there was room to stretch out.

"I shouldn't be a swim teacher then, huh?" Quenti's voice was light, but she heard the tinge of worry.

"I thought I did pretty good until I almost drowned," she said with a choking laugh.

"Ha. How about we get some light in here, so I can see you when you lie?"

Alara rolled onto her stomach, unhooking her arms from her pack. She dug into the bag and gave a small cheer when she felt the flint dry at the center.

She pulled it out, along with the small iron ring, and worked them into a spark, touching her magia to the flash of light. A small flame sprung into the air and lit the surrounding cave.

It worked.

Quenti let out a gasp.

Shadows from the twinkling flame jumped onto the walls of

the enormous cavern. Above them, the rock stretched up into blackness, the ceiling out of sight, but bright stars danced across every visible surface, a multitude of colorful gems embedded in the stone.

After a few beats, she shook herself and pulled the rope tied around her waist twice. A minute later, Runeo and Lili popped up from the pool.

Quenti and Runeo helped dry their supplies and clothes, while Alara slipped the flint cuff back onto her wrist, feeling the weight against her skin. It was lighter than the gold cuff that adorned her other wrist and slightly less comfortable.

The passage from the cavern was obvious, a thin crack in the wall—the only doorway out. She felt a shiver of familiarity as they ducked through the opening and into the black tunnel beyond. The ceiling ran just above Runeo's head, and the walls were too narrow for her to stretch out her arms. A sense of calm settled over her at the feeling of being surrounded by soil and stone once more.

"Is now a bad time to share that I'm claustrophobic?" Lili said, her voice trembling and her eyes darting between the walls.

"Just take deep breaths, and pretend you're in a very… dark forest," Quenti said.

Lili shook her head. "I don't think that's going to help."

The tunnel wound as they moved forward and Alara lost track of their direction, assuming they were going south, deeper into the mountain. She wondered where the passage could lead. She'd been wandering the Haven since she was young, and she'd never found this route before.

Nearly an hour later, Quenti stopped without warning. Alara heard a small yelp as Lili ran into Runeo.

"Are we there?" Alara asked.

Quenti cursed.

"What?"

"There's a split. I don't remember seeing a split when I was leaving."

"Did we make a wrong turn?" Lili asked.

"A wrong turn where? There's been only one tunnel this entire way."

Alara looked ahead to see the tunnel fork in two separate directions, with nothing to distinguish the two options. "That's probably because the tunnels just converged on your way out."

"That doesn't do me much good right now."

Alara bit her lip. "I guess we just choose one. These belong to the Network, so either way, they both lead to somewhere friendly. Probably."

Quenti nodded. "Right it is," she said with no confidence.

They walked for a while longer, the darkness draining away any sense of progress. Alara grew lost in her own thoughts, her mind back in the forest with Ardo. His eyes on her, dark with confusion and betrayal.

For as hard as she fought to return home, what would be left for her now? Would Ardo forgive her? The flame she held above them swayed with each spike of fear and dread that danced through her body, though she didn't have the energy to care.

Alara bumped into Lili as the group came to a clumsy stop again.

"Another split?" Alara asked.

"A wall," Quenti said, her voice glum.

Lili let out a sound—something between a groan and a cry. She closed her eyes and took a deep breath.

Happy to have her thoughts dragged from Ardo, she placed a hand on Lili's shoulder. "Move behind me and keep your eyes trained on the open space of the tunnel. Don't look at the walls."

Lili nodded and did as she said. Alara moved around her and

pushed past Runeo, who was scowling at the obstacle that stood in their path.

"We went the wrong way." Quenti looked defeated as she stared at the stone.

"It doesn't make sense. Why have a tunnel to a dead end?" Alara brought her flame closer and examined the edges, trying to find some sign of a crack or a door. The stone was smooth, perfectly melded with the rest of the tunnel. She pressed her hand to the stone. It was warm to her touch.

She looked closer, her fingers tracing a small ridge in the center. As the flame hovered near, the ridge in the stone glowed as the outline of a condor appeared. It seemed almost familiar, but she couldn't quite place it.

"What is that?" Quenti was leaning over Alara's shoulder, looking at the symbol.

"I'm not sure," Alara said. She moved the flame away, and the glow disappeared. "Step back a second."

No one moved. In fact, the group inched closer as their eyes focused on the image in front of her. "I said"—she pushed her palm into Quenti's chest with a nudge—"step back."

As the footsteps shuffled behind her, she brought the flame back toward the carving. Again, the edges of the bird appeared to glow, a light coming from within the stone. Alara took a deep breath and pressed the flame against the stone with her palm. She felt the heat of her fire sink into the cool surface and then a shudder of movement.

The entire wall shifted, and a gap appeared to the left. A doorway. Alara turned back to the others. Her flame had gone out, but a trickle of light came from the newly opened doorway, and she could see their faces bathed in shadows.

"You first," Runeo said with a smirk, whispering the words.

She stepped forward, feeling the others follow. They were in a stone room. This time, clearly man-made, and the floor made of flattened dirt and hay. A sharp light descended from above them, accenting the darkness from which they emerged.

She looked up, trying to understand what she was seeing. Slats of light stretched from the wood planks above them as figures moved in and out of view. And then she heard voices— one very familiar voice.

She looked around again at the straw that scattered the ground and breathed in the smell of manure. Her eyes widened, and she couldn't stop the grin that stretched across her face.

They were under Adelmo's stables. She was home.

CHAPTER 38

ALARA

They stayed silent as the voices above them continued their conversation. Her mind was still reeling from the fact that the underground tunnels used by the Network led to Adelmo's home.

A realization hit her, and she turned to look at Quenti, her eyes full of accusation.

Had she known?

Quenti looked away sheepishly, but nodded to the others.

When the voices above them faded, Runeo sent a curl of wind through the floorboards to tug at Adelmo's arm. Through the slats, she could see his shadow flinch and then lean toward the floor. She lit her flint and set the small basement room aglow.

"El'dyo!" Adelmo's voice was soft, and Alara smiled at the familiarity.

A few moments later, a beam of light filled the room and Alara saw a piece of the flooring lift away. A rope ladder fell through the opening, and they climbed out into the stables.

Before Alara could even get her bearings, Adelmo pulled her into a tight hug. "El'dyo, child, what are you doing here?"

She opened her mouth to answer, but he shushed her with a raised finger. "Hold on, give me a minute." He disappeared through the doorway where his house attached to the stables, and she heard the shutters close.

"Come in, just be quiet."

They followed his waving hand into the small home. The fire was lit, burning bright in the hearth, and the air was already growing warm with the shutters sealed.

"So… you're a part of the underground Network?" she said, not knowing whether to be grateful or upset. "You're working against the Council?" The words came out harsher than she expected, and she softened her voice. "Did you help Quenti escape?"

"The Network has many hands," Adelmo said. "No one knows everything. It's what keeps us safe. But yes, I helped. I am sorry that I could never speak to you about these matters before. You were so close to Senye Emaru and embedded in the rhetoric. I hoped this day would come when we were on the same side."

She was silent, unsure of how to respond. Was she on his side now? If Emaru discovered what she was doing, she certainly wouldn't be considered on the side of the Council. "I'm not on anyone's side. I'm just trying to right a wrong."

"So, tell me all about it." Adelmo's voice was soft as he looked between their faces.

Together, Quenti and Alara explained their situation, Lili occasionally adding a few details. Runeo was silent as he watched the exchange, distrust in his eyes as he watched Adelmo.

"We're here to free their people," she finished, nodding to Runeo and Lili.

"That's easier said than done," the old man said, his eyes sad. "If it were as simple as freeing bruyas from dungeons, we would have done that long ago." His eyes focused on her as he said this, and she shuddered.

"But they did nothing wrong!"

"Right," Adelmo said. "Innocent or not, the Network will not support a rescue mission."

"Why not? Isn't that what they're supposed to do? Help people?"

"The Network is about the long game—keeping those with magia safe. They save people when they can and stand back when they need to. Running into the dungeons and trying to free random bruyas is a surefire way of getting caught and blowing open the entire Network." He shook his head. "If we get exposed, thousands of future bruyas and magites will suffer."

She stared at him, trying to understand what she was hearing. How could the Network claim to want to help bruyas when they wouldn't even save the innocent ones?

"We need to try," she said, her voice desperate.

"The Network can't help." Adelmo's voice was soft, but Runeo tensed up.

"And are you going to stop us?" he asked, his voice cold.

Adelmo shook his head. "I'm one blameless. I'm no match against the four of you." He stepped back, his hands up and open. "I will not stand in your way. But know that if the Network finds out what you're doing, the councilguards aren't the only ones you'll have to worry about. If you get caught—you'll get no help from us." His hand was warm on her shoulder, and he squeezed. "So please, do not get caught."

She nodded and placed her own hand over his. His skin was dry and soft. "Can we get your help with one thing?"

"Perhaps." Adelmo lifted his eyebrow, hesitant to commit.

"We need two more magite outfits for Lili and Runeo."

"And perhaps one that isn't torn for you," he said, eyeing the ripped cuff of her tunic and the mud stains along the hems.

"Oh." Alara tugged at her outfit and gave him a crooked smile. "Yeah."

"That I can help with." He walked over to the chest in the corner of the room where she used to keep her fighting gear. He dug for a moment and then pulled out a pile of different-colored tunics. She gave a small gasp to see that he even had some black mage attire in the trunk.

He spread the clothing out, the fabrics wrinkled, but clean. "Take your pick."

The four of them made their way through Cielo, and all the while, Alara and Quenti tried to keep their heads down, not making eye contact with those as they passed. They still weren't sure how many people knew her face or that she had been "captured" by the evil bruyas. Lili's eyes were wide as she took in the city's architecture, while Runeo had a perpetual look of disgust as they passed through the streets.

"Can you look less like you want to kill everyone?" Alara hissed under her breath. "It's a little conspicuous."

His eyes flashed to the side, and she knew he had heard her. He said nothing, but his face shifted, his lips softening on the edges. His dark eyes were still intense as they took things in, but at least he looked less angry. The four of them had chosen magite outfits—thinking people would be more likely to pay attention to a wandering mage. Lili had found an earth magite's clothes that fit well and Alara had replaced her tunic with another red one. Runeo, on the other hand, was left with a blue tunic of a water magite—the only clothes that fit his longer limbs. It was clear in his walk that he was uncomfortable in the thin fabric. More than a few times, she had caught him tugging at the hem of his tunic.

"I'm more worried about your face than his," Quenti whispered from beside her. Alara ran a finger along the ridge of her scar. She knew the other girl was right. Her eyes darted around. They were almost to the entrance to the Haven, where the chances of running into someone she knew would increase significantly.

Suddenly, she saw something in the distance that made her lips turn upward into a smile.

"Runeo?" Alara asked. "Can you do me a favor?"

He looked over at her and followed her gaze to the woman who walked down the street, a l'lama in tow with wares strapped to its back. He nodded, seeming to get the message.

With a small wave of his hand, a red hat with a large flat rim flew off the back of the l'lama in a gust of wind. It glided twenty yards before landing in the street just in front of them. Alara gave a quick glance around before scooping the hat up and placing it on her head, tilting it to cover her face.

"Thank you."

He grunted in response.

A minute later, they had reached the entrance to the Haven. She took a deep breath as they stepped into the shadowed tunnel. It was the same entrance Adelmo had led her and Quenti through so long ago. They kept their pace steady as they passed by the healer quarters, though she saw Lili staring into the open doorways, her eyes studying the movement of the other healers.

Alara had taken the lead, sending strands of magia out to piece together where the dungeons would be. She was taking them through the school and toward the councilrooms. Going through the market was more direct, but she wanted to avoid the crowds. Thanks to Adelmo, she knew it was Sunday, which meant that most of the magites would be in the market or around the city—away from the school on their day off.

They got through most of the campus without running across anyone. And she knew the tunnels well enough to take them around any magite she sensed in their path. But even as they went, she wasn't sure where exactly they needed to go. She guessed the dungeons would be somewhere near the councilrooms, but where, she wasn't sure. The councilrooms were the one area she had always avoided, having been chased off by Senye Cruz one too many times.

She put her hand up, signaling the others to slow down. She could feel some magites up ahead of them in the hallway. They were near the dorm rooms, on the edge of where the councilrooms started. She needed time to think. She saw a door ajar up ahead and darted inside, letting the others follow behind her.

The room was a small study area with scattered tables and a handful of books left abandoned.

It wasn't until Lili let out a soft yelp that Alara realized it wasn't empty. Sitting in one chair and holding a small book was a young boy. His face was pale and cheeks pink. His curled hair fell into his face as he looked up at the small group in surprise.

Lili was the first to react, she jumped forward and laid a hand on his head. He gave a small gasp and slumped forward. "Oh Sol, I'm going to be punished for that." She moved the boy carefully, so his head lay on the table, her hands fluttering as she stepped back.

Quenti gave the boy a strange look.

"What's wrong?" Alara asked.

"Nothing. I just—this is the kid that brought me my bed when I first got here." There was a hint of guilt in her voice.

Alara ran a hand over the burns on her face again, feeling the shame well up and threaten to engulf her. "This is all my fault. I just got distracted—I shouldn't have."

Quenti put a soft hand on her shoulder, "This is the most I've seen you use your powers—ever. We all make mistakes."

Lili nodded in agreement, but Alara still heard Runeo's grunt of annoyance.

"Where to, then?" he said. "Or are you out of power?"

She shot him a glare. "Give me a minute. I've gotten us this far, haven't I?"

She slumped into one of the other chairs, away from the sleeping child, closing her eyes. Reaching toward the warmth in her chest and snagging a thread of magia, she sent it out toward the councilrooms. These tunnels were like second nature to her, and she had little difficulty finding the main councilchamber. With a small thrill, she recognized Emaru's energy. She could almost picture the councilwoman sitting at the table alone, her energy shifting as she read some particularly moving passage from a book.

Alara felt a small twinge of pride and warmth. She'd have to tell Emaru about this when she saw her again. But how would she explain all her decisions over the past several weeks? She shook those thoughts away. She couldn't worry about that until Khuna and Micos were safe.

Khuna and Micos. Her eyes flew open, and she shot a look at Quenti.

"I have an idea."

She closed her eyes again and continued her search of the councilrooms, heading down below the main chambers. It took a few minutes, and she felt beads of sweat forming on her hairline from the effort, but then she opened her eyes, smile wide.

Two floors below the main councilchamber, she felt the distinct but dulled energy of Khuna. She wasn't moving and something seemed off, but it was definitely her. Alara felt around the room in her mind, touching on a few other magia cores. At least one of them was pacing, while the others remained still.

"I know where the dungeons are."

CHAPTER 39

ALARA

"What're we gonna do about him?" Runeo looked over at the boy still slumped unconscious on the table. "The second he wakes up, he'll alert the Haven."

"Can you cleanse just a few minutes of his memories?" Quenti asked, looking at Lili.

The tierren's face was pale, and she shook her head. "Even on a good day, I wouldn't have enough power to do that. There are few in Arbol who would. That's why we couldn't send Alara home sooner."

"We'll have to work fast then," Alara said.

"I can jam the door," Lili said, running a hand along where the wood frame met the cold stone of the walls. "It'll at least buy us a little time."

Alara nodded. "Okay." She mentally ran through the passageways that led to the dungeon. "I'll lead everyone again, but we'll have to be careful. Once we get past the main floor, even magites would look suspicious."

With that, the group slipped back into the hall, Lili taking up the rear. She paused for a moment as they left the room, hand in front of her. A small root broke through the packed dirt of the floor and curled in front of the closed door.

Alara turned and headed toward the councilrooms. There was a stairwell nearby that would hopefully lead them down to the dungeon level. If her hunch was correct, they wouldn't have to pass by the councilmembers' offices. The last thing she wanted was to walk by the room where Emaru was camped out and accidentally run into her. She would have to wait for a reunion until after she had helped the others escape.

And hope to El'dyo Emaru never finds out what you did, her thought came unbidden.

Silently, she led their small band, ducking into the shadows as she sensed movement ahead of them every few minutes. She let out a sigh of relief when she saw the passage ahead, veering off from the hallways to the left. A long set of stairs led down.

Signaling, they turned into the passage and made their way down the winding staircase, the narrow walls pressing in on either side. She held her breath as they raced downward—there was nowhere to hide if a mage or councilguard came their way. But they made it to the bottom, where it opened into a wider hallway.

The torches down here were few and far between, casting wide shadows along the passage. The air was colder on this level, as if highlighting the absence of life. She sent out a thread of magia toward the dungeons and felt Khuna's energy in the distance. They were so close. As she pulled back, her excitement died, replaced with an anxious dread.

Two mages were headed toward them. Alara pulled the others back, and they ducked into the stairwell. Runeo's eyebrows furrowed in concern, and she held up two fingers before pointing down the hall. She ducked around the corner to see if there was any place to hide. A few yards down was a door, but they wouldn't have made it before the newcomers rounded the corner.

Still, if they stayed, even the most distracted mage or council-guard would notice the brightly dressed magites huddled together. And that was even assuming they weren't planning on taking that stairwell.

She eyed the torch across the hall from them, then pulled at the thread of magia and directed it toward the flame. Taking a deep breath, she tried to pull at the fire to make it go out. The heat in her rose and the flame jolted. A spike of fear hit her as the flame shot up even higher.

A hand rested on her shoulder. Quenti, nodding, solemn and supporting, even in silence. Quenti raised her hand, and a small bubble of water formed above the torch. It fell into the flame and the torch went out with a small puff of smoke and steam.

A second later, footsteps rounded the corner down the hall. Her heart pounded in her chest, and she wondered if everyone else could hear it.

The mages were getting closer, and she could hear them talking. It was two women she didn't recognize, but with a sickening lurch she heard one mage say, "Update Senye Emaru."

At least one guard was headed directly into the stairwell where they were hiding. Eyes wide, she turned to the others. She didn't need to use words. It was clear they understood the conclusion she had just come to. They needed to get out of here and now.

Runeo motioned, and Alara looked at him, trying to understand. He motioned again and pushed around her, inching into the shadowed hallway.

She wondered for a moment if he planned to ambush the two guards before his hand moved and a rush of breeze emerged from his palm. A door down the hallway slammed shut.

"What the——"

The two guards bolted past them and down the hallway. They burst through the slammed door, and Runeo out of the stairwell and led them running in the other direction. Alara tried to send out a thread of magia to see if there were others around, but she couldn't focus her mind as they ran.

The group slowed as they turned the corner.

"This way," Alara whispered. It was a few more turns before she came to a large, heavy door. She closed her eyes, breathing deeply and letting her body relaxed. She tried to push the thoughts of Ardo and Emaru from her mind. After a few moments, she stretched her consciousness out to touch the people beyond. She could still feel Khuna and a few others, neither moving nor sleeping. Another three were more active, pacing and moving within the room.

She turned back to the others and whispered, "Three guards, I think."

"We can take them, easily," Runeo said with a look that made her stomach twist.

"Remember. No killing." Her voice was a sharp whisper.

He sneered. "Remember, I'm no monster. Besides, we wouldn't want to harm your friends."

"Not to mention it'll be easier on all of us to not leave a trail of blood."

"And you don't think those councilguards out there will talk?" he said.

"What're you talking about?" she said, annoyed. Where had this come from?

"Don't think I don't know the true reason behind this. No, you don't want anyone to die because killing anyone will make it that much harder to come crawling back after all of this. But even if that's the case, do you really think the councilguards we take out won't rat on you when it's all over?"

The truth of it was a stone in her stomach that she refused to acknowledge. "I can deal with them after this. But if you want my help, we aren't killing anyone. Agreed?"

His jaw muscles twisted, but he gave a stiff nod. "Fine. But we'll need to disable them before they can send out an *envia*," Runeo said, looking at Lili. "Can you do it?"

Lili was pale, but nodded. "If you can distract them, I can."

Runeo gave a grim nod. "No killing required, then." He grabbed the dagger from his hip and readied himself to lunge into the prison cells, leaving her wondering how this wouldn't end in bloodshed.

But then, she had an idea. She gripped his shoulder and pulled him back.

"Change out of your magite clothes."

"What?"

"Put your bruya tunic back on." She grabbed the pack that swung on her shoulder and shoved it into his hands. "Quickly."

She watched the thoughts flicker across his face. His eyes were narrowed with suspicion, and she had to wonder if he thought this was some elaborate trick to get him arrested. But he conceded, taking the bag from her and shrugging off his blue tunic. She averted her eyes at the sight of his bare chest.

She turned back as he slipped the brown tunic over his head and fastened the flowered and woven belt around his waist. The blue magite pants stuck out from beneath the tunic, but it would have to do.

Alara signaled for Lili and Quenti to stand behind her, and she wrapped a small piece of rope around Runeo's hands. He palmed the ends without tying them and gave her a nod.

After taking a deep breath, she swung the door open and shouldered her way through, tugging Runeo after her by his arm.

"Thank El'dyo, that was the longest walk ever," she said with an over-the-top sigh. "This bruya would not shut up!"

Alara glanced around the room, taking in the scene. Her jaw clenched as she saw five councilguards looking at her in utter confusion. Three mages and two blameless—all giving the duo a suspicious look. She was happy to see that while a few had placed hands on their weapons, none had been drawn yet.

"Why is there a magite delivering us a prisoner?" one guard said, eyeing Runeo with disgust.

Alara stepped further into the room, leaving the door behind her open. She pushed Runeo into the center of the room.

"That is a brilliant question," she said, having no idea what to say next. She tried to put on a large innocent smile, but the looks she was getting made it falter. *Screw it.* "Now!"

Runeo dropped the ropes that had been around his wrists and sent a wave of air crashing into three of the guards sitting along the wall. Lili and Quenti charged in behind them and Alara ran back to shut the door, not wanting the commotion to draw anyone else down to join the fray.

She turned back and saw Lili incapacitating her second guard with a touch of her hand as Quenti and Runeo fought with the other three. Alara swore under her breath. All three remaining guards were mages. She grabbed a simple wooden club hanging on the wall and snuck up behind Runeo. He was struggling with two mages, but she whirled the club around and drove the blunt end against one man's head. A crack echoed in the room, and she jumped back as the man crumpled. She held her breath until she saw the downed man's chest move slightly. Runeo's eyes widened for a moment, looking at her.

"Not bad for a magite," he said with a smirk before returning to the other guard.

She didn't like that coming from him, but didn't let the thought linger. She had to help with that final councilguard, further ensuring the scuffle didn't end in bloodshed.

It was another wind mage. He and Runeo danced around each other, dodging gusts of wind and jabs from their daggers. Alara shifted the club in her hands, hoping to help him, but they were moving too fast for her to get a clear shot. She could only watch as they spun around each other, their feet making arches on the dirt floor as they circled. She thought back to her fight in the dark marketplace.

"Runeo, dirt floors!"

Runeo's eyes widened as her comment registered. He didn't hesitate, sweeping his hand and sending a flurry of dust at the man's face. She used the moment of distraction to swing the club at the man's knees. He fell with a loud grunt and Lili jumped forward, placing a hand on his head before his body went limp.

Her feeling of triumph cut short, yanked from her like air after a punch to the gut as she heard Quenti cry out. Alara turned to see her holding her side as a blameless guard lunged forward with his blade.

She acted on instinct. Sweeping forward, low to the ground, she picked up the fallen spear she had been fighting with earlier and threw it, bronze-tipped blade first, into the man's chest. He twisted for a moment, blood smearing down his chest, and then he fell, unmoving.

Alara let out a small gasp as nausea roiled through her at the sight. The sight of death and failure. Her inability to stay loyal to her oaths. Her inability to protect her own people from herself.

El'dyo, what have I done?

"Quenti!" Khuna's voice! Her gray face was pressed against

the bars of the cell, focused on the ground a few yards away where Quenti lay crumpled.

All Alara could see was the thick stream of red blood seeping through Quenti's fingers as she clenched her side.

No.

CHAPTER 40

ALARA

Torn between the sight of her injured friend and the murdered guard, she knew she had to help Quenti. She could dwell on her treasonous act forever, but Quenti needed help now.

She caught Runeo's eye, half expecting the bruya to call her out on her misdeed, but he too was focused on Quenti.

Lili moved first, diving across the floor and spilling her pack onto ground. Her face was pale, and she was shaking, but her fingers moved quickly as she picked out some bright red leaves from the grounded contents.

Alara watched as Lili pulled back the torn fabric of Quenti's robes. The wound in her side was jagged and deep, and Alara's stomach lurched. Lili pressed the leaves into the wounded bruya's side and pressed her hands against it. Alara could feel the rise of Lili's magia as she poured it into the girl. She could also feel the weakness of it and see the cold sweat forming on the tierren's forehead. She'd already been straining herself all day putting people to sleep.

After less than a minute, Lili faltered and swayed, her face a sickly white. Runeo leaped forward, just in time to catch her head before it hit the ground.

"Is she…?" Alara's heart pounded.

"She just fainted. Pushed herself too hard. Check on Quenti."

She was still ashen and shaking. Pulling back the leaves, Alara looked on with both hope and dread. The wound wasn't as deep as before, but blood steadily flowed from it. It hadn't closed. This was bad.

"It's not healed completely." Alara looked around the room, helpless. Nothing stood out as healing materials—not that she would know. Her eyes searched the surrounding cells.

Khuna pressed against the bars, her eyes wide. Zinita stood next to her, eyes not meeting Alara's.

"Is anyone a healer?" She didn't recognize anyone, but those who registered her question shook their heads.

"Alara," Runeo said beside her, "you could seal it."

"I'm not a healer," Alara said, looking at him like he had grown two heads.

"You can cauterize the wound. Just close it. Keep her from bleeding out."

Alara thought she would be sick. "You mean…?"

"She will die if it's not sealed."

"I can't," she choked out.

"Yes, you can," Quenti groaned.

Alara shook her head. "Using my abilities on a rope is one thing, but this…"

"Do it, you coward." Quenti's voice was firm. "Or are you the only one allowed to have a scar?"

Alara bit her lip at the jab and saw the ghost of a smile on Quenti's lips.

"El'dyo help me," she said, kneeling beside her rapidly paling friend. She closed her eyes and pulled at the threads of her magia, feeling the heat rising in her body. She shuddered, but let it flow into her hands as her flint ignited the flames. "Runeo, hold her down."

He nodded, moving forward and ripping a piece of leather from a nearby guard's vest and placing it in Quenti's mouth.

Alara gulped. "Like a l'lama. Like a l'lama," she whispered.

"Huh?" Quenti said, voice muffled by the vest.

"Nothing. Nothing." Her hands burned with fire, and she reached out to touch Quenti. As she made contact with skin, she felt the girl's cries echo in her mind. She locked her eyes on that small patch of skin, doing her best to ignore what she was doing.

This is nothing. I'm definitely not *burning a human being's skin.*

The skin sizzled, slowly sealing beneath her fingers.

And then the smell of burning flesh reached her nose, and she gagged. Her magia flared, and the flames jumped under her palms. She threw herself to the floor—away from Quenti—as a piece of fabric on her tunic caught fire. *No. Not like this!* Alara could only watch wide-eyed as Runeo quickly grabbed at the flames and squashed them out with his hand.

"It's… it's done," Alara said softly, wrapping her arms around herself.

Runeo gave her a grim look before checking back on Quenti. It was an ugly wound—puckered and white and red—but it was sealed. Sweaty and pallid, Quenti pushed herself up.

"Remind me never to get stabbed again. It's not nearly as cool as it looks."

"Can someone let me out now!" Khuna was still leaning hard against the bars, as if she could sink through them and out of the cell if she thought hard enough.

Runeo jumped up and grabbed a ring of keys from the wall.

It took a few tries, but he finally opened Khuna's cell and Zinita's right after. Khuna took the keys from him quickly and unlocked the cuffs on both their wrists. She turned to Alara and threw her the keys.

They clattered to the floor next to her. Her eyes widened as she watched the gold cuff fall from Khuna's wrist. She looked down at her own, her stomach churning with some emotion she couldn't quite place.

She heard the snort of derision from Zinita as the bruya watched her hesitate. Alara refused to look at her, instead focusing on the cuff.

"Where's Micos?" Runeo said, his voice on the verge of panic.

"They took him away. We haven't seen him since." Khuna sat on the floor holding Quenti as she gave Runeo a frown.

He shook his head and looked back at Alara. She sat half-frozen on the floor. Keys were now forgotten in her hands as her eyes swept over the prison cells, searching fruitlessly.

"We need to find him," Runeo said. "*You* need to find him."

Alara bit her lip, unsure. She'd already used so much of her power, but the desperation in his eyes stung.

"Please," he said.

"I can try."

She closed her eyes and yet again felt for her magia. It took a few minutes to grasp on to it, the smell of burning flesh still fresh in her mind. She picked at the threads and sent them out, stretching them as far as she could, searching for the energy she associated with Micos. But her senses were muddled. She pushed harder, but it kept slipping further away with each push. She finally opened her eyes, shaking her head and refusing to make eye contact with him.

A few feet away, Lili was coming to, still shaken with her head in her hands. Khuna and Quenti sat, their foreheads pressed together and lips moving in unheard whispers. Zinita was the only one emboldened by the situation. She moved swiftly around the room, collecting the weapons from the fallen guards and distributing them. Alara took a spear and threw a set of arrows at Runeo. He took them, distracted.

"We need to get going," Zinita snapped.

"We need to find Micos," Runeo said, voice just as sharp.

"What about the rest of them?" Quenti pulled herself to her feet. She motioned to the other cells, where a scattering of others sat, wide-eyed at the scene. "We can't leave them."

"We don't have time for this. We've already stayed too long." Zinita's voice was cold, but Alara heard the truth in her words.

"She's right."

The female bruya's head whipped around, eyes narrowing. "Don't think I'm going to trust you just because you agree with me."

"Let's not talk about trust," Alara said. "I wasn't the one who planned to kill someone."

Zinita smirked. "And yet you were the only one here who actually killed a guard."

Alara bit her lip. Amid Quenti's injury, she'd almost let herself forget about the blameless councilguard she pierced with the spear. About the man she *killed*. Her eyes found their way back to the guard, whose body was splayed out on the dungeon floor, eyes open, chest stabbed, and running a sickening dark red.

El'dyo, what have I done?

"That was an accident." The words rang hollow, even in her own ears.

"And who's to say another accident won't happen to one of us next? That you won't turn on us just as you did on them?"

Khuna stepped between Alara and Zinita. "We have bigger problems right now."

"We need to find Micos." Runeo's voice was tight. "We can't leave him."

Zinita opened her mouth to reply, but before she could, the door behind them swung open.

"What are you doing here?"

Alara's eyes widened at the familiar voice and she let out a cry, louder than intended, "Micos!"

"Thank Sol!" Runeo leaped, his arms opening to wrap around his brother, but Micos stumbled back, hand reaching for the dagger at this belt.

He wasn't wearing his bruya clothes anymore, and he didn't even have a guard escorting him. He was alone in the garments of a fire mage, with a dagger and bolas strapped to his waist. Something was very wrong.

Alara pulled at the threads of magia deep within, again feeling for elemental users. While she felt the presence of the boy in front of them, it in no way resembled the bruya she knew in Arbol.

"Micos?" Runeo said, stepping toward his brother once again.

"Runeo, don't—" But she was too late. Micos lashed out, a spit of flames flying from the torches at Runeo. Quenti acted first, sending water spinning through the air to divert the attack.

He didn't even flinch at the fire that spun toward him or the steam the water let out as they collided. Alara pushed him aside and stepped next to Quenti as Micos stared them both down.

"Don't do anything stupid, Micos. We're trying to help."

Alara wasn't sure anything Quenti could say would matter. She could feel the shift in his energy as her magia brushed against him. This wasn't Micos anymore. She let out a shudder. This was *wrong*.

The young bruya—now mage—didn't make a move to attack again, and neither did Quenti nor Alara. The room was still and quiet.

And then Micos lifted a hand to his temple.

Son of a bruya. He was sending out an *envia*.

Alara pulled back her arm, and without thinking, threw her fist at Micos's face, the impact putting up more of a resistance than she expected. All the same, he fell back, blood spurting from his nose, though she knew it was too late.

"Well, I guess they know we're here now," she said.

Runeo was still unmoving, staring at his brother with wide, unblinking eyes. She counted herself lucky he didn't attack her for punching his brother.

"We need to go," Quenti whispered.

"What's wrong with him?"

"Runeo—we can't..." Alara grabbed his shoulders and swung him around to look at her. "We can't take him now, but I'll help you get him back. *Later.*"

He shook his head and snapped out of it. He nodded once and let himself get dragged from the dungeon, Alara's hand still on his arm.

Chapter 41

Alara

All stealth was gone as the group escaped the dungeons. They couldn't afford to waste any time slinking around the halls. Their best bet was to get back to the secret tunnels before whatever message Micos had sent out brought the entire Haven to them.

They made it up to the main floors and were headed back toward the school when Alara's head cracked open with the harsh voice she recognized as Senye Cruz's.

"Bruyas have infiltrated the Haven and have assisted in the escape of several prisoners. Be on the lookout for suspicious activity and report to the councilguards. These bruyas and fugitives should be viewed as extremely dangerous."

The message repeated a second time, and when it died away, she felt the familiar ache following a mind-talker's mass *envia*. She looked at the others, who were as shaken as she was.

The group stopped and looked at each other in silent dread and unease. It was Quenti who spoke first, eyes on Alara.

"You should leave."

"What?" Alara said.

"Pretend you used us to get back here. You can even run to give them information—they know we're here now, anyway."

Her thoughts spun, and she almost moved to follow the instructions. But then she looked at the wan face of Quenti, the sickly pallor of the other bruyas around her—all drawn with hunger and exhaustion and grief.

"No," she said, voice firm. "I promised to see this through. I can at least get you back to the tunnels before I leave."

She almost believed the words.

"Are you sure?"

No.

Her mind flashed back to the dead guard in the dungeon. Could she even call this place home again after what she'd done?

She took a deep breath. "I'm sure," she said, adopting an overly confident tone. "But first, we need to blend in. No more running," Alara said, looking around the empty hallway.

"I don't think five bruyas and a beaten up magite are going to blend in anywhere," Runeo said. He waved a hand at the disheveled group.

"Do we have any rope left?"

Runeo shook his head. "I dropped it in the scuffle back in the dungeon."

Alara looked around. They still had their bags. She pulled Runeo's magite robes from one and tossed the fresh tunic at Quenti. Without needing instruction, Quenti slipped the torn tunic over her head and put on the fresh one, moving slowly to avoid irritating her wound.

"You three put your hands behind your backs," Alara said, motioning to Khuna, Runeo, and Zinita. "We can at least pretend you're already captured."

"You don't think a handful of magites marching around with captured bruyas are going to draw attention?" Runeo asked.

"Less attention than them running through the halls together," Alara said. "Hopefully."

She then grabbed Runeo by the arm, taking a little joy in squeezing his elbow harder than she needed to. He shot her a glare, but after an exhausted sigh, played the part as they continued forward.

The ruse seemed to work. Magites rushed by, looking panicked and confused, whispering to each other and exchanging shifty glances, but no one noticed the group walking calmly through the halls. Only an occasional pair of roaming eyes would fall on them, but Alara just smiled brightly and nodded at each. They were lucky to pass by no one she recognized, particularly as they made their way through the main thoroughfare of the school.

"Alara Ayar!" The voice was cold and sharp behind them.

Her heart stopped and she turned on her heels, the taste of fear metallic on her tongue. Any hope she'd held in her heart drained away.

A group of familiar magites stopped in front of them, Raquel at their lead. Behind her stood Mitteo and several others Alara only vaguely recognized.

"I heard you were running around with the bruyas, but I didn't believe it," Raquel said. "I mean, I wanted to, but didn't think you'd actually turn into one of them. So, it's true? Are you really a bruya lover now?" Her eyes lingered on Runeo, and her lips twisted into a sneer. "I guess I can see *some* of the appeal."

Alara took in the girl's black tunic and brightly woven *aguayo*. "I can see you've become a mage. Congratulations."

Raquel smirked. "Not all of us were failures." Her head tilted, taking in the others behind Alara with silent appraisal.

"Please—please—fight back. I've always wanted an excuse to kick your face in."

For a moment, the hallway was still. And then Runeo grabbed the bow from Quenti's back, Khuna clenched a spear, and Zinita whipped out her dagger in a reverse grip.

Raquel's smile widened in contempt. "Oh, this is perfect. I never really liked you, anyway."

With that, the Raquel pulled her own bow from her back, and the magites shifted into fighting stances behind her.

Before she could could blink, an arrow was already flying toward her heart. She could only curse internally at her slow instincts, and waited for the inevitable piercing.

But the hit never came.

Her eyes widened in surprise as Raquel and her arrow both went flying against the tunnel wall. She cried out as she was slammed against the stone and fell to the packed dirt floors.

A black-haired wind mage rounded the corner, hands raised in a fighting position. Alara flinched, but the girl's brown eyes flickered over her before she turned on the other magites, sending a wave of air at one of them, knocking him over.

Out of the corner of her eye, Alara saw Raquel scrambling back to her feet. Not wasting a moment, she jumped forward trying to snatch her bow up from the floor.

But before she could make a proper move, Raquel was already lunging forward, eyes wide with anger. A small voice in Alara's mind yelled at her through the fog of her racing thoughts: Raquel wasn't fighting to disable, she was fighting to hurt her—to kill.

Raquel let out a feral growl from between her clenched teeth, but was dragged to the floor. A tangled mess of roots writhed and grasped at her feet.

Thank you, Lili!

Alara whipped around, looking for her, but she was farther down the hall, holding up a pale Quenti and trying to dodge attacks.

Then who…?

On the other side of the corridor stood Mitteo, both hands moving as the roots twisted around Raquel, pinning her to the ground, arms caught at her sides.

He met Alara's wide eyes and gave a wink. "I've always wanted to do that."

"You?"

Before she could question him further, a spit of fire flew at her from the side. She threw herself down, wincing as her knees scrapped across the floor. She turned back, getting to her feet as she took stock of the group. There were still five magites from Raquel's group left, and none looked willing to back down.

A jet of water, cold and hard, hit Alara in the gut. She doubled over and lashed out with a wave of fire from the torches. It didn't hit its target, but pushed back her enemy enough to recover. Another mage was charging her, spear at the ready. She rolled to the side and adjusted her grip on her own, turning as her assailant lunged toward her, jabbing it at his side.

He shifted, sending her stab wide, and stabbing back. Before she could gain her footing and before the attack landed, the magite was blown across the hall.

Runeo, panting, lowered his arm and turned back to help Khuna against her opponent.

A cry caught Alara's attention, and she spotted Zinita on her knees, cradling her arm as a fire magite stepped toward her, dagger raised.

Without thinking, Alara threw her hands forward, fire pulling from the torches along the hallway. The flames swirled together, collapsing on the magite in a chaotic mass, engulfing her robes.

The girl cried out but the flames dissipated into smoke, magically choked out of existence. Her burst of power hadn't lasted long, but it was long enough. Zinita had already taken the opportunity and lunged, piercing the magite's side.

The girl fell to the ground, clutching her wound. Zinita looked up, briefly meeting Alara's eye. She didn't react, but the usual twinkle of hate was nowhere to be found.

Alara wished she could feel the same about Zinita, but she just couldn't. "Leave her," she commanded as the bruya raised her spear for the kill.

Surprisingly, she listened with a scoff and simply kicked the magite again before moving on to her next opponent.

Alara ran over and checked the magite's wound. "Please stay still," she said. "Help will be on the way. I promise."

But the girl spat at her feet. "Burn in hell, you filthy bruya."

With a pained expression, Alara turned back to the rest of the group. There were still three more magites left fighting. They needed to end this skirmish and get out of here. She reached down again then attached her magia to the torches and pulled. The torches exploded into flame behind the cornered magites. A jet of water from Khuna engulfed her flames, and steam billowed throughout the tunnel.

Runeo condensed the steam and spun it, conjuring a steam tornado that chased the magites down the hallway. They turned and ran, their yells echoing as they retreated. Great. More alarms. They needed to get out, now.

The mage who had attacked Raquel cursed and chased after them. Who was she, and why had she helped them anyway?

Shaking her head, Alara took in the current situation. Four magites were pinned to the ground while Raquel was alive and well, her protests shrill and grating.

They had cut it close, but they'd managed to at least make it through this fight without killing anyone—though her prospects for being allowed to return to the Haven seemed to dwindle with every waking moment. But she couldn't let her thoughts linger. She had to get her friends out safely. Everything else could wait.

"Who are you?" Runeo asked, pointing his bow at Mitteo.

Alara stepped between them. "Mitteo is someone from my class." Someone who was apparently risking just as much as she was, though she didn't know why.

"So, a magite," Zinita said, brandishing her weapon.

"A magite who helped us," Alara said, still in front of Mitteo. She turned toward him, her eyes wide with questions. "But why? Why did you help us?"

Mitteo opened his mouth to answer, but was cut off.

"Enough chit-chat, kids," the wind mage said, making her way back down the hall. "We need to get out of here. I don't know how long we have before those magites out our positions."

Runeo opened his mouth to speak, but she shot him a look and he shut up.

El'dyo did she need to learn how to do that.

"We'll do introductions later. You've angered the Network, and getting caught is not going to make it any better."

She turned her eyes to Raquel, who was squirming and shouting on the ground, trying without much luck to untangle herself from the roots.

"Can someone please shut her up?"

Lili stepped forward, looking less pale than she had been earlier. "Gladly."

CHAPTER 42

QUENTI

"What are you doing here?" Adelmo's voice shook as he saw the group filing through his door. The still-unnamed wind mage followed up behind and looked surreptitiously over her shoulder as she closed the front door and locked it.

"You were supposed to be out and gone by now." Adelmo looked across the group, his eyes widening in surprise as he noted the newcomers. Confusion now replaced panic as he turned back to the wind mage. "Suri?"

"I'm afraid that plan won't work anymore," the wind mage, Suri, answered. She ran a hand through her short hair and looked over the group. Her skin was paler than even Adelmo's, contrasting with the rich black of her hair. Worry lines etched deep on her forehead. She looked like an exhausted parent, despite likely being only a few years older than Quenti, herself.

Adelmo's eyes roamed over the group in front of him. They were admittedly a pretty sorry sight. Mitteo timidly stood to the side, his magite clothes wrinkled. Alara's hair was tangled and spotted with blood, her clothing askew and *aguayo* lost in the battle. Beside her, Lili and Runeo's own outfits were torn and stained with what Quenti realized with a lurch was her own blood. Lili's skin had taken on a grayish hue, and Runeo looked... broken. Khuna and Zinita were still wearing their prison garb—drab brown sacks—and their faces were thin and pale with exhaustion. Zinita still had her arm cradled to her chest. Quenti didn't dare look down at herself—at the ripped and stained fabric that would only remind her of the sharp scent of her own burnt flesh and blood that she was trying desperately to forget.

Suri's voice broke through Quenti's thoughts like a knife. "Even if they wanted to leave, they can't."

Quenti snapped to attention, but it was Alara who spoke up first. "What?"

Suri didn't seem to register the interruption. "The Council has sealed the borders of Cielo until they can sweep for the fugitives." She finally looked at the group, her eyes flaring with anger. "Apparently you've upset some people in very high places."

"They've sealed off the exits?" Lili asked, eyebrows furrowed. "But they don't know about the tunnels. Surely those will still be open."

Suri shook her head. "It's a magical seal. There will be no way for anyone to cross the threshold from any point until it's disabled." She pursed her lips tight in a grim line. "And they won't disable it until you're caught."

It was as if the air had been sucked from the room. Quenti struggled to take a breath. Trapped. They were trapped. A cold, rough hand slipped into her own and she turned to see Khuna standing beside her, eyes focused straight ahead.

She squeezed Khuna's hand and took another breath, touching the coolness of her magia for reassurance. "So, now what's the plan?" Her voice was firm despite the taste of fear that sat on her tongue.

Suri slumped into a nearby chair. "I don't know. You've really screwed this up. The Council is after you, and that's now putting our entire Network in danger."

"Maybe if the Network had helped us in the first place, we wouldn't have made such a mess of things," Alara said.

"The Network," Suri's eyes bore a hole through Alara as she spoke, "survives through caution. If the Council were to know there was dissent from within, no one would be safe from the sweeps."

"We didn't have a choice. We had to save them."

"And look where it got you," Suri said coldly. "Now no one can leave, and we're all in danger of being caught and cleansed —or worse."

"Cleansed?" Runeo's voice was shaky and soft, but it still jarred Quenti to hear him speak. He hadn't said anything since the dungeon.

"Mind-wiped. The Council has multiple mind-walkers they utilize for the task."

"Is that what happened to my brother?" Runeo's voice was hoarse. "He didn't remember me; he—he wasn't..." It cracked and his words fell away.

Suri's eyes almost held pity as she looked at him. "Sounds like it. That's how they deal with bruyas or magites who don't consent to the Council's rule. Cleanse their memories and pasts away then remake them as the perfect followers of the Council and El'dyo."

Her words were almost casual, but the implications made Quenti's stomach churn. She had heard the stories whispered behind closed doors when she was younger. It was yet another reason her mother never trusted the Council, but she had never understood the implications of it all until now. Would her memories have been cleansed if she had stayed longer and kept resisting? Would she have lost her entire past—her entire being? A restless energy settled in her bones.

"The ones that get cleansed are lucky, perhaps," Mitteo said, voice soft. "Cause enough trouble, resist a few too many times, and you disappear for good."

Alara looked like she'd been struck by lightning, her face pale and eyes sharp. "They wouldn't." But the words were feeble, and she fell silent. Quenti remembered the look on Micos's face again. There was no arguing with the reality.

"They'll cleanse us—if we get caught," she said.

"If we're worth it," Mitteo muttered off to the side.

Adelmo's eyes were sharp as he looked around the room. "Let's just focus on you not getting caught."

"We need a plan—a real one," Suri said, sitting up straighter.

"Let's just stop talking and get moving, then," Quenti said.

"She's right. They'll start the sweeps soon and you'll be found here easily enough," Adelmo said. His eyes were on the closed door.

"We need to move into the tunnels first," Suri said. "Then we can formulate a plan to get you all out of here. *Without* exposing anymore of the Network. That part is key, and arguably more important than anything else."

"Or maybe the Network can stop hiding with its tail between its legs and actually do something," Alara said.

"You stupid child."

"You're not much older than we are!"

"Then start acting like it," Suri fired back. "This could start a war. Balance between blameless and mage is delicate at best." The air in the room seemed to shift with her powers.

"The bruyas are already fighting a war," Quenti said, no

longer able to keep silent. "They've been fighting for generations. The blameless and mages declared war on them from the moment they stopped bowing down to the Council. Maybe it's time to stop pretending this is any kind of peace or balance."

Everyone turned to her. She could see the surprise on Khuna's face, but couldn't bring herself to care. She was tired, angry, and more than a little scared.

It was Adelmo who spoke first, face creased with concern, and Quenti remembered with a jolt that he was blameless. She felt a small pang of guilt, but pushed it aside. She didn't have time to examine her emotions toward Adelmo right now.

"Perhaps tomorrow we can worry about wars, but let us try to win this battle first." He clapped his hands together. "We need to get into the tunnels. There is a meeting chamber. If others within the Network wish to help, that's where they will be."

"You think others will come?" Quenti was hopeful, if hesitant.

"We can hope," Adelmo said. He paused. The room was silent, and no one moved. "Come now. We need to head out."

He pulled aside the rug and pulled up the loose planks of wood, motioning for them to follow as he climbed into the basement.

Alara followed first and then the rest, finally shuffling toward the opening. Khuna followed behind Zinita and Quenti looked back to see Runeo still standing in the corner, unmoving. His face was gray and his eyes unfocused. He hadn't moved or acknowledged the conversation after his brief words regarding Micos. He had been broken.

Quenti hadn't known him for long, but she had never seen him looking so young. He looked like a child who had lost their parent—or a brother who had lost his family. Empathy sliced into her like a hot dagger and she looked away, unwilling to feel that ache right now.

Grabbing his hand, she pulled him behind her and they followed the others into the basement without another word. Now was the time for action.

Adelmo led them through the tunnels, back through the passage they had originally taken, and toward the other fork. They walked for another hour before Adelmo finally stopped them. They were still in the tunnel, the darkness pressing in on them, but not completely enveloped, thanks to the light of the torch Suri held.

Quenti looked around expectantly, but saw nothing to indicate they had reached any particular destination. Suri pressed the torch flame closer to the wall and a small carving lit up in the tunnel. It was the same condor that marked the entrance into Adelmo's stables. Suri passed the torch to Adelmo as she held her hand out, a small whirl of wind spinning on her palm. She pressed her hand against the carving, and it glowed with an inner light, then the wall melted back, opening into a doorway.

Light flooded the tunnel and Quenti squinted, blinded by the change. Perhaps it was this adjustment that delayed the revelation of what stood behind the door.

As Adelmo stepped forward, the others followed. Quenti and Runeo ducked in last, looking around the large, lit room. Torches lined the walls and a large table stood at its center. And at the table, a single woman—a woman in mage garb—sat. She gave a tired smile as she saw Adelmo and the others filtering in.

"Elna," he said warmly, moving to embrace her. "It's good to see you."

"It's good to see you, too." Her voice was soft. She was younger than Adelmo, although older than anyone else in their group. Her hair was almost gold in the light of the torches, with strands of silver sparkling among the golden threads. Though, despite her graying hair, the woman's skin was still smooth. She wore a blue *aguayo*, indicating she was a water mage.

Mitteo took a seat at the table, a few chairs down from where Elna stood with Adelmo.

"You look strangely comfortable," Alara said to her fellow magite, mouth agape. "You knew about this place?"

Mitteo suppressed a smile. "For longer than you can imagine."

"Mitteo," Adelmo said, "has been a member of our ranks for many years now, and most recently, an informant on magite missions."

"And all that bumbling around?" Alara said, "was it just for show?"

"Not all of it," he admitted. "But on missions, I always tried to give our bruya brethren a chance to escape when possible." Mitteo looked around the room. "How long until the others arrive?"

He looked more comfortable and confident than Quenti had ever seen him before.

The woman, Elna, gave a sigh, and she sat back down into her chair heavily. "There won't be any others."

"This is it?" Alara bit out.

Adelmo's face looked drawn as he sat down beside Elna. The rest of the group followed his lead.

"When the *envia* went out," Elna said, "it was chaos. The Network was unprepared and didn't know what to do. It was quickly followed by another message—one indicating we were to stay out of this." She paused, looking at the group, her eyes falling on Mitteo and Suri. "In fact, we were to fall in line with the Council's orders. We were told to capture the fugitives and bring them to the councilguards ourselves, if it came to it."

"The Network wants us working for the Council?" Mitteo's face was red and his brow furrowed.

Elna remained calm, her eyes soft as she took in Mitteo's anger. "This was an unsanctioned operation that puts the entire Network in danger. We can't afford to be unveiled because of a hotheaded few."

Alara flinched at this. "So, we should have left them to die?"

Elna didn't reply to this and the group let the words sit, the silence heavy. Alara's eyes were distant, cast downward onto the table.

"What happens now?" Runeo's voice was soft.

"Well, we get you all out of here as fast as we can. If either side catches you, it's over."

Mitteo slumped back into his chair, "Us too?"

"The second you revealed yourselves, your affiliation with the Network ended." Elna's voice held no sympathy. "You'll need to leave with the rest."

Beside her, Alara stiffened, knuckles white as she gripped her spear. *You'll need to leave with the rest.* The implication was clear. Quenti didn't move to comfort the other girl—she knew there was nothing that could be done or said.

"How do we get past the barrier?" Quenti asked.

"It's a *sosteya* spell that's holding the border—a wall of air and fire magia that keeps anything from moving through. A powerful one," the older mage said.

"Who's holding it?" Alara asked. "Take them out and we can take out the barrier." Her voice was higher than normal, but her face was set in a grim look of determination.

"Most likely, there are more than two mages holding the spell. Maybe even receptives," Elna replied.

"What does that mean?" Quenti asked.

"That it would be almost impossible to find and stop it at its source," Mitteo answered. Elna gave him a nod.

"We can't shut it off, but maybe we can break through it," Alara said.

"Break through the barrier with magia, you mean?" Quenti asked.

Elna pursed her lips in thought. "In the end, though powerful, the spell is just air and fire. If we attack it from multiple points at the same time…"

Khuna looked around the room, her face drawn with anxiety. "How many do we have for this?"

"Nine," Mitteo said, his own eyebrows furrowed. "Do you really think that's enough?"

"No," Elna replied, "but it'll have to be."

Chapter 43

Alara

Alara's head spun. This couldn't be real.

There was no series of underground tunnels in the Haven. There was no bruya network. There was no threat to those she cared about.

She was still asleep in her dorm room, or perhaps just sleeping through her history class again.

You'll need to leave with the rest.

Except, no. This wasn't a dream. This was all too real.

She understood the truth of those words the second she killed that councilguard.

She was going to lose her home—everything she knew—for the second time in her life. Nothing made sense anymore. She looked at Adelmo's face as he spoke, remembering all the conversations she had had with him about the Council and El'dyo. Had all of that been a lie? Was he just spying on Emaru through her?

And Emaru. Could she have known about the bruya mind-cleanses? Alara knew the answer before she even finished asking herself. Nothing happened in the Haven that Emaru didn't know. The thought of it made her stomach twist and her throat tight.

Micos's grim face flashed through her thoughts.

The ground fell away beneath her.

You'll need to leave with the rest.

The words sunk into her body and settled in her stomach like a rock. She felt the wood of the spear gripped loosely in her hand. The grain was smooth and warm beneath her palm.

She took a deep breath and focused only on this sensation. There was no time for self-pity right now. There would be time for that later. During a battle, all you can do is focus on your next move. Focus on not getting killed.

Alara looked at the worn profiles of the group gathered around the table. The torches in the room cast long and dark shadows across their faces. Zinita and Khuna were still pale and thin from their time in the dungeon. Runeo's eyes were glassy and distant. Lili and Quenti looked just as exhausted as she felt. Mitteo, Suri, and Elna were the only ones not strung out. They were ready to fight a battle—or, in this case, break through a magical barrier.

"We'll split into groups of two or three," Elna said, pulling Alara from her thoughts. "The smaller the groups, the less attention we'll draw. We'll need to make our way to the edges of the city without being caught."

"Make sure a magite or mage is in each group—the bruyas won't know where they're going." Alara's voice sounded strange to her own ears. "It may also help us blend in."

"Who's with who then?" Suri asked.

No one moved for a minute, their eyes roaming the room warily. It was Lili who stepped forward first, grabbing Mitteo's arm with a smile so bright only Lili could have managed it. "Partners?"

"Aren't you a tierren?" Suri said, frowning. "He is as well. We should split ourselves up into more diverse groups. We don't know who we'll be up against."

It was Zinita's turn to step forward, her lips tight. "I can go with him."

Mitteo turned to look at the bruya, his focus honing in on her sharp black eyes. He nodded, giving Lili a weak smile as he stepped away from her.

The rest of the group split up hesitantly, trying to make an even split of power. A deep frown creased Elna's face as she saw the cuff on Alara's wrist, though she didn't comment.

Elna pointed to Lili and Quenti. "I can take you both with me. I don't plan on leaving. Can you find your way out after we break through?"

They nodded in agreement.

Once Khuna and Suri formed their own group, Alara and Runeo were left standing next to one another. She gave him a weak smile, and he answered with a stiff nod.

She looked away, her smile dropping quickly as she turned to Adelmo. "Are you coming with us?"

"I can help get you to the border, but my place is here," he said.

Alara didn't know how to feel. Her heart instinctively sank at the thought of never being able to see him again, but the reality was that the man had been lying for years. No. Her entire life. She was torn grief and distrust.

Would I have trusted myself with the secrets he held? No.

"Okay." Elna's voice was firm as she looked around the room. "Everyone needs to make it to their section of the border before dusk. That should give us all a couple of hours."

They then made their plans to meet up in the woods after they broke through the barrier. From there, they would head back to Arbol. Those of them with blood on their clothing changed into the spare pieces they had stored in the chamber. Alara almost found herself laughing as Quenti pulled on a mage's tunic that was clearly two sizes too small, leaving a line of her stomach bare. Quenti let out a growl at her face.

"Just know," Elna continued, "by doing this, we are not just going against the Council, but against the Network as well. Outside of this room, there is no one else we can trust. Those in the Network will turn you in just as fast as anyone. You are all leaving—for good." Elna's eyes fell on Alara on this last line, and she felt the icy cold knowledge of what she was doing sink into her chest. But she held Elna's gaze unflinchingly, unwilling to show her fear. Elna nodded after a second and looked away.

Before they left, the group said their goodbyes. Quenti and Khuna gave each other a tight hug and Alara watched as Lili placed a soft kiss on Runeo's forehead, whispering something into his ear. Alara stood off to the side, awkwardly watching the exchanges. She gave a small jump as Quenti threw her arms around her. Lili followed suit, and Alara's chest squeezed tight as the two bruyas wished her luck.

She'd be lying if she'd said it didn't feel good. It was a warmth she had never really felt, even with Emaru.

"Do you have your lucky letter opener?" Quenti asked, eyes searching Alara's belt.

Alara frowned at the dull dagger that still sat at her hip. She pulled it out, fingering the dull blade lightly. "I don't think this thing has brought me any good luck. Maybe you should take it." She pushed it forward toward Quenti, who frowned and pushed it back.

"It brought you to Arbol. I'm calling that good luck. Keep it and hopefully it will do so again."

Alara bit her lip and slipped the dagger back into her belt, next to the sharpened one. She, Runeo, and Adelmo then re-entered the main tunnel, heading back to Adelmo's stables. Behind them, the other groups split up in different directions.

As they rushed toward the stables, Alara placed a soft hand on the dull dagger at her side and whispered a small prayer to El'dyo. And, for an extra bit of luck, she added a prayer to the bruya god, Sol.

When they left Adelmo's home thirty minutes later, the city was in chaos. People rushed by, eyes sweeping the streets and alleys, as if waiting for an army of bruyas to jump out.

Mages, magites, councilguards, and blameless alike all combed the city, in search of the elusive fugitives—though it was clear they had little idea who to look for. The bustle of the hunt made it all the easier to slip through the streets unnoticed. So worried were they about the bruyas on the loose, they didn't think to look at those in their own uniforms.

At one point, Alara's heart halted in her chest as a group of councilguards called for them to stop. But as the three of them were pushed to the side of the street and onto the narrow walkway, they marched by without so much as a second glance.

Alara let out a small curse at the incompetence of the councilguards before thanking El'dyo for their luck. Cielo wasn't a huge city—cities up north were more sprawling—but it was densely packed, and the streets wound along the mountainside, making it difficult to find any direct route to anywhere.

As they made their way toward the borders, turning toward the eastern edge, the chaos quieted. Adelmo took them down ever thinning streets, the number of villagers dwindling with each turn. As they ducked to the right, the street transformed into a set of stairs weaving between the tall buildings. The sun hung low in the sky, blanketing the narrow alley in deep shadows. It almost felt like entering the tunnels again. The staircase was just wide enough for two people to pass by each other, shoulders brushing against the stone walls.

"Hurry," Adelmo said as Alara paused at the top of the alley. She didn't respond, but bounded after him, Runeo close on her heels.

Only a few others were on this street, but each time Alara had to brush by them, she held her breath, waiting for inevitable discovery. She was so absorbed by this dance, she hadn't noticed when Adelmo stopped, and she bumped into him, catching herself from falling backward onto the stairs.

As she looked over Adelmo's shoulder, her breath caught in her throat. A man she didn't recognize stood in the middle of the street, his face grim and eyes narrowed. He wore the garbs of a councilguard, his hair a mixture of black and silver.

"I went by the stables to ask for your help with the fugitives. You weren't there." The man's voice was low. "I'd hoped I was wrong."

"Get out of our way."

"I'm afraid I can't do that. The Network's been ordered to turn in the escapees."

"No one here is an escapee. You can let us by and forget you saw us."

"You'd put your future at risk for a stupid pack of bruyas acting on a whim?"

"I'm doing what's right."

"So am I." The man moved his hands and a blast of wind hit Adelmo. His body jerked to the side, smacking against the wall of the building next to them.

Runeo launched a gale of wind the mysterious man. He

dodged the brunt of the gust, but fell back a few steps, giving Alara a chance to check on the downed Adelmo, who groaned softly.

Runeo followed up his attack with a second blast. It hit the man before he could counter, crumpling him to the ground. Runeo stepped forward, bow raised, arrow pointing unerringly at the man's chest.

Adelmo lifted his hand and tugged at Runeo's sleeve. "Don't. He's on our side."

"He has an interesting way of showing it."

"He's just following orders to protect the Network."

Alara looked between Adelmo and the other man. He sat against on the alley wall, heaving as he looked up at Runeo.

"If we leave him, he could turn us in." Alara's voice was colder than she expected.

Runeo hesitated, but dropped his bow. "He's right. We should go."

"We can't just leave him," Alara said.

"Alara." Adelmo spoke softly, pulling himself up from the ground. His eyes were focused on her with an understanding that made her scowl.

"We can't trust him," she said, chest burning with an emotion she refused to acknowledge.

"I know, but we have to go."

It was Runeo who moved first, tugging at her arm as he tucked his bow back away. Adelmo turned with a nod and continued to lead the way. Runeo kept a steadying hand on her as they moved down the thin path.

Alara didn't know whether to be relieved or worried that the man didn't pursue them.

A few minutes later, they had reached the outskirts, which saw them at the bottom of the mountain, Cielo rising in the sky above them. The sun had ducked behind the whole of the city, shadowing the forest that stretched before them.

After only a moment's hesitation, the group moved forward. The trees were twisted and wild, but the forest itself was thin. It ended abruptly only a hundred yards after it had begun. They broke into a clearing, and she saw the tall wall that encompassed Cielo stretching in front of them.

But that wasn't what brought Alara up short. Shimmering in the approaching dusk, the air a few yards short of the wall undulated. As she approached, the air thickened. After a few more steps, she had to stop short, her ears popping from some unseen pressure in the air and her face flushing red with the heat.

Runeo was beside her, a drip of sweat forming at his brow as he tried to press his own hand forward into the invisible force field.

"The sun is setting. You need to act now." Adelmo's voice echoed in the silent clearing.

Runeo and Alara made eye contact before they both stretched out their arms. Alara closed her eyes and pulled at the thread hot in her chest. The heat intensified around her and she could feel Runeo's powers building beside her. She opened her eyes and bit her lip, pressing her magia toward the barrier.

She could feel the pull of her magia meeting resistance, the air sizzling. She tugged, trying to put it out as she would a campfire. Beside her, she felt the edge of Runeo's own magia slam into the wall. She could see the ripples in the air moving, the barrier pushing and pulling between their magia, wavering under the pressure.

She was probably imagining it, but it seemed like she could feel the others along the border pushing their own magia into the wall, weakening it with each wave. The shimmer in the air sparked, and the heat abated as she tugged at the boundary.

"Wishing you took your cuff off now?" Runeo's voice was loud in her ear and she realized the hum of magia she was hearing was in her head, the surrounding clearing still silent.

"A little late for that, don't you think?" Alara said, out of breath from the effort.

"Just wanted to know if this was an 'I told you so' moment."

Alara clenched her teeth and pressed hard against the magia. "Nope."

She could feel the barrier weakening, the ripples in the air quaking. Her ears popped again, and she knew the pressure around the wall was starting to decrease. A small thrill of excitement and pride shot through her, and the flame of magia at her core burned brighter.

And then there was a loud crack. She had only just registered the sound when Runeo slammed into the barrier, his body bouncing off like a stuffed doll. Alara's thread of magia immediately snapped away from her grasp and the barrier pushed forward against her. She stumbled back and whipped around, eyes frantically taking in the clearing behind her.

The first thing she saw was Adelmo, face white and eyes wide, but he wasn't looking at her. He was looking at the edge of the forest where Emaru stood, hand still stretched out.

Her eyes were dark and focused on Alara.

CHAPTER 44

ALARA

The shock on Emaru's face probably matched Alara's. She didn't move or make a sound as their eyes met, but her lips were pulled tight and her eyebrows sank low on her face. Alara had seen the look of disappointment on her guardian's face many times before, but even after all she'd been through, she still felt the sharp stab of shame.

"Emaru!" Alara's voice seemed to shake the older woman out of her stupor.

"Alara," she said. "I thought you were dead."

This was the first time she'd ever heard Emaru's voice crack. The councilwoman had always been careful to present a strong front. So seeing even the slightest sense of humanity in her was enough to completely disarm Alara.

Without thinking, she flung herself forward, throwing her arms around the woman who had raised her.

She felt Emaru's own arms tightening around her, a warmth she had never felt before. Something inside of her unraveled.

"El'dyo," she said. "I don't know what's happening anymore.

I just missed home, and I wanted to come back, but Khuna and Micos—"

"Shh, shh. Everything is going to be okay. I'm just glad you're back."

Alara let herself sink into Emaru. She could count the times the older woman had comforted her on one hand, and in that moment, it was all she had ever needed. The exhaustion and confusion and grief of the past few weeks melted away.

Behind them, Runeo groaned, and she pulled away to see him pushing himself off the ground. Immediately, she stepped toward him. His face was twisted in pain, and he was clutching his side.

Emaru gripped her arm tight with her hand. "Stand clear, Alara."

"No! He's…" Alara stopped, unsure of how to even end that sentence. How could she make Emaru understand?

He's not bad. He's one of the good ones. He's a friend.

"Alara." Emaru's voice was sharp, and her grip almost painful.

"But—" Before she could finish her thought, Runeo was to his feet, hands thrown forward, ready to fight. Emaru sent another wave of wind and it cracked against him. He flew back folding in on himself, coughing.

Alara tugged against Emaru. "Stop it!"

"Back away, Alara."

"No, listen to me!"

Emaru snatched at her wrist as she tried again to stop the woman from throwing an attack. "Stop this, you stupid child!"

The flame inside Alara flared to life, and her body glowed with heat. Emaru let go with a hiss and Alara stumbled back.

"I need you to listen to me," Alara said as she tried to tamp down the power flaring inside her.

"Honey," Emaru said, "I know you've been through a lot, but you're not thinking clearly. I was so scared when you fell over the cliff. I thought you were lost for good." Her eyes shone and her teeth flashed in the dusky shadows. "But you were so much more resilient than even I could imagine. You will make a wonderful councilguard and a powerful mage in whatever way you want."

Alara's eyes went wide at those words.

"Yes," Emaru continued. "You've shown your strength, your power, and your drive. No one could doubt that now. No further tests would be needed to prove it."

"I'd be a mage?" Alara said. After everything she'd been through, she'd almost forgotten how it all had started. How close she was to failing out. And that whole struggle could pay off.

"You'll be a councilguard," Emaru said.

"Councilguard…" Alara repeated the word under her breath. Given the circumstances, she shouldn't have cared, but she felt a lump form in her throat all the same.

Emaru leaned to look over Alara's shoulder. "But councilguards can't let bruyas run wild in Cielo. We need to keep the Haven safe."

Alara shook her head. "Runeo isn't dangerous."

Emaru's lips twitched ever so slightly at her words. The emotion was brief, but clear. She had been on the receiving end of it more times than she could count. "You're tired. We can discuss this all later, but you need to step away."

But Alara didn't move. It was an easy decision. A single step to the side is all it would take to achieve her dreams. But she didn't move. She *couldn't* move.

Runeo stumbled back up from the ground, a trickle of blood running from his ear.

"Alara," he said. "Move, so I can take care of this."

"No."

"She took Micos. She took my brother." His voice was cracked and brittle.

Alara's stomach twisted, and she looked back at Emaru's face, flushed with anger.

"Did you know?"

"What?" Emaru asked, her anger just barely suppressed.

"What they're doing to the bruyas? Wiping their minds? Killing them if they don't fall in line?"

Emaru's shoulders went rigid. "We do what we need to protect our realm."

"I thought we were helping them," Alara said, feeling stupid even as she suggested it.

"We are helping them. Sometimes it's better when people don't remember."

"When you take away their identity."

"You've spent too long letting the bruyas and traitors—" Emaru spit the words out as her eyes flashed to Runeo and Adelmo "—fill your head with lies and nonsense. We protect those with magia from themselves. And we protect the blameless from their influence. From their capacity to corrupt. You've always known that. Sometimes that takes sacrifice."

Alara let her hand fly up to run along the ridge of her scar. She *had* always known that, hadn't she? Her shoulders slumped, and she looked over to see Adelmo, eyes shining with disappointment and fear as the resolution melted from her face. She turned away from him, not wanting to see his thoughts so plainly written in his expression—accusing her. And she stepped to the side.

Emaru's lips lifted into a smile. "That's better."

Alara sagged as the councilwoman casually flicked her hand, raising Runeo in the air. He gasped and choked, as if hanged by his neck. Alara watched, pale, her breath stuttering as his face went red. His eyes searched hers out, but they weren't filled with the anger and hate she expected to see there. In them she saw a plea, the same plea he wore in the dungeons as she had pulled him away from Micos. Heat shuddered through her body.

"You're strong, I'll give you that," Emaru said. "Stronger than the bruya whose mind we cleansed. Your brother, was he? He begged us to let him go before we fixed his mind, but he's much happier now. I promise."

With a crack, the flame inside Alara's chest burst from her and the air sizzled with heat. Emaru dropped Runeo with a small gasp and turned on her, eyes wild.

Alara's mind buzzed, and any sane thoughts quickly dissipated amid her fury. She shot her hand out, sending a crackling whip of flame toward her, toward Emaru. In the back of her mind, she realized she was using the fire from the boundary spell to feed her magia, and a rush of power thrummed through her blood.

Emaru fell back as the flame bit into the air where she had just been. But she recovered quickly and sent a burst of wind at Alara, knocking her off her feet.

She hit the ground and felt the air stutter out of her lungs. She didn't wait to recover before she wildly threw her magia, sending tendrils of sizzling flame to wrap around the councilwoman.

But Emaru flicked her hand casually, and the heat dispersed.

"What are you doing, child?"

"I should have listened to you sooner. I shouldn't have been holding back my powers." Alara sent another flame at Emaru. It spun behind her, but she still blocked it with ease.

"It's a lesson you learned too late. Perhaps when we cleanse your memories, we'll do a better job of teaching you."

Alara growled as she sent another flare toward Emaru. It shot out, fast and hot, and she smiled with satisfaction as the councilwoman stumbled as she dodged it. A second flame had Emaru falling to her knees, face turning red—though with anger or embarrassment, Alara couldn't tell.

Emaru didn't even seem to move her arm, but suddenly Alara was flying backward, feet off the ground. She crashed into a tree behind her and felt the crack of flesh on wood shudder through her. Though she didn't have the air in her lungs to cry out, her entire body screamed.

Adelmo stumbled toward her, his face pale and drawn before a streak of air sent him stumbling back. Emaru didn't even bother to look his way; her eyes focused solely on Alara.

"It would be such a waste if I was forced to kill you, Alara. Come to your senses."

"This is what the Council has become?" Alara's ribs ached with each syllable uttered.

"You don't understand the Council at all. This is what it needed to become to survive. To keep the citizens of Sombria safe. To maintain peace."

Emaru raised her hands toward Alara, and she felt her stomach clench, waiting for the blow. Her own hand reached out automatically, the thread of magia weak, but there.

Then everything happened at once.

Alara felt the wind from Emaru's attack raging toward her at the same time she saw Adelmo jump between the two of them, his spear raised toward the councilwoman's heart. And then the sparks of magia that Alara had thrown were caught in Emaru's wind blast. The air between them exploded in fire and heat.

Alara flew back against the tree and the world went from white to black.

Chapter 45

Quenti

Quenti felt the fear traveling down her spine, ice cold and sharp.

"You saw that, right?" Lili asked, voice thin. She slumped against the nearby tree and stared up at the barrier. Her skin was pallid again.

Quenti could feel the drain on her own powers. She could only imagine what Lili was feeling after all the healing and mind-walking she had done. Absently, she fingered the tender and jagged scar that burned against her stomach.

"Something happened," Elna said. "Something bad." Her hands were outstretched as she pushed against the barrier with her magia.

A ripple of hot air traveled along the wall and brushed back a strand of Quenti's hair, but the barrier remained unaffected.

Just a few minutes before, the air had shuddered and cracked. Quenti had let out a shout of glee as the wall of fire and air seemed ready to shatter. But then there was a flash of light so fast she wasn't sure she had really seen it. And then silence and stillness. The ripples had calmed, and the barrier had stilled, as if nothing had happened.

Groaning in frustration, Quenti pulled water from the small drainage ditch nearby. She threw it straight at the wall where Elna stood. With a hiss, it turned to steam, the barrier unperturbed by her attempt.

"Now what?" Quenti asked, slumping down next to Lili.

"We should head back. One of the others might know what happened," Elna said.

Defeat fell heavy on her shoulders. They had been so close to getting free. But she pushed herself up from the ground. "I hate Cielo," she spat. "It smells like human waste."

Something had shifted in the city. They were on the outskirts where the forest met the oldest buildings of Cielo. The painted rooftops here were faded and scarred. The stonework forgotten, clogged with moss and dirt, even as people continued to live their lives.

On the way out, the streets had been almost empty as they slipped through alleys, but now they overflowed with activity.

"People look—excited," Lili whispered.

"That's not good for us," Quenti said.

"Not good at all. Once we get back, we'll have time to come up with a new plan. Adelmo always knows—"

"Elna!"

Elna's steps faltered at the voice behind them, then she swiveled around, face shifting as she greeted the councilguards coming down the side street.

Quenti's stomach clenched, and the blood drained from her face. Eight sets of eyes were focused on the three of them. She didn't need Alara to tell her that two of the councilguards standing with flint cuffs on their wrists were fire mages, and the other six looked just as intimidating.

"Where have you been?" one guard asked. "Senye Cruz was asking about you."

"I've been searching for the escaped bruyas. Same as everyone else."

The guard smiled. "We've caught some. On the other side of the city."

Quenti's head swam. Beside her, Lili's body went rigid, but to her credit, she didn't make a sound.

"Senye Emaru thinks the rest will be scattered along the outskirts," the councilguard continued.

"I've already been searching this area," Elna said. "I've seen nothing yet." The mage's voice was exhausted, though she couldn't tell if it was genuine or part of her act.

She then caught the eye of one of the fire mages. His lips turned down in a frown.

"Who are they?"

"Magites, Senye," Quenti said, hoping addressing the man as such wouldn't be out of line. She didn't exactly focus on basic magite etiquette in her short time there. "We're here to help with the search for the bruya scum." *Was that too much?*

Elna frowned. "And what I was telling *them* was to return to their dorms. The councilguards and mages have things under control!"

"But we can help fight!" Lili shot back, catching on.

"You can help by staying out of anyone's way. And not being seen," Elna hissed the last part.

Quenti grabbed Lili by the arm. "Clearly we're not wanted."

As they turned, Quenti heard the fire mage speak and her

shoulders tightened. "Don't those two look a little old to be magites?"

"They're from one the outskirt villages and were picked up later than most. They seemed a little slow, if you ask me," Elna whispered. "Come on, I haven't checked south of here."

With that, the councilguards marched away, down the way the bruyas had just come. Quenti and Lili tried to keep their stride steady, even as her heart hammered in her chest.

They'd lost their only ally in the city. But even worse, one of their own had been caught. Who was it? A wave of panic hit her as she pictured Khuna's gaunt face when they had first found her in the cells.

"The entrance to the tunnels isn't far," Lili said, squeezing Quenti's arm. "We'll know what's happening soon."

When they arrived at the meeting chamber entrance, the door was closed, but light leaked from underneath. Quenti paused, hand on the cold wood. She almost didn't want to know who'd been caught. She didn't know what she'd do if it was Khuna again.

Lili's warm hand covered her own. Quenti felt the cool trickle of calming reassurance move down her arm and into her chest. And then Lili pushed open the door.

Quenti saw Zinita first, dagger unsheathed and poised as her wary eyes watched them enter. Mitteo and Suri sat at the table, whispering. And then there was Khuna, pacing up and down the room.

Khuna looked up, eyes flicking from Lili to Quenti. She ran forward, pulling her into an embrace.

Quenti let herself be held, just for a moment. Khuna's entire body trembled. She gently pushed Khuna back and placed a hand on either side of her face, looking into her eyes.

"We're both okay."

Khuna nodded.

Quenti kissed her, ignoring the cracked dry skin and taste of dried salt, relief flooding her body. Everything was going wrong, but at least Khuna was still safe.

"So, do we know what happened?" Zinita's voice was cold and snapped Quenti out of her reverie.

She took stock of the group and it hit her. All the groups were back, except one.

"Alara, Runeo, and Adelmo were caught," Quenti said.

Lili let out a curse.

"Now what?" Zinita said.

"Now, we come up with a new plan," Suri said, looking around at the others. "We still need to get you all out."

"We aren't leaving Runeo behind." The anger in Zinita's voice surprised Quenti. "Not like Micos."

"You may not have a choice. Breaking them out may have been an option before, but things are different now. You'll get nowhere near where they're holding them."

"Right now," Mitteo said, "we need to lie low. The entire city is looking for you—for us. El'dyo, it feels weird saying that."

"So we sit around waiting and just hope no one finds us?" Quenti said.

"We wait and we plan," Mitteo replied.

"I'm sick of planning. Our plans haven't worked so far, anyway."

"So, what would you suggest? A full frontal assault on the Haven?"

"We need to do something," she said, rebelliously.

"We need to stay here," Mitteo said, more firmly.

"We can't just wait around for something to happen." Quenti grabbed the small dagger tucked into her belt. "I'm going. Anyone who wants to join can."

"And what actually are we going to do?" Mitteo asked, exasperated. But Quenti saw even he was standing now.

"If the Network can't be bothered to come and help us, we'll go to them."

Chapter 46

Alara

Alara was awake before she was aware. She lay with her eyes closed, feeling every bone and muscle in her body protesting against the movement of her breathing. The dirt beneath her was cold, and the air was icy and smelled of something familiar that turned her stomach. She was no longer outside in the forest.

The sharp realization of what had happened hit her, and a new pain stabbed in her chest. Her eyes cracked open to a dim darkness, a stone ceiling only just visible above her. And out of the corner of her eye, a set of metal bars. She was back in the dungeon, lying on the ground of the cell she had saved Khuna from just hours before.

It took her another few minutes to get the strength to move her head, and she heard an immediate whisper of movement in response to her own.

"Alara?"

She tried to speak, but her throat was tight and dry. She swallowed and tried again, wincing as her voice cracked. "Runeo? Are you—okay?"

"I'm okay, but..." He paused and seemed to choke on his words.

Alara turned over with a groan, trying to find him in the dimness. He was in the cell next to her, sitting up, but she could only just see a silhouette of something large on the ground next to him.

"I tried to save him," Runeo said, his voice maintaining its uncharacteristic softness. "I tried, but I didn't know what to do. Lili could have..." The words died on his lips and Alara lurched forward, eyes straining in the darkness as she took in Adelmo's slumped form.

Alara realized the smell she had registered when she had awoken. Adelmo's face was white and red, the skin burned away to show the muscle underneath. She only glanced down long enough to see that the rest of him had shared the same fate. She looked back at his face and looked into the hollow blue eyes of her friend.

Alara turned and gagged, her stomach wrenching painfully even though she had nothing to give. She hadn't eaten since the night before.

"I'm sorry." Runeo's voice was soft.

Alara shuddered, a numbness sinking into her body. "It's my fault. If only I had had better control. If only I had listened to Emaru." She thought again of the look of cold disappointment on Emaru's face. She chuckled humorlessly. "Ironic how listening to her could have saved us from her."

"That was the woman who raised you?"

"Yes," Alara said. She expected to feel something as she confirmed her relationship to the councilwoman—Sadness, guilt, anything, really. Instead, the hollowness in her chest only expanded.

Only silence from Runeo followed, and she slowly took in their surroundings. There was only one torch left burning across the room. The prisoners they had left behind only a few hours before were slumped in their own cells, the dim light outlining their pathetic bodies.

Her cell was only a couple of yards across at its widest. A single bucket sat in the corner and Alara tried not to think about what it was for. She was wearing her magite robes, although they were stained and torn beyond redemption now. Her weapons were gone, and she felt a pang of sadness when she realized that the dull dagger that Quenti had returned to her was also gone.

She also noted the twin cuff that sat on her left wrist, matching her right. After attempting to pull at the thread of magia in her chest, she realized she couldn't even feel the heat of it anymore. This realization left her hollow, causing her to shiver in the damp air of the prison.

She fingered her cuff—the one that had been on her since she could remember. Hadn't she always been a prisoner?

"I should have listened to Emaru. I shouldn't have been so stupid, so afraid of my own magia." Alara bit the words out. The continued irony only frustrated her further the more she thought about it.

"It wouldn't have mattered," Runeo said. "They would have never let you truly embrace it. They wanted you to fear it. The Council sees our powers as a tool, but they aren't. They are a part of us, as much as an arm, a leg, or even a heart."

"But it could have saved him still. It could have."

Alara heard a shuffling and looked over to see Runeo leaning against the bars between their cells. "You've been fighting with one hand tied behind your back your entire life. It's a wonder you had any power to show for it at all." He stretched his hand out toward the torch across the room, the cuff glinting gold in the wane light. The shadows in the room shifted as a small breeze cut through the air.

Runeo's eyes studied her. "It feels like trying to breathe underwater having this cuff on. How strong did you have to be to wear this cuff your entire life and still use your powers?"

Alara looked down at the cuffs on her wrists and felt the cold hollowness in her chest like a sharp blade to the gut. The image of her family home in flames and Adelmo's burnt skin flickered in her mind, turning her stomach. "It doesn't matter now. Do you think it will be a memory cleanse or execution?"

Runeo's laugh was rough and humorless. "I may be executed, but I doubt they'll give you up after even this." His dark eyes met hers in the dark again. "I bet you could still use your powers, even now, if you wanted."

"I can't even feel them."

"Try."

She flicked her hand toward the torch, its flames undisturbed.

He huffed. "Okay, now actually try."

She sent a sharp look of annoyance toward him, but pushed toward her powers at the center of her chest. She was somehow relieved to feel the slightest breath of warmth there. She reached out with it, and the flame flickered. The shadows danced across Runeo's face, smug and satisfied.

"What good does that do me?"

"I didn't think you were one to give up so easily. You seemed like you had more fight back in Arbol."

"Maybe I've learned my lesson."

"The wrong one." Runeo was pressed against the bars, and his black eyes seemed to glow in the darkness. "I'm not giving up yet and neither should you. We can fight them when they come for us."

Alara looked at him, trying to muster the same passion and hope he still seemed to possess, but from the corner of her eye, she could still see the shadow of Adelmo's form crumpled on the ground. Her eyes burned with tears and emotion.

"I'm done fighting."

Runeo pushed off from the bars, moving to sit on the other side of the bars, his anger clear in the jerkiness of his movement. Alara tried to care, but she couldn't. She stayed slumped against the wall and stared blankly into the darkness. She wondered, not for the first time that week, what it might be like to have her mind cleansed.

The thought didn't escape her that she had somehow run home only to find herself in the same predicament she had been in Arbol. Would they erase Adelmo from her mind? Perhaps it wouldn't be so bad. Perhaps it would be better to not remember and go back to blissful ignorance.

She lost track of time. How long had it been? Hours? Days? What about the others? She focused on the flame across the room, its flickering hypnotizing. And then there was the grinding of metal on metal and wood on stone, and the prison shone with light.

Alara blinked into the sudden brightness, trying to adjust and make sense of the forms that stood before her.

"Senye Cruz," Alara said as her eyes focused. Councilwoman Lena Cruz stood before her, two councilguards flanking her, and someone Alara recognized with a stab of fear: Luis, a mind-walker employed by the Council. Did that mean…

Runeo was right. They *were* there to cleanse her memories. She hadn't even thought that the person doing the cleansing would be someone she recognized, but there was a lot that she hadn't known.

Senye Cruz's smirk was cold and unflinching as she stared down at Alara in the torch's light. She had grown to hate that smirk over the years. But this instance told a specific story. *This* smirk was the look of someone who had wanted the worst for her since day one and was finally seeing it come to fruition. Alara lifted her chin, sending a glare back at the woman, refusing to give in to the look of loathing.

"Well, well," Senye Cruz said. "I always told Senye Emaru that one day you would end up here. She didn't believe me. She thought she had you completely under her wing. Goes to show how much she really knows."

Alara didn't respond to this, but she felt herself flinch at the words. She saw Emaru's face flash in her mind again—the look of disappointment as they fought on the border. And the look of cold disgust that had flashed in her eyes right before Alara had sent out the attack that had killed Adelmo.

"Leave us," Senye Cruz said, glancing between the two councilguards.

They hesitated, looking at each other but not moving.

"The prisoners are behind bars and cuffed. What possible threat could they pose?"

"We've been given orders to escort you all to the councilroom for the sentencing and cleanse," one guard said, shifting by the councilwoman. Neither of the councilguards were mages, and she could almost feel their discomfort standing next to Senye Cruz.

"I'm giving you new orders."

"But Senye Emaru—"

"Yes, yes, Linda is ever by-the-book, isn't she?" Senye Cruz said. With a wave of her hands, the torch she was carrying flared up, sending the guards scrambling back for a second. Before they could register what was happening, Senye Cruz had her dagger in her hands. She slashed the blade across both councilguards' throats, sending a bright red flash of blood through the air.

Alara fell back with a small scream as blood spilled onto the floor of her cell. She looked back at Senye Cruz and saw that she had stopped moving, her blade dropped to the ground and eyes wide. Behind her, Luis had a large hand gripped on the councilwoman's head and Alara could feel waves of power flowing from him.

She didn't stop to think. She pulled hard at the thin, frayed thread of magia in her chest, fumbling for as it danced and spun from her grip. She sent it to the torch still gripped in Senye Cruz's hand. The fire's flare was only a quarter of the size of the one Cruz had managed before, but it was enough. The fire sprang toward Luis's arm and he jumped back with a small cry of pain.

His eyes turned to her, anger clear as his hand stretched out to Alara.

The ground shifted under her, roots clawing out to grab at her legs. But the distraction had been enough. Senye Cruz had dropped to the ground and found her fallen dagger. Alara watched with wide eyes as the older woman turned with a smooth motion and stabbed him repeatedly, viciously.

The roots at her feet stopped moving, and the man gave a strangled cry before he crumpled to the ground.

Senye Cruz stood up from the ground, stepping back from the man. Her eyes glowed gold when she looked up at Alara with a small smirk.

"Clearly, Senye Emaru has been underestimating you from day one."

CHAPTER 47

ALARA

"You've made quite a stir, Alara," Senye Cruz said, looking through the bars. "You have both the Council and the Network up in arms."

"The Network?" Alara said, eyes widening. "What Network?"

"You've always been a terrible liar. It just doesn't fit you, child," Senye Cruz said with a tilt of her head. "I know about the Network. I'm one of those who run it."

"You're what?" Alara wasn't sure what Senye Cruz saw in her face, but the woman laughed and shook her head. She made her way toward the wall, plucking the keys from where they hung near the door.

"Who do you think helped Quenti escape?" she asked with a smile. Unlocking Runeo and Alara's cells, Senye Cruz stepped back and made room for them to pass.

Runeo stepped out first, eyeing her with suspicion. He allowed her to take his wrist and unlock the cuff. As he rubbed his skin where the cuff had been, a breeze fluttered through the dungeon. For the first time since Micos's capture, he looked alive —just a little. He smiled at Senye Cruz. "Thank you."

Her golden eyes winked in the firelight and she nodded at him before turning to Alara.

She stepped out of her cell and over the slumped body of Luis, being careful to not get blood on her boots. Senye Cruz approached her, the keys for the cuffs in her hands. Alara allowed her to unlock the first cuff, feeling the weight of it lift from her chest. The silver-haired woman nodded to her second wrist and Alara looked to where the cuff laid against her arm, scuffed from years of use.

"You were trained," Senye Cruz said, "to fear your abilities— to keep them under control. Are you ready to embrace this part of you?"

Alara looked between the cuff and Senye Cruz. She felt like the world was shifting beneath her and she was just barely holding on. She wasn't ready for much of anything at this moment, and all she could do was anxiously run her fingers along the wrinkled burn along her neck.

Senye Cruz stepped forward with a frown. "The fire only burns you if you let it. Your magia is a part of you, like any other limb or organ. You're better than this. Got it?"

Alara felt the queasiness in her stomach shift.

"I said, do you got it?"

While the feeling in Alara's gut didn't quite lift, she nodded anyway. She would never be ready, but if there was a time to do something crazy, this was it.

Alara lifted her wrist and allowed Senye Cruz to unlock the cuff. Her skin felt icy as it fell to the ground, but it was quickly replaced by a surging wave of heat flowing through her. The flame that always flicked in her chest flared to life. The torches in the room bloomed and danced, filling the room with light.

She felt a cool hand on her shoulder, and Senye Cruz leaned down to look her in the eye. "Take a deep breath and remain calm. Remember that your power is a part of you. It isn't something to fight or control."

Her voice was soothing and Alara found herself nodding as the flame within her calmed. The heat didn't dissipate, but she adjusted to the thrill of fire pulsing throughout her.

The flames on the torches calmed and returned to their normal flicker. "Much better," Senye Cruz said. She looked back up, her eyes taking in the room. "It looks like you are the only two. Who else were you with?"

Alara felt a small weight lift off her shoulders as she too looked around. No one else had been caught. She told Senye Cruz who else was in the group and felt as the older woman tried to send out an *envia* to Mitteo, Elna, and Suri, letting them know where they were at. She shook her head after a second. "I can't find them, but the Haven is always difficult to send through. The fact they aren't in here is a good sign, though."

Alara nodded at this, but it was Runeo who spoke up. "What does it matter? If the barrier is up, we're still trapped."

"I know where the receptive holding the spell is."

Alara's eyebrows raised at this. "The spell is in a receptive?"

"Break the receptive and the barrier will go down. If you get out fast enough after, they won't have time to put the barrier back up. And I can help delay that."

"I didn't know there were receptives powerful enough to hold such a spell," Runeo said.

"There aren't many. It will be sad to see this one broken, but I fear we have no choice." Senye Cruz looked around at the other cells as the small group of prisoners stared at the scene playing out in front of them. She made eye contact with one man, and he quickly backed away from the bars, his eyes widening in fear. But another man was leaning against the bars of his cell, a smirk on his face.

"Do you need help with any of this?" His voice was gruff. It matched his unshaved face and dark, shadowed eyes.

No. They didn't need help from some strange prisoner. She shook her head at Senye Cruz, but she was ignored.

"What's your name?"

"Tony."

"And your crime?"

"An unregistered mage. I got caught outside of Lejon trying to cross the Ruinedlands."

Senye Cruz nodded and looked at Alara, as if looking for approval.

"Do you trust him?" Alara asked.

"I remember the story of his arrest. They don't hold people for violent crimes here—only crimes against the Council. It is likely these people are on our side."

"And if he's not?" Alara's eyes narrowed as she turned to look at the man. He was thin and dirty from his stay in the prison, but he held himself with confidence. She realized standing there that she could feel his magia rolling off him, even cuffed. It was cool and clear. "You're a water mage?" she asked, eyeing him.

He looked a little surprised, but nodded. "Technically, not a mage, but I trained in the Haven before I defected. I know my way around."

Alara hesitated, looking at the keys in Senye Cruz's hand. She shook her head. "It's too dangerous." Her eyes met Runeo's, and she saw he was studying her. He said nothing as he moved toward Senye Cruz, shoulders straight.

He offered his hand out and Alara watched as Senye Cruz dropped the keys into his palm. He silently walked over and unlocked the man's cell, stepping back to let him out. He smiled at Runeo, rolling his shoulders back and forth before leaning down to wrestle the weapons out of one of the dead council-guard's hands.

Runeo threw the keys back to Senye Cruz. "We should let the rest out, too."

Alara's mouth opened in protest, but Senye Cruz's golden eyes sparked in the light. "Since we're breaking all the rules anyway, I don't see why not. I can help the rest out and find your friends. I will let them know the plan and make sure you all find each other at the end of this."

Alara didn't like it, but if the past few weeks taught her anything, it's that the world wasn't always as it seemed. Plus, they could use all the help they could get.

She turned to Senye Cruz. "Are you coming with us?" She looked over at the tall mage in her bright, neatly pressed clothes. She wore the red and orange shawl of a fire mage with white thread woven throughout to show her status as a mind-talker, a thin bronze headband wrapped around her head to show her status as a councilmember. Alara couldn't help but respect her. In spite of her status within the Haven, she was ready and willing to risk it all.

"My place is still here. I can help you escape, but I've done more good staying here than I could ever do out there."

"Won't you get caught, for all of this?" Alara said, a hand waving over the bodies that were scattered around the room and cell doors flung wide.

Senye Cruz raised her eyebrows in surprise. "I have no idea what you're talking about. I was in my quarters when the pris-oners all escaped. Speaking of which, the councilguards were supposed to bring you up to the councilrooms with Luis. Emaru will notice soon that you haven't arrived, and I am supposed to be there soon as well."

She rushed to open the cells of the last few prisoners and then turned back to Alara. "The receptive is in the main worship hall. Destroy it and the barrier will go down. I will delay its reinstatement as long as I can, and I'll send an *envia* when I find your friends. But for now, you should go!"

Alara nodded, and before Senye Cruz could question it, Alara threw an arm around her. "Thank you."

"Go, child!" Senye Cruz said, awkwardly peeling the Alara off of her.

With that, Alara, Runeo, and Tony left the dungeon. Runeo and Tony had changed into the councilguards' gear and collected their weapons. He handed a small dagger and spear off to Alara as they left.

"Where to?"

They both looked at her expectantly, and she straightened her shoulders and took a breath before turning to the left.

"You heard her. We're headed to the worship hall."

CHAPTER 48

ALARA

As they made their way up through the lower level and to the main level of the councilrooms, they didn't pass a single other person, mage or otherwise. Alara had never seen the halls so empty in all her years at the Haven. It was… an unsettling sensation.

"Well, how many city-wide bruya searches have there been?" Runeo reasoned with a smirk.

It was a good point, and given how many others in their party remained, having even the lowliest of magites involved in the search made sense.

"I, for one, won't question our luck," Tony said from behind her.

Alara shot a glare behind her, still unsure of whether she trusted this man.

Though regardless of how much an empty Haven made sense, she knew she wouldn't be happy until they made it out of the Haven—and out of Cielo. They needed to keep their guards up.

She sent her awareness out ahead of them again, keeping a feeler out for mages or magites heading their way. She realized as they walked quickly through the halls just how easy it was to tell the people she felt apart. She felt every movement and use of their powers, and could even differentiate the magia being used. From the heat of a fire mage's magia to the cool breeze of a wind mage, each one felt distinct. It was as though she was seeing the world through her powers for the first time, every sensation crisp, clear, and so very full. What could she have learned had she just done this from the start?

She snapped back into the moment, and her mind-stalking abilities snagged the presence of a few mages around the next corner. There would be no easy way to avoid this group. The corridor they were in led to the worship hall, and any other route would have them circle the entire Haven, putting them at further risk of running into other groups.

She raised her arm as they approached the corner and the group slowed to a fast walk. She pointed in the direction before holding up four fingers. Runeo and Tony both nodded, the grips on their weapons shifting. Runeo pulled his bow and Tony tightened his fist along the wood of his spear. Hopefully, they wouldn't have to use their weapons, though, as both Runeo and Tony were dressed in councilguard attire. They couldn't afford to waste any more time on unnecessary fights.

Still, she held her hand steady on her spear, and they turned the corner at a casual walking pace, heads down as they approached the small group.

"Are you kidding me?"

A stone sank in Alara's stomach and her head whipped up, eyes meeting Raquel's.

"Sol," Runeo cursed, obviously recognizing her as she

rounded on them, the three other magites behind her now alert to the threat.

Raquel squinted for a moment, a finger touching her forehead right as Alara felt a magia flare.

Son of a bruya.

She was sending an *envia*.

Fugitive Alara Ayar has been spotted. She is in the Haven by—

Before she could finish the message, Runeo had sent a burst of wind, knocking her to the ground. The other three magites moved forward, weapons at the ready.

Alara ducked as a swinging bola whipped just over her head, smacking hard into the stone wall behind her. She scrambled back to her feet and whipped her spear around, the shaft crossing with an enemy's own spear with a thud.

The magite gave a small twist of his hand, and Alara felt the pull of his magia, though she couldn't do much as the ground beneath her shifted. A root snapped around her ankle, and she stumbled sideways, trying to keep her balance.

With every moment, she only felt the roots tighten around her calf. Frustrated, she sent a spark of fire from a nearby torch at the root and it burst into flames. The heat of the fire, though intense, didn't burn her as it ate the root away. With a scream, Alara pushed back at her opponent, who fell back, eyes wide as the flames sizzled around them. There was fear in his eyes; a fear of her abilities. Though, for the first time in her life, Alara didn't care. She raised a hand to send the flames in the magite's direction, but was thrown to the ground by a gust of air, her spear clattering to the floor.

Her bruised body protested at the jarring movement as she tried to catch her breath. What she saw wasn't a surprise: Raquel coming at her, a look of pure loathing twisting her face. The girl was always looking for an excuse to pick a fight with her.

Alara moved her hand and threw the flames of a torch toward her charging enemy, but the wind mage batted the flames away with a burst of air—or at least tried. The first flare dissipated but was immediately overrun by the remaining flaming gale. A loud scream pierced the air around Alara, somehow breaking through the roaring of flames. It was an all too familiar sound, one that plagued her nightmares. With a panicked breath, Alara pulled back her magia. The flames dissipated, revealing Raquel, out of breath, clothes tattered, hair singed, and eyes red and watery.

Alara swallowed. She could have kept going. If she did, who knows if Raquel would even be standing there.

A gust of wind blew Alara back and onto the hard marble floor. Leaping back to her feet, she narrowly dodged another blow from Raquel before pushing her hands out in front of her. She pulled again at the threads within. This time, she'd go all out and make sure Raquel was done, for sure. An image of Adelmo's charred remains flashed in her eyes, the smell of burnt flesh singeing her nostrils.

And then nothing happened.

"You still suck at this, you know?" Alara winced at the look of satisfaction on Raquel's face. The hollowness in her chest threatened to suffocate her as she looked into her eyes. It wasn't a feeling of shame, as she expected. It was fear. Fear for Raquel's life. She knew in that moment that she could end it. The thought terrified her.

Her eyes searched out her spear, but the weapon was too far for her to reach.

Raquel followed her gaze. "You always thought you were better than us. That rejecting your magia made you special. But you're nothing without your stupid weapons."

Alara felt her chest flare with heat at Raquel's words. Alara *had* thought she was better. But she wasn't nothing without her spear. Not anymore.

"Fine." Alara threw her hands forward, pulling tight on the threads of her magia that swirled in her blood. The torches on either side of the hall burst forward, filling the air in front of her. Alara crawled back in surprise. She heard Raquel's strangled cry through the flames, but couldn't see her through the brilliant wall of fire.

Alara stumbled to her feet, pulling on the flames, a little queasy as she pictured Adelmo's burned face again in her mind.

A ribbon of wind shot through a weak spot in the flames, A ribbon of wind lifted her and threw her against the wall. She caught her breath and she pulled at the torch flames behind Raquel and sent them soaring toward the other girl's head. Her brown hair sizzled as it caught, and she screamed, dropping to the ground and using her shawl to put out the flames.

"I don't want to hurt you," Alara said, noticing the burns along the side of Raquel's face. They almost mirrored her own.

The girl let out a growl and leaped toward Alara, air throwing Alara back to the ground. Before she could catch her breath, the mage lifted her again and Alara felt her body, like a rag doll, being thrown against the other side of the hallway.

"I've wanted to do this for so long!" Raquel screamed.

Alara fell to the ground, sharp spikes of pain pricking her ribs. And then Raquel was on top of her, eyes flashing and teeth showing in a wolfish grin. The wind mage had her hands around Alara's throat, her thumbs pressing into her windpipe, magia forgotten.

Alara scratched futilely at the girl's hands, trying to lighten the grip. She stretched a hand out beside her and weakly tugged at the threads of her magia, pulling the torch flames toward them, but she couldn't keep a grip.

Blackness creeped along the edge of her vision.

This was how it would all end. At the hands of one of her former classmates…

And then the flames reached Alara's hands, exploding into a roaring inferno, engulfing Raquel's head completely. She could see it. The wicked smile of the jealous magite, face turned black in the heat, skin melting away. She could smell it. A sickening steak, putrid and nauseating.

And all through it, Raquel's determination shown through. She didn't scream. She didn't yell. After the longest several seconds in existence, her hands simply fell away, her head falling limp onto Alara's outstretched hands.

Alara screamed. She was a child once again, pushing away the carnage of her own doing. She pushed Raquel's heavy body away and scrambled backward against the wall, shallow breaths marring the otherwise now silent hall.

A familiar face popped into her view, blocking the sight of Raquel's body.

Alara expected Runeo to scold her—to yell at her for being weak or not fighting better. Instead, he nodded and handed her the spear she had dropped. "Not that you need it at this point." He smirked.

Only then that she realized the rest of the carnage of those around her, brought on by her fellow bruyas. Was that what she was now? Was she considered a bruya now?

Tony was cleaning the blood off his own spear as he stood over the body of the last magite, red blood on red cloth. There was a moment of silence as Alara took in the surrounding bodies. They belonged to students of the Haven. Students she had dined with and studied with.

Whether or not she wanted to believe it, in the eyes of the Haven, she was a bruya now.

"It isn't easy killing, but sometimes it's necessary," Runeo said, as though reading her thoughts. She nodded, the truth still making her stomach churn. The safety of her world had been shattered to dust the second she and Emaru fought and Adelmo had fallen. But looking into Runeo's and Tony's eyes now, at the cold indifference to what had just happened, she realized that the world had never been safe—not for them. They'd always seen it for what it was.

She stood up, no longer shaking and queasy. She glanced down at Raquel's body one last time, squaring her shoulders in determination. She couldn't pretend the world was perfect anymore.

Bruya or not, it was time she learned how to survive this world, too.

They were only a few turns away from the worship hall, but time seemed to slow and stretch as they ran through the corridors. At each turn, she expected to find another group of mages ready to fight, but each time they only found emptiness; it was unsettling. It was only a matter of time before the *envia* that Raquel had sent brought the mages and councilguards back toward them, even if Raquel hadn't communicated their location. Someone had to know where she was stationed, and they'd know exactly where to send their troops. The trail of blood left behind by their battle would only serve as an easy guide to bring the mages to them all the quicker.

But then they turned the last corner and there it was, the intricately carved blue doors of the worship hall, unguarded and ajar.

CHAPTER 49

ALARA

Alara pushed open the oversized doors and saw the large empty hall spread out in front of her. In her time in the Haven, she was used to seeing the sun shining through the glass at the top, lighting the floor below with a thousand colors. Now the roof was shadowed, the bronze and gem decorations hollow in the dark, and only a few small torches were flickering along the walls.

But there was something else glowing. At the center of the hall, where Wila usually stood for her sermons, the spire that marked the top of the Haven swirled down into a column. At the base, a small divot of stone circled it, and around that, a white fire sparked, fueled by nothing but the stone itself.

Her eyes widened as she took in the spire stretching above her and to the ceiling. She had seen it a hundred times before, but never really looked at it closely. It was carved of white and pink quartz. This was no ordinary fist-sized receptive… The spire itself was the receptive.

"Oh no," she said.

"We need to destroy that?" Tony asked, his voice holding the same awe her face must. She nodded, not trusting herself to speak.

Runeo didn't waste any more time. He ran toward the center of the room, hands up, ready to send an attack at the column. But when he was only a few yards away, she felt a familiar tug of magia threads behind her. The very next moment, Runeo's feet left the ground, and he skidded across the wooden floors of the worship hall.

Alara's head whipped around to see Emaru silhouetted in the doorway they had just come through. Her face was stretched into something resembling a smile. "I've been underestimating you all these years."

"You've forced me to underestimate myself," Alara said, taking a step toward Emaru, the spire behind her forgotten.

"You're the one who insisted on never using your powers to their full extent. I saw your potential, and I tried to raise you to embrace your powers. You never understood what you are capable of and now…" She stopped and shook her head. "Then again, perhaps that was my failure." Emaru looked at Alara, eyes pleading. "Stop this before it goes too far. You're smarter than this. I raised you better."

"You raised me with lies and fear."

"I protected you."

"My whole life, I thought we were helping bruyas. I thought we were just trying to show them a better way, to teach them. But you were wiping their minds, turning them into mindless zombies for your own gain. For the Council."

"Not for the Council," Emaru said. "For all of Sombria. We take the measures we need to keep the peace for all. History has shown us what happens if we let magia run twild. I know you know the history. You've seen the Ruinedlands. Death, destruction, deformities. That's the alternative. The Council is the only thing standing between our realm and a perpetual civil war. In order to save lives, I am willing to keep this delicate balance." Emaru's face was red as she spoke, her voice full of the passion that Alara knew so well.

For an instant, she pictured them sitting at the dinner table, debating the use of magia in Sombria. It was a conversation they had had a million times, but Emaru's eyes had never shone brighter as she made her point. She used to admire that.

She shook her head to rid herself of the memory. "Don't lie to me!"

"Lie to you?"

"It's what you've been doing to me my entire life."

"Alara, I have *never* lied to you," Emaru said. "Kept you in the dark, perhaps. But with good reason. Not everyone can understand why we do what we do."

"Then maybe you're just lying to yourselves, then. But I know the truth. You do what you do to stay in power. It's what the Council has always wanted. It's what *you've* always wanted."

"I'm sorry you feel that way," Emaru said, almost in a whisper. "But we only stop those who would seize power without thought for the consequences. Perhaps we suppress more than we should. Perhaps we could do better. But the realm is full of bruyas who care nothing for the lives of the blameless. Just like your new friends. You don't understand how fragile this country has always been."

Something along Emaru's belt flashed in the light of the receptive, the white and bronze dagger—her dagger—tucked in the councilwoman's belt. Her eyebrows furrowed, and she looked up at her old mentor. "You stole my dagger."

Emaru's eyes flickered down to the blade at her waist and her eyebrows shot up, a hint of a smile on her lips. "*Your* dagger? Where did you get it?"

Alara bit her lip. "I… found it."

"You have no idea what you had, did you?" She took a step toward Alara, who moved back without thinking. "This is why we need each other. I have so much more to teach you. And you. You still have a mountain of untapped potential. That is why I saved you. Why I took you in and raised you out of all the children in your village. These wild, untrained bruyas can do nothing for you. You are so much more than them."

Alara's fists clenched. "I am so much more than you."

Before she could question herself again, she gathered the heat that was seething through her blood. Flames shot out from the surrounding torches, swirling toward Emaru. The hall suddenly lit brightly in the firelight.

Emaru didn't even flinch as she raised her arm. Wind blew the fire off course before it could touch her. Her eyes lit up with anger and all pretense dropped from her face. "I guess we're doing this, then. It's clear you didn't learn your lesson the first time."

She threw her hand forward just as Alara ducked, the air still hitting her like a wall and throwing her back against the floor. Her already-bruised body ached, but she stood back up, quickly. She saw that Runeo and Tony had been thrown back with her, and they, too, were recovering. Tony quickly summoned a cloud of fog as Emaru took aim toward them again. The thick fog wrapped around her, obscuring her from view, the group scattering while she was blinded. Emaru only struggled for a moment before the fog was blown away. But that second gave Runeo a chance to take aim. The arrow darted straight toward Emaru's chest, and Alara felt her own heart squeeze at the sight.

At the last moment, Emaru flicked her wrist, and the arrow streaked to the side. Alara ran at Emaru without thinking, throwing flames from the torches to her left. As the councilwoman dodged the attack, Alara flung the flames from her other side and felt a small jolt of satisfaction as the second attack seared and lit Emaru's sleeve. The woman's eyes widened slightly in surprise.

Tony was beside Alara. He threw his spear as Emaru quickly put the fire out on her sleeve. Alara thought it might hit, but Emaru flicked her wrist, and the spear jutted off course and clattered to the ground.

Alara let out a scream of frustration as fire shot toward Emaru once again. The air in the room whipped Alara's face and a strand of her hair came loose as her fire swirled around Emaru's body, the flames licking the air uselessly around the councilwoman. The flames buzzed in the room, circling like a tornado. And then it flew back toward Alara, Tony, and Runeo.

They flattened themselves to the ground as the inferno danced over their heads. Sweat beaded across Alara's back. Wind howled through the room, and the torches blew out, throwing them into darkness. The only light in the room remaining was the glow of magia that sparked along the base of the spire.

She jumped up as the darkness fell, throwing her hand out as she felt for her magia. But the cool darkness of the room was all that met her. There were no fires left to manipulate, and she had lost her flint somewhere along the way.

Emaru's face looked skull-like in the waning light. Shadows danced across the ridges of her face, and her eyes glimmered with satisfaction. Alara's stomach turned. Was this the person she had been following her entire life?

A gust of wind blew Alara off her feet. She skidded along the wooden floor, stopping when she hit the spire. She pulled herself up, using the warm crystal behind her.

Emaru strode across the room, not toward Alara, but toward where Tony scrambled to his feet. Before anyone could move, Emaru picked up a spear laying abandoned on the ground using a gust of wind. She snatched it out of the air and hurled it at Tony, piercing him through the chest in an instant.

Alara didn't move or make a sound as Tony fell to the ground with a brief grunt. She watched as Runeo shot toward Emaru, dagger in hand. He countered her wind as she tried to blow him off course. Alara didn't even see her hand twitch as the bolas lifted from Tony's own belt and whipped at Runeo's head. She had never seen such a precise use of wind magia before. The ability to lift objects and control them using air required a finesse that few took the time to learn.

The bolas cracked as they hit Runeo's skull and he fell, stumbling to the ground. Emaru swiftly pulled the dagger from his hand, a grim smile on her face.

"Stop!" she screamed before she could stop herself. She walked toward Emaru, eyes shining with tears she wished she could stop. "What's the matter with you? I've always thought of you as a mother."

Emaru straightened, her eyes narrowed as she looked down at Alara. "And you were a disappointment of a daughter."

Alara stabbed the spear in her hand forward, but Emaru parried the blow easily. She twisted again and swung the weapon down toward Emaru's knee. The wood of the spear hit her, but she only stumbled back slightly then brought her dagger slicing down toward Alara. She fell back, the sharp metal brushing against her tunic, just barely breaking the threads of the weave.

Emaru looked at her as she fell back. "I thought you'd be worth something. Look at you. After years of trying to convince me you were better without your magia, and you can't even fight me without your fire."

Alara jumped up in one smooth motion and shifted on her feet, the spear in her hand cool under her touch.

"You were always useless," Emaru said, breath heavy. "Just like your parents."

A sharp stab of pain shot through her as the heat of her magia rose from within. She sneered at Emaru and dropped her spear. It clattered in the hall.

Alara felt as if her skin might start glowing as the heat shimmered just underneath the surface. The darkness still settled around them, but heat flickered in the distance. The torches' burning embers sparked at the edge of the room. She looked down and met Runeo's eyes.

He was still on the ground, looking bruised and pale, but his eyes were hard and focused on her, and she saw his fist clench. She nodded her head and wished she were a mind-talker. But he seemed to get the message. A soft breeze whistled around the room and Alara stretched out her magia to meet the embers of the torches.

Fire and heat flared, and this time she didn't command it; she *was* the flame. She burned and surged. She consumed and destroyed. She reached out to Emaru and squeezed, wrapping her in flames.

Runeo jumped to his feet, bolting away from Emaru before the flames hit as the room roared into light. Emaru disappeared behind the wall of flames.

"Alara! We need to destroy the receptive." Runeo was behind her. She glanced back to see him hacking at the quartz spire with a heavy spear, his wind batting at it uselessly. She turned and focused on Runeo, sending a stream of flames to meet with his wind. The magia hit the spire and sparked, an enormous chunk of quartz falling from the column as Runeo hit it again with his spear.

Alara felt a surge of strength as she sent another wave of fire with Runeo's wind spiraling around the quartz receptive. She could see the cracks forming and the magia at the base wavering.

A wind-empowered arrow blew past her cheek, burying itself into Runeo's shoulder. Blood splattered across the crystal, and he fell back with a cry. *No, Runeo!*

The roaring of fire and wind suddenly stopped as Alara lost focus. The temperature in the room plunged and her blood turned cold as she looked up, trying to make sense of what was happening.

Emaru was a few yards away, her hair charred and robes blackened, but she was breathing as her eyes flashed with an odd mix of hatred and glee. Alara saw where the arrow had come from. A magite stood, bow taut and pointed at her, a smile on his face. Around them, more mages and magites were entering the hall, spreading out to encircle them.

She didn't move, but the fire reacted, living and acting at her thoughts. Streams of fire rained down on the room, scattering the mages as more flames protectively sealed Runeo, Alara, and Emaru away from the rest of the room.

But as Alara watched, more magites and mages filtered into the room. The array of colors dizzying as they filed into the room and began to manipulate their magia. Beside her, Runeo breathed unevenly, a hand gripping the shaft of the arrow in his shoulder, trying to keep it from moving.

"I don't know what to do." Her voice was hoarse as she and Runeo looked at each other. He was silent, but he reached for her hand, squeezing it as he trembled at her side.

She took a deep breath, feeling the fire as it danced through the room—through her—wondering perhaps for the last time what having her memory cleansed would feel like. Or perhaps she had gone too far for that to be a viable option.

Then she heard screaming, and she wondered for a second if it was her—if she had lost all sense of herself. But then the energy in the room shifted. She heard another scream, sharp and rich in her mind.

We've cowered in the shadows for too long, apologizing for sins that were not our own. The Council does not fight for us. They fight for the blameless, they fight to control us like l'lamas for their will.

Alara was briefly confused at how she could hear anyone so clearly amid the roar of fire before realizing the voice had come through an *envia*.

A look of recognition and fear flickered across the mage's faces around them. Emaru stood, head swiveling sharply as she looked for the source of the *envia*. For Councilwoman Lena Cruz.

Alara watched as a new group of magites and mages filtered into the room—surrounding the others. And at the front, Senye Cruz stood, her eyes glowing as she met Alara's own.

Behind her, Quenti stepped forward, smiling with Khuna by her side, and beside them both, Lili and Mitteo. Relief flooded her exhausted body.

She almost laughed when she recognized the small boy they had knocked out in the study rooms standing among the rebel magites. And there were even more teachers and fellow students that she vaguely recognized from her time wandering the halls.

"Today," Senye Cruz's actual voice echoed in the hall as even the shuffling of bodies seemed to fall silent in response. "We are done hiding!"

Chapter 50

Quenti

A silence fell across the room and Quenti tightened her hand around the handle of her club. She felt separate from her body as she watched the small army of mages shift, turning to face the new arrivals, weapons in hand.

Cruz and Khuna stood on either side of Quenti, and she let out a breath as she swept her hair back from her face. That she was there at all was… strange. She had never been one to jump headfirst into a physical altercation, and yet this is what she had practically begged the Network to do. To join them in the struggle against the Council.

What in Sol's name was she thinking?

At that moment, she wanted nothing more than to grab Khuna's hand to turn and run.

But there was nowhere for them to run. Unless they succeeded, there was no escaping the Haven.

And then, not with a clear cry or a single surge, but with a disorganized shuffling, the two lines moved forward, converging into a clashing of wood and metal. And Quenti was back in her body, all too aware of the spear being thrust forward toward her stomach.

It was Khuna who blocked the blow with her own club before cracking the middle-aged man across the knees. His cry of pain was lost in the hall's noise, but Quenti felt the crunch of his bones in her chest.

"Move back behind me!" Khuna yelled over the noise, pushing her body in front of Quenti's. Before Quenti even had time to register her words, she was already moving again.

Parrying a blow from another spear, Khuna ducked under the mage's arm, grabbing them by the shoulder and twisting until they fell. A second later, she had thrust the fallen mage's spear into the thigh of another approaching mage before he could even raise his own weapon.

Quenti watched it all, club forgotten in her hand. Khuna moved like water around the fighters, ducking blows and twisting around mages, sending them sprawling before they could even turn. She was so mesmerized by her movements, she didn't see the dagger. Neither did Khuna. Quenti saw the blood afterward though, bright against the dark skin of the bruya.

She didn't think. She only moved.

Her club cracked down onto the mage's head and then his knee. He stumbled back, but raised his arms and she felt the crack of air around her, ears popping uncomfortably as he pushed her back. She dropped her club and raised her own hands, feeling the cool rush of her powers.

The water hit the gray-haired mage hard in the chest. Before he could react, Quenti had twisted the water around his face. She held it there, watching his eyes go wide and his hands scrambling to move the water from his mouth and nose. But his hands only passed through the water, uselessly. Her powers rushed through her like a waterfall, and she let them pour out of her. Every ounce of anger and fear she had been holding in these past weeks flooded from her. Her eyes never left his.

It was Khuna's warm hand on her shoulder that finally brought her back to herself. The water fell to the ground along with the mage, heavy and forgotten.

Quenti turned to see her leaning heavily on one leg, but standing. She expected a reprimand for going too far, but Khuna was smiling.

"That was amazing. A little scary, but amazing." She nodded toward the center of the room, backlit by the raging inferno that Alara had created. It was thick with fighting mages and rebels. "Now, perhaps you can use that aggression to get us to Alara?"

Quenti didn't respond. She tugged at her powers and pulled back the water that had spread along the floor. The water whipped around Khuna and her, circling them.

Khuna grabbed the dagger that had stabbed her in her right hand, her club still in her left.

Quenti and Khuna moved together through the hall, jumping to the aid of their allies as they passed—presuming they could actually tell the difference between mage ally and mage enemy.

Though when they could tell friend from foe, Quenti would send a ball of water around the enemy mage's head while Khuna would break their knees with her club.

Fire, water, and air swirled around the hall in a confusing jumble, and the ground beneath them rumbled precariously.

Quenti truly couldn't tell who was winning, though she knew the odds were not in their favor. Even with the Network on their side, they were outnumbered two to one. And more enemies were on the way.

"If we can't win fast, we won't win at all," Quenti said, stepping over the body of a young magite who couldn't have been older than twelve. A piece of her died inside for the young soul. She couldn't even tell what side of the conflict he'd been on.

"Which is why we have to remember," Khuna said, "that escape is our only way to win."

The pair looked to where Alara and the others were fighting against the center pillar. They were only a few yards away.

A sharp cry caught her attention. She turned around searching for a minute before she saw Ander—the young rebel who had first slipped her a note about escaping the Haven. He was crouching on the ground, hands up, barely holding back the flames that threatened to engulf him. She could see the smoldering sleeve of his yellow tunic from where his powers had slipped.

She looked between Ander and Alara for only a second.

"Go help Alara!" Quenti said to her partner. "I'll be there soon."

Khuna opened her mouth to argue, but Quenti sent a sharp wave of water pushing her away as she turned her attention to Ander.

She didn't watch Khuna leave, only taking hold of the water again and throwing it with all her strength straight at the stream of flames. The air hissed as water turned to steam. It did little, but it weakened the flames enough for Ander to give a final push. The inferno veered off to the side, and the young boy stood, pale and shaking.

She stepped up beside him and faced the tall councilguard who stood, glaring at them both.

"Picking fights with children?" Quenti said. "Is that what the Council trains you for?" She narrowed her eyes and tried to pull as much water from the air as she could. But the air was dry from the fire, she barely had enough to pull together another small globe.

"We're trained to exterminate the threat of bruyas," the dark-eyed man sneered, "no matter how small and insignificant."

"Well, then. Let's see how that works out for you." She shifted the grip on her club and lunged, channeling every piece of Khuna's own grace as she could muster. The councilguard moved with a trained ease as he knocked the club off course with his spear. Quenti stepped to the side and swung again. And again. Each time, her blow was blocked, but she kept moving, forcing the councilguard to swing and spin after her.

She had hoped to exhaust him, but it didn't take her long to realize what a foolish wish it was. His breathing barely hitched as they continued, but Quenti's club got heavier with each swing.

She tried to pull at the threads of her magia, but the air barely stirred with water, still dried out from his own powers. She let out a gasp of frustration as the liquid she pulled out dropped from her grasp.

"I thought this would be an actual fight," the councilguard said, "but the kid seems better trained than you."

That's because he is.

The guard twisted his hand and thrust a jet of fire at her. Her sleeve smoldered as she gathered just enough water in the air to put it out. He was teasing her now. He could easily beat her with his powers. And he knew she knew it. His eyes flashed with malicious glee as she struggled.

"You may not be small, but you're still insignificant," The councilguard taunted her as they moved, his eyes dancing.

"I can still beat you with my club," Quenti said, lunging clumsily toward him, knowing full well she couldn't.

They moved again, twisting around each other. Every other sound in the room had turned to a dull buzz as she focused on only him. He was almost laughing now, stepping around her with a relaxed ease, spear held loosely in his hand as he blocked each swing.

"Why are you just toying with me?" She thrust forward, feeling the wood of her club just brush against his leg.

He laughed.

"I thought the Council was supposed to train honorable warriors," she said. "You're dressed like a mage, but you're nothing."

"This coming from a filthy bruya?"

Quenti stopped moving, breath heavy. "That's right. I am a bruya. And an aguen. And you?" A smile stretched across Quenti's face. "You're screwed."

With that, Quenti pulled the water that had been gathering behind him as they sparred through the hall. The air had cooled as he had stopped using his magia, too busy taunting and dancing around Quenti.

Her arms may have been heavy, but it was enough. The water surged forward and wrapped around his face, just enough to cover his mouth and nose as his eyes went wide in surprise.

The councilguard tried to light the flint at his wrists, but to no avail. Quenti had splashed his sleeves earlier on in their struggle. It didn't take long for him to panic, though each time he tried to move his head outside of the water bubble, she moved the bubble to match.

She walked past him as he fell to his knees, not bothering to watch him take his last breath.

He was insignificant. But she needed to get to Alara.

Chapter 51

Alara

The hall ran thick with cries and chaos as the rebels surged forward into the line of mages. Alara's instincts told her to jump straight into the thick of the brawl, but she knew there were more important things to do. Even if the rebels won against the mages in the hall, there would be more to come. Wait too long, and they wouldn't have enough time to take it and the barrier wouldn't come down.

The rebels had given her the distraction and time she needed. Emaru, who had been standing in front of her a second before was gone now, lost in the confusion. She needed to take advantage.

Alara turned away from the fighting and looked at the spire. She dropped the ring of fire that surrounded them and felt the slight relief of releasing the magia. Her body was heavy and sore from how much she had been using her powers—more than she'd ever used them in her entire life—but there was no time to rest. She could see a few cracks had formed in the receptive, but the magia in the base still glowed strongly.

Alara flung fire toward the spire, hitting it and sending sparks and flaming wisps bouncing into the air. The surrounding air seemed to bend with the heat, and she threw another blast toward the base.

Nothing happened. No cracks or rumbles. The spire sat, unaffected.

"I need help," Alara said, looking down to Runeo, who panted on the ground beside her. He met her eye, face slightly pale, but nodded. With a wince, Runeo snapped the shaft of the arrow in his shoulder. The point was still embedded in his muscle, but he let the rest of it fall to the ground as he stood.

That little move would make the arrow harder to pull out, but for now, it'd at least be easier for him to move around.

"Okay," he said.

With that, he and Alara sent magia crashing toward the spire again. At first, there was no change. Just a stubborn crystal giving no way to their magia. Thirty long seconds passed, and as the fire and wind pelted the quartz, cracks began to form.

Exhaustion bled through her body, somehow permeating her very core in a way she had never felt before. She wondered how Runeo was feeling. Her companion was pale and only using one arm as he flung his wind at the receptive. And he had more to worry about than spent magia.

Alara felt her energy flag. While the cracks had widened, she didn't know if she and Runeo could do it alone. And then a new column of fire hit the spire. She turned to see Zinita smirking at them, the trademark malice reserved for Alara gone. Suri stood beside the bruya, sending her own magia toward the receptive.

And then Alara glimpsed the fighting and carnage for the first time since the Network had entered the hall. She couldn't help but feel a twinge of anxiety as she saw a rebel magite crumple after getting stabbed with a spear.

Zinita and Suri ignored the chaos, focusing on the spire. Together, the fuegen and wind mage sent another column of magia at their target. Alara and Runeo took their cue and joined in. She felt her energy renew just slightly as new cracks started forming along the spire, the room almost trembling as it weakened.

Suddenly, Runeo broke off his attack. Alara turned just in time to see a spear being knocked away as it whistled past her. A magite glared back at them, and she recognized him at the same moment that Runeo did.

It was Micos.

She heard the sharp intake of breath beside her. But before she could say anything, Runeo had already picked up the loose spear and was gone, running to meet him.

Alara watched wide-eyed as the two clashed. Before Micos could recover, Runeo shoved the butt of his spear into his knees, trying to push him down. But he stood his ground, twisting his own spear toward Runeo's thigh. It tore at the fabric of Runeo's tunic as he stepped back. Micos wasted no time swinging the spear again, this time toward Runeo's chest.

Alara watched in horror as she realized the truth of the fight. Runeo was trying to stop Micos. Micos was trying to kill Runeo. That wasn't even mentioning the arrow that had pierced Runeo, moments earlier. She knew who'd win the fight, and it made her stomach twist. She turned to assist him, but before she could break off toward the fight, Zinita was beside her, hand gripped around her wrist.

"Your magia is stronger," she said. "Focus on the spire." With that, Zinita broke off her magia and ran toward Runeo and Micos.

Alara watched for a moment, her eyes traveling the room.

She saw Emaru a few yards away, defending herself against five other mages.

"Come on!" Suri was beside her now, bringing her attention back to the spire. She nodded, and the two attacked the quartz once again. While the two of them weren't as strong, the cracks within the spire had expanded. It was another few minutes before Alara felt her legs shaking.

She paused for a moment, letting go of her magia and looking at the chaos that surrounded her. Khuna was beside them now, fending off attacks. She found Quenti fighting against a black-garbed councilguard.

Senye Cruz fought off a handful of mages that Alara only vaguely recognized in the distance. Nearby, Runeo and Micos still struggled, Runeo's eyes red and shining even as he crossed spears with his brother.

Alara's eyes searched for Zinita, when she finally caught the movement of her dark hair behind Runeo and Micos. Alara's heart stopped. Zinita had a dagger clenched in her fist and was swinging it wildly at a councilguard that danced around her, spear raised. Alara would have recognized the young councilguard's movements anywhere, even if she hadn't seen his gray eyes.

"Alara, the spire!" Suri's voice was loud in her ear, but she barely understood the words.

Zinita was lunging now, her dagger whipping toward Ardo's unprotected hip.

"No!" Alara said, her feet moving toward Ardo with no thought. But she was too far away. The dagger's blade made contact with his hip, but before it could pierce deep, he had twisted and the butt of his spear slammed into Zinita's jaw. She was too far away to hear, but she felt the crack as her head jerked back, stumbling over a fallen body behind her.

Ardo wasted no time bringing the spear down into the Zinita's stomach with a sickening spin. She spat up blood, sparing one final venomous look toward her enemy before she fell back, unmoving and twisted among the other bodies.

Alara lurched forward, but felt the pull of arms behind her, wrapping her around the waist. Khuna's voice was soft in her ear, murmuring something she couldn't understand. As she felt the prickle of tears in the corner of her eyes, Ardo stumbled back into the crowd of mages, disappearing into the throng.

This wasn't what she wanted. She didn't trust the Council or Emaru, but she felt like everything was falling apart. There were dead bodies of mages and magites scattered all around the hall. She couldn't even tell which were rebels and who wasn't. Her stomach twisted and her breath became shallow.

It was in her moment of panic that Alara saw Emaru cut down the last two mages fighting her. Before Alara could make a move, the woman's eyes had swiveled to her, pupils blown wide. Alara felt the wind on either side of her as Suri and Khuna flew back.

And then Emaru was in front of her. Before Alara could even reach for her own powers, she felt the air get pulled from her lungs.

This wasn't like getting the wind knocked out of her—that sensation she was used to. No, this was an instance of air literally flying from her lungs. Alara tried to breathe but felt like she was underwater. Her eyes bulged and Emaru grabbed her by the arms, pulling her against her body and immobilizing her.

"I tried so hard with you," the councilwoman said, her voice just above a whisper. "But I should have done this years ago.

With a sinking feeling of dread, Alara saw the mind-walker Luis wading through the crowd of fighters a few yards away. His face was pale, and his tunic was still torn and bloody, but Alara could see the white scar of a healed wound on his stomach. An earth mage had saved him from his wounds down in the dungeon.

Alara tried to pull herself from Emaru's icy grip, a feeling of panic rising in her chest as she struggled to breathe. She could feel Emaru's nails digging into her skin and felt blood seeping down her arm. Luis was grinning widely as he seemed to float toward her, his hand outstretched.

Still, she writhed, pulling at the flames around her, but Emaru set out her own burst of wind. It radiated from her on all sides, dissipating the flames. Emaru hadn't let go of Alara—hadn't even flinched as her wind magia exploded.

As panic set in, Alara struggled to find a soft place to hit Emaru—anywhere to escape the inevitable. And then Alara felt the hilt of a dagger in Emaru's belt. She twisted her hand, trying to get a grip on the cool hilt, but found it to be anchored in place. She tugged desperately one more time before she registered Luis's hand coming down on her head, his palm calloused and warm.

She felt her vision going black on the edges as his magia surged, threading its way into her mind, plucking at her thoughts, searching for something. As he pruned the thread of a memory, Alara could feel the essence of it slowly disappear.

The sense of mourning lasted a moment. But then it was gone. Along with whatever memory was cleansed. Was anything even missing? And then he plucked again, twisting, yanking. She saw Mama's face as the man plucked at the memory of her.

Alara's anger rose and her hand clenched the hilt of the dagger tighter. It grew warm as she gripped it. Suddenly, Alara felt magia flowing not from her own core, but from the dagger in her grip. She felt Emaru stumble back, dagger slipping from her belt. The air returned to Alara's lungs in full force. She took a deep breath, pushing back at Luis, whose eyes were now wide as his hand still held to her head. It was the first time she had seen any semblance of fear in his eyes.

She pushed back at his memories, twisting his own magia back on himself. Now she was in *his* mind, seeing *his* memories. She saw him, younger than he was now, hair a pure golden brown and forehead missing his deep set wrinkles.

And she saw herself, only four or five, kneeling in front of him, eyes empty as his hand rested on her forehead.

A scream rang out in Alara's head. A scream she recognized but could not place.

CHAPTER 52

ALARA

The scream was followed by a high-pitched squeal and then a laugh.

"Come on, Lara and just do it already!" Alara turned to see the boy behind her, his brown curls falling into his face, brushing his forehead. His skin was a deep brown, freckles black against it, and his eyes a sharp blue. The corners of his lips were creased from his constant smiles.

She recognized the boy. She was no longer in the worship hall in the Haven. She was in her memories.

One specific memory.

She felt herself turn and flick the coin, knowing what was going to happen next. She saw it hit the lip of the frog and heard the small splash as it fell into the fountain pool.

"I knew you couldn't do it. My turn!" Ro was pushing her out of the way now. She felt her foot shoot out, almost against her will, and the boy went tumbling down in front of her.

Alara winced as she felt the bite of stone against her knees as she jumped the boy and wrestled his coin from his hand. She felt the sting as if it were happening to her, even though a part of her recognized it wasn't. She wasn't bleeding. At least not on her knees.

The second coin hit its mark, landing with a soft clink in the open mouth of the frog. The water that sprayed from its mouth faltered, finding a fresh path around the coin.

"Ha!" She elbowed the boy and pointed to where the coin had landed in the frog's mouth. "That's a point for me!"

"That was my coin! My point!"

"Oh, please. It doesn't work that way."

And then Dela was speaking behind her, voice high and soft. "Lara won fair and square, Ro. Don't blame her because you're a loser."

Alara urged herself to look back, to look at her friend Dela's face, a face she had forgotten years ago. But her past self didn't listen. And then they were laughing and Alara felt the dread creeping up her back and into her mind. A knowledge of something to come—of something she didn't want to happen. Didn't want to relive.

The arrow made no sound as it passed through the air and into Ro's chest. His smile didn't even leave his face as his hand came up to feel the shaft protruding from his body. And then he crumpled, blood leaking onto the cobblestones and near Alara's bare feet.

Alara watched in fascination, the world seeming to stop, as the blood nudged at her big toe. She had relived this memory over and over her entire life. But something felt different. She looked down at the still body of her friend and noticed the fletching of the arrow. They were black feathers. The color of the councilguard.

Then Alara was running, and Dela's hand was clenched in her own. An awareness hit her hard. The councilguards were here. The two kids were in trouble. The awareness of the young Alara warred with the confusion of older Alara. The councilguard meant safety.

No, the councilguard meant death. "Never show the Council or mages what you can do," her mama's voice whispered in her mind. "Stay silent. Stay hidden. Stay safe."

And then Mama's voice was loud and coming from ahead of her.

"Faster, Alara!" Mama's voice was hoarse and eyes wild as she ushered Alara and Dela through the door.

A distant piece of Alara expected to head toward the cellar where Dela was being ushered down with the others. She wasn't even sure why, but then Mama was kneeling in front of her, a dagger in her hand.

The same distant piece of Alara recognized the dagger—the one she was now holding in her left hand, its hilt hot under her palm. The other Alara knew the dagger, too.

"Go, hide the dagger and run. Don't look back, no matter what!"

She nodded and grasped the dagger. The blade was sharp under her grip and she wrapped it in a piece of cloth before jumping out the back door of the house and running. Her lungs burned and her knees and legs ached, but she bound through the trees as silently as she could. Jumping over roots, grabbing on to low-lying branches to swing over shrubs.

She had trained for this. She had spent hours in the forest learning to move like a spider monkey, silent and sure. Often trying to see if she could sneak up on Mama or Papa when they were out fishing.

The sounds of screaming and the breaking of wood were muffled as she passed deeper into the woods. She came across a large rock wall, her eyes passing over the loose boulders before picking the crevice she wanted. She felt her hand scrape along the rock as she tucked the dagger into it, biting her lip as a thin layer of skin was taken off. She pulled her hand out and looked back at the crevice. She smiled. The dagger didn't show, the crevice was barely visible, and from where she stood, it appeared as nothing more than a small lip in the stone.

Satisfied, Alara looked back toward the village and the muffled sounds of war. She knew what Mama wanted. She wanted her to run, hide, even go to the Arborelis if she could make it. But she had never been good at listening.

She looked back at the wall one more time, searching for any sign of the crevice or the blade hidden there. When she was sure there was none, she darted back toward home, just as silent as she had been before.

She slowed as she got closer to the village. The screams of the villagers and calls of councilguards rang out as they broke down doors. Alara hoped the chaos would drown out any sound she made as she snuck closer. Her family's home was on the edge of town and she saw the guards were just making their way to it. She knew what they would find when they broke the door. An empty room.

She held her breath and watched from the tree line. She could just see into the windows as councilguards marched around the room. They knocked over tables, tore up furniture, and scoured the floors, all in search of something—the dagger.

Then there was a sharp cry of a child and Alara saw a shift in the councilguards' movements. Their heads disappeared from the windows and more cries echoed in the air, making her heart pound. She recognized the shout of Mama and the roar of wind as she fought back.

All logical thought left Alara, and she sprinted toward her house. She had to help. She didn't bother going around to the door, but jumped through the opening of a window, screaming. Eyes swiveled to her in surprise and she saw Mama, half dragged out of the cellar, face pale, eyes looking at her with such deep sadness that Alara almost backed away and ran. Almost. But then she met the eye of the guard that held Mama's arm, a dagger against her neck.

Alara dove toward him, pulling at the threads of every fire she could find in the village and bringing them to her. She jumped on him, grabbing the knife from his hand as he burst into fire. She pushed him away from Mama and turned on the other guards. She could feel the mages in the room pulling at their energy, readying themselves to fight. Even the blameless guards clenched their weapons and stared at the small child that tried to defy them.

Alara swallowed, her heart quickening in a sudden realization of what she was up against.

"Alara, help!" Mama shouted.

Alara felt her mother's powers rise behind her. She threw out a fireball as Mama's gale of wind hit, and the flames exploded at the gathered guards. They scattered, dodging the flames as best they could, but they fell down all the same as flames ate at their clothes.

She and Mama threw another gust of fire at the guards, pushing them back, trying to keep them away from the others still gathered in the hidden basement of the house.

And then a roar filled her head so loud she fell to her knees, pressing her hands against her ears. Through watering eyes, she saw the door of the house fly off its hinges and hurtle toward her. It soared over her hunched body, but she could almost feel the crash as it hit Mama behind her. She didn't even cry out as she fell into the basement below.

Alara stood up on trembling legs and looked at the doorway as a woman she didn't know walked through.

You know her, a voice whispered in her mind.

Her hair was darker than she remembered, but her eyes were still the deep gray that Alara knew so well. They shone with a confidence and a surety that she had always admired. Emaru.

Heat danced through her blood as she looked at this woman. This woman who had hurt Mama, who had destroyed her home. Anger swelled, and she launched a shot of fire toward the woman, who didn't even flinch as the flames dissipated around her.

Alara screamed this time as she threw herself and her magia toward the woman. A glimmer of a smile tugged at the corner of the woman's mouth as the fire streaked toward her. With the slight wave, her magia was tugged from her control. It turned, the flames twisting in the room and back toward Alara.

Her hair caught fire, and she felt the flames biting at the skin of her neck and face. With a strangled cry, she fell to the ground, clutching her hands over the flames, putting them out as they danced across her skin. Then the fire was out and Alara was calm. But the screaming continued.

Alara turned herself back toward the basement, back toward her parents and her friends, and she saw the fire licking at the wood floor, dropping burning wood into the small pit below. She saw Dela scrambling up the stairs, trying to escape the fire. And Papa, dragging Mama toward the wood stairs, struggling under her weight as he dodged falling pieces of wood.

Before she could even think to help, before she could recover from the shock, she heard the roar of wind and Emaru was behind her, cold eyes glaring as the helpless villagers tried to escape. She waved her hand lazily and a scattering of arrows shot through the air, piercing those in their way. Dela fell from the top step of the stairs and into the dust floor below with a thud. Five other children and adults fell where they had stood.

Eyes wide with horror, she saw her parents below still, Papa glaring up at Emaru unarmed and unprotected, but chin still held up in determination.

And Alara watched as Emaru waved her hand at the flames that danced around them, and the fire roared up higher, engulfing her parents in white hot flames. Right before they disappeared behind the flames, Alara saw Papa's warm eyes holding her own.

A screech flew from her throat, and her entire body shuddered. She snatched a spear from the ground and turned on the woman a few feet away. She swung the point of the spear and sliced down toward the woman's heart. The woman moved at the last moment and the spear missed her chest, but it scraped along the woman's face, splitting open her cheek. Alara felt a wave of satisfaction as red blood poured from the wound.

Her arms were suddenly wrenched behind her and she felt herself being lifted from the ground, like a small doll. The guard didn't even struggle as he held her and placed a dagger across her neck.

The woman, blood dribbling down her cheek, made a sound.

"Don't," she spoke, stepping closer and looking at Alara in amusement. "This one has heart. Cleanse her memories, but keep her alive. We can use someone like her."

Chapter 53

Alara

Alara felt the hand fall away from her head, and the world reshaped itself into the worship hall of the Haven. Luis crumpled to the ground, a hand clutching his throat as blood leaked between his fingers. Khuna stood behind him, her dagger dripping red.

She turned to see Suri and Quenti both warding off Emaru, dodging the club she was wildly throwing around. Without even thinking, she flew at Emaru. The others jumped away as she tackled her to the stone floor.

She clawed at Emaru's face and smashed her fists against her. "You!" Alara screeched, unsure of what she even wanted to say. All she could think of was how much she wanted Emaru to hurt.

"Get off me!" Emaru said, voice uncharacteristically ragged and fatigued. Still, she knocked Alara back with a blast of wind, pulling herself up to her feet.

Alara sneered as she looked at the woman that had raised her. Her eyes traced the silver scar that stretched thin across Emaru's left cheek. "I wish I had killed you when I gave you that scar."

Fire burst into life and collapsed toward Emaru from every direction. She didn't even blink as she threw her hands up, stopping the flames before they reached her. A gust of wind hit Alara in the chest, knocking her off her feet. Her body hit the floor but didn't feel any pain. Her mind just continued screaming. With a snarl, she jumped up and launched multiple waves of flame toward her again.

A stream of fire grazed her shoulder. And with a flick of her wrist, Emaru collected the flames and pushed them back toward her in a raging squall of flames.

She rolled aside and continued screaming until her throat was raw. She was going to burn her to ash. She created more, more fire, more heat, more light. She threw everything she could pull out of herself at Emaru who continued dodging and deflecting them. Beads of sweat were the only proof that her flames were even doing anything to her.

With each dodged flurry, hopelessness weighed down on her through her rage. Every deflected stream was more proof that she was truly just untrained and inexperienced. Was there any true hope that they could even defeat her?

Around them, the mages still fought one another other. Suri continued her assault on the spire, her energy flagging, and the cracks no longer growing. It was only a matter of time before the Haven's backup arrived, and this would all have been for nothing.

Emaru continued sidestepping barrage after barrage of hellish flames, diverting some across the room and searing clusters of fighting mages around the room. She had an idea.

She dodged another attack, running a few yards away. Emaru twisted and sent another strong gale at her. Alara ducked, the wind sailing over her head.

Emaru smirked as she redirected more of the fires inside swirling winds, forming a series of small fire tornadoes in Alara's path.

Again, she jumped out of the way, letting the swirl of wind and fire sail past her. There was a crack and a burst of light as the fire tornadoes careened straight into the weakened spire receptive. The quartz shattered, and the floor of the hall shook as stone pieces rained down onto everyone below—including a large chunk that smashed into Emaru's face.

The woman crumpled in on herself.

The cries over the din in the hall shifted as crystal and ceiling collapsed down onto the combatants. Clashing ceased and mage and magite alike set about dodging the falling debris.

"We need to get out," Senye Cruz's voice rang out in Alara's head. "The entire structure of the hall is collapsing!"

"Come on, Alara!" Quenti said, grabbing her from behind as stone and crystal rained down around them.

Alara shook her head and pulled her hand away. She ran over to the corpse of Luis, the fallen mind-walker, and pulled out a dagger from his belt—her special dagger. An exhausted smile played across her face as she slipped the too-warm trinket into her belt.

The room shook again and Quenti grabbed her with both hands and started dragging her away.

"We need to go, now!"

With a breath and a final glance, she found Emaru lying in the rubble. Was her chest still moving? Another tug by the now-frantic Quenti. Together, they turned and ran, ran over the carnage of both the battle and collapse.

She passed Khuna, who struggled to pull Runeo. Following his gaze, she saw Micos was running in the opposite direction, trailing another mage. She bit her lip as he disappeared into the hallway and placed her hand on Runeo's shoulder. He was no longer fighting, and after letting out a raw yell, he slumped against Khuna's shoulder.

"We have to go," Alara said, feeling heartless as she did. Though, to his credit, he didn't argue, and he silently fell in step behind them as they made their way through the hall, catching up to Lili, who ran alongside Mitteo and Suri.

Senye Cruz was nearby directing the flow of rebel mages and bruyas out of the hall, the woman's eyes meeting her own.

"We all need to leave, now," she said.

"Isn't that what we're doing?" Quenti said, somehow unable to hide her snark, even in their dire circumstances.

"Not just leave the building. Leave the Haven. All of us. The entire Network. The Council and all of Cielo will know what has happened, and that will put targets on our backs."

Alara tried not to think about the bodies they'd left behind in the hall, but she couldn't help but remember the empty eyes of Zinita. *Ardo*, her head whispered against her will, and she bit the inside of her cheek, pushing away the thought. She hadn't seen his body among the rest.

"Where are we going, then?" she asked, voice distant. She had been acting on instinct up to this point, and the reality was just hitting her that she'd no longer be able to call the Haven home.

"I don't know," Senye Cruz said, looking tired and older than Alara had ever seen her before. "This was never a part of our plan. But we need to get out. We can meet in the Outlands, where the River Mied meets the River Muerta." She sent the *envia* out to the rebels gathered and still running. "Separate into small groups and don't travel a direct route. Meet in two moons' time. I will bring other bruyas. Others who can help our cause.

We can't just hide in the trees and outskirts any longer. The Council won't let us."

Alara nodded, trying to picture a map of Sombria in her mind. They were to head southeast.

"We need to get back to Arbol and warn them what's happened." Runeo's voice was hoarse and dry. It was as if he hadn't spoken in years. "Quil'la needs to know."

Senye Cruz looked at him, studying him before nodding. "Go then. Meet us at the fork after. Do you know where it is?"

"Yes," Mitteo said firmly behind Alara.

She turned to see Lili, Mitteo, and Suri still standing together. "I can help them find it."

Senye Cruz looked at the seven of them. "All of you, then?"

Suri gave a nod.

"Stay safe, and we'll meet again soon."

Alara jumped in surprise as Senye Cruz set a hand on her head and pulled her to her shoulder for an unexpectedly warm hug.

"Now go!"

With that, Quenti pulled Alara down the hall toward a split to the left. It took a few turns to realize where they were headed. She smiled. It was the same route they had taken on their first tour of Haven together. She had never realized that her mischievous friend was even paying attention.

They made it to the large cavern at the mage's main doorway to the Haven. The l'lamaga and l'lama pens were empty— someone had already stolen the carts and the tacking, too.

Suri pushed open the large doors, and the light of the new day burst through, blinding Alara. As her eyes adjusted, she could see that the sun had just breeched the tree line on the east, sending long shadows along the ground and lighting the city in high contrast.

It was then that Alara heard the cacophony breaking through the cool morning air. Cielo was in chaos.

Blameless, magites, and even mages, scampered through the city, making for the exits in waves as councilguards struggled to keep them calm, all the while scanning the crowds for wayward rogues. Did they know the enemy was no longer restricted to bruyas now? That their own fellow mages and magites could have turned on them?

"How are we going to get out of here?" Quenti's eyes were wide as she took in the chaos.

"Can we just join the exodus?" Lili asked, eyeing the fleeing masses.

"With these crowds, who knows how long that'll take," Alara said. "And every second we spend here is a second more they have to find us."

Suri smirked and grabbed Lili's hand. The others followed without question as she darted out of the gates to their left.

"Where are we going?" Alara asked. And then she saw where Suri was looking. The River Sura cut in front of them, flowing under a large stone bridge between them and the Via Sura, the main road out of Cielo. Beside the river were a few reed boats, tipped on their sides and forgotten. Runeo and Suri used their wind powers to lift the boats up and into the water, holding them there as the others piled in. Lili helped Alara in and was about the step in herself when there was a shout.

A sole councilguard noticed them and charged toward them. Alara stood up, unsteady in the boat, but ready to attack.

Lili was faster. She darted forward toward the man without hesitation, her movements nimble. She ducked under the spear he swung at her and jumped up, gripping her hand on his head.

The man fell with a muffled thud into the grass and Lili bounded back toward the boats without looking back.

Suri looked between the councilguard's prone body and Lili with wide eyes. "El'dyo, you have to show me how you did that!" Suri said as she and Lili hopped into the boat. Runeo joined Mitteo and Khuna in the other craft, and then with a flick of Quenti and Khuna's wrists, the party was off, bolting through the water, the wind whipping in their faces.

They passed others who paddled madly to escape. And as they approached the gated arch that served as their exit, she sighed in relief as she saw the opening. Others had already made their escape, somehow blowing a hole in the grating.

"One last thing," Alara said over the sound of splashing. "There's a short waterfall on the other side of that grating."

"A what?" Runeo said.

"Don't worry," Alara said. "Between the airen and aguen in these boats, you all can slow the fall and help lessen the impact on the water, right?"

The others looked at each other as the grating drew closer.

"Right?" Alara repeated.

"Stop it right there!" a councilguard cried from the top of the wall. He didn't wait for their response, instead launching a barrage of flames at the group.

Alara stood up, meeting the soldier's fire with her own, which dissipated on impact.

"Looks like we don't have a choice," Suri cried out, palms facing the outer side of the boat.

The others followed her lead as Alara continued warding off attacks from the overzealous fire mage standing guard on top of the wall.

She had at least expected Quenti and Khuna to slow somewhat as they approached the grate, but in true Quenti style, they only increased their speed, hurtling toward the falls. As if going faster made it easier to jump off the cliff.

To their credit, it did. She didn't have a chance to panic as they passed under the wall, through the grate, and off the top of the waterfall. Out into the open air.

It gave her even less time to panic as they plummeted fifty feet onto the river below.

CHAPTER 54

ALARA

The wind whistled around their two boats as they descended. Her heart sinking as her stomach rose to meet it. Had she made a mistake? Maybe not all airen could move heavy objects like she had always seen Emaru do all of her life.

If that was what Runeo and Suri were doing with their abilities, she didn't feel it—at all.

"El'dyo take it!" Alara swore involuntarily as an uncomfortable falling sensation pierced her stomach, forcing her eyes shut.

As they fell further, the boat's bench pressed up against her rear and there was a tangible slowing of momentum before they crashed into the water. The impact felt… impossibly soft.

It was only when she opened her eyes that she saw the ten-foot-wall of water on all sides of their boats. Somehow, Quenti and Khuna had helped cradle the boats as they landed. She could only stare in awe as the couple spread out their hands, pushing the walls away, and launching the boats upward to the surface.

She let out a shaky breath as she stared back at the falls. She hadn't actually been sure that would work—without someone getting hurt. She was glad they'd proved her wrong, but there really was no other choice.

The rest of the party was silent as they continued to speed along the river, sharing ecstatic glances with each other.

Alara swallowed as she bit back the excitement, and her smile turned into a frown.

"What's the matter?" Quenti said.

"It's nothing," Alara said. "Just that… I'm happy to be leaving the Haven. It's my home. I didn't think I'd *ever* be happy to leave. I spent so long trying to fit in." She looked back at the towering city, a bittersweet flavor caught in her mouth. She reminded herself of the truth. That it had only been her home for as long as she *recalled*, following her mind cleanse.

Quenti put a hand on Alara's shoulder. "You'll just have to make a new one. I think we might even be able to help with that." She grinned.

Alara watched as the Haven disappeared behind the tree line and they moved deeper into the forest.

She turned to the front of the boat, looking south. Alara only pondered briefly the insane events that had landed her here, racing back toward Arbol and away from the Haven.

She met Quenti's eye and the young woman smiled back at her.

"Yeah, I guess I will." She closed her eyes and let the morning air blow her hair back. Somehow, the prospect of making her way back to Arbol felt right. Something like home.

Epilogue

When she opened her eyes, the blackness pressed in on her. She blinked a few times, ensuring that her eyes were, in fact, open. The blackness remained unchanged. She wiggled her toes and fingers, feeling the strain of her wrists in the rough cuffs, but reassuring herself that everything still worked.

She racked her brain, attempting to put her thoughts in order and piece together what had happened. She remembered screaming and blood and fire. And then blackness.

Stone scraped against stone somewhere in the darkness, muffled by what she assumed was a door or two. And then came voices.

"She's alive."

"Has she been questioned yet?"

"She was in and out after the battle. Wasn't making sense before."

"Stay out here. Make sure no one else comes in."

"Are you—are you sure, Senye? Even chained, she's dangerous."

"I will be fine." The voice was clearer now. Closer. Easier to recognize.

As the door creaked open, torchlight filled the room. She turned her face, wincing in the sudden brightness.

Senye Wila stepped through the room, one hand wrapped around her torch, the other fingering something in her pocket. "Senye Emaru," she said in a melancholy tone.

"Why so formal, Ria?" Emaru said, chin raised.

"Linda, we have a lot to talk about."

"I'd love to start with why I'm currently chained to a wall."

"Your protégé, who, if I remember correctly, we told you to get rid of years ago, just staged a rebellion and made off with the weapon we've been searching for—for decades. A weapon you recently had in your possession and then lost."

Emaru moved in her bindings, trying to adjust herself, but no matter the angle, she was still looking straight up at Wila. It wasn't a circumstance she'd normally allow. "We all underestimated the girl. Clearly, that won't happen again."

"Clearly, it won't. But you won't be around to make that mistake again."

Emaru twisted her wrists, hidden behind her back. "I don't think I can abide by that."

She reached for her core, the swirl of air that moved constantly through her chest.

And she touched nothing. There was nothing there.

"I'm sorry I didn't warn you," Wila was looking at her with something resembling pity. "But there will be none of that."

"You've made us move up our timeline. Well, Ayar and Cruz have. I always knew that woman was only one step above a bruya." Wila spat the words out. She paced the room, eyes not settling on any single place. "We knew this day would come, but I thought we had time to plan and perfect…" She cut herself off before her voice raised too much. "But now…" Her eyes swiveled back to Emaru, who leaned against the wall silently, her wrists still twisting uselessly behind her. "I'm just monologuing now."

"I'm used to the sermons," Emaru said.

"You know, I always thought you'd be on our side of this."

"I still am."

"No, no. You'll be much more useful to us as a lesson…" She paused. "A lesson of what happens when you betray the Haven."

"Betray the Haven?"

"Intentional or not, your mistakes have resulted in what amounts to a betrayal."

Again, Emaru reached for her core, only for it to come up empty.

"I admit," Wila said, "we had to be a tad more aggressive to stunt your abilities." She pulled a small stone out of her pocket and tucked it into the chained woman's belt, patting it with a sad smile.

"Goodbye, Linda. The Haven really could have used you."

END OF BOOK ONE OF
THE MAGE WAR CHRONICLES

Want a Free Book?

Yes, we're a little crazy. We're offering you a free ebook, on the house!

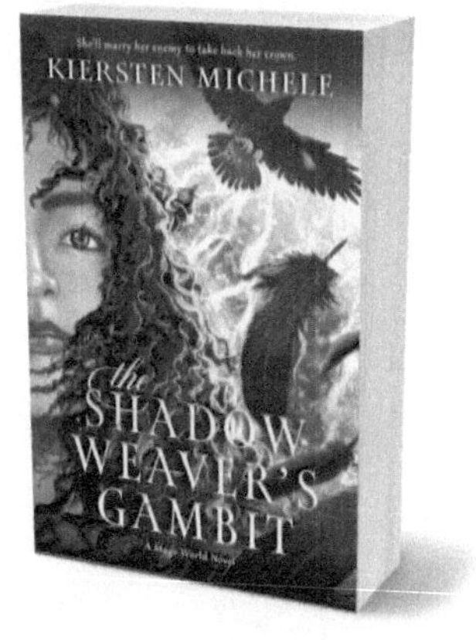

Journey across the Ruinedlands in the same world as *City of Mages*, to the warring city-states of Anillo and Xaca. Witness Mariela as she tries to reclaim her country from her stepfather—with a little help from a talking firebird and a generations-long enemy, the leader of Anillo.

This action-packed Romantasy is perfect for lovers of *Dance of Thieves*, *We Hunt the Flame*, and of course, *City of Mages*.

Pick up your free copy at: https://BookHip.com/CKFMXRQ

Thank you, Patrons!

This book was a couple of years in the making, and in the deepest midsts of drafting, editing, and everything in between, I (A.J. Cerna) had a handful of loyal Patrons at my side. I want to thank each and every one of you for your loyalty and support.

I hope *City of Mages* was worth the wait!

PATRONS

<u>Specter Seeker Tier</u>
J Soderberg

<u>Bruya Tier</u>
Steven Beal

<u>Magite Tier</u>
Bernardo Nuno
Derek Alan Siddoway

Join us on Patreon and get featured in A.J. Cerna's next book:
Patreon.com/magiabooks

Acknowledgments

And, of course, even outside of Patrons, books aren't made in a vacuum. Though many of us have this ideal of an author writing deep into the woods, Henry David Thoreau-style, the reality is much more collaborative.

As authors, we have have our own shortcomings. My own are outweighed by my coauthor Kiersten Michele, and vice-versa. However, even the two of us have our limits. We can only re-read our own words so many times before they become a veritable alphabet soup.

To start with, I'd like to thank the members of Eddy Street Authors, who suffered through initial, gross, untested drafts of the novel. I'd also like to thank the Sarah Keno and Cambria, who took the time to read the beta version of the story and provide necessary feedback to bring the novel to where it is now.

Additionally, I'd like to thank our line and copy editor Anthony Holabird, whose work was also crucial to adding that extra layer of polish.

I'd also like to give a shoutout to frequent collaborator Derek Alan Siddoway, who was always there to give advice, mostly on the advertising and presentation side of things.

About Kiersten Michele

KIERSTEN MICHELE is an author and bookworm who spends her mornings, evenings, weekends, and in-between times reading. She grew up on mysteries, fantasies, historical fictions, and any other story that would take her on an adventure. Her love of reading turned into a love of writing, and she took that love to college and…got a PhD in counseling psychology. Plot twist. But when she's not writing *extremely fascinating* academic articles, she's creating stories to take her on more adventures.

The Mage War Chronicles is her first (fiction) publication.

When not tucked into her reading chair, she's out adventuring in the real world, climbing rocks, hiking rocks, and taking way too many photos of rocks.

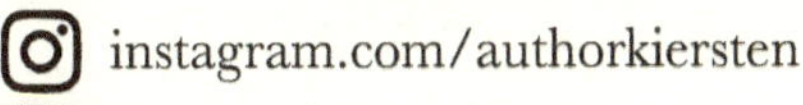 instagram.com/authorkiersten

 youtube.com/@magiareads

About A.J. Cerna

A.J. CERNA is an author, film-lover, gamer, and all-around story junkie. Like any healthy kid, he grew up imbibing fantasy novels, anime, manga, and movies, and realized at a young age that writing stories was the best way one could spend their time. Eventually, he found his way into film school, where he got his degree in screenwriting. In his time in Hollywood, he pitched animated series around town and worked in the anime dubbing industry in various capacities. He also ran the film site *LRM Online* as editor-in-chief for several years, which allowed him to write about the stories he loves when he wasn't writing stories himself.

His series consist of *Djinn Tamer*, *Champions of MythRune*, and now, *The Mage War Chronicles*.

When not reading or writing, he can be found hiking, podcasting, gaming, or checking out the latest craft beer breweries.

Books by A.J. Cerna

THE DJINN TAMER SERIES

Djinn Tamer: Starter (Bronze League Book 1)

Djinn Tamer: Rivals (Bronze League Book 2)
Djinn Tamer: Evolution (Bronze League Book 3)

Champions of MythRune

facebook.com/ajcernawriter
x.com/AJCernaWriter
instagram.com/ajcernawriter
youtube.com/@magiareads